"A great page-turning choice for a read-it-in-one-sitting airplane ride or lazy afternoon on the back porch . . . The novel transports readers to another world, giving a solid dose of action-adventure and a kick-butt female protagonist. *The Catch* . . . is a great escape."

—*STAR-TELEGRAM*

"[Stevens] makes her protagonist more empathetic and likable than ever. . . . [An] exceptional novel."

—*DALLAS MORNING NEWS*

"[An] adventure tale about a woman who thinks on her feet (that is, when she is not using them to kick bad-guy booty) and always stays one step ahead of her adversaries. My prediction: This will be one of the summer's most popular beach reads."

—*BOOKPAGE*

"[Munroe] can play people and entire countries against each other while never being more than one step away from the action at all times. [Stevens] is fabulous and the characterizations are thrilling. . . . You get what you see, and that includes the cleverness, the grit, and the pain. A definite keeper!"

—*SUSPENSE* MAGAZINE

"A fast-paced action thriller that vividly shows why Munroe is probably the best new action hero."

—*HUNTINGTON NEWS*

"Thriller fans will immediately be sucked into this life-or-death tale as Stevens's fast-paced plot and indomitable and justice-driven heroine keep the pages turning."

—*LIBRARY JOURNAL*

TAYLOR STEVENS

THE
CATCH

A NOVEL

B\D\W\Y BROADWAY BOOKS • NEW YORK

Copyright © 2014 by Taylor Stevens
Excerpt from *The Mask* copyright © 2015 by Taylor Stevens

All rights reserved.
Published in the United States by Broadway Books,
an imprint of the Crown Publishing Group,
a division of Penguin Random House LLC, New York.
www.crownpublishing.com

Broadway Books and its logo, B \ D \ W \ Y, are trademarks of
Penguin Random House LLC.

Originally published in hardcover in the United States
by Crown Publishers, an imprint of the Crown Publishing Group,
a division of Penguin Random House LLC, New York, in 2014.

This book contains an excerpt from *The Mask* by Taylor Stevens.
This excerpt has been set for this edition only and may not
reflect the final content of the forthcoming edition.

Library of Congress Cataloging-in-Publication Data
Stevens, Taylor.
  The Catch: a novel / Taylor Stevens. — First Edition.
    pages cm
  I. Title.
  PS3619.T4924C38 2014
  813'.6—dc23   2013038572

ISBN 978-0-385-34895-9
eBook ISBN 978-0-385-34894-2

Printed in the United States of America

Book design by Jaclyn Reyes
Cover design by Eric White
3-D rendering by Brian Levy

10 9 8 7 6 5 4 3 2 1

First Paperback Edition

For my readers.
Your support for the earlier books in this series
made it possible for Munroe to ride again.
This one is for you. Thank you.

THE
CATCH

CHAPTER 1

DJIBOUTI, DJIBOUTI

On the rooftop edge, she waited, eyes tracking down the length of the street while she sat with one knee dropped over the side, the other tucked under her chin, ears attuned to the small sounds that marked the climber's progress toward her.

Here, four stories up, the smell of rotting garbage was a little less putrid, the air a little cooler, and if she chose to stand and stretch, she could see beyond the expanse of treetops and dusty low-slung houses, through to the port, a barely visible patch of primary colors against the ocean. This was Djibouti. Dirty. Quiet. Corrupt. A world far removed from the rain forests and humidity and familiarity of equatorial Africa where she'd been born, yet so much the same. Pinprick on the map between Somalia and Ethiopia, a desert nation of less than a million that bottlenecked the mouth of the Red Sea, this, the capital, was where half the population lived.

Chatter rose from below as women, heads wrapped in colorful scarves and dressed in ankle-length sheaths, passed by with their bundles. Scratching from behind told her that the climber had pulled himself over the ledge, that he'd stood and dusted his hands off on his pants, that he strode slowly, deliberately in her direction.

Vanessa Michael Munroe didn't turn to look. Didn't acknowledge him when he stopped beside her to peer down at the street. Ignored him when he sat a few feet away and with a satisfied sigh dropped his legs over the side, leaned back, and surveyed the area.

Most of what surrounded them was single- and double-storied buildings, mainly residential and strung along in both directions, some nestled within dirt-strewn walled compounds and some not.

"It's a good view," Leo said. "Better breeze up top. Not so much smell."

She didn't answer; continued to ignore his presence. He could have spared himself the effort of the climb—spared her the effort of small talk—if he'd simply waited until she'd returned. Instead, he'd come for her, which was his way of marking territory: a reminder that he was familiar with her routines and could invade them if he cared to. She allowed him to believe it, just as she allowed him to believe that he knew who she was, where she'd come from, and why she was here.

They sat in silence, and in spite of the lowering sun and the evening breeze that had begun to cool the air, sweat still trickled down her back and neck, soaking her shirt. The heat didn't bother her the way it would him, so she let him have the discomfort and the lengthening quiet until finally he broke and said, "We board at two this morning."

His English was thickly accented, and that he chose to use her language instead of the French with which they typically conversed was more of his pointless point-making.

She said, "I'm still not interested."

He nodded, as if contemplating her defiance, then stood and, with his toes poking over the edge, studied the ground. Wiped his hands on his pants again and took a step back. "It's for you to decide," he said. "But if you don't board, I want you out by tonight."

Chin still to her knee, focus out over the dirt alleys, rooftops, and laundry flapping on many lines, she said, "Why? If I come, I'll just get in your way."

"That may be," he said. "But still you come. Or you leave."

She glanced up, the first she'd deigned to look at him. "And then who'll be your fixer?"

He took another step away from the ledge. "I managed before you got here," he said, and began to walk away. "I'll manage after you're gone."

She straightened and her gaze followed him. "It's not you who has to manage without me," she said. "You shouldn't be the one to make the decision."

Leo paused but kept his back toward her.

She studied his posture, counted seconds, readied to slide out of the way if in response to her provocation he moved to shove her off the building.

"You'd have been better off making arrangements to board in the afternoon," she said, "when the khat trucks come into town."

His hands, which had tightened into fists, loosened a little. He turned toward her, and she watched him just long enough for him to catch her eye, then she shied away in that guilty manner people caught staring often did.

This was part of her persona here, hesitant and nonconfrontational. Made it easier for the men to dismiss and underestimate her, kept her beneath the radar, though for how much longer was up for debate. Like the rest of the guys, Leo had lived more life than his forty-something years indicated; he wasn't stupid. But he was often gone and when he was around she went out of her way to avoid him to keep from giving him enough access to her that he grew curious.

With her back still to him, and his eyes boring into her, Munroe said, "Who're you trying to avoid by boarding so early? Ship's agent?"

"Yes."

"Even if he's not there, he'll hear about it. If you go when the khat trucks arrive, every man in the port is going to be focused on getting his fix—no one will pay attention to you."

"To us."

"Maybe."

"You'll come, Michael."

Not a request or a question, an order.

"Maybe," she said.

Leo turned again and strode toward the portion of roof they'd both climbed over, the part where there was less of an overhang and it was possible to get from ledge to balcony and down to the dividing wall without as much risk of slipping and breaking a neck. Louder, Munroe said, "If it wasn't for me, you wouldn't even get into the port tonight."

Leo didn't answer, waved her off and kept walking. He lowered himself over the edge and, at some point on the way down, let out a grunt. Munroe stood. A thud marked his drop from the wall to the ground of the compound next door, so she turned and followed the rooftop edge to the opposite corner, where she caught the colors of the port's shipping containers stacked four and five high.

Somewhere near there the freighter *Favorita* would soon dock, if she hadn't already, and Leo expected Munroe to be on it. He forced her to pick between poisons: board the ship as part of his team of armed transit guards, risking her life on the water to defend his client's ship if attacked by pirates, or leave the team—and it wasn't difficult to guess why. No matter what she chose, he got her out from under his roof and away from his wife.

Munroe crossed the roof to the spot where Leo had gone over. Lowered and dropped from the ledge into the narrow balcony. Through the glass on the door a five-year-old girl peered out and waved, and Munroe waved back. The girl laughed and hid her face and Munroe grinned.

Months of coming up here, of being noticed and smiled at, so many nights of hide-and-seek with sleep, of watching the stars fade under the rising glare of the sun, and not once had any of the apartment occupants spoken to her. She'd learned their routines, sometimes left gifts of nuts and fruits on the balconies when only the children were at home. Occasionally handcrafted presents waited for her in exchange, but not today, which was fitting for a good-bye. The girl peered out again, and Munroe smiled, then slipped over the rail and maneuvered into position to drop to the next balcony, perhaps for the final time.

For six months Djibouti had provided the comforting chaos that only the Third World could offer, and for these six months, navigating the nepotistic politics, the culture of graft and paranoia, the stench and the sounds and the maze of a society steeped in khat drug addiction, had played snake charmer to the serpents inside her head.

She'd come full circle, back to the African continent: had maneuvered herself into the arms of a mercenary team as she'd done a decade ago, and as it had also been then, she wasn't here as one of Leo's ship-jumping little army for hire, but as a linguist and a fixer. She'd wanted nothing to do with the weapons and the machismo. Though she had the skill to be one of the boys, she'd come to him as an errand runner. This was her past, comforting in a way that home might be comforting, if anything could ever be home. English-teaching parents had been her cover story—one that didn't invite questions—and really, Leo and Amber Marie had no reason to doubt. She got things done, soothed the abrasions that came with working in the grit: Familiar and rote—what clocking in for a data-entry job might be to anyone else—Djibouti had kept the inner voices quiet, gave her a way to keep busy without the responsibility or the burden of life-altering decisions or people depending on her for survival. She didn't need Leo's job for the money but for the sanity, and though she could eventually find something else, she didn't want to. She was dead here, liked it that way, and wasn't ready to come back to life.

Munroe went hand over hand, from second balcony to wall, and dropped into the compound that housed the two single-story buildings that were Leo's base of operations. She crossed caked dirt and passed beneath the one large tree to the rearward house, which was three small bedrooms and a few common areas that she shared with two other team members.

Natan lay lengthwise on the living room couch, his bare foot wrapped in an ankle bandage propped up on the wooden armrest. In place of ignoring her as he typically did, he watched her, and when she'd crossed half the room he said, "Leo is looking for you."

"He found me," she said, and stopped. Doubled back and stood in front of his foot. "How bad is it really?"

Natan shrugged.

"That's what I figured," she said, and his expression gave away what his words didn't: He knew just as well as she did why Leo had made this switch, and whatever resentment Natan may have felt at staying behind over a minor injury was probably compensated for by watching Leo's jealousy reach boiling point.

Munroe continued down the tiled hallway toward her room.

She'd never claimed to be male, not to Leo, not to Amber Marie, not to any of the rest of the men. Unlike so many other misrepresentations in her line of work, this one hadn't been calculated or deliberate, was just a continuation of the way she preferred to dress and operate in countries where being a single woman had the potential to cause endless complications. She was long and lean, with an androgynous body; it wasn't a difficult transformation and over the years the pretense of behaving and working as a boy had become more natural than assuming her own identity.

She'd shown up in Leo's office unannounced and asked for a job. He'd given her two weeks to prove her value, and with her skill set and experience it had been easy to ingratiate herself and create dependence, to become part of an operation that, for all of its excellence in weapons and security, lacked the finesse needed to inoffensively grease the daily bureaucratic gears. The side effects of coming onto the team as a male had been a bonus: She didn't have to endure sexist quips, no one hit on her, and Leo's men all respected the boundaries of man-to-man personal space.

Except she'd done her job too well, her name had been uttered once too often on the lips of the boss man's wife, and because Munroe had never bothered to clarify her gender at the outset and it was too late to clarify it now, appearances had turned her into the only guy the wife hung out with and repeatedly talked about during the long stretches the others were away. Call her oblivious, but a husband's jealousy was a complication Munroe hadn't planned on.

Munroe paused in front of her room to listen down the hall for Victor.

If the Spaniard was in, he wasn't moving about. She opened her door to a bare room: a bed she rarely slept in, an empty desk shoved up beside the bed, and a narrow armoire with a few changes of clothes. None of the furniture was from the same set much less the same decade. Her room had no pictures. No personal items. Nothing that said she belonged here.

Munroe sat on the bed and pulled from beneath it a backpack that had been with her for nearly ten years and twice as many countries. Held it in her hands and stared at it without seeing while Leo's options chased each other around her brain: Board the ship, or leave the team.

To keep his marriage calm, Leo needed to make her departure look like her own doing. She had no attachments that would make walking away difficult, but his clumsy, indelicate, ham-handed attempt to back her into a corner irritated her just enough to prod her into proving points of her own. A little manipulation, a little back-stabbing, and the fight in her had breached the surface again.

Munroe sighed. Perhaps she wasn't as dead to the world as she'd thought. She stood. Unzipped the pack and then dumped the few clothes from the armoire into it. Against her better judgment, she'd board that ship tonight, Somali pirates be damned, and when she got back, when she was ready, she'd leave Leo's company and Djibouti on her own terms.

Movement and a knock at the door interrupted her thoughts. Amber Marie, the other half of the company, the real brains behind the operation, stood in the door frame, blond hair tied back in a severe bun, baggy clothes hiding both her shapely figure and her age, which was a good ten or more years younger than her husband's. It was Amber who Munroe truly worked for, solving problems in a world that created new ones daily.

"Leo says you're going with him," Amber said.

"I might."

"You don't have much time left to decide," Amber said, and paused. "I guess either way you're leaving tonight?"

Munroe nodded. "Seems that way."

Amber smiled, making it difficult to tell if she understood that Natan's injury was really just a conveniently timed excuse that allowed Leo to force Munroe's hand. Amber said, "I figure once you get a taste for the ships, Leo will steal you away and you'll never want to be my go-to guy again." Gave a halfhearted attempt at another smile. "Either way I came to say good-bye and to thank you for everything."

Munroe returned the half smile. "It's been a good run," she said, and in response, Amber shifted, anguish in her body language. If Natan hadn't been in the living room, Leo's wife would have invited herself in, sat on the bed, and in response Munroe would have walked her through logic as she'd done so many times before, would have reassured her that based on probability alone, Leo would be home soon and that stress was pointless. Or they would have sat and laughed about the local inefficiencies and exchanged stories that played to similarities in lives that had left them both strangers to their homeland, citizens of a planet on which, no matter where they went, neither of them ever really belonged. But given the way things were now, Amber remained leaning against the wood, arms crossed, trying to look brave.

"So I'll see you when you get back," she said.

Munroe shoved the last of the clothes into the backpack and gave her the same answer she'd given Leo. *Maybe.*

Amber Marie nodded and with a mock salute left for the living room. The few words she exchanged with Natan filtered back as a mumble, and then the front door closed to quiet. Munroe stared through the empty door frame.

Amber's parents had been English teachers, not missionaries, but the dynamics were the same. Like Munroe's, Amber's loyalties, few as they were, were to people—not to any place or culture or flag. Born abroad, raised abroad, ever on the move and anxious if she stayed in one place too long, caught between cultures, with no allegiance to the country stamped on her passport—the easiest way to answer the question *Where are you from?* was to lie.

Munroe slung the pack over her shoulder and shut the armoire with finality. In the living room Natan, still on the couch with his ankle propped up, called out as she strode through. "Where are you going?" he said, and she ignored him, just as she had Leo.

CHAPTER 2

The two beat-up company vehicles were parked in the dirt space between the houses, which meant that everyone was accounted for and on the property. Like everything else, the cars were Leo's, made available if Munroe wanted them for work, provided none of the other team members had need of them. She paused in front of the Land Cruiser, the easy way out with its keys beneath the front seat, and, with the evening dimming, walked out of the compound through the pedestrian gate.

Touches of light from the recently set sun guided the way, augmented by the artificial glow that streamed out of nearby houses. She strode along the side of the road, over hard-caked dirt and sand and outcroppings of weeds, toward a larger junction several hundred meters away, where she could flag down a taxi.

Voices and conversations rose and fell within lengthening shadows, clusters of people gathered on doorsteps or in gateways, part of the vitality that the cooling darkness brought to the sleepy daytime streets. The white of her skin marked her as a beacon and men called out as she passed, then followed with shocked laughter when she responded in their tongue. Language was what protected her, had guided and guarded her throughout the years, the ability to understand, to communicate in a way that, because of her foreignness, most assumed she couldn't.

Munroe reached the crossroads, a thoroughfare more heavily trafficked, where proper streetlights obscured the stars and clusters of pedestrians followed along the edges, while vehicles, some decrepit, some shiny and new, competed for right-of-way in an orchestrated dance of chaos. Occupied taxis slowed for her, shared rides that would charge a lesser fare, and she waved them on in favor of an empty car. She argued with the driver over the rate and, knowing he was under khat influence, climbed in, numb to the risk and the casual recklessness with which he drove, life-threatening and yet so commonplace in a galaxy of Third World experience.

It took but a few minutes to reach the heart of Djibouti, where, like the thoroughfares that had brought them here, new money had paid for new roads, and the potholes were few and far between. She'd once heard the city described as a French Hong Kong on the Red Sea, but whoever had said it had clearly not been to the parts of the city she more often frequented—the parts where the roads were pitted and shacks were assembled with whatever material was to hand, and camels and goats played backdrop to the encroaching desert.

The taxi stopped a block over from her destination, and Munroe paid and stepped out into the night and into early evening noise that had only just begun to trickle out from the nearby bar and restaurant that catered mainly to foreign military, expats, and what few tourists had discovered this stop on the far, far edge of the map.

Off the sidewalk and under a portico, she pushed open a narrow door and headed up an equally narrow staircase, wooden, poorly constructed, and dimly lit by a loosely hung bulb. At the landing she knocked on the door. There was no answer, so she knocked again, and when still no one came, she let herself in with a key.

The apartment was small, part of the repartitioning that went on in a city where the population increased faster than new construction. Light filtered in from the short hallway, and she turned on another so that the common room was fully lit. The area had been tidied up, bright colored floor pillows organized, though two opened cans of 7UP and scraps of khat said that she hadn't missed the home-owners by much.

Munroe stepped into the kitchen at her right and into the smell of burnt cooking oil, cumin, and cardamom. Passed around a double gas burner and counter space to get to the end wall, and another door, which she surveyed for disturbance of the random threads she'd left, before pulling them away and unlocking.

The room was half the size of the one she kept at Leo's place, probably maid quarters in its prior life, dusty and stale, the air hot and difficult to breathe. A bare mattress on a crude wood frame filled the longest wall, and beside it stood a padlocked trunk, turned so that its hinges faced out. She tugged a frayed string to turn on the light, another single bulb that put out less wattage than the one in the stair-well, and opened the window to let in oxygen. It had been a month at least since she'd last been here.

Munroe knelt at the trunk and turned it toward her. Unlocked and lifted the lid. Not counting the Ducati she'd left behind with a friend in Dallas and the few possessions she stored along with the bike, everything she owned was in this room, and still, these were emergency necessities more than possessions.

She didn't need things, or want them, trappings to hold her hos-tage, clutter that had to be fussed and worried over and protected from theft and rot and ruin. Even these items were a ball and chain, but the tactician in her had refused to let them go, and in the mo-ment that seemed wise enough.

Munroe shuffled through clothes for the brick of bills buried among them, and when she found it, broke off a wad of dollars and euros to create a dozen small rolls that she stuffed into pockets and shoes and undergarments. She dropped the last half of the money into the backpack, pulled a tactical vest from the trunk, studied it for a moment, and with a long inhale, reached into a pocket and drew out one of the knives. Palmed the weight and felt the heft. Waited for a reaction, for the cravings and the urges to come, and when they didn't, she let out the air.

Munroe shoved the knife back into the vest, wasn't about to unsheathe it to find out how far her newfound calm had taken her, dropped the entire thing into the backpack, and followed with a single box of ammo and a handgun she'd brought with her from Europe.

She preferred the knives, silent extensions of her body, but considering the territory she was about to wade into—attempted hijacking or not, Leo wouldn't weep if she had an accident—the gun was a necessary evil.

She pulled a small fireproof safe from the bottom of the trunk, and balanced it on her knees to unlock it. Inside were the rest of her documents, and photos stored in ziplock bags, the only mementos she allowed herself, personal touches of her former life that she would never bring onto Leo's property as an invitation for someone to dig through her stuff and try to find answers to the questions left open to speculation.

She added the documents and a few pieces of clothing to the growing collection in her pack, tossed in a roll of duct tape, weapon and tool of choice, the one thing she never allowed herself to forget, replaced the items she would leave behind, and then paused at the photographs. Slipped one out of its protective covering and glimpsed the faces she hadn't dared look at these past months, smiles she'd once felt, peace she'd briefly had. With the picture came the sense of loss, and the pain, a knife slice against her torso that she blocked out, stomped down, and buried.

She turned the image facedown, caressed the back of it with her thumb, and then pushed the picture in with the others and dropped them into her pack. Shut and relocked the trunk. This was as close as she ever got to good-bye, and if she never returned, her hosts would eventually figure she was gone for good, would commandeer what she'd left and rent the room out to someone else; if she never returned, she had with her what she couldn't afford to lose.

Munroe opened the door and nearly bumped into the teenage sister working in the kitchen. The girl lowered her eyes and stepped aside to allow Munroe to pass.

"Where is your brother?" Munroe said, and the girl motioned

toward the front door. Munroe put one of the small rolls of bills on the counter. "Tell him I came. Tell him to keep my room for another month."

The girl nodded, and Munroe, not wanting to make her more uncomfortable than she was already, standing alone in the presence of someone she believed was a young man, left the house, shut the door, and headed down the stairs checking her watch.

In spite of her recommendation to delay the embarkation until tomorrow's khat hour, Leo would proceed with his own plan to board early in the morning dark. She had time. Not a lot, but enough that she could make the return across town on foot, and so she walked, long strides in the dark, mind churning, running what she knew about this contract against everything Leo hadn't said.

She reached the compound with forty minutes to spare and waited out the time on the street, where she could watch the gate and catch glimpses of the activity that went on beyond it. Waited until the cars were loaded and the men were inside, and Leo, hand to the roof of the Mitsubishi, Amber in its passenger seat, paused to scan the area. He looked for her, waited for her, was so convinced of her attachment to Amber Marie that even in light of what Natan had surely told him about her leaving the property, he couldn't imagine that she would have simply taken the other half of his offer and walked away.

Munroe strode for the gate and stepped into the path of the security lighting. When Leo saw her, his head ticked up in acknowledgment. "You're late," he said.

She paused and made direct eye contact, something she'd never done before. Gave a sly half grin that should jar his perception, then continued for the Land Cruiser where Natan, with his boo-boo hurt ankle, was behind the wheel eyeing her now-fuller backpack.

She grinned at him too, all the way to the back of the vehicle, where she dumped her pack on top of the other bags that filled the storage area, and then climbed into the backseat beside Victor, who nodded: a gesture that said welcome and also provided notice that now he, and probably every other member on the team, knew the unspoken reason she'd been ordered to come along.

She nodded back.

Victor, levelheaded and older than the others, was perhaps the only one who saw beyond her façade of youth and inexperience, and because the rest of the team treated her as an outcast, a necessary evil that they used but didn't trust, Victor had set about to mentor and protect her. She allowed him that. Even in her indifference she appreciated the kindness and, under the circumstances, expected that he'd be the only one who wouldn't let chest-thumping war-bonding and loyalty to his boss completely overwhelm reason.

Munroe slammed the door, and Leo, who'd been watching her all this time, turned, and got behind the wheel of the lead car.

CHAPTER 3

They headed out in convoy, dark streets to better-lit thoroughfares, then on to the northernmost shore of the city and the older of the port facilities, where, unlike the newer construction across the bay with its gantry cranes stretched out like giant manacles over massive container ships, the more humble mixture of local dhows and ancient breakbulk freighters berthed to load and unload the piles of boxes and bales lining the dock.

At the guard post, Leo handed over documents that would allow them entry, documents that had required effort for Munroe to procure, that would guarantee no one looked at what they carried into the port, the type of work for which clients in her past had paid a premium—done here for minimum wage and taken for granted because Leo had no idea of the skill it took to do what she did. In his eyes, all she was and all she'd ever be was a flunky, an expendable underling, unlike the big boys who carried the guns, and that was fine by her.

The guard waved them through and the lead car navigated along de facto streets formed by shipping containers stacked four and five high, toward the breakbulk wharf and finally to the freighter for which they'd been conscripted.

Four ships filled the wharf, and a few men still milled around, remnant stevedores sweeping the docks from a ship recently loaded or unloaded. Mostly the port was quiet, all the agents long gone, which had been Leo's reasoning for boarding at this hour.

In the world of shipping, nothing happened for a crew or a vessel at port without the ship's local agent. The agent, eyes and ears and hands of the ship's owner or charterer, should have been the one to secure the port clearance. Going behind his back as they did tonight meant going behind the back of whoever controlled the ship. And because they were avoiding the agent, they were sneaking armaments into the port for no legitimate reason.

Unlike many countries, Djibouti permitted the transport of weapons—even had systems in place to facilitate maritime security teams who needed to transfer from airport to seaport. This was one of the reasons Leo had chosen to base his team out of Djibouti—the law of the land spared him the logistical headache and expense of maintaining a mini arsenal in international waters and meeting client ships at sea. There were fees, there was paperwork, there was time and expense, yet none of that had been an issue before, and still tonight Leo made every effort possible to avoid legalities. Which raised the question: If the person who owned the ship and the one responsible for the freight weren't paying for this armed escort, then who and why? Because Leo and his team, although less expensive than some of the larger, better-known maritime security companies, still didn't come cheap.

The lead vehicle continued to the end of the wharf, pulled to a stop near the center of the last ship, and Natan, following close behind, stopped the Land Cruiser alongside. The freighter was larger than Munroe had expected, Liberian flagged, maybe six or seven thousand tons, about 150 meters long, with three hatches and two deck cranes. She sat low in the water with a freeboard that couldn't have been more than five meters, and by initial assessment was either an old ship or not well cared for.

Munroe stepped from the car and, together with the others, collected the gear. The captain came down the gangway while several of the ship's crew looked on from the deck. He was short and stocky with a healthy midsection. Under the glare of the port lights his weathered face and thinning hair pegged him as in his sixties, but his posture, physique, and more, the way he carried himself, said early fifties on the outside, and Munroe would have guessed there was military buried somewhere in his background.

Leo moved to greet the man and the two shook hands, exchanging words with imperfect English as the common language between them. Munroe knelt to tighten the straps of her backpack, keeping far enough away to avoid drawing attention, close enough to listen in as the captain bantered good ol' boy to good ol' boy with a level of camaraderie that came off with far too much exuberance to be genuine. And then, after a moment or two, as if exhausted from the effort, the captain swung his arm in a wide motion toward the gangway and said, "We hurry. Please. Put your men quickly so we go on the way."

Leo turned toward Victor and nodded him toward the ship. The Spaniard picked up his gear, started upward, and the other three followed. Munroe let them pass, hoping to catch the last of what was said between Leo and the captain, but they didn't speak as the men trudged up, and when her delay turned awkward she stood and grudgingly followed, leaving the boss men to whatever they had to discuss.

On deck, the ship rumbled beneath her feet, the main engine's oil pumps already running, which explained the crew loitering about: waiting to cast off lines as soon as they were given the order. The men acknowledged her when she boarded but didn't move to shake hands or speak to her, didn't have the faux friendliness of their captain, though from the curiosity written on their faces it would seem that Leo's men were the first armed escort to have boarded with this crew, if not the ship.

Munroe paused beside the gangway, let her bag slide off her shoulder, and set it by her feet. Victor and the others continued aft, toward the working and living quarters, which rose five levels above a deck long and wide enough that it could be used to lash down additional freight, if needed, but at the moment was empty. The ship's cargo was limited to the holds below—bags of rice, according to Leo, humanitarian aid for South Sudan by way of Mombasa, Kenya—and scanning the deck for the nearest access hatches, Munroe could only wonder if he was really that stupid or simply believed that she was.

The captain reboarded while Leo, arms around Amber, lingered on the dock. Unlike the crew, who kept to themselves, the captain approached Munroe and offered a hand, and when she took it, he gripped hers and pumped it in a move of dominance.

"English is your language?" he said.

She nodded.

"Good. Very good," he said, and welcomed her aboard with more of that same too-genuine-to-be-true friendliness: A minute or two of chitchat, just as he'd done with Leo, and then, duty finished, he turned and called out an order to one of his men. He continued on toward the door that the rest of the team had passed through, and Munroe turned back to the docks, searching out anyone who showed undue interest in the security team's arrival and departure.

The lighting and distance worked against her, and finding nothing, she leaned forward to stare at Leo and overtly watch the last of his good-bye. It was childish to needle him like this, but given the circumstances, the immaturity of it only made her want to do it more. He caught her eye, gave his wife a final kiss, and Amber turned from him and climbed behind the wheel of the Mitsubishi.

Munroe couldn't see her face but, having been through this with her eight times now, knew that as soon as Amber was alone inside that car, the veneer would crack, and the pain and neediness she'd held back on the dock would seep out and the tears would flow.

The vehicles circled around, and by the time Leo reached the deck Amber was already out of sight. He paused when he got to Munroe and flashed a grin, his way of showing that her behavior hadn't bothered him. She picked up her bag to follow him.

"Have you been on a ship before?" he said.

"It's not my first voyage."

He frowned, almost as if he'd been counting on her falling seasick on their first night out and was disappointed that it might not be so, then headed up the ladder—stairs in land-based terminology—for the bridge, and she in turn passed through the same door that the rest of the crew had.

The bosun pointed her up one level to where the helmsmen and mechanics bunked. Her berth was farthest down the passageway, accommodations for one that would be shared by two because Leo's guards would rotate watch.

Munroe found Victor in the room, which suited her fine, and she suspected he'd been the one to arrange to have her bunk with him. Munroe dumped her gear on the floor, and without looking up from the array of equipment he'd already spread out on the bed, Victor said, "Leo says you take first."

"Is he on first too?"

Victor nodded and said, "You know the ships?"

His was the same question as Leo's, only this one came from a place of concern instead of wanting to see her lose breakfast.

"I've been on a few," she said.

Victor grinned and wagged his finger. "You keep secrets," he said, and the way his gray-streaked beard twitched with his exaggerated speech forced her to return a smile. He'd already unloaded half his bag and unpacked his weapon, had laid out the equipment: handheld VHF radios, protective gear, and supplies—backups to his backups. He busied himself with his AK-47, which was what all of Leo's team used because parts and ammunition were so easy to find in this part of the world and the telltale staccato blended in with the enemy's.

Courtesy of Leo, she'd be keeping watch unarmed, just a warm body to fill his obligations. Victor handed her a radio and an earpiece, then nodded to his ballistic helmet. "You can use if you want," he said. "We trade when we trade shifts."

"You don't want me dead like Leo does?" she said.

He chortled and, noticing her interest in his weapon, said, "You use this before?"

"Something like it," Munroe said, and this time he laughed as if she'd let him in on a private joke. He wagged his finger again, as was his way. "You go on the ships, you use the guns." He ran a palm over his weapon, but paused and shook his head. "You make up stories."

She smiled and shrugged. In all, she'd probably spent more time on the ocean than he had, mostly in cigarette boats and in gutted and refitted fishing trawlers that had hauled the smaller boats longer stretches, up coastline in the Bight of Biafra, all part of the gunrunning operation she'd abandoned when she was seventeen. On ships she'd laughed, and loved, and killed, and on a ship she'd fled one life for another. Now here she was, more than ten years later, another circle completed.

Victor put the weapon in her hands, pointed out its working parts, and she listened, allowing him to teach her what he felt she should know, and when he was satisfied that she'd been properly schooled, he took the rifle away and returned to his own work.

The ship shuddered beneath their feet, indicating that the lines had been cast off and the voyage was about to begin, and Munroe left the berth for the passageway and the main deck, for Leo who had no idea of the sweet talk and magic that had been involved in guaranteeing the tug and the pilot would be available, arrangements that he'd never had to make before, would probably never make again, a task that shouldn't have fallen on her shoulders but had, due to his hiding their boarding from the agent.

CHAPTER 4

Munroe stood on the open deck of the *Favorita,* night-vision binoculars dangling uselessly from her wrist, staring out over the water and the pinpricks of light that dotted the vast blanket of darkness while the ship rolled a gentle back and forth in its forward churn through the ocean swells.

They traveled at about twelve or thirteen knots—fourteen or fifteen miles an hour in land-based language—a slow and easy target in high-risk-area terminology. Leo had put her in this spot an hour ago with the instruction to keep watch, and knowing it would frustrate him, she'd stood exactly here and had done nothing more. The ship and the people on it weren't her responsibility; she couldn't care enough to pretend that they were.

Another two hours and dawn would come, and if she had it her way, with the passage of time he'd become more irritated with her ineptitude until eventually he'd give up on her and wish he'd left her in Djibouti.

Munroe glanced aft and caught the movement of his silhouette on the bridge port wing, some fifty feet above the main deck, where he patrolled, war-gamed up in a combat vest and helmet, cradling his automatic weapon: a contrast to the flashlight and whistle that he'd given her, both of which she'd tucked into pockets in the tactical vest because she had no intention of using them.

He'd laughed when he'd first seen the vest, as if she were a child playing dress-up. Had asked where she'd gotten it, wanted to know what was in her pockets. When she wouldn't answer, he walked away in disgust and she watched him go, trying hard to see what kept Amber Marie attached to him. Smart and independent, Amber humored his Napoleon complex and committed herself to a lifestyle she hated, for a man more often away than home. Whatever Leo gave, whatever Munroe couldn't see, Amber loved him enough that for her the rest was worthwhile.

Munroe turned from him to the water, to the invisible danger that might or might not lurk in waiting. The captain had taken them northeast, presumably into the Internationally Recommended Transit Corridor, an unmarked sea lane between Yemen and Somalia where warships from two dozen nations patrolled nearly six hundred miles along the world's busiest sea route.

Fortune had turned against Somali piracy in recent years; the rate of hijacking attempts had fallen far below the heyday when dramatic confrontations and multimillion-dollar ransoms made international headlines. But the threat hadn't gone away. Ships were still hijacked, just not as often. Travel in the Gulf of Aden was a calculated risk: The ocean was too vast for the warships to respond to every distress call, yet the odds were slim that any one ship would be the losing pocket on a roulette wheel of twenty-two thousand a year. Armed guards made safe transit a sure thing; in spite of attempts, no armed ship had ever been hijacked.

Defending a moving fortress, guards had the advantage of the high ground; they were also better trained and better equipped, and three or four could do what twenty pirates on skiffs below could not. Even so, most merchant ships traveled without them. Armed transit was expensive, controversial, and, depending on the ships' flag state, in many cases illegal.

Leo moved out of sight to the far side of the bridge, so Munroe sat on the deck and leaned against the bulwark. Across from her, not more than a smudge of shadow beyond the crane, David held watch the way watch was meant to be held. He was Leo's friend from their years together in the French Foreign Legion: two men already used to working as a team, now on the same sentry cycle to compensate for her perceived uselessness. That would be the order of things until they reached Mombasa—four hours on, four hours off, in a schedule that would turn days and nights into eight-hour segments and force her to wait several shifts before her off time rolled around at an hour that most on the ship would be sleeping and she'd be free to explore unobserved and unhindered.

Munroe stood again, and, almost as if on cue, Leo's voice sounded in her earpiece. She made a show of fiddling with the bud and then spoke too loudly so that he yelled at her in a whisper, and that made her smile. He instructed her to walk the port side of the ship, to keep alert, and so she made a slow amble, aft to fore and back again, with ocean spray carried up by the wind stinging her face and probabilities playing against facts, because as much as she didn't care what happened to the ship, she cared what happened to herself. No matter what Leo claimed, this wasn't a standard voyage or standard contract, and she fully intended to get back to land no matter how badly anyone else fucked things up.

The sun rose, and Victor came as part of the relief of the next watch. "You do good?" he said.

She pulled the flashlight from a pocket and handed it to him. "Your weapon," she said. "Just in case." His beard twitched and he wagged his finger, so she gave him the whistle as well.

When he laughed, she grinned and turned away for the galley to grab food and see what more she could learn from her shipmates. Leo's team was far too egalitarian to fit neatly into the formal segregation of officers and crew, but at sea they followed the patterns of their hosts, and on the *Favorita* that meant Leo and David ate in the officers' mess, socialized with the officers, and had their berth on the officers' deck while the rest of them were relegated to the crew's mess and crew's quarters.

The arrangement was how Munroe preferred things—it kept Leo away from her—and in any case, the crew interested her most. She ate in silence, listening to the cook hash out an issue with the mechanic, understanding nothing of the words rattled off in Tagalog, but plenty of the body language, and references to the captain, who came up in the conversation more than once.

From what she'd observed, overheard, and coaxed out of the cook during a brief conversation before they'd fully embarked, the ship had three officers and thirteen crew—a Russian captain, first and second mates and engineer from Poland, and the crew mostly from the Philippines with the exception of three who were from Egypt. She didn't know how long the captain had been with the *Favorita,* but it was longer than the cook, who'd been with the ship for four years.

The mechanic left, the cook went about his work, and Munroe returned to the berth in an attempt to sleep, a fight against memories that were sometimes easier to forget than others. She tossed fitfully and, when the effort seemed futile, pulled the packet from her vest pocket and brushed her finger against the back of the facedown photo. Held it there a long while, connected to Miles Bradford, lover, lifesaver, companion, and friend, in the only way she could be.

She'd contacted him once in the past eleven months, had sent him a newspaper clipping of a burned-out yacht, the end of a monster who'd nearly destroyed both their lives in his purchase of female flesh, a newspaper clipping that would have told him that she'd succeeded and was alive. She'd kept up with him from a distance, through status updates and news on his company blog, breadcrumbs that he put there for her because he had to know she was in the shadows, lurking, watching, though lately the breadcrumbs had become fewer, and her temptation to return stronger.

The separation hurt, but it was better than the death that inevitably followed her, destroying the ones she loved most. This way, maybe they'd both stay alive.

MUNROE WOKE TO the sound of the door handle turning, a firm yank out of a sleep she'd had no recollection falling into: a yank that pulled her out of bed and onto her feet ready to fend off an attack before the door had swung fully open.

Victor stood in the doorway, one foot over the threshold, body frozen in place, muzzle of the rifle raised halfway in her direction, surprise etched onto his weatherworn face.

Munroe raised her hands in a show of backing off. Said, "Bad dreams," and stepped a retreat toward the bed. "I didn't expect to sleep," she said. "I'm sorry I'm late."

Victor lowered the weapon and moved past her, into the berth. He unsnapped, unzipped, and pulled off the tactical gear. Munroe stooped to scoop the fallen packet of pictures off the floor, reached for her vest, and with her head down and avoiding eye contact, stepped out, away from the shame of having given evidence of the emotional disequilibrium.

Leo glowered when she arrived late. She turned her back to him and faced the water, allowed monotony to take from her what sleep could not. Time became routine and followed a rhythmic pattern that rose and fell with the motion of the sea and passed into the rotating of the watch.

Leo gave up on her after her third turn at not even pretending to care, and, cautious to keep out of sight, she didn't bother showing up again after that. They rounded the Horn of Africa and turned south along the Somali coast, presumably routing far off course as was standard procedure to evade pirate sightings, running dark at night to escape attracting attention with the lights.

She spent daylight sleeping or talking with the crew, avoiding her bed, the berth, and the potential of being compromised around people she didn't trust. When she did sleep, she did so on deck, among supplies or in hidden nooks that she'd discovered in her exploratory forays, and in the deep night and early morning she slipped down the access hatches and into the holds.

There was something on this ship that made the crew nervous, caused huddled talk, shifting glances, and tension in their posture and interactions. With Leo's flashlight she searched for inconsistencies in the way the bags of rice had been loaded, and it took over two days of incursions into the belly of the freighter before she found the first storage crate buried two bags deep, directly beneath the center of the number one cargo hatch.

A touch of splintered wood had led her to more until she'd uncovered a portion of what had to be a larger cache, a mixture of small arms, Russian-made assault rifles, and antitank and antiaircraft weapons. There were possibly additional stockpiles, perhaps even larger munitions, buried deeper or that she'd overlooked in the other holds, but discovering this was enough for her questions and suspicions to find answers: If these weapons were legal and intended for discharge in Mombasa, they wouldn't have been hidden, which meant they would have to be offloaded before reaching Kenya, and the only place to do that was Somalia.

Munroe reburied the cache and made for the ladder, moving hand over hand, anger at Leo rising higher with each rung toward the deck. He hadn't been hired to protect the ship, which was old and carrying worthless cargo; not even hired to protect the crew. Instead of diverting hundreds of nautical miles out of the way to avoid the hazard area, at some point they would be traveling directly into it. He'd been brought on to stand guard over the arms delivery itself.

She reached the top of the ladder, disgust rising at the audacity, not the gunrunning—given her history she could hardly be a hypocrite in that regard. Leo had played God with her life, had deliberately taken choice away from her by withholding information: an act made all the more vile because as far as he knew she was young and inexperienced, and if things went to hell, he'd knowingly written her a death sentence.

Munroe moved through the opening and crouched onto the deck, resealed the hatch, skirted between the coamings, and waited in the shadows, watching for Victor to pass on patrol. Strategy and tactical possibility laid themselves out on a chessboard inside her head, cold calculation muting the fury.

It was one thing for her to play the fool and willingly allow someone to use her, another entirely to be played and used as if she were a fool.

Certainly Victor, too, knew what lay beneath her feet, and his betrayal in the face of his act of concern stung worse than if this entire venture had only been Leo's doing. And Amber Marie? What of her?

Munroe drew in a deep breath and let the anger seep out, pulled rationality into its place. Detachment would serve her far better.

She felt Victor's approach before she saw him, instinct long honed during the years of hunting and being hunted in the dark. Waited for him to pass and then rose to approach from his blind spot, moving soundlessly, steps drowned by the wind.

Victor startled when he felt her, said, "Christ!" and spun to face her. "Are you crazy?" he said, and then trying to cover the surprise gave her his bearded grin and said, "What new secrets do you bring tonight?"

She kept beside him, stride matching his. "I think it's you who've been keeping secrets."

"My secrets?" he said, and his voice betrayed a genuine earnestness that she'd truly hoped wouldn't be there.

"Where is this ship headed?" she asked.

"That's no secret. Mombasa—we all know this."

"Before Mombasa."

He stopped walking, turned to study her, and in the moonlight his expression twisted and his eyebrows lifted as if he'd begun to understand.

"I've been exploring down in the hold," she said. "Found a few interesting things. So where do we stop to deliver them?"

Victor started walking again. "You didn't know?" he said.

"Didn't know what exactly?"

He didn't reply.

"Obviously, Leo knows," she said. "And you know, and I assume that David knows. What about Emmanuel? Marcus? Am I the only one that Leo neglected to tell?"

"He briefed me alone," Victor said. "Told me he would do the same for the others and that we were not to speak of it again."

"What's your cut?" Munroe said.

"If Leo finds out," Victor said.

"He's the last person I'd tell anything."

"One-sixth," he said. "On top of the voyage pay."

Munroe stopped walking. Whatever indifference she'd maintained after boarding the ship shed like the last of a snake's old skin. Leo had gall forcing her on a gunrunning mission while cutting her out of the hazard pay.

Victor paused, waiting for her, but Munroe had nothing more to say. She turned and strode away, and after a hesitation he continued on again.

Munroe kept to the shadows, breathing in the dark and timing movement to skirt the others on patrol, went up on the inside, where, although she might be spotted, possibly caught, she wouldn't cast shadows and invite a bullet the way she would outside. She'd not yet been on the officers' levels, but she knew where Leo bunked and how to find him thanks to innocent questions and friendly banter with the bosun that had given her enough to map out the deck in her head.

She reached the level and turned down the passageway, quiet like the rest of the ship, and when Munroe found the berth that she understood to be Leo's, she thrust the door open.

Leo was already upright on his bed, reaching for a sidearm, when she strode through.

"There's no point in shooting," she said.

The light in the room switched on, brilliantly painful, and Munroe shut the door, leaned back against it, and crossed her arms.

Weapon two-fisted in her direction, Leo swung his legs over the side of the bed and said, "What are you doing here?"

"Demanding my cut," she said.

"Are you insane? You walk into my room in the middle of the night and start nonsense."

"I've been down in the hold," she said. "I understand basic math. There are six of your people on this ship. I'm one of them. I want my cut."

"Ah," he said, and he smirked, then put the weapon on the floor beside the bed, swung his legs back up, and lay down as if she were a trifling inconvenience. "That cut goes to Natan," he said.

"Natan isn't here, I am."

He laughed. "Your body may be here, but you're of no help and there's no way I'm giving you a cut."

"Natan's body isn't here," she said. "That makes him even more useless than me."

Leo propped himself on his elbow in a brief pause, then sat up again. Swung his legs over the side of the bed again and rested his bare feet on the floor. "You had no reason for being down in the hold," he said. "You are digging into things that don't involve you." He paused for emphasis. "It could get you hurt."

She maintained eye contact, a deliberate challenge to his authority, which, if he'd been capable of seeing beyond his idea of who she was, should have given him pause, made him wary; but his body language said otherwise.

"It involves me," she said. "You left out a lot of important details when you demanded I come along."

In response, Leo slowly stood, shoulders back, chest out, hands slack at his sides, as if his implied threat should cause her, the purportedly weaker of the two, to retreat out of fear of whatever would come next.

Munroe followed him with her eyes but didn't move. "Natan wasn't hurt that badly," she said. "He could have come if that was what you'd wanted."

In a space so small that Leo could have reached her if he'd stretched far, he took a step in her direction: another challenge.

"I won't be as easy to throw overboard as you imagine," she said.

"You are far out of line."

"Hardly. What's your plan for the discharge? We get close to the

Somali coast, offload at sea, and be on our way? Is this the captain's doing or is someone else pulling the strings?" And because the muscles in his legs tensed as if he were preparing to take another step, she said, "It would be a mistake to get any closer."

Leo paused at her warning, then laughed. "Okay," he said, "whatever you say." He turned away from her and sat on the bed. The laughter stopped. He glanced up and said, "Get out."

"I want my cut."

"I'm done talking," he said. "Get out or I make you leave."

She didn't move. Didn't speak.

Shorter than she was, he came after her, hands first as if he would grab her collar and toss her to the bed. Time slowed. Instinct overrode thought, and with a speed hard-won in her struggle to stay alive, she blocked and parried. History that had made her who she was called out for the kill, was held in check by years of controlling the urges.

The attack and smack back lasted less than two seconds, and in the wake of her defense, Leo paused and stood hunched over, hands clenched, confusion and anger advertised on his face, a message on a well-lit marquee. Munroe nodded and opened the door. Stepped into the passageway and shut it behind her. If deceit-and-revelation was the deed by which score was kept, tonight had evened the game.

CHAPTER 5

Late afternoon the next day, Munroe left the relative solace of the engine room and headed out to the main deck, blinking back against the blinding sun, staring up to where Leo patrolled on the bridge wing. She'd avoided him since her confrontation, had snuck into the galley to grab food when she knew his men wouldn't be around and slept when most of the ship was awake.

She took her time in the climb to be certain he knew she was coming, each slow footstep reverberating against the metal. Leo didn't speak or acknowledge her when she reached him and so she leaned her forearms against the rail, kicked a foot up on a slat of one of the many shipping pallets lining the railing, and allowed him the silence while he continued the slow pace along the wing, a small circuit from which he could see the full length of the ship, miles of ocean ahead and around, and everything that lay in their wake. A minute passed. Two. Five. Ten, and finally Leo stopped beside her. "What do you want?" he said.

"What do you know of the captain?" she asked.

Turning back to the ocean, he said, "Why?"

"He committed us to delivering arms off the coast of Somalia— would be nice to know something about the hands we're in."

Leo snorted. Patted his rifle. "Not his hands."

Munroe nodded toward the weapon. "That's fine while we're moving and out on the open sea," she said. "But to make this handoff we'll be stationary and vulnerable—not just to whoever we're dropping off with, but to warring clans and pirate factions."

"What would you know about keeping a ship safe?" he said.

"More than you'd imagine."

He was silent again, perhaps replaying their last encounter and the truths he'd uncovered in those seconds, perhaps debating whether she was worthy of the discussion. "I'm not expecting complications," he said.

"Have you done business with him before?"

"He comes recommended from a trusted source."

"But what of his history? His enemies?"

Leo stretched a hand toward the empty ocean and drew his arm around in an arc. "Whatever enemies he might have, they're certainly not here."

Munroe shrugged and turned from him, back to the water.

Leo could be right, she hoped he was right, but she'd experienced far more than her share of treachery in remote places of the world, had felt too much of humanity, too deeply, to believe that anything was ever what it appeared to be. Without knowing what strings the captain had pulled to get these weapons, whom he might have pissed off along the way, it was impossible to predict what traps lay ahead and plot a strategy to avoid them; but if Leo didn't already see this, hadn't been concerned enough to vet the captain for himself, explaining her reasoning now wouldn't change anything.

"How far out are we?" she said. "One day? Two days?"

"Around thirty hours."

"I want my cut for the delivery."

Leo shook his head.

"If I turned out to be useful after all, you'd still give it to Natan?"

"Yes."

"Why?"

"We've already had this discussion."

"You're certain you won't change your mind?"

He glared as if she were a fool for asking and so she straightened, nodded, said, "Okay then," and turned for the ladder.

This conversation had been her final attempt at reconciliation, an olive branch. Leo's decision severed her path from his completely. Had he given her what was her due, she would have been more useful than all four of his men, and not just in her ability to understand the whispers behind their backs. She'd lived her own store of experience from that previous lifetime, had survived when betrayal had come while they were anchored and men with guns, as well trained as any of Leo's team, hadn't been enough to keep the ship safe.

In passing the door of the bridge, Munroe spotted the captain, who, like Leo, had become her enemy: He had put the lives of his crew at risk—a violation even greater than what Leo had done to her, because even if he'd compensated them for this detour, unlike her, his men weren't in a position to say no. They were poor, had families to feed, and if the ship was taken for ransom, they had no resources to raise the money should the ship's owner refuse to pay. And even if they were fortunate enough that the *Favorita* carried kidnap and ransom insurance, the captain's violations, if they came to light—and insurance companies being what they were, this breakaway excursion *would* come to light—would cause the policy to be voided, and the crew, like so many ship's crews before them, would be abandoned to their fate.

The weight of it made her head hurt, made her nauseous. She had run to Djibouti to get away from the killing, from monsters who played and toyed with people's lives, had run to get away from the burden of caring, and here, the yoke of life's injustice had found her again.

Munroe reached the main deck and headed through the open door to the interior, hating humanity, hating that she felt anything at all. Jogged up a level and strode the passageway to the berth where Victor slept. Stepped into the room quietly, trying to avoid waking him, but his eyes opened and he said nothing as she knelt and reached for one of his bags.

"I need to borrow your backup radio," she said.

Victor nodded, and in what was probably the greatest repair of trust that he could have offered, he closed his eyes and rolled toward the wall.

WHEN IT WAS dark again and Victor was back on watch, Munroe left the supply room and returned to the berth to retrieve her pack. Carried it with her to the deck and walked the full length of the ship, skirting the patrol, until she'd passed beyond the foremost coaming. Here there were shadows that even the sporadic light of the clouded moon wouldn't reach.

Sheltered from the wind, she settled for the night with her pack as a pillow, the pictures in her pocket for company, and for entertainment the three men on watch trading crude jokes in her earpiece.

In the rhythm of the ship as it rose and fell, Munroe watched the map in the sky, same as she had done so many, many nights before in that land of superstition where rumors of her juju, her magic, went out before her and kept her team ahead of conflict and out of trouble. Here on the *Favorita*, thousands of miles and over a decade away, the story could have been the same had she not, in her running, worked so hard to develop the reputation of a nothing.

Munroe closed her eyes and drifted into the constant of the engine's hum, swallowed by the soothing comfort of the monotony until the ship shuddered, tossing her from her place of repose as if she were on a toy boat rattled by a child in a bathtub.

Confusion erupted in her earpiece.

Victor's voice came first in a series of swears, followed by Marcus on the starboard wing of the bridge in a heated exchange with the chief officer, arguing in a French that Nowak couldn't understand, while Nowak used broken English that meant nothing to Marcus. A simple flick of a switch and in less than a minute Munroe could have settled things, but the decision to intervene or not had already been made by Leo. They were on their own.

Munroe grabbed the strap of her bag and belly-crawled out from the shadows and in the direction of the starboard railing. Far down the deck so that they were shapeless blurs in the dim, Victor and Emmanuel paced at their respective rails, too focused on scanning the water to get involved in the argument up top, which continued, increasing in volume if not clarity.

Three shadows rushed through the doors of the upper deck, and all of them moved quickly toward the bridge. Again in her earpiece, another discussion, this time the captain's voice, first in English to Leo, it seemed, something about the propeller getting caught in a fishing net or ocean garbage, about it not being unusual, about sending a man to look, then something in Russian to Nowak, which she would have understood if she could have heard, but the words were garbled. These were two wholly distinct reactions by the different factions: the captain and the *Favorita*'s officers, as if the propeller stoppage could have come from a number of different sources; Leo's crew, as if an attack was the only possibility—which was what Leo was here for, of course—though logically, tactically, the captain's reaction made the most sense.

How did you stop a freighter, a pinprick of black against more black, in the middle of the goddamn ocean at night, without warning, and nothing to worry the radar? And yet Munroe sided with Leo.

Not because of the weapons in the hold or her misgivings about the handoff, but because she'd heard of similar happenings, knew how she would have stopped the ship if it needed to be done.

The lights didn't power on, and from her earpiece the captain's logic was clear: If there was nothing on the water, he didn't want to attract something. Leo didn't argue. If there was something on the water, he didn't want to give the invaders a map and create targets.

Munroe continued the low crawl toward the railing, covering the distance tentatively, knowing that Marcus in his nest up by the bridge would inevitably spot her and, amped up and trigger-happy as he was, might not register that it was she until after he'd already shot her.

Nothing in her earpiece indicated he'd seen anything out in the darkness.

Nothing of value came from Victor or Emmanuel, or from David, who'd by now joined Marcus on the wing. All of the men were equipped with night vision on their scopes, had low-light binoculars, but little good those would do as they hunted, hunted through a hazy green for small specks in the vast emptiness.

Without the propeller the ship moved on momentum alone, and Munroe could feel the slowing while the pacing of the men intensified. The silence dragged on for long, long minutes until the ship was dead in the water and at the mercy of the wind and the currents.

No armed ship had yet been hijacked off Somalia because guards were able to fend off attacks from a distance, made it impossible for the marauders to get close enough to fire at the bridge or put an RPG round through the engine room: the guards kept the ship *moving,* but tonight that strategy had been thwarted.

Munroe scanned the ocean again, saw only blackness, and in the continued eeriness of the ship gone quiet, the only sounds were the water lapping and the whispered coordination in her earpiece while the jolt of adrenaline that had come in the wake of the stoppage settled some.

The longer they went without any sign of attack, the more the tension subsided. Fifteen minutes passed, twenty perhaps. The engineers and the mechanic had been roused, and problem solving had gone into full swing. And then Victor whispered a slur, as if he'd found an enemy that even Marcus and David up by the bridge hadn't spotted. He fired several quick bursts. A warning to whatever was out there, assuming something was out there.

And then more silence.

Even the radio went quiet and Munroe could feel the focus as each man studied the water, trying to find the threat that eluded them.

Another five minutes passed and then Marcus, a tremor of excitement in his voice, gave coordinates for an approaching attack boat, though no sound of an engine came in over the water. Then new coordinates. And new ones again. And again. The tempo on deck picked up. Not confusion so much as tension in trying to home in on multiple moving targets far enough away that they were not easily spotted among the swells even with the aid of low-light goggles.

Munroe lay flat near the railing, watching, waiting, analyzing, puzzling.

So much about the scenario was wrong.

Pirates might follow a well-lit ship at night waiting for dawn before they launched an attack, but she'd never heard of a night strike that targeted a ship out in the dark like this.

Victor fired three more bursts.

Wrong.

Even a calm ocean dumped four- to six-foot swells against the ship's hull and turned waterline boarding into a climb up a sharp, wet, rocking, bucking wall. It was hard enough using grappling hooks and ropes and ladders when there was no armed resistance and you could see what you were doing.

This made no sense.

Flashes sparked out in the dark, far behind the freighter, and a barrage of weapon reports returned from the ocean, though it didn't appear that the attack drew closer. And then there was silence again. An elongated stretch of minutes where the automatic weapons went quiet and the armed guards, finding protection behind strategically placed sandbags, searched again for the enemy, and in that eternity, the first flash-bang grenade hit the deck.

Even this far fore, dulled by the distance, muted by the open air, Munroe felt the concussion wave. David screamed, and Munroe knew his pain. Through the night goggles, looking at the moon was like looking into the sun—how much more the searing light that had just exploded in front of him.

Without the night vision, the men on the ship would be forced to fight blind.

And then another explosion, another flash.

Wrong, all wrong.

Munroe struggled to pick Victor out from the darkness but couldn't find him. A shadow or two moved down from the bridge, another one up, but she could no longer tell who was whom. The ship's foghorn blew, signal to most of the crew to gather in the safe room. Another explosion followed, and then another, and then from the port wing of the bridge a staccato of weapon reports more sprayed anger than targeted shooting.

Munroe closed her eyes, breathed in the sounds of silence and the fragrance of the impending battle. She saw the strategy, knew the reason for the suppressive fire, understood that it wouldn't be long before the fighting escalated and whatever was out there closed in: Leo's team had the high ground, presumably had superior training and better weapons, but the ship was the length of a football field, and they could no longer see in the dark and hadn't come prepared for a full-on assault of a standing ship. Leo's team didn't have the capacity to hold the *Favorita* indefinitely.

The silence lingered and Munroe knelt, palms to the deck. The cool of the metal bled into her hands. The first rush burned through her veins and, with it, release in abandoning herself to fate, to the predator's instinct: tranquillity in the knowledge that death had come for her again.

CHAPTER 6

Munroe crawled along the edge of the coaming in the direction where she'd last seen Victor. The muzzle flashes out on the ocean stayed dark and, without targets at which to aim, so did the weapons on deck. How long before Leo's men pulled the night goggles back on and began hunting the water once more? Probably never—being blinded again was too great of a risk. And then as if to confirm the thought, another concussion grenade landed midship and brought more searing light.

This was Leo's war. He and his men could do what they'd been paid to do, but she wasn't sticking around. No matter how far away the suppressive fire might be, something was close enough to get those grenades on deck, and that was her way out.

A minute passed, then two, while she continued a cautious stop-start in Victor's direction; she'd drag him with her if she could, if only for the kindness he had shown, and then she heard the thud, soft and sick: a body being hit with a metal pipe or a rubber-coated grappling hook laying hold somewhere along the railing.

Munroe paused. Heard the thud again. Was fifteen feet away when the first man, dressed in commando getup, reached the deck and slid over the rails. A moment later a partner came up behind him.

The second man untied a rope from his waist, pulled hand over hand, and hauled up a grenade launcher, which he gave to the first man, and a Kalashnikov rifle that he kept for himself. The man with the launcher passed within a few feet of Munroe, and he carried his weapon with the casual confidence of one who'd handled rifles since childhood, yet his gait, clumsy and ill-timed, betrayed him as an amateur playing dressed-for-war, as if he mimicked moves seen on television without understanding the reasons for them.

Munroe breathed down the quandary. The boat they'd come from was her way of escape. And yet these men were far enough fore that without the night vision, Leo's team would never see them, and there was no way to give Leo a warning without alerting the invaders to her own presence. Munroe moved from her belly into a crouch.

The man with the launcher spoke, and she froze.

The words came in Somali. "Remember, don't shoot the captain."

"How do I know which is the captain?" said the other.

"You saw his picture."

"But they are all white men."

"Only shoot the legs," said the grenade launcher, and the man with the rifle signaled something and lay prone on the deck, face toward the bridge, while the man with the launcher crept away from his partner, as if he intended to continue around the foremost side of the hatch to the port side. Munroe strained to pull images from the dark, far down the deck. Still no Victor. Waited until Grenade Launcher approached the corner of the hatch and then slunk through shadow after him.

She came on him from behind. Hand to head, foot to knee. Slammed his face into the metal edge of the coaming and his body went limp in a fight that had ended too fast to be fair. She'd killed more often than she wished to remember, had fed off the hunt and suffered from it all the same. The law of the jungle cried out to her to finish what she'd started, to answer treachery with treachery and dump him in the ocean, but this wasn't her battle, it wasn't personal enough to upend the numbness of Djibouti.

The silence on deck ticked on.

Munroe left the unconscious man where he'd dropped.

The attack boats were out there. Couldn't be much longer before chaos erupted, and she needed to be gone before it happened.

At the corner of the hatch she leaned out toward the man with the rifle, still prone on the deck, playing warrior with his face toward the bridge.

"*Halkan kaalay,*" she hissed.

The man turned in her direction but didn't rise and so she called louder, trying to mimic the accent she'd heard so briefly before. On the second call, the man with the rifle moved to his feet, scampered in her direction, and when he passed the corner, she grabbed his neck, pulled him off balance, and shoved him into the metal as she'd done with the first. But he didn't go down.

Instead he clawed. Twisted. Tried to regrip the rifle and get a finger on the trigger. Munroe smashed her forehead into his face and he crumpled. She grabbed the rifle and struck him hard, and when he collapsed completely she stood over him breathing heavily, wrestling through the desire for blood and violence that had enveloped her in those seconds he'd fought back.

Munroe knelt and searched his clothes. Found a small handheld radio, snatched it up, clutched the rifle, and returned starboard. On the water she discerned the outline of an inflatable boat tethered to the freighter by the tails of the grappling hooks, and one man below working to keep the little craft from being washed into the hull of the ship.

If he'd only planned to deliver his accomplices, then he would already have been gone. Instead, he waited. She could use that.

Munroe searched the deck for Victor again. Couldn't see him and so ran along the coaming in the direction he'd last been. Three minutes to find him and then she'd be gone, three minutes of time ticking off inside her head, and all she happened upon was empty deck.

She crossed between hatches one and two, glanced fore and aft.

Spotted a motionless form several meters in the direction she'd come and skirted through shadows toward it and found not Victor but the ship's captain.

In the burn of disappointment Munroe punched the man. He didn't move. He wasn't dead, she could tell that much, but was unconscious and bleeding from a head wound—as if he'd been on his way to the hold with the weapons and had been too close to the last flash-bang when it had gone off.

In the heat of the moment, direction change in the midst of battle, a decision that had as much to do with frustration over not finding Victor as it did with scorn and loathing for this lump of a thing that meant something to the invaders, Munroe reached for the captain's collar and dragged him toward her escape. She couldn't guess what they wanted with him, but by getting him off the ship she'd deprive them of a trophy, and maybe find answers, maybe purchase a foothold for Victor, for Amber.

Another round of automatic fire from the water shattered the temporary stillness and this time the muzzle flashes appeared to be moving closer.

Time. She had no time.

Munroe pulled the captain into the shadows and foot by foot wrangled him to the rope that the intruders had used to pull the weapons on board.

In the dark where she had left them, one of the battered men had crawled to his knees. Hand on his head, he swiped at the blood. Counting every wasted second and regretting her decision not to dump him overboard, Munroe strode toward him. He opened his mouth but no sound came out, and he scratched backward to get away from her. Munroe slammed the butt of the rifle to the side of his head and he stopped moving.

The battle on the bridge intensified.

She returned to the captain. Pulled the rope beneath his back, looped it under his arms, twisted and tied it into a bowline knot. The rope was thinner than she would have liked, was enough to carry his weight but would probably cut into him. Face to the rail, focus on securing the man, she missed the scrape from behind. Felt the movement before it reached her, let go of the captain and stood at the same time the rifle muzzle pressed into her spine.

The adrenaline uptick fed into her veins, clarifying thought into rapid calculations. One hand raised slowly in a show of surrender, her other inched toward the sheath for the knife.

The muzzle punched into her back was accompanied by a rush of Somali, ordering her to turn around, the volume and tempo of the words telling her the person holding the gun was overadrenalized, scared; words she ignored because there was no logical reason she should have understood them, and if the man with the rifle followed the same instructions as his predecessors, he couldn't kill her until he'd confirmed she wasn't the same white face he'd seen in photographs.

Ears straining, Munroe stretched past the battle, searching for clues to the number of men behind her, calculated the risk of turning to fight. Another flash-bang exploded somewhere on the deck, instant answer, instant out.

In the concussion wave she dropped. Spun. Knocked the muzzle up and followed with the knife. Hand wrapped around the weapon, she shoved it away. The rifle discharged beside her ear, deafening, while the young man fought for control and her knife answered with a life of its own, the dormant demons ascending from deep sleep, instinct and speed in the face of death.

His body dropped, the warmth of his blood trickled down her hand, and Munroe knelt, predator over prey, breathing in the fragrance of fear, scanning the deck for his companions, cursing Leo.

There had to be one more man in the dark, someone with the launcher. Likely a three-man crew identical to the one she'd already encountered. She searched the shadows and didn't see him. Turned back again to the rail.

Paused only a moment and then leaned toward the water. She was finished here. Would not stay to fight a war that had never been hers to begin with.

She called to the man below, "*Waxaan hayaa kabtankii.*"

"Where is the signal?" he said back.

"It is broken," she said, words kept short out of fear that with so many variants of Somali, her dialect would be wrong. "Take the prisoner."

The man in the boat shifted and made a poor attempt to stand, and that was enough to know that he didn't suspect. Munroe wrapped the rope around the top rail and then around her waist, heaved the captain up, leveraged him against the rail, and tipped him over. His deadweight pulled hard against her, and the rope burned her hands as she let it out. She fought to keep from dropping him, grateful for the short descent to the waterline.

The man below guided the captain in and Munroe released her hold.

"*Waan soo socdaa,*" she said, and the man in the boat didn't object. She pulled the 9 mm from the small of her back and shoved it into the front of her waistband. Snagged her pack, shrugged through the straps, and, leaving the rifle on deck because she couldn't carry it too, slipped over the railing, took hold of the base of the grappling hook, wrapped the line around her leg, and let herself over the side.

She was vulnerable in those long seconds that she worked her way down, white skin against the night, hands, neck, and face a certain giveaway had the watchman been suspicious. It would have taken only a small bit of clarity for him to notice what he should have seen from the beginning and shoot her in the back. But in speaking his language she'd designed her own protection. Why should he doubt what he'd heard? He was too busy keeping the boat from getting rubbed bare against the ship to concern himself with her.

Last few feet before the waterline, Munroe let go one hand, pulled the handgun from her pants, shoved her feet against the hull to push out, and dropped into the center of the boat. The little craft rocked hard and her shin landed on the captain's arm, bone-crushing pain softened by the partial flexibility of the boat's bottom.

Munroe pointed her weapon at the watchman, but preoccupied as he was with keeping the craft steady, she might as well not have bothered. He didn't fully look her way until she'd shrugged out of her pack, one shoulder first and then the other, gun and focus always steady on him.

Only when he saw the weapon pointed at his face did he lower the oar he'd been holding against the hull and slowly raise his hands in surrender.

The man was older than she would have guessed, had at least ten if not fifteen years on the young men who'd gone up the *Favorita.* Like theirs, his clothes were black, but his were closer to rags, mismatched, torn, and ill-fitting.

Eyes never leaving his, handgun never lowering, Munroe reached for the rifle at his feet, and when she'd secured the weapon for her own use, she returned the 9 mm to her waistband.

"Untie and shove off," Munroe said.

The man knelt to let loose the lines, then picked up the oar again and pushed hard against the ship. The inflatable responded, and Munroe braced for his retaliatory lunge, expected him to take a swing, but he didn't.

Once away from the ship, he put down the oar and, taking the engine just above idle, turned the nose of the boat toward open water, then shifted his face toward hers to look askance. Munroe stole a glance at the bottom of the boat and confirmed what she'd seen earlier. Aside from the captain, who still lay unconscious, the little craft was empty. To leave the freighter and head into the open ocean like this would be a death sentence, but there was no way these men had gotten so far out with just the gas in the engine's tank. Somewhere nearby, and yet far enough away that Leo's men with their night vision hadn't picked it out, was a mother ship that held what she wanted.

"Where is the fuel?" she said.

The man pointed away from the *Favorita,* waved far ahead.

"Take us there," she said, and so he sat in front of the engine, pulled a small compass and a flashlight from his pocket, and placed his hand to the tiller.

The whine rose louder and the inflatable surged away from the ship, dead ahead, in the opposite direction of the muzzle flashes and sounds of battle, which carried loud and long over the water's surface.

Her willingness to leave the ship, to run from a fight she might possibly win into the arms of certain death if lost at sea, had been based entirely on the innate desire to stay alive—not hers, but that of the man in the boat, who wanted to live far more than she did. She trusted her instinct and his desire for self-preservation; the *Favorita* disappeared entirely into the night that swallowed them, and only the explosions in the distance were left to punctuate the dark.

Three minutes out and Munroe found nothing that could guide her; five and she first saw the pinprick of light, a candle flame that flickered, and with this as her beacon, she had the boatman idle the engine and motioned him around the captain, toward the front of the craft.

"Hands behind your head," she said. "Face to the water."

But instead of doing as she'd instructed, the man dropped to his knees and clasped his hands in a form of prayer and pleading. She only partially understood the dialect and the jumble of words, a stream of excuses and begging, most probably lies no different from Leo's.

She read past speech for the body language, for the truth that words obscured, and touched the muzzle of the rifle to his forehead. "Tell me," she said. "Who is your boss, and what value does the ship captain have to you?"

The man had no answers, only stories of fishermen unable to make a living, of being a simple man hired to watch the boat. She punched the rifle into him and he stopped. His was an old tale based on an even older truth that might have meant something back when Somali piracy was in its infancy and hadn't yet turned into the multimillion-dollar cutthroat business that it had become.

As if he read her face, read her distrust, the man put his hands behind his head and pleaded again. "On the boat," he said, and motioned toward the light. "He knows what I don't know."

Information from him would have been a bonus, but what she really wanted was a way to get to land. "You live if you do as I say," she said. "If you don't—" She punched him again with the weapon. "Understand?"

He nodded emphatically. "Everything as you say," he said, and she lowered the muzzle and motioned him toward the tiller.

They started up again and the flicker on the water grew larger until it materialized fully into a wide flashlight beam swung in the hand of another man who was, as far as Munroe could tell, the only occupant on a V-hull about twenty feet long without any overhang or shade, definitely not the dhow or mother ship that she'd expected.

When they were within shouting distance, her watchman idled the engine, stood and waved, called out the news that they carried the captain with them, and the man on the boat motioned them in closer.

The inflatable slipped in behind the larger vessel where an outboard engine was tipped up, and beside it a ladder extended into the water. Munroe grabbed hold of the ladder, pulled herself onto the bigger boat, was over and standing by the time the guard got close enough to see her face. Butt of the rifle to her shoulder, muzzle toward his head, she said, "I don't want to hurt you."

In response to her words, he gaped and stood staring.

"Drop your weapon," she said.

He didn't move, but his body language screamed shock more than threat. Surprise, perhaps, at the white man partially dressed in military camo, intruding on his boat to put a gun to his head—a white face speaking his language.

She didn't want to fire a warning shot. Hadn't been able to check the magazine in the rifle, though from her watchman's reaction when she'd pointed the weapon at his head, she assumed it was loaded and functional. She took a step forward and the man flinched. "I don't want to hurt you," she said, "but I will if I have to. Drop the gun."

The man lowered the weapon and straightened.

"There's a white man in the boat," Munroe said. "Bring him up."

The man remained mute and motionless, wasting her time, trying her patience, amping the adrenaline higher. Munroe pulled the 9 mm from her waistband and fired in the air, a deafening blast against the night that would, if there were other boats like this out there, probably send the curious in their direction.

The weapon report was enough to get him moving.

The man dropped the flashlight and scurried for the inflatable.

Munroe scooped up the light and switched it off. Knocked his rifle out of the way and followed him to stand guard while he climbed down; kept watch as the two men wrangled the captain upward.

When at last they'd heaved him up and deposited him into the bigger boat, she demanded her pack, which they brought up, and then she motioned them both back down into the inflatable and, while they waited, did a quick inventory of her boat. This wasn't the mother ship by any means. No generator or air compressor, not much in the way of food or water, and no spare ammunition. But what the vessel did have was fuel in several large containers, and the fuel was what she'd come for.

Munroe leaned over the outboard and tipped the propeller back into water. The men in the boat below guided the inflatable away. She fired a warning shot with the rifle, confirmation that the weapon was operational, enough to keep the men from veering off too far. She opened the tank vent, adjusted, primed, and pulled the engine to life.

The men stared, faces upturned, bodies motionless.

Rifle on her shoulder, voice raised to carry over the engine, she said, "Who do you work for? What do you want with the ship captain?"

No response.

She fired again. Closer to the inflatable and both men flinched.

"The ship captain," she said again. "Why?"

"I don't know," the second man said, and when she raised her rifle toward his head, both men held hands up and wailed over each other in a pleading chorus of ignorance that wasted her time.

Munroe stepped back and set the rifle on the boat's one wooden bench. Pulled out the smallest canister of fuel, dragged it aft, and dropped it over to the men, who came in closer to take it. Grabbed three water bottles, tossed them down, and then followed those with the short-range radio she'd taken from the grenade launcher. Setting these two free was a promise kept, and she didn't know what was worse: that she left the men to possibly perish on the open sea, or that they might survive and go on to other plunders and other killings.

CHAPTER 7

Munroe stood watch as the small boat shoved off, waited until the men faded completely into the night, and then turned to further inspect the upgraded version of escape and the supplies it carried. This boat was longer, wider, probably heavier than the cigarette boats they'd used when running guns in the Bight of Biafra, and the engine had less horsepower, but a rough estimate of consumption and the fuel on board said she could probably make about four hundred nautical miles before running dry.

According to Leo they'd been less than twenty hours from rendezvous. At the *Favorita*'s speed that put her somewhere in the range of three hundred nautical miles from the meeting point, and because it made no sense for the captain to hand off the armaments far out on the ocean—not in this remote part of the world, not if he'd hired an armed escort for his trouble—it also meant that with a hefty give or take and a dollop of assumption, she was within three hundred nautical miles of the coast—probably less, depending on what course the *Favorita* plotted.

Munroe inclined back to trace out the map in the sky, then pointed the bow to the west and opened the throttle, and the boat lurched forward, a pounding rise and fall against ocean swells that jarred her body and promised to cover distance in less time than the *Favorita* would have. Without food, without shade, and with limited water, reaching the coast would be a long, hard slog, but as long as she reached land she could turn south and follow the shoreline into Kenya. If she didn't make it that far before running out of fuel, so be it. Land was land. She spoke Somali, she'd find a way to survive, always did, and this wouldn't be the first time fate had taken her across an ocean just to dump her on shore to figure her way from the clues at her feet.

That had been that other lifetime, the missionaries' daughter who'd fled the continent with the blood of the sadist who'd trained her to fight, taught her to hate, still fresh on her hands. And as it had been with the *Favorita* in Djibouti, bribes had also paved the way for her flight from Cameroon when she'd boarded the *Santo Domingo* in Douala. She'd snuck off the freighter when the ship had reached Valencia, and without more money, it had taken two months of working the docks as a stevedore to figure out a way to get from Spain to the United States. She'd lived among the containers and in abandoned offices until a man had come in the dark with a knife and had made her a killer for the second time. He'd taught her how easy taking a life could be, showed her a first glimpse of the predator that the knife of her tormentor had created.

MUNROE LOCKED THE tiller in place and, struggling to keep her balance, tracked down the pieces the pirates had used to refill the engine fuel tank: makeshift funnel, smaller container, scooper to ply gasoline from the larger drums. Then she inspected the rifles and their magazines, each of which had been only half full, as if ammunition had been rationed out among the lower ranks and saved for the battle with the ship.

She consolidated ammunition, snapped the one full magazine back into place, and set the rifle aside. Scooted for the bench and for the third time made her way around a large twist of black-painted two-inch polypropylene rope that lay in the middle of the boat. Stopped, turned, and flicked the flashlight beam over the one item that should have jumped out at her the moment she'd set foot on this craft. Rope of this thickness had no business here.

Munroe knelt and put her hand on a braid fat enough that her fingers didn't meet on the underside and after a moment she stood. The captain had been close when he'd said fishing lines had jammed the *Favorita*'s propeller. A few hundred feet of rope like this, stretched out and floating in the freighter's path, and the propeller would have sucked it right in and been wrapped to a complete stop. But to lay the rope out far enough in advance to avoid being spotted by the armed guards, to do it on the pitch-black of the ocean without the ship's lights to guide them, the attackers would have had to know the ship's speed and coordinates and exactly where the ship would be.

This wasn't a random hijacking.

Munroe maneuvered herself over the bench, picked up her pack, and carried it fore, then took off her vest and put it beneath the captain's head as a pillow of sorts to protect him from the pounding rise and fall and possibly prevent more damage than what had already been done.

She checked his pulse, his breathing, lifted his eyelids and shone the flashlight into them. His pupils weren't dilated, which meant that it probably wasn't brain bleeding that kept him out like this. She studied the lines and creases on his face, hints of secrets he hadn't told, might never be able to convey again, and then shut off those thoughts.

The need to know was automatic, a desire to understand, to problem-solve, an analytical skill that had served her well over the years but which had no purpose in a present when reaching shore was the only thing that mattered. Munroe switched off the light, and in the boat's repetitive pounding and the engine's roar, in the endless water and the lightening sky, she had nothing but empty exhaustion that had followed on the heels of the adrenaline dump. In the monotony the memories came for company, prodding at her soft spots like calloused fingers picking scabs off a wound that had only just begun to heal.

She studied her hands and felt the blood, a stain that she couldn't wash away no matter where she went or the distance she ran. Death followed her, embraced her, and beckoned her. She'd become one of Pavlov's dogs, salivating for blood when her emotional dinner bell was rung.

Munroe stood and reached beneath the captain's head for her vest, pulled out the picture pack, and held the photo of Miles Bradford close. She'd been forced to join forces with him on a job that hadn't turned out as they'd expected. They'd worked together a few times since, had risked their lives for each other, and killed to keep the other safe. Had lived together as lovers. "You have a gift and you have heart," he'd once said. "Let them serve you."

She'd killed again since then, several times over, sullying herself while cleansing the world, and had finally said good-bye when that seemed to be the only way to stop the pain. The strings of attachment to him pulled at her even now, half a world away.

She hurt, and hated that she hurt.

Whatever peace Djibouti had given her was over. Maybe the run was over. Maybe it was time to go home.

Home.

Munroe turned the word over inside her head, then shut it down, shoved it aside. Tucked the picture away again, but wouldn't lie to herself over what this was. In this fear there was no honor, no adrenaline, no release into the path of death, simply cowardice. She'd finally known peace, known happiness in being accepted and loved for who she was, and for the first time in her life, instead of rushing into the arms of what terrified her, she hid from it.

FOURTEEN HOURS ON the water, stomach churning and head throbbing from the constant pound against the waves, and Munroe caught her first sight of something solid. A mirage, the glimpse of this thing filtered in and out and finally strengthened into a green-splotched dirt-gray that stretched out long in both directions, and so she turned the bow south.

———

SHE WAS DOWN to the last of her water and twenty liters of fuel when clusters of white and swaths of color along the shore took on the form of construction far too organized, too much in one place, to be Somalia. Munroe turned west again, ventured closer, passed a wide waterway that led inland, and when she finally came upon buildings more Polynesian than African and the only explanation was that at some point she'd crossed into Kenyan waters and had reached something of a resort, she tossed the extra rifle overboard, stuffed the banana clip inside her pack, and slid the remaining rifle behind the fuel containers.

MUNROE SLOWED AND continued beyond pristine beaches, past occasional wooden fishing boats, and finally, spotting a jetty stretching into the water, she drew in for a better look.

To the right of the pier a wooden fishing boat sat, sail collapsed, with its bow snug on the white sandy shore, and not far from the fishing boat, three men, barefoot and in tattered T-shirts and cutoff pants, watched Munroe's approach with open curiosity. She assumed the boat was theirs, although the pier itself probably belonged to the nearest hotel, or to one of the houses that abutted the beach. Not far off to the left a man washed his bicycle in the ocean, and a few children scampered along the sand, chasing one another in shrieking laughter that she could hear even as far out as she was.

Beyond this, the area was thick with the impossible-to-hurry that so often accompanied detachment from urban life; laid-back quiet that said wherever this was, it wasn't anywhere near a big city; a place where violent crime was nearly nonexistent, and where a local face was enough to keep curious, entrepreneurial hands from running off with fuel and machine parts.

Munroe slipped in along the far end of the pier and, finding a place to tie off, cut the engine, tossed the lines up, and climbed after them.

She glanced again at the three men on shore, stretched her legs, and worked out the kinks in her neck while measuring the responses in their body language, the nuances of their expressions. Adjusted her posture to reflect the no-hurry of the heat, and with hands in her pockets, strolled toward the front of the pier.

The men by the fishing boat, leaned back on the sand, stopped talking as she approached. She paused a few feet away and looked out over the water, measuring minutes with the hands of African time, and finally greeted them in English. She would have tried Arabic next, then Somali if the first two failed, but the one who appeared to be the youngest among them—eighteen, nineteen tops—responded in kind.

She nodded toward the sailboat. "Is that yours?" she said.

The English speaker motioned to the man at his left. "My friend boat," he said, and then staring at Munroe's black cargo pants and boots: "You army man?"

"On holiday," she said.

He smiled, stood, and said, "You want private tour? I know good fishing, pretty place. Or maybe nice lady, I have sister, you come meet her."

Munroe smiled wide enough to show teeth. "I might," she said, and since he'd saved her the necessity of making small talk before moving to business, she turned toward the ocean and nodded in the direction of the waterway. "How far does it go?"

"She go all way around island."

"You know the island well?"

"Know Lamu Island very good," he said. "Know all islands very good."

Munroe nodded, turned toward the water again, and let the quiet speak. "I could use a guide," she said finally, "and a watchman. Do you and your friends want work?"

"What is watchman?" he said.

"A guard. For the boat."

"You want *askari*?" he asked, and without waiting for a response he turned to the others and spoke to them in a language with which

Munroe wasn't familiar but that pinged inside her head and sent sparks of Arabic and English and German colliding against each other.

The English speaker pointed to one of the men still seated and said, "Mohamed, he work five thousand shilling for day."

"And you?" she said. "What's your rate?"

He smiled. "I go five thousand shilling for day."

The men had told her where she was and that was what she'd needed. Hands still shoved into pockets, she said, "Let me think about it," and turned and walked for the pier.

Behind her the discussion started up again; got louder, carried closer.

"We go three thousand shillings for day," the first said.

With no idea what the dollar-to-shilling exchange might be, she pointed to one man first, and then the other. "Two thousand, two thousand," she said, and the English speaker stuck out a hand.

"I am Sami," he said, and Munroe shook on the understanding that she'd just been robbed. She turned to glance at the setting sun. "I have no shillings," she said. "Does Lamu Island have a bank?"

"Yes, closed now," Sami said. "I have friend, he buy dollars, give good price."

She had enough fuel to get through the night, and hotels would probably accept dollars.

Munroe turned toward the boat, toward the captain, still unconscious, deteriorating from heat and dehydration. There hardly seemed a point in trying to get him medical care, but if she didn't, she might as well just slit his throat.

Munroe clenched her fists, pushed back the invisible blood that stained her palms, and said, "Where is your friend?"

"In Lamu Town."

"Do we take a taxi? Bus?"

"No car on island, only donkey. We go your boat."

"I need a hospital first," she said. "Do you have one of those?"

"We have."

She nodded toward Mohamed. "You take me to the hospital and he brings the friend with the good price to meet us."

Sami turned to interpret for Mohamed, their dickering started up again, and after a minute of back and forth Sami said, "He show you hospital, I bring my friend," and so Munroe swung her arm wide toward the pier, gestured Mohamed to the boat, and to Sami said, "Bring a liter of drinking water with you when you come."

CHAPTER 8

Munroe followed Mohamed's guidance back to the waterway and farther up the island's coastline until they passed a collection of small resorts and hotels. Mohamed waved toward the beach and in a tone that was more explanation than instruction said, "Shela," as if it had some importance, and perhaps to him it did because he believed she was a tourist.

She acknowledged him with a nod.

In an area this remote, where there were resorts there also had to be a landing strip and a place where commerce and money changed hands and where she could buy fuel and supplies. Beyond the hotels the shoreline thickened into foliage again, and by the time Mohamed pointed and nodded, waved and urged Munroe toward the shore, she'd still seen nothing that could stand in for what Sami had referred to as Lamu Town.

They coasted on momentum into the shallows. Mohamed hopped out, waded ahead, and used the lines to drag the boat until the bottom scraped.

Munroe unlaced her boots and pulled them off. Draped them over her shoulder, nudged her vest out from beneath the captain's head, picked up her pack, took everything with her over the bow, and trudged up the beach toward a building that backed up to the sand.

Around the front under the last of the day's sunlight, Lamu District Hospital greeted Munroe in big painted letters. The area was quiet, no crowds milling about the main entrance, and she continued on through an open walkway with dirty whitewashed walls and patterned brick that allowed the ocean breeze to circulate and keep the smell of rot, sickness, and overripe body odor to a minimum.

In a layout similar to that of so many provincial hospitals and clinics on the continent, the structure was courtyard-style, with concrete floors where there wasn't dirt, and under the porticoes on rough-hewn benches women in color-splashed *abayas* and in tribal wraps held sickly babies and small children.

Munroe found a nurse who spoke English well enough to understand her problem and mediate in locating a doctor; then she sat on the concrete and pulled her socks and boots back on. The nurse returned with a man Munroe pegged for a volunteer. Light-skinned, dark-haired, and with several days of beard stubble, he wore faded scrubs and the look of numbness that often attached to foreigners who, working too long in impoverished conditions without supplies and equipment, were forced to witness sickness and death they would otherwise have been able to prevent. He greeted her in fair English and with an air of forced patience.

Within his words of introduction Munroe heard the accent and for her own benefit answered in Italian, utilizing language, that special form of magic that increased in potency the farther the spell was cast from where it was expected. The doctor's expression shifted into a cautious smile, and in micro increments his posture relaxed with relief, almost as if he'd been holding his breath.

Munroe mirrored his response, shook his hand. "*Ho bisogno del vostro aiuto,*" she said. "I have an unconscious man in a boat, can I show you?"

On the shore Munroe climbed into the boat and the doctor followed. While Mohamed waited on the sand, she shone the flashlight down onto the captain, who might already be dead, and then handed the light to the doctor.

He knelt and, as Munroe had done earlier, shone the beam in the captain's eyes. Then he pinched at his skin, then picked up his wrist, and listened through the stethoscope. He turned toward Munroe. "He's still alive. No sweating. Rapid heartbeat, probably low blood pressure," he said. "How long has he been like this?"

"I found him drifting," she said. "I've had him for about twenty hours."

"He needs fluid urgently," the doctor said. "Needs to have the head wound stitched, but fluid is an emergency."

"I'm on my way to Mombasa," she said.

"In Mombasa they have better equipment, but you can't take him like this."

"How long would you keep him?"

"At a minimum, twenty-four hours for the dehydration. But even after that he's not in any condition to travel."

"I can't stay in Lamu," she said. "If you want, I will leave him."

"Better not," he said.

"I can wait for twenty-four hours, but not more than that. I'm traveling by sea—how long to Mombasa by car?"

The doctor pursed his lips and blew a long exhale. "These roads?" He shook his head. "It depends on the day. Twelve hours? Eighteen? Could be three days if there are issues."

She felt his exhaustion, the Third World weariness. "There are always issues," she said, and he nodded, wiped his forehead.

"All right then," she said. "I'll cover the expenses for his stay for as long as I'm here."

"You know how it works with medical?"

"Yes," she said, and knew all too well. Different part of the continent, but the same concept everywhere: Except for the rare clinic that catered exclusively to foreigners and to the rich, hospitals in Africa worked on a payment-first basis, and it wasn't unusual for the injured and dying to pass away unadmitted because they didn't have the money to put up front to get in the door.

"I'll get you a list," he said. "I'm already off for the night, but when you have the supplies, ask for help at reception and they will come get me."

"Is there anything I can do for you?" she asked. "Perhaps a donation to a worthy cause?"

"Just ask for me when you're ready," he said. "I'll leave the list at reception," and the doctor stood and helped himself off the boat.

Munroe watched him walk up the beach, silhouetted by the small amounts of light that reached out from the hospital, until finally he disappeared entirely.

To Mohamed she said, "Where is Sami?" and although as far as she knew the man didn't understand English, he understood the intent of her question and pointed to the boat to her left that hadn't been there when they'd arrived.

THE CURRENCY EXCHANGE took place behind the hospital, haggling kept short while Munroe chugged down the entire bottle of water that Sami brought, and then she traded three hundred dollars for far fewer shillings than they had to be worth; enough to get the captain into the hospital and her through till morning, when she could find Lamu Town and figure out the next step. Tonight she just wanted the captain off her hands and a bed where she could collapse, and she'd get there faster if the boys assumed she was gullible and that money flowed freely.

The three of them got the unconscious man off the boat, and Sami and Mohamed carried him inside. As promised the doctor had the list ready, and Munroe paid for admission, then followed Sami and Mohamed while they carried the captain to the assigned room. The windows were holes with wooden slats, and dirty mosquito netting hung over four low metal beds with sagging mattresses.

There were four other people in the room, two of them sharing a bed, one of them in a hacking fit that racked his frail body and left blood on the cloth he held to his mouth. If the captain survived the night he'd be fortunate not to take with him the seeds of tuberculosis, but at least his own sheets were clean, and above the smells of spoiled food and body odor, the air hinted faintly of antiseptic.

The pharmacy, on the other side of ill-fitting shutters that opened a window to the portico, was a room that held only a small wooden desk and chair, and along one wall were mostly empty shelves. Munroe handed the pharmacy tech the doctor's list. Meticulously slow to the point of painfulness, he collected the items, and when he had everything, he wrote out the bill by hand with a well-worn sheet of carbon paper placed between two notebook pages.

It took Munroe a hunt to find the cashier to pay for the items, and with a handwritten receipt she returned to the pharmacy, where the man exchanged her items for the paper.

The receptionist sent a runner for the doctor. He arrived more quickly this time and Munroe suspected he'd never left. She gave him the IV bags, needle, tape, gauze, disinfecting wipes, and the rest of what he'd asked for, then followed him back to the captain's room, though because of the coughing she waited outside the doorway, watching as the doctor inserted the port, hooked up the bag of fluid, and hung it off an ancient IV stand.

If the captain lived, if she chose to take him rather than abandon him here, she'd be the one handling the medical routine: a burden she hadn't anticipated when dragging him off the ship had seemed simple enough.

She should have just left him there to die.

BY THE TIME Munroe returned to the boat, hunger and exhaustion had become a sharpened edge that made it difficult to play nice or play dumb. She arranged for Sami to accompany her as watchman for the night, and left him to sort out with Mohamed how and when the two would reconvene.

A few kilometers along the shore, clusters of light began to peek out of the surrounding darkness. With Sami's help Munroe found a jetty that she could tie off to, and before leaving him with the boat, she marked off and pointed out the last of the fuel so that he knew she was aware of the levels and he wouldn't be tempted to steal from what little she had left. Her actions weren't a judgment against him, nor an implied accusation, simply an acknowledgment of the way the continent worked when it came to petty theft, notice that she wasn't as gullible as he might believe. And then, even though he'd not worked a full day, she handed him two thousand shillings, told him that she wanted fuel and would add an extra two hundred if he found a way to get it to her before midmorning.

"I get it, no problem," he said, and so she patted him on the shoulder, left him for the night, and wandered up the darkened beach to the nearest cluster of lights.

The hotel, when she reached it, was like pictures out of a magazine, with secluded thatch-roofed bungalows overlooking what would, in the daytime, be white sand beaches and crystalline turquoise water: the tourist version of East Africa. In the unwalled main house guests lounged on oversize rattan furniture under sweeping ceiling fans and gawked as she passed by, as if she were some swamp creature crawling in.

A mixture of languages followed in her path, some unfamiliar, some that sent off flashes of illumination in her brain, all part of the easy way people talked in foreign places when they assumed they wouldn't be understood: a cacophony of mixed conversation that added to Munroe's burnout and made her head hurt.

She surrendered passport and money in exchange for a key, and a teenage boy showed her to the bungalow, breezy with a high ceiling and a fan with wide blades that took the sea air and turned it into something cooler.

On the dresser were two bottles of water and a bowl of fruit, which Munroe ate, one piece after the other. And then there in the room, with the burn of the sun and the salt of the ocean spray still crusting on her skin, she let down the mosquito netting, lay on the bed, closed her eyes, and slipped away.

How long she slept, she didn't know. Long enough to feel rested, not enough for the dreams to overtake her or for the sun to rise. Over the ocean the first hint of color change began to paint the sky, and she followed the pedestrian paths to the great room, quiet and empty.

Munroe called out a low hello and a woman shuffled out from

the back with a slow indifference that said Munroe had woken her and she could only half-pretend to be happy about it.

"I need to use a phone with an international line," Munroe said.

"It needs a deposit."

Munroe placed a fifty-dollar bill on the counter. "Enough?"

The woman nodded and led her to a door just beyond the wide front desk, a small business center, with a computer, a printer, and a phone all on one narrow table. When the woman left, Munroe sat, sighed, and picked up the handset.

Of all the people who'd screwed her over during this past week, Amber Marie made her the maddest, and there were things to say before Munroe could cut completely free. She dialed, waited out static and hiss while the phone rang long, and eventually, with sleep in her voice, Amber picked up.

Munroe said, "Hey, it's Michael."

"Michael?" Amber repeated, and the tone in that one word conveyed disequilibrium and a hundred questions that had no voice or articulation. Munroe waited a second, an exclamation to the silence, and then said, "Yeah, Amber, Michael. And thanks a fucking lot for stabbing me in the back."

CHAPTER 9

Munroe heard movement on the other end of the phone, as if Amber had sat up, swept the sheets aside, and swung her legs over to the floor. "Wait, what?" Amber said, and the phone was repositioned, one shoulder to the next. "What are you talking about?" And then after another pause, "Michael, where are you, and why are you calling?"

"I can tell you where I'm not," Munroe said. "Not out on the fucking ocean on a craptastic freighter carrying illegal weapons, that's where I'm not. And you know what? After everything I've done for you, Amber, after the friendship, the times we've worked together, and the fact that I've watched your back, it would have been real solid of you to at least clue me in on Leo's little gunrunning mission before I agreed to take the job."

There was a pause before Amber said, "Gunrunning?"

In the hiccup of that hesitation Munroe heard the bewilderment and breathed down the anger of betrayal. Wished she could take the seething venom back, could rephrase and reword. Understood in that drop of time that of all the people Leo had deceived, his wife was at the top of the list, and that this phone call, which had been meant as a kiss-off and a way to vent her rage before cutting ties forever, had turned into one of being the bearer of the worst kind of news.

Amber, still several mental paces behind, mellow and pleading, said, "Michael, where are you? Where is Leo?"

Munroe said, "Who brokered the deal to get Leo on board the *Favorita*?"

"I don't know," Amber replied. "Someone Leo was tight with in his military years, came by way of a phone call or something." Then, voice twining higher with desperation, added, "Why, Michael?"

"I'm going to break this to you as nice as I can," Munroe said. Pinched the bridge of her nose and closed her eyes. "The *Favorita* is running illegal weapons and Leo wasn't hired to protect the ship and the crew, but to guard the shipment and make the arms delivery."

"That's not possible," Amber said. "Leo would never have done that without telling me."

"You're certain?"

Amber hesitated, and in that delay Munroe found her answer.

"But gunrunning," Amber said. "The only place they could offload between here and Kenya is off the Somali coast."

"Exactly."

"Oh God, Michael, no, he wouldn't."

"I discovered the weapons," Munroe said. "Brought the issue to Leo and he was pretty pissed that I found them—didn't think I was worth telling—didn't want me meddling. I figure Natan has answers for you that I don't."

"Natan knows?"

"The whole team knew. Everyone except me. And apparently, you."

There was another long spell of silence, Amber pulling in these details to reconfigure them, make sense of them, and Munroe didn't rush her. "If it's you calling and not Leo," Amber said finally, "then something went wrong. Where is he?"

"Go talk to Natan first."

"Hang on," Amber said, and in the background a door slammed

and Amber's breathing picked up tempo, as if she'd jogged from the main house to the annex. Another door opened. Slammed. And after that came the pounding of Amber's fist on Natan's door. Then Natan's voice, muted, as if Amber pressed the headset to her chest—arguing, then yelling—mostly Amber—and then more pounding, this time the headset itself, being beaten repeatedly against something while Amber swore in time with the beat, words Munroe had never heard from her before.

And then a door slammed again, and Amber, still breathing heavily, said, "I'm pissed off and angry, but mostly scared. Michael, where is Leo?"

"The ship was hijacked," Munroe said. "I got off before the fighting got bad. That was around thirty hours ago. Last I saw him, he was still alive on the *Favorita*, about three hundred nautical miles somewhere east of Mogadishu."

Amber responded with silence—no tears, no hyperventilating. She was in that scary quiet place she went when an emergency struck and she plotted how to fix it. When the reality of what had happened fully sank in, Amber would break down and lose it completely.

"How is it possible," Amber said, "that the first armed ship ever taken by pirates happens to be Leo's ship?"

The question was rhetorical, without inflection, emotionless and numb, but Munroe answered anyway. "I can tell you that it wasn't a typical hijacking," she said. "Was something closer to a military assault but carried out by people with no military training. It's possible the ship was targeted because of the illegal cargo."

"Oh, Michael," Amber said, but in her tone of patronization what she left unspoken was *What could a boy like you possibly know about a military assault?*

Munroe said, "Did the *Favorita* carry kidnap and ransom insurance? Do you know anything about the owners? The charterer? The captain?"

"If a ship carries K&R, then the contract requires that it be kept a secret," Amber said. "I could try to find out. Leo handled all the coordinating on this one, so I don't know what due diligence was done on the ship or the principals."

"You were okay with this?"

"Work has been really slow, Michael."

Amber's justification for mediocrity and sloppy work was a maddening headache, one more frustration Munroe didn't want to deal with. "I've got to go," she said. "Ask around, see what you can find out about the ship. I'll call you back in a couple of days."

Amber said, "Please wait."

Munroe paused.

"I just," Amber began, and then stopped.

Munroe waited a moment longer and then, unwilling to be a surrogate for Amber's tenuous connection to Leo, hung up.

She shut her eyes and breathed away the frustration of feeling Amber's pain, of knowing that no matter how badly she despised Leo or how much this wasn't her problem, for the sake of the rare individual she related to and truly respected, she couldn't walk away just yet; she laughed at the irony of having run to Djibouti to get away from being responsible for other people's lives only to have fate, in an emotional joke of cosmic proportions, encumber her with an unconscious captain who she wished would die already, and a woman whose husband wanted Munroe dead.

MUNROE LEFT THE hotel, walked to think and clear her head, and wandered inland without any destination or purpose through the tiny township. Shela was an oversize village that even in its remote poverty catered to those with money—perfect if she'd been looking for a friendly escape from civilization, a place to drop off the map and remain lost for years, but she wouldn't last a week before her insides started to itch and the perpetual restlessness that raised the hunger for a challenge called for her to come and play.

Munroe found Sami on the pier swapping money with a barechested and barefoot man for an assortment of soda and water bottles. At her approach, the man who'd taken the payment greeted her with a wave and a friendly smile, then left them and padded back to shore. Sami pointed out the eight bottles lined up near her boat, about eleven liters of liquid total. "My friend bring gas," he said.

Munroe handed him two hundred shillings.

She needed to get a gauge on exchange rates and prices and find out how badly Sami was hemorrhaging her cash. "We go to Lamu Town," she said.

"Hospital first?" he said. "Go see you friend?"

"Lamu Town first."

Sami hopped into the boat and Munroe tossed him the bottles of fuel. Together they dumped them into the tank, set the bottles aside, and let loose the lines. On their way again, Sami guided Munroe up the same stretch of coast that she'd traveled yesterday, past the hospital and a water ambulance beached uselessly on the shore, to where the thinned-out clusters of buildings began to thicken into a tightly packed township. Gleaming whitewashed buildings with arched windows and doorways, porticoes and rust-brown rooftops, stood sentinel along a stone wharf—an old, old city that had passed through many hands and many cultures and yet maintained an Arabic base note.

The number of wooden boats lining the piers and jetties grew, as did the crowds along the waterfront. There were no motorized vehicles that Munroe could see, everything done on foot as Sami had said, with supplies transported by so many laden donkeys: a rural haven that appeared to continue on as it had for centuries.

On the upper edge of town where the shore activity began to thin again, Munroe left Sami with the boat and tracked back along the wide stone shorefront in the direction of the bank that Sami had pointed out, and was accosted at regular intervals by men trying to sell what she didn't need.

Language erupted and ebbed around her, wave after ocean wave crashing upon her in the form of laughter, talking, yelling, and movement: the cacophony of a thousand voices inside her head, shouting for attention, dizzying mental chaos while her mind tried to create order and structure and make sense of the clamor and wouldn't let go, a sensory overload of too many tongues, too many dialects, background noise that most people could simply ignore, even when it was pointed directly at them. For her, always present, demanding attention, without a pattern to hold on to, the turmoil would rush onward, cresting higher until she'd be forced to hurry away into quiet.

Two men continued to tag after her, offering food, boat rides, donkey rides, curios, and wanted to know where she was from and where she stayed; giving the only response that wouldn't encourage them further, she refused eye contact, refused to acknowledge their presence and kept on walking. Their harassment served her right for coming into town looking like a full-on tourist. She knew better than to mark herself as an outsider, which was the same thing as an invitation, but she hadn't exactly expected to jump ship when she'd packed for the security escort.

Munroe stepped into the Gulf African Bank, and across the threshold, door shut behind her, she breathed a rush of quiet and the cool of the air-conditioning, relief to her skin and to the tumult inside her brain. She exchanged a thousand dollars for shillings and directions to an Internet café, then rolled the Kenyan money into separate bundles to spread throughout her pockets and smiled at Sami's audacity: His starting price had been nearly a hundred dollars a day in a country where most worked for a dollar or two, and in agreeing to half of that she'd dropped him into a small fortune.

When Munroe exited the bank, one of the men from the wharf picked up his wheedling, pressed after her between old stone buildings and streets only wide enough for bicycles and donkeys. He gave up when they reached the town's fort square and she'd still not acknowledged him, and off this open market area on another narrow street, where signs in Arabic and English spanned the few feet from building to building, Munroe found the Internet café.

She could have used the computer at the hotel but old habits and watching her back wouldn't allow her to work where she was vulnerable. Answers to the easy questions came fast. She'd come ashore on the major island of an archipelago, less than 70 nautical miles from the Somali border—had another 180 to go to get to Mombasa. She could cut the journey by half if she was willing to take a flight from Manda Island across the channel, but she wasn't in a hurry and didn't see the point in sacrificing the boat, and the doctor had been right in his assessment, going by road wasn't worth the risk with or without the captain.

The harder questions, those about the *Favorita*, took longer. Queries on the ship turned up nothing about the owners or the charterer, much less the captain, whose name she didn't know. Neither were there reports or notices by any of the newsgroups or antipiracy watchdogs within Somalia who would be the first to report the ship's arrival once it showed up offshore in any of the pirate-haven coastal cities—assuming the ship showed up at all. There was always the possibility that the propeller stoppage had damaged something mechanical and that repairs, if they could even be done at sea, would take time, or that the hijackers had only been after the armaments and without interest in the ship itself, and the crew was already dead on a deserted vessel.

The obvious stated that whoever expected delivery of the armaments had decided to take them without paying for them, but easy assumptions were often wrong. Answers to why the pirates had specifically wanted the captain alive and had gone to the trouble to track down the *Favorita* at night would never be discovered in databases and by Internet sleuthing. These were specifics found only on the ground, blending, mingling among those who knew: the type of information hunt upon which she'd built her career.

None of it mattered. The *Favorita* was no longer her problem.

But there was Amber.

Munroe sighed. Typed in the URL for Capstone Security Consulting, clicked for the blog. The thought of calling Bradford, of letting him know that she was still alive and hadn't abandoned the ties that bound them, played itself around inside her head.

The most recent post was a week old already: news links that

Capstone's clients and potential clients would find relevant, and security updates to the various regions in which the private security teams worked. The clues were hidden gems among press release–type details. He was in Afghanistan again, though there was nothing to say how long he'd be away this time.

Munroe cleared the history and temporary files. Paid for the computer time and slipped back into the narrow street, crowding between bodies and sidestepping donkey excrement and the sewer runoff that flowed in gutters toward the ocean.

Mohamed was at the boat and he stayed behind while Sami accompanied Munroe to the outside of town, where the streets were dirt and far wider, and they could hire out a donkey and its owner. They hauled the plastic containers off the boat and carried them to purchase more fuel. Moved on to food supplies, water, and sailcloth: simple transactions made one by one, merchant by merchant, that took most of the day.

They returned to the hospital and Munroe asked for help in finding the doctor and then sat waiting on the concrete for a full thirty minutes before he arrived.

"You're still in Lamu," he said, and she stood to shake his hand.

He took hers with a tired smile.

"How's the patient?" she said.

"His vitals are much better, hydration much better, though he could use another day of fluid."

"I'm leaving for Mombasa in the morning. Can he travel?"

The doctor shrugged and Munroe didn't press.

"He's also showing some signs of response," the doctor said.

"He's conscious?"

"We would say a minimally conscious state," he said, raising and lowering his hand to mimic a wave. "The reactions come and go, up and down, small here and small there. No talking yet, no direct response to requests."

"But he might wake up completely?"

"It's certainly possible."

The unconscious captain had caused no trouble, but when he

finally woke, if his memory functioned as it should, the fight on the *Favorita* would be where he'd left off and there was no guarantee he'd view being pulled off the ship as a good thing.

"Sedatives will keep him more comfortable until I can get him into another hospital," she said.

The doctor eyed her just long enough to state that he wasn't an idiot. Then, with a sigh that said he was indifferent, he pulled a notebook from his pocket and began to write.

CHAPTER 10

The same four people who had been in the captain's room last night were still there, the coughing just as bad and the smell of decaying body fluid a whole lot worse. The captain was in his bed as Munroe had expected, wearing the same clothes he'd come in with, eyes closed, mosquito net down, IV hooked into his arm with the pack completely drained.

All of the supplies she'd paid for yesterday were gone; pieces most likely pilfered one at a time by family members of the sick, if not the hospital staff themselves. Theft was the way of the continent; anything not welded in place was so likely to disappear that even gas caps and engine lids were often padlocked shut.

Munroe went through the multiple steps to reprocure the items on the doctor's list as well as extras and, because she wanted it, also paid for the sheet on the captain's bed.

She returned to the room long enough to detach the empty IV bag and hook up another, then left for the boat with everything else she'd purchased. She handed the supplies up to Sami, climbed in after them, dried off her feet, put the boots back on for the umpteenth time. Sami said, "I go with you to Mombasa."

Munroe paused and looked up. "Do you know Mombasa?"

"I know good," he said. "My home in Malindi."

Munroe recognized the city name from the research earlier in the day: a tourist-based town about a hundred kilometers north of Mombasa—close enough that Sami had the potential to be helpful, and he, apparently interpreting her contemplation as doubt, added, "I watch boat for you, give good price."

She finished lacing her boots and glanced up again. He smiled, confident and cocky. She liked the kid. He'd proven trustworthy and reliable, hadn't stolen anything from her yet, and it would be helpful to have him as an extra set of hands.

"What about Mohamed?" she said.

"Mohamed two wives here, he stay."

She stood and stepped across the boat for the bench. If she planned to keep the boat running, she would have to hire a full-time guard for it in Mombasa anyway. "I won't pay two thousand shillings a day," she said. Paused and returned his cocky smile. "That's Lamu-only price."

Sami grinned, then laughed. He interpreted for Mohamed, who also laughed, and still smiling, Sami nodded. "Five hundred shilling for day," he said. "Mombasa price."

Munroe stretched out her hand and Sami shook it. The offer was still overpriced, but she needed him loyal, and although a good pay-check didn't mean he wouldn't eventually steal from her, it notched the possibility down slightly.

"Have Mohamed stay with the boat tonight," she said. "Go get whatever you need. We leave before the sun. If you're not here, I travel without you."

"I be here."

"Bring a flag with you," she said.

"Flag?"

Munroe used impromptu sign language to indicate what she wanted: a Kenyan flag to fly aft so that on the small chance they encountered officials on the water, there'd be less inclination to stop the boat and check for papers.

—————

MUNROE FOUGHT FOR sleep throughout the night and, unable to find it, finally rose in the early-morning dark. Showered off the sweat again, which in the humidity tended to collect as a permanent layer, pulled down the two hand-washed shirts she'd hung before going to bed, and then redressed, button-down over the T-shirt, protecting her skin, shielding her gender.

She tossed the last of her things into her bag, pulled a pillow off the bed, debated calling Amber Marie then opted against it. Without any news to add, the conversation would turn on itself with long lingering silences, and Munroe didn't have the desire or the emotional energy to be Amber's life support.

At the front desk she traded payment and the room key for her passport, and when she carried her stuff down to the boat, she brought the pillow. Sami was already at the pier when she arrived, and together the three of them returned to the hospital to collect the captain.

They beached the boat, trudged past the reception desk and down the open breeze-filled hall, and when Munroe stepped across the threshold, the captain, who'd been unconscious for more than two full days, turned to face her and opened his eyes, expressionless and unblinking.

She stepped closer, waved a hand in front of his face, got nothing, and gradually his lids shut again.

Munroe injected the sedatives into the IV tube, waited a few moments, then untucked the bottom sheet from the bed and showed the boys how to use the sheet as a sling to carry him out.

The captain stank. She didn't want to touch him, didn't want the boys to touch him either. With effort they got him and the IV attachment into the boat, and when they had him situated under the makeshift sailcloth tent, Munroe put the pillow under his head and, with the duct tape she'd taken from Djibouti, strapped him to it. This would do better than her vest at protecting him, though not by much.

She balled up the soiled sheet and threw it onto the sand. Someone would find it. Wash it. Use it. Not even disposable containers meant for single use in the West would go to waste here. Munroe paid Mohamed and sent him off. She attached the flag that Sami had brought, and without any fanfare they began the slow journey down the channel, back to the open ocean, back to the full throttle of the engine's cry, where time and monotony would allow her mind to wander freely and the puzzle of the captain and the *Favorita* to become the chew toy that would keep the demons quiet and the memories at bay.

THIS CLOSE TO the equator daylight began and ended at nearly the same time year-round, making it possible to pace and predict by the shades on the horizon, and so the rise of the sun in its arc across the sky marked the progression of time and the concept of distance and brought, with its rising, the heat.

In between the long spells of silence Sami pointed out markings on shore and narrated a travelogue that tied in with his own history, and after he'd interrupted her thoughts for the fifth or sixth time, Munroe said, "How many languages do you speak?"

"I have five."

"Perfectly?"

"Three perfect," he said. "I have Swahili, my mother Kikuyu, my father Kalenjin all perfect. And I have English, Arab, and some words here there for more."

"Good," she said, and scooted slightly on the bench. Patted it to indicate he should move in closer. "Come talk to me in Swahili."

"Then you cannot understand," he said.

"You can interpret," she said. "Tell me the story twice."

He smiled again, his cocky smile, and she liked him all the more for it. He sat next to her and throughout the hours recounted one tall tale after the next, first in Swahili and then with equal animation and flourish in English, each story growing longer, larger, and more animated as his audience prompted and questioned. Through snippets and flashes, between water and food and the occasional reapplication of sunscreen she'd picked up in a tourist shop in Lamu, Munroe learned his family's history, of his many siblings and half siblings, his education—or lack thereof—and his adventures on the water as a fisherman that had started when he was ten.

By the time they passed Malindi in the early-afternoon hours, Munroe could feel the syntax, the grammar, the resonance of patterns of the country's lingua franca beginning to form, could feel the tension relaxing now that the key to the aural lock had been handed over, and soon enough, over time and of its own accord, her ability to speak would grow and she would rapidly become more and more fluent.

This same poisonous gift—this savantlike ability to visualize the way the words configured into shapes—had defined her life and turned her into what she was now. Without language, there would have been no gunrunning, without the gunrunning no nights in the jungle fighting off the worst of human predators, without the nights, no instinct of self-preservation and the speed and the need to kill that had marked her every moment, waking and sleeping, since.

THEY REACHED THE outer stretches of Mombasa in the late afternoon. Beach houses and large hotels spread out between palm trees and lush manicured greenery, and the rate of sea traffic seemed fast-paced and hectic after the idyllic slow quiet of Lamu.

The beach shallows sloped out far into the ocean, and jetties and docks were plentiful. Munroe chose one at random, tied off, and then utilized the easier and less attention-garnering option of sending Sami on ahead to discover whom the pier belonged to and if space could be rented. In his absence, she knelt to untape the captain from the pillow, was overwhelmed by the strength of his stench, and held back the gag reflex.

Sour body odor and perpetual decay were part of the pungent bouquet that made up the sub-Saharan landscape, but the body fluid and days without bathing, amplified by the humidity and the hours in the sun, had turned his stink into something else altogether. With only one IV pack left she needed to get him to a hospital soon, and there was no way to take him into a city like this.

Munroe emptied a plastic container, dipped it over the side, and dumped the water over the captain, and when he didn't react, she did it again and again until he was thoroughly soaked and the runoff took with it the harshest of the smell.

Sami returned to the pier with a local watchman, an *askari* as Sami called him, a man Munroe pegged as in his early fifties, who wore a worn-out button-down shirt, pants two sizes too large, and shoes made from tire rubber, and carried a handmade baton as a symbol of authority. The *askari* negotiated with Munroe for the price of berthing, money that would go directly into his own pockets—or more likely a beer bottle—but as long as it kept the boat from being disturbed for a night or two she was fine with that. She paid the few hundred shillings he wanted and then, with business settled, pulled her pack and vest off the boat and left Sami to stand guard over the captain and her supplies.

On Mombasa's North Shore, the hotels were larger, more spread out, covered far more length of beach apiece than they had in Shela, and in the search for a place that suited her purpose, Munroe walked a kilometer or two.

She settled finally on a hotel that was a cross between one of the larger block-style monstrosities and the smaller boutique locations and, in a repeat of what had happened in Lamu when she'd come strolling in after the hard journey at sea, hotel patrons stopped and gawked. She passed through to the front desk and languages started up behind her.

HER ROOM WAS on the first floor of a three-story building, one of five in the complex, at the far end of a wide tiled hallway and with a porch that opened to the manicured gardens and the ocean. Munroe drew the curtains, though they didn't close completely. Turned the air conditioner down a notch. Eventually she'd shut it off altogether because the cool air would only make it harder to stay adjusted to the climate.

She dumped her belongings on the bed and pulled the irreplaceables from the vest and the backpack. The toilet tank, a ziplock bag, and duct tape became her storage for the handgun, and the bottom pockets of the legs on the bamboo bedframe safekeeping for the money and documents that she didn't want to carry. Munroe stayed long enough to rinse off the ocean spray and change her clothes, and then with the help of the front desk staff called for a taxi, and the driver took her to the hotel that fronted the pier where she'd docked. She instructed him to wait and then walked through the hotel grounds back to the boat.

Until she knew the area better, had gotten friendly with the eyes of the beach—the *askaris* and the beach boys who spent each day hawking wares and attempting to separate tourists from their money, those who felt the pulse of their own strip of sand—she couldn't leave the boat alone. Not unless she was willing to return to a stripped-down empty shell. So she waited with the boat and sent Sami to find a boy who'd be willing, for a small fee, to help carry the captain.

He returned fifteen minutes later with two men about his age.

They got the still damp and stinking captain from the boat and to the pier, carried him up the beach to a dirt track that ran between houses and hotels, and finally to the coast highway—if it could be called a highway—where the taxi waited.

She didn't need to know the city to understand that the viable options for medical facilities narrowed into two choices. Easiest and cheapest would be a government hospital, which, for whatever modern medical equipment it might boast, was still the place to take the captain when she was ready for him to die. In a city this size there would have to be private facilities, smaller and more expensive, that catered to expatriates and tourists and the local population of rich: The doctors would treat first and bill later and save her the hassle of making a daily visit to a pharmacy to replace stolen items or to buy whatever the captain might need next, and this is what she asked for.

THE HIGHWAY TOWARD the city was a two-lane patchwork of asphalt, potholes, and worn-off edges, and in both directions cars, dilapidated trucks, and brightly painted vans blew by in a treacherous dance of road share with overladen bicycles, pedestrians, and animals. An orange spray-painted van with metallic stickers on the rear window spelling TOTAL INSANITY crossed into oncoming traffic, cut off the taxi, then rushed to the side of the road to let off passengers.

The taxi driver muttered words that couldn't have been polite in any language, and Munroe thumbed toward the van. "What is that?" she said.

"*Matatu*," the driver said, and for his tone might as well have lifted a shoe to reveal dog crap. "They are crazy."

There were more minivans at irregular intervals, packed beyond capacity, sometimes with the side door slid wide and a man or two hanging from the opening, sometimes at the edge of the road while people got on and off. Different name here, and maybe a bit more ostentatious than what she'd seen elsewhere, but the concept was the same all over Africa: Privately owned vehicles pumped the lifeblood of humanity within the cities, filling the gaps in public transportation, plying the routes without a schedule, departing only when full and, if they had space—and sometimes when they didn't—picking up anyone who flagged them down along the way. The faster they drove, the more people they shoved into the seats, the more money they took in, which made safety the last priority.

The taxi driver took Munroe all the way to Mombasa proper, past five-star establishments and hovels off the side of the road, while woodsmoke and diesel exhaust blew in through the open windows. They continued across the Nyali Bridge to the island itself, Kenya's version of Manhattan, bypassing the thickest of downtown, traversing sections of the city that changed scenery one street to the next, single-story storefronts, restaurants and multistory office buildings, petrol stations and car showrooms, large private homes hidden behind compound walls and thatch-roofed shacks. With the exception of the poorest of the places, every compound, every store, every building had an *askari* or two or three. Some were in uniform, some not, but their role was unmistakable.

If there were private medical facilities closer to where they'd started, the driver had bypassed them, taking her to the south center of the island to the Aga Khan Hospital, which from the street side of the compound appeared to be more of an oversize block-shaped house than anything medical and only grew to clinic proportions once they were inside the compound walls.

An orderly and two nurses came to Munroe's aid; quick questions were asked in the face of the emergency she presented, and they whisked the captain away. In the tacit agreement of the continent, the color of Munroe's skin, of the captain's skin, had allowed them entry before the talk of money.

Racism in the West had nothing on racism within sub-Saharan Africa, where prejudice against color was perpetrated at every walk of life against those a shade darker. In the worst of times lighter skin created targets and victims, but in the routine of everyday life, through minute reactions and a million assumptions, it opened doors, brought better treatment, and accorded privilege for no other reason than a collective unconcealed prejudice that valued a person based on his or her melanin levels.

Munroe filled out paperwork, paid a deposit for the captain's first day of stay, and asked for help in locating a cell phone provider, and with the information scribbled on a piece of paper and stuffed in a pocket, she sat in the waiting area, eyes closed and dozing, until the doctor came to find her.

His last name was Patel, probably early thirties—not much older than she—and in a lie that bordered the truth, Munroe explained the circumstances that had brought her here and added to them fabricated secondhand reports of the captain's violence and volatility and the suggestion that if he should start to come around, for the safety of everyone, it would be better to sedate him and then call her. The doctor took notes and didn't seem inclined to argue, and she could only hope that in her desire to keep the captain under control until she figured out what to do with him, she hadn't gone overboard in her description of his mania.

CHAPTER 11

It was after eight by the time Munroe stepped back out into the coastal air and she breathed in the night with its musk of rotting verdure and the exhilaration of having at last rid herself of obligations.

Sami was on the sand by the base of the pier, and with him were the two men who'd helped carry the captain earlier. Even though the conversation was in Swahili, they stopped talking when she approached. She nodded hello and asked Sami away, led him down the pier beyond prying eyes and paid him for his work for the day and, because she liked him, added an extra thousand shillings, then stayed with the boat so that he could find a hot meal.

He returned some forty-five minutes later, same friends in tow, all of them a little louder, a little drunker—most likely courtesy of Sami's newfound wealth—and with the boat back under watch, Munroe walked the return to the hotel, showered, and collapsed.

THREE HOURS OF sleep, just after midnight, and she woke to the noise of her neighbors in the hallway either returning from or heading off to something that required far more cheer and laughter than the hour warranted, noise echoing off tiled floors and high flat ceilings. Music and the party atmosphere of the tropics also seeped in from beyond the glass porch door, making it pointless to try to sleep again, so Munroe left her room for the front, where she could use the international line in the business center to make another call to Amber Marie.

The phone rang only once before Amber picked up, and her voice had a disjointed breathless quality to it, as if she'd jolted out of hard-earned rest only to plunge back into the nightmare she wished were a dream.

"Have you found out anything about K&R on the *Favorita*?" Munroe said.

"I've spent so much time trying to get answers and I'm still not sure, but from everything I've gathered, I think there's no policy." Amber's voice caught and she took a few slow breaths. "I've been to the port several times to talk to the agent," she said, "had to pay him to give me the name of the charterer, and finally tracked them down in Germany, but the ship seems to be owned by a shell company and if anybody at the charterer knows who the principals are, they're not telling. I can't dig any further from where I am and that's where the trail to the owners ends."

"Have you been watching for Internet news?"

"Yes," Amber whispered. "Haven't found anything, and I've got feelers out with some of the other maritime protection agencies, but nothing yet. I'm going to keep bugging. Eventually someone, some-where, is going to know something and at least we'll find out where the ship ended up and we can start from there."

"Have you checked into the AIS?"

"I can't find anything there either. It's like the ship has disap-peared."

The AIS was puzzling. Large vessels were equipped with the Maritime Automatic Identification System, transponders that trans-mitted position, and although it was primarily used as a way to avoid collisions, it was also a tool anyone could use to track any particu-lar ship's speed and course and coordinates at any given time. For the sake of ship security, most interactive maps didn't display vessels in pirate waters, but that the ship couldn't be located at all was something different—and it was hard to imagine that a ship the size of the *Favorita* hadn't been fitted with a transponder.

Although Amber hid them well, Munroe could hear the tears, the agony, the nightmare of having been cut off from someone she loved with no way to know where he was, if he was alive, or what would happen to him if he was ever found. She had lived it herself less than a year back.

Compassion swirled in a beaker of conflict.

Paraphrased words from the Book tumbled inside Munroe's head, scripture committed to memory as a child to please a father who could never be pleased: *If a sister be destitute of daily food and you say be warmed and filled, but give not those things which are needful, what does it profit?*

Leo's betrayal and stupidity still stung, and time away from him only hardened her anger. After what he'd done it was not a small thing to offer a little assistance, but this wasn't for Leo. "I'll see if I can find anything from down here," Munroe said. "Give me a day or two."

"Thank you," Amber said, though the words were rote and tinged with hopelessness. Unwilling to drag the conversation out, Munroe hung up and then stared at the phone. Clenched and unclenched her fists, squeezing away death and responsibility.

Indeed. What *did* it profit?

Depending on how hard and how long she tracked this path, she *would* inevitably pick up clues to the mystery of the *Favorita,* and then what? Given that Amber Marie would never be able to ransom the crew, to find the *Favorita* and do nothing more was, perhaps, worse than never looking in the first place.

Now was not too late to walk away. Munroe had the captain off her hands. The Aga Khan Hospital had a charity arm and so was possibly the best place she could have brought him to abandon him. She could give Sami the boat and catch a plane out of Kenya tomorrow. To where, though? Back to Dallas? To do what? Pick up where she'd left off—as if that were even possible?

Purposelessness was madness.

The pictures tucked away in her vest pocket returned, those images together with Miles Bradford during happier times. Had the roles been reversed, if he had been trapped on the *Favorita* right now, she would move heaven and hell to find him and wouldn't stop until every person responsible for his capture was dead.

Munroe picked up the phone to dial again and her finger, trembling slightly, rested above the touchpad. She replaced the handset. Drew in air to calm her heartbeat and then, in a movement quick enough that she didn't have time to think it through and change her mind, punched in the numbers for Capstone Security. It was 1:00 A.M. Mombasa time, 5:00 P.M. Dallas time, just on the outer edge of business hours, assuming someone was in the office to man the phones.

When the line connected, a woman answered, and Munroe recognized the voice though she hadn't expected to hear it.

"Sam?" she said. "This is Michael."

Samantha Walker had once been a vivacious bombshell of a sniper, had been one of Miles Bradford's closest allies, and had nearly been killed in an attack on Capstone's facility. Shrapnel had taken her spleen, part of her liver, twenty feet of intestines, and forced her into months of physical therapy. Bradford's best friend had died in the same blast, and Samantha was lucky that the worst of her damage was the scars and permanent limp. That explosion had taken lives, changed lives, changed everything, really, and were it not for Munroe, it never would have happened.

"It's been a long time," Sam said, tone friendly enough, but there was an undercurrent that cut like knife to skin and told Munroe what the blogs and Internet breadcrumbs never could. "We weren't sure if you were still alive."

"Still alive and swimming hard," Munroe said. "Is Miles around?"

"He's on assignment," Sam said, and left it at that. Didn't offer any indication of where, though Munroe already knew, and made no suggestion to patch him in, though Munroe knew she could.

"Would you tell him I called?"

"Sure," Sam said, "I'll tell him." But where she normally would have asked if Munroe wanted to leave a message or if there was a number where Bradford could get back to her, there was only empty silence.

Munroe put down the receiver, nausea mixing with heartache. At least in Samantha, Bradford would find someone stable, someone whose nightmares didn't make her try to kill him in her sleep, who didn't feel the driving urge to take off for developing countries every time things got quiet. She was happy for him. For them. And she had her answer now, even if it wasn't the one she wanted.

What did it profit?

Better to start work tomorrow cutting the trail that would lead her to the *Favorita* and give Amber the gift of possibly saving Leo, if he was still alive to be saved, than to wander aimless and homeless while turmoil devoured her from the inside. There was peace in the compartmentalization of shutting down, in switching off emotion, and for the first time in a long time Munroe slept beyond sunrise.

MUNROE REACHED SAMI at noon; found him sleeping beneath the tarp and let him be. Headed back up between the hotel and the bordering houses, up the same dirt alley they'd used to carry the captain to the ocean highway, and at the weed-eaten and eroded edge of the road she approached the first woman she came upon and in childish and broken Swahili asked where to wait for a *matatu* to the city.

The woman beamed a smile at Munroe's botched attempt to communicate. She raised a hand to steady the overladen pot nestled upon a rag rolled atop her head and shifted the baby carried in a sling on her back. Motioned up the road to a bright red building with a high thatched rooftop, a restaurant it seemed, and in English replied, "You stay there, he come."

The wait wasn't long, and with two others who lingered at the spot, Munroe climbed into a lime green van named SPHINX EYES. She scooted bent-over and sideways along a narrow walking space and squeezed into the second bench from the rear as the others squished in behind her. There was no air, albeit plenty of smell.

The *matatu* operated on a pay-as-you-go system, in which everyone seemed to know the price and clunked change into the tout's hand as bodies, bowed, climbing over laps and belongings, squeezed in and out of the van at irregular intervals.

Munroe watched. Counted. And when the van came to a final stop in the midst of a potholed and mud-spattered lot somewhere still on the outskirts of town, she got off with the remaining passengers and handed the tout her coins.

Another woman pointed her to a second ride, and Munroe climbed into a nearly full van with a tumult of words and voices trailing behind her. *Mzungu* was the one most often repeated, one she would have understood even without the patterns and comprehension picking up faster now; the same mocking whisper that followed her any time she submerged into local cultures on the continent: *white person.*

MUNROE STEPPED OFF the *matatu* somewhere along the north end of Moi Avenue, a main artery that ran through the center of Mombasa. Far up and down both sides of the multilane thoroughfare, cars, trucks, bicycles, hand-drawn carts, city buses, and *matatus* juggled for road share in the clog of diesel fume and dust, all part of the vibrant chaos that made Africa's big cities what they were.

The sidewalks, cracked and littered, were a slow rush of pedestrian bustle, and Munroe oriented herself to the rough map she'd drawn on her palm, followed the lines and got lost several times, which she expected and which was part of the process of breathing in the ambience, the sounds, the heartbeat, of a new location.

She paused on a corner to get her bearings and a young girl, three or four years old, held her hands up, begging for coins, saying *jambo, jambo* in the high-pitched voice of toddlerhood. Munroe shook her head and the little one pestered her for a block at least and Munroe fought the urge to look back, to see which adult kept track of the child; it would only make her angry. Street children were endemic Africa-wide, the young ones often put out to beg by their parents or relatives though a few were orphans, all of them drawn to the tourists, easy marks in their softheartedness and unwitting propagators of the blight in their giving.

There were nonprofits that worked exhaustively to get kids off the streets, housed them, educated them, clothed them, but the street was an addiction hard to shake with its easy money, glue sniffing, and freedom from rules. Most returned to begging, and eventually as they grew older and their cuteness wore off, to lives of hard crime, prostitution, and early death: Like everything else in Africa, there were no easy answers and no easy fixes.

On Digo Road Munroe found the Safaricom shop, a branch of one of Kenya's largest telecom carriers. She purchased the cheapest phone available and set up and paid for a noncontract account. First call was to the Aga Khan Hospital and Dr. Patel for an update on the captain.

"He's showing signs of responsiveness," the doctor said.

"He's lucid?"

"Not with words, but his eyes follow movement and he responds to voice prompts."

"You think he'll pull out of it completely?"

"It's highly likely."

Munroe lingered over the answer, strategized over the possibilities and the dilemma they forced her into. There were things the captain could tell her, answers she wanted for Amber Marie, and she needed him conversational to get them. Problem was, she could only get answers if he didn't take off first, and there weren't a lot of options to ensure that one didn't happen before the other. She said, "I told you, he needs to be sedated."

"At this stage, I don't feel the need," the doctor said. "There are signs of agitation, but that's normal in his condition. There's nothing of the violence you mentioned."

"Put it this way," she said. Paused, and chose her words for highest impact. "As long as your patient remains sedated, I'll continue to pay for his bed and medical expenses. If you choose not to keep him sleeping, then chances are when he is fully awake and when no one is watching, he'll get up and walk out of your clinic. If he does that, I refuse to foot the bill for his stay. What's more, if he doesn't fully recover, it will fall on your shoulders to turn him out of your clinic. It's your decision, but it seems to me sedation would be the simplest for everyone."

There was a long hesitation, then he said, "You are blackmailing me?" and in the gaps between his syllables she could hear the bewilderment and frustration.

"Just making a request."

"This is not a request you make."

"It's very much a request," she said. "Let me know what you decide."

The doctor was silent for another space and then there followed a discussion in the background, something between him and the front desk that lasted a minute or two. "All right," he said finally. "I will keep the patient under mild sedation for the next seventy-two hours while he continues to recover, but you need to pay the fee for his entire stay in advance."

"I'll be there this evening," she said, and flipped the phone closed.

Seventy-two hours to sort out the next step.

THE SOMALI MARKET was on Nehru Road, a potholed street in which stagnant muddy water filled what asphalt didn't, a street vibrant with color and chaos, where cars came and went at an impatient crawl, and people and porters crossed between them at will and without regard for the rules of the road, slowing traffic down further. In both directions tailors and merchant shops hid behind glass doors and windows that could barely be seen for the collection of wares displayed on the sidewalks in front of them, mixed among and sandwiched between open-front bodega-style stores, with products stacked up the walls, each establishment brandishing a specialty of sorts: expensively priced cheap electronics, used and new clothing in bright, almost neon colors, piles of hats or handbags or trinkets in cheap plastic sheaths, all inevitably imported from China, laid out on make-do wooden tables or under umbrellas, or draped over vehicle hoods and sometimes spread out on burlap between parked cars on the street itself.

Munroe strolled the street, browsing merchandise, dodging clustered foot traffic and mud puddles, a game of street chess that involved thinking many moves ahead to avoid ending up spattered with filth, searching for the familiar signs to indicate that she'd arrived at what she'd come for, but by the time she'd reached the far end of the road where the congestion eased, and the pedestrians and shops were far fewer, she'd still not found it.

She hadn't known where this market would be, had simply known that there would have to be one somewhere in the city—perhaps more than one. Decades of wars and clan fighting had bled the Somali diaspora out across the globe, but Kenya, because of its proximity, played host to the largest refugee population. The poorest were abandoned, living in squalor, unable to work and restricted to camps, though many others under better circumstances had become part of the Kenyan landscape, and in spite of rampant xenophobia, they had entrenched themselves as entrepreneurs of sorts, businessmen who worked hard and plied a variety of trades. There had to be a place where the culture remained intact, where those far from home could buy what little familiar comforts home had once provided. In answer to her inquiries, the East Indian proprietors at the Safaricom shop had pointed her to Nehru Road.

She paused outside a clothing bodega and ran her fingers along the seam of an ornately stitched *guntiino*. The proprietor, a man on the upper end of fifty years, neatly dressed and with a *koofiyad* atop his head, was beside her almost immediately, high cheekbones and angular nose giving away his ancestry before he opened his mouth. She knew his look as he sized her up, and while he tried to determine the level of her interest in his wares, she rated his potential effectiveness as a mark.

In English he asked where she was from, a handy question before negotiations because stereotyping worked well when intending to separate a target from his money. Munroe replied in Somali, and as always, when language appeared when least expected, the welcome widened.

"You know my country?" the man said, and she smiled for an answer.

They made small talk, a lighthearted conversation that ebbed and flowed as customers came and went: a sale here, a sale there, until Munroe had no more time to spare and asked the man where she could go to do *hawala.*

"You want do *hawala,*" her host said, repeating her words as if perhaps she'd misspoken.

"I have a friend in Galmudug," she said, and the man nodded politely as if it all made sense now.

"There are a few places," he said, and with a broken ballpoint pen and a scrap of paper, he drew basic directions that relied on store signs, building color, and alleyways for markers. At the sidewalk, Munroe paused in front of a beige tunic. "How much?" she said.

She would willingly have paid whatever price he named, compensation for the knowledge he had freely given, but he cocked his head, clasped his hands, and asked a fair price, probably exactly what the garment was worth. Munroe paid and slipped the tunic over her head. The extra clothing added to the heat, but this would allow her to cover the shirts and mask the pants, which, although perfect for working on a ship, had continually marked her as a stranger on land and so made her a perpetual target.

It took time to track down the spots that coincided with the three sets of directions and descriptions the proprietor had given her, and once she had, she looped back to each, watched the entrances and waited for clients to come and go, analyzed one location against the next. And then, having seen all that limited time would allow, she wound back through the noisy street to the door sandwiched between a handbag bodega and a tailor shop.

The entry was solid wood, built into cinder-block housing, raw and makeshift in a way that indicated it had been built long after the other shops along the street, that it more than likely blocked off what had once been an alley, and here she would find that thing for which she searched.

All Somali hijackings were financed business endeavors, not the result of a group of rabble-rousers gathering in a boat and setting out to see what big fish they might find. The money to purchase boats and fuel, weapons, ammunition, and food sometimes came from individuals acting as venture capitalists in a start-up undertaking, but was more often paid by a consortium of investors, local as well as foreign—money from Kenya or Yemen or even farther abroad—black-market investors, word-of-mouth investors, who bought shares in upcoming hijackings expecting to make the money back with a hefty return when the ransom came in.

This was the reason that the naval forces in the Gulf of Aden, and more, the armed maritime security companies, had done so much to deter piracy over the years: There were still plenty of desperately poor men willing to risk their lives on the promise of financial gain, but investors were far less willing to put their money on the line when the risk had increased to losing the entirety of their investment: skiffs, fuel, and arms blown up in a raid or a hijacking gone wrong.

Hawala was an informal money transfer system based on trust and honor and personal connections, a transfer system that operated outside of and yet parallel to traditional banking. Local Somali boys hadn't figured out on their own that the *Favorita* had armed guards and then come up with the strategy to stop the ship and overpower them. Someone, somewhere, had paid for the hijacking of the *Favorita,* and as it was impossible for money to flow into Somalia without some form of information flowing with it, there was no one better to talk to about the money movement that funded piracy than the men whose hands were on the taps of currency flow.

Munroe opened the door and stepped inside a de facto hallway created between the concrete walls of two buildings and a Plexiglas roof. Humidity mixed with heat and robbed the narrow passage of air.

The alley continued fifty feet inward, dead-ended at the back of what had to be another building, and in front of the dead end stood what she assumed was a bodyguard. He was within an inch on either side of her five foot ten, with Somali bone structure, had on a well-worn earth-brown Western suit with tennis shoes; arms crossed, he studied her as she shut the noise of the street behind her and headed toward him, hands by her sides where he could see them.

Instinct and self-preservation drew her into reptilian calm. Like an injection into an addict's vein, the first hit of adrenaline was soothing and jarring, a rush that pulled thought and action into a narrow focus where nothing mattered but survival and acquiring the thing she'd set out to get.

CHAPTER 12

Munroe walked slowly enough to buy time, to assess the level of threat in this enclosed space. The man uncrossed his arms as she drew near, sizing her up the way she did him, his face creased with the wearied disinterest of a soldier who'd seen too many fights and wasn't looking for another: attentive nonchalance that said he was capable of slitting her throat but wouldn't seek out violence for the thrill of it.

Munroe drew nearer and a recessed doorway became apparent. Inside the shadow of the door frame was another man, dressed similarly to the standing man, seated on a stool, legs kicked out across the entryway showing bare ankles. She stopped a few feet from the door and looked askance at the standing man before attempting to enter.

He hesitated and his gaze shifted, first to the sitting man and then back to her. She'd assumed she wouldn't be the first white face to show up at this place, but his behavior indicated that she was an anomaly. He spoke in Somali to the man on the stool, his words accented and in a dialect different from what she was most familiar with, but she understood.

"Tell the boss there is a white man here."

The man on the stool got up and unlocked the door. He let himself in and the door shut behind him with the click of the lock's reengagement. In the resultant stillness and the several minutes that it took for him to return, neither Munroe nor the other man spoke, although he did step back to his spot by the wall and allowed Munroe her space.

When the door opened again, the second man held the door wide, motioned Munroe inward to where a third guard stood. This hallway, too, was empty, a bare concrete strip adorned by a wooden chair by the front door where the third guard had sat, a light that hung limply from a plywood ceiling, and another solid door that filled the far wall.

Munroe stepped through and the third man closed and locked the door behind her. She felt no malevolence: These were precautions meant to deter murderers and thieves from going after cash in a country where crime was high and Somalis were the enemy and easy targets.

The inside guard walked with her to the end of the hall, knocked on the door, and then opened it slightly. She stepped into an air-conditioned office with a wall of shelves and meticulously marked ledgers on one side and two chairs on the other. In front of her was a wide, polished wooden desk, and behind it, a middle-aged gentleman in a suit far more costly than what his men out front wore. He smoothed down a tie when he stood, and stretched out a manicured hand in greeting.

"How can I help you?" he said.

His English was crisp with the enunciation of education somewhere posh in England.

"I need to do *hawala*," Munroe said. "I was told you were the man to see." She glanced at the chairs off to the side of the room. Walked to the nearest, grabbed the back, and tipped it toward her. "May I?" she said, and when he nodded, she dragged it across serpentine tiles to the front of the desk, turned the seat toward him, and then sat down.

He remained standing, grinning, chin cradled against his thumb. "You Canadian?" he said. "American? What?"

"Cameroonian."

He raised his eyebrows and she sighed with mock impatience. "I carry passports from a few countries," she said. "I was born in Cameroon."

"You're white African?"

She shrugged.

"You do this often?"

"First time."

"And you found me how?"

"I asked around."

"Okay," he said, and he sat in an oversize leather chair. Made a show of pulling out a ledger and poised the pen above a page half filled with enigmatic squiggles and figures. "How much do you want to send? To who? Where?"

She smiled and, reading the nuance in his posture, the micro expressions that danced across his face, took the route of playfulness. "A thousand U.S. dollars," she said. "To Abdi Hasan Awale Qeybdiid, in Galmudug."

He glanced up from the ledger for a second and then burst out laughing. Put the pen down, leaned back in his seat, and grinned again.

He pointed a finger and said, "A young white boy wants to use a Somali *hawaladar* to send dollars to a warlord turned regional president." Shook his head. "I'm pretty sure he doesn't want or need your money. So really, why are you here?"

From her boots and from her pocket, Munroe retrieved three of the small bundles that she'd rolled when she was in Djibouti and slowly, theatrically, unfurled them and laid the bills flat on top of the desk. "It really is a thousand dollars," she said. "The money's yours if you don't want to send it, but I'm here because I need to learn something."

"I transfer money, not information," he said. "Are you CIA?"

"I'm not, but if I was, I don't expect I'd tell you."

"I've known a few officers. They tell if it benefits them."

She paused at the little piece of intel that meant she wasn't the only one who had come to him for things, which meant she'd come to the right place. "If I was CIA, it would benefit me," she said. "But I'm not."

"What then?"

"Just an individual trying to discover something."

"In the form of *hawala* to a man wanted for war crimes?"

"It's a challenge," she said. "A game, if you care to play, which you should, because either way, you win."

He leaned forward in his chair. "I'm amused," he said, "but just because the room is empty doesn't mean I'm not busy."

Munroe switched to Somali, said, "I'm looking for a ship."

The *hawaladar*'s smile faded, his expression and his body tensed, as she expected they would, and the good nature shifted into guardedness.

Knowing she had his full attention, Munroe said, "A hijacked ship, taken somewhere east of Mogadishu a few days ago. There's been no news, no claims for ransom. I am trying to find something that has become invisible."

"I've got nothing to do with pirates," he said.

"I'm not asking," she said. "It would never benefit you to tell."

His shoulders relaxed slightly, and he nodded.

She leaned forward, hands folded on the desk to mirror him. One couldn't understand Somalia, its history and culture, its infighting and warlords and nonstatehood, without understanding the centuries of treaties and blood feuds, alliances and suballiances of clans, a shared cultural knowledge that only those raised within it were able to completely comprehend. Without knowing the *hawaladar*'s alliances, or who hijacked the ship, or why, even innocuous questions had the potential to blow back.

"I am an outsider," she said. "I understand that even though you were educated abroad and have probably lived more years away from Somalia than at home, clan identity is still part of who you are." She paused to analyze his nonverbal responses, and with no visible opposition, continued. "It's difficult to know how ludicrous my request might be to you, which is why I'm offering a game that will allow you to win no matter what, and will never challenge your loyalties to your people."

He waited a second to see if she had more, and when she remained silent, he leaned back in his chair again and studied her a long while.

"Not CIA?" he said.

She shook her head.

"What agency then?"

"None," she said. "Just an individual."

"With money to spare, and you speak my language."

She nodded.

"There's no way to guarantee you're telling the truth?"

"None," she said. "But I don't want anything from you that might incriminate you."

He shifted forward again, deeper against the desk than he had before, so that his face was closer to hers, his expression clouded with mistrust and accusation. "If there are no demands for ransom and the ship disappeared, where does your information come from? How do you know a ship was hijacked?"

"I was on it," she said.

"You were on it."

She tipped her head in response and he started laughing again.

"How?" he said, shoulders shaking, and she allowed him his moment of self-reveling humor. He sighed. "You were on it," and then with a forced straight face said, "How did you get here?"

"I stole one of their boats. Followed the sun to the coast. I'm not as innocent or as young as I look." She paused for effect and then scooted the small stack of bills in his direction. "If the hijacking was paid for by Somali money, then tell me nothing, return me half the money, and I'll be on my way. If it was foreign investment, then I only ask that you give me whatever rumors are passing through on the wind, and the payment is yours."

"All you want to know is if there was foreign investment?"

"Yes," she said, "and if it is foreign, from where the investors hail."

His focus skimmed over the money, then returned to her, and he held eye contact a long time before replying. "What makes you so certain I'm able to learn anything?"

"Everyone knows something," she said. "Everyone has ears. Eyes. Intuition. And because your business relies entirely on trust—and it involves money—you're in a better position than most to hear, see, feel."

He tapped a forefinger on the bills, refused to break eye contact in a way that under other circumstances would have come across as a threat, but which she read as a search for words. "I don't need this," he said.

"I know."

"Then why did you offer it?"

"Earnest money."

"What for?"

"To prove I'm not wasting your time."

"I'm opposed to piracy," he said. "I'm a religious man and pirates are *haram*. If you understand my culture, then you understand *haram*, yes?"

"I do."

"I'll play your game," he said. "I will ask and see what I can find, only because I am curious about the implications in what you've left unsaid."

"That's all I ask," she said, and stood to go.

"Communication moves slowly," he said. "It'll be a few days before I have anything for you—assuming there's anything to be had. Do you have a number where I can reach you if I come by anything?"

"I'd rather just stop by for news," she said. "Unless you have a number you want to give me."

"Do you have a name?" he said.

"Michael."

"Michael what?"

"I'm not asking for yours, so how about we just leave it at Michael."

"Abdi," he said. "Like your warlord friend." Paused. "You are really Cameroonian?"

She nodded and stretched a hand forward and he shook it, gripped hard and tight and held on long enough to communicate the silent message that fucking with him would be a mistake. When he released her and she turned to go, he picked up the stack of bills and slid them into a pocket in the ledger. "I expect I'll be giving half of this back to you," he said.

She paused at the door. "I doubt it," she said, and when she left him, she did so with the conviction that no matter how many other lines for information she might lay out, or whose path she crossed in this search, she had already found the man whose connections would lead her to what she needed.

CHAPTER 13

Munroe exited the *hawaladar*'s alley for the cluttered confusion of Nehru Road, for dodging cars and crowds as she walked the street to its beginning to trace her way back to Moi Avenue and begin again. The next destination came with a street name, and since she'd found pictures of nearby buildings posted to online street maps, it would hopefully be easier to find than the *hawaladar* had been.

Munroe paused at the periphery of a crowded bus stop to glance at the map on her hand and in her slowing felt a tug on her pants leg. In violation of the natural inclination to look down, her head ticked up in the opposite direction of the pull, searching for a threat that, if it came, would come from elsewhere: a skill taught by a continent where safety was never taken for granted.

The teenage boy who'd grabbed at her pants continued to follow her, reaching for her leg, pointing at her shoe, supposedly calling her attention to something at her feet. She refused to acknowledge him and in her peripheral vision spotted his partner coming up behind her on her left.

She pivoted to face him slightly. Hand to his chest, she shoved him back, not hard enough to injure or cause a disturbance, just enough to keep him beyond arm's length and allow her to get through the crowd unmolested.

A woman inadvertently blocked Munroe's path, and when Munroe stepped around her, the boys, unwilling to let go of their target, closed in again. If they continued to follow her, a pack of wild dogs on the hunt, they'd eventually draw others in, and Munroe didn't want that fight.

Not today.

In a heartbeat she reversed a half pace. Right fist across her chest and under her arm, she punched the boy hard beneath his sternum. Felt his expulsion of breath. Spun fully around just long enough to glare at the one on her right, giving notice that she'd fight back and that they'd be better off with an easier target, then continued away from those thirty seconds of conflict and another part of what made Africa's big cities what they were. At some point today, a tourist wouldn't be so lucky.

On Mombasa Road Munroe found the bright blue two-story building that marked the turnoff to a side street where, supposedly, she would find Kefesa, a local NGO whose mission statement claimed to advocate for Somali refugees within the Mombasa-area prison system. Not exactly the type of outfit she was looking for, but the organization had current connections to Somalia, and its blog contained pictures and stories less than two weeks old that made the office easier to find than any of the dozens of potentially outdated data-aggregated listings available for other Somali-centric NGOs. If nothing else, someone at Kefesa should be able to point her to a government branch or aid-oriented outfit better suited to her needs.

Bars ran up the face of both fronting windows, but the grille that would have been pulled down over the entry was still up. Inside, peeling paint mixed with mildew and just enough cool to take the edge off the humidity.

From the back a woman's voice, pleasant and lilting, said, "A minute please," and a moment later she rounded the corner. Munroe recognized her from the blog photographs, and she approached now, short and plump with a purse slung over her shoulder, keys and clipboard in her hand, and a welcome on her face.

Munroe's story wasn't long: a journalistic interest in local xenophobia against Somalis and the desire to interview one of the directors, and this scored her an appointment for tomorrow afternoon, because they were already gone for the day.

The woman reached into her purse and fished out a fat wallet stuffed with scraps of papers and clinking coins. She found a dog-eared business card and offered it to Munroe. "You call tomorrow, ask for Peter," she said. "He can confirm."

Munroe accepted and for the sake of pretense took a moment to read the card. Courtesy of the blogs, she knew the name and the face, knew where to find the number printed on it. Counting on inter-office gossip to pave the way before she called, she said, "I'll do that."

THE STREETS WERE less crowded now, most of the sidewalk merchants having packed up their cardboard and their goods, most office workers already on *matatus* and buses headed toward home. Munroe left Kefesa for the Aga Khan Hospital, her long stride picking up the pace the emptier the streets grew, thoughts matching speed as she plotted the lines for information she'd put out today against the one she would throw tomorrow.

There was danger in working too many too fast: The more people asking questions, the greater the odds that word would leak that she was on the hunt, and those who might previously have been willing to talk would become suspicious and grow silent. After Peter Muthui at Kefesa, she would make the effort to ingratiate herself with someone inside the local office of the Ministry of Foreign Affairs, and when that was finished, she'd return to the Somali market to converse again among the merchants, and then she would wait before beginning once more.

This was always the way of learning what went unspoken, of listening for rumors and absorbing details from the undercurrents: a time-consuming cycle of pretenses and follow-up, of establishing trust and allaying defenses, of creating one ruse and then the next and so becoming whatever her mark needed to allow him to talk.

MUNROE PASSED THROUGH the front doors of the Aga Khan Hospital, where the woman at the desk was distracted with a file. Bypassing her, Munroe continued on, made it across the foyer, up one flight of stairs, and all the way down the hall to the captain's room without being noticed.

She stepped inside the small private suite and shut the door behind her.

Accommodations here were a far cry from where he'd been stashed in Lamu: This room had only one bed and its own attached bathroom, though he'd never have the opportunity to put it to use. The floor was tiled and the walls were painted white, and the room was climate-controlled and smelled faintly of antiseptic and medication. The captain's sheets were clean, his port was recently bandaged, and the IV bag was half full; the filthy clothes had long since disappeared—hopefully had been destroyed.

The air conditioner groaned on and the curtains rustled with its breeze. Munroe sat, watching the captain, studying the tranquillity on his face, waiting for a reaction and for his instinct to kick in—that uncanny ability of the human animal to sense, even during sleep, that it was being watched—waited for him to open his eyes. But either he was still trapped in his state of unconsciousness or the doctor had been true to his word and had put him under, because the only movement was the rise and fall of his chest.

She returned to the front desk and paid for the next three days. Burning through cash as she was, the room and medical attention didn't come cheap, but costs were a small fraction of what a similar stay would have been in the U.S. Pockets lighter, she stepped back out into the nighttime air and made the long walk back to where the *matatu* had left her earlier in the day.

MUNROE EXITED THE *matatu* not far from the hotel beyond the pier and, in a pattern that had become familiar enough that now was the time to alter it, followed the dirt road down toward the beach. Knew something was wrong before she reached the sand.

The menace came in spaced silences, gaps in conversation and laughter where the night should have been fully alive: the urban equivalent of the scattering of birds fleeing danger in the jungle canopy. The immediacy of death crawled up her spine, an animal instinct honed in her savage teenage years, and the uptick in aware-ness primed her for a fight and drowned out everything but the focus of the moment.

Munroe slowed and scanned for clues to this thing that lurked. Slipped out of the beige tunic, which had been camouflage on Nehru Road during the day and which was now a neon light beneath the moon. Left the dirt path for the low stone wall that hedged in the hotel grounds, went up through a break and onto manicured grass, then balled up the tunic and shoved it under a bush.

CHAPTER 14

Munroe's breathing slowed and she took each step forward in measured calculation, followed the hotel grounds inward toward lampposts and the winding paved trails they illuminated, followed toward the pool and the thatched cabana with colorful lights strung about, to where hotel staff catered to drinking and partying guests oblivious to the possibilities that lay outside the boundaries of their perceived haven.

She slipped past the edge of the pool and continued to the foremost retaining wall, beyond which was the beach under the moonlit sky, and on the beach a crowd where there should have been no crowd: shadows without gender, without race, without any purpose but to gawk and hover around a lump of something at the foot of the pier while at the far end of the dock the empty boat lifted and lowered with the rolling waves.

Had this been in the heat of the day when Sami typically slept, Munroe would have found no oddity in the seemingly empty vessel, but in the evening, when the world came alive, the shape of Sami's form should have been visible—on the boat itself, or the pier, or somewhere nearby as it had always been since the beginning—but she couldn't pull his silhouette from the crowd.

Munroe strained to see clearly. Had nothing but a history of violence and the roiling in her gut on which to draw, but that was enough to know that Sami had been stolen from her.

She clenched and unclenched her fists. Turned from the scene and inhaled the night, a long deep breath in countermeasure to seething violence, hatred toward an invisible hand that had once more moved against her.

Calculation turning against calculation, she walked beneath palm trees and around flower bushes, back to the lighted pathways. Found one of the hotel staff on his way to the pool, a stack of towels in his arms, and stopped him. Nodded toward the beach and said, "What's going on with the crowd down there?"

The man tensed with a hesitation that said he'd been told to keep what he knew to himself because worrying guests was always bad for business. Munroe relaxed into nonchalance, handed him a hundred shillings, and with her tone mellow to ease his tension, asked again, "What happened?"

He pocketed the money and his focus drifted toward the ground. "A man die," he said.

"A white man?"

His face jerked up. He shook his head and, as if the lifeless form still sprawled out on the sand meant nothing, said, "Everything finished now, you don't worry. No problem for any guest only with men on the beach, everything okay."

Munroe would have asked him if such *problems* were a regular occurrence on this stretch of coast, but there was no point to that. He continued on and she listened to the noise of the night and, when the pathway emptied, returned to shadow to slip through the dark for the far edge of the periphery where stone retaining wall met sand, where the only light was that which came from the sky, and where it was possible to observe the pier without being seen.

She would have preferred to be on the beach among the loiterers, where learning could come faster and she could place blame and find culprits, but fear and uncertainty infested the air, and as it was no secret that the owner of the boat had been a foreigner, she would draw suspicion and anger from the moment she stepped into their midst. Crowds were easy to incite, difficult to control—pack mentality turned rational individuals into an unthinking, brutal mass, and she didn't want to wind up on the receiving end of that kind of mob justice.

An argument erupted between several of the men near the pier: pushing, shoving, yelling in a language Munroe only partially understood and which brought on mental anxiety that amplified the inner tumult. The crowd parted slightly and among those shoving and being shoved were the two young men who'd helped carry the captain and whom Sami had later befriended and fed.

The fight ebbed, and with the crowd still pushed back, Sami's body was clearly visible, surrounded by the darkness that had bled from him, left behind and out in the open for show-and-tell. Permutations danced and collided inside her head, answers to questions she hadn't thought to ask, and anger for never having asked them.

The rate of crime near the big cities and the cheapness of life on the continent said Sami's death was a statistical inevitability, a coincidence, bad luck and timing: He was new to the area; he'd had money and had flashed it around. Instinct, and the confusion and fear written within the actions of Sami's new friends, said otherwise.

This death had followed from the *Favorita,* had finally caught up with her because she'd stayed in one place long enough, but it was a statistical improbability that someone hunting for the boat would have found it by chance among the thousands along the entire Kenyan coast. Munroe closed her eyes and filled in the gaps with what had no words, breathed in the tenor and again watched the crowd, the young men.

If his killers had wanted the boat, they would have taken it already and gone, and she understood that these boys had not been the ones to commit this atrocity, understood that they, like her, would never know if Sami's killer or killers now hovered together with the curious.

Munroe studied the beach and counted those who came and

went, mentally retraced each step since her arrival in Kenya: the Internet searches and hotel stays, merchants and hospital visits, the few precautions she'd taken out of habit, not out of concern that she would have been tracked or targeted.

If it was the captain they were after, they should have just asked her nicely. She'd wanted him off her hands, would gladly have traded him for Victor—for the whole of Leo's team if he was worth that much—and then walked away, but now this was personal, now she had her own dog in the fight. Now she wanted blood.

The mood on the beach shifted, whispers upticked on the wind, and glances turned toward the dirt road. Several of the bystanders walked away, some of them passing close enough that Munroe could clearly see their faces, though none of them were familiar. By the time the two local policemen reached the base of the pier, the entire crowd had bled off, no one wanting to be hauled in for questioning and, regardless of guilt or innocence, forced to bribe his way to freedom.

The men stood over Sami's body. One knelt and poked him, as if to confirm he was dead. They spoke for several minutes, conversation carried away on the wind, and at last one of them left for the dirt road. When he had gone, his partner sat on the pier and pulled out a pack of cigarettes. He showed no interest in the boat moored at the far end of the dock—perhaps hadn't even noticed it—struck a match and casually smoked a cigarette.

The wait dragged out longer than an hour and one cigarette turned into six, while the man kept watch over the body. What would have been a crime scene elsewhere left nothing for him to investigate. Even if someone better qualified had arrived to handle the case, or there had been technicians trained to collect the evidence, even if the city had forensic equipment to lead the investigators to culprits, there were still no databases through which said evidence could be compared, no hair samples or fiber samples or DNA or fingerprints, nothing at all but eyewitness testimony to sort out what had happened tonight, and the eyes had all long since vanished.

Detectives might return tomorrow, knocking on doors, asking

questions, might even make arrests based on hearsay, but the investigation would be limited to first- or secondhand accounts, and because Sami was a stranger without family making demands for justice, the truth had likely died with him.

The first man returned carrying a sheet or cloth or possibly burlap, and was accompanied by two others not in uniform. The two new men wrapped the body and the four carried it away, and Munroe was left to face the empty beach with nothing but rage to keep her company. Sami was lost to the night, lost to her, lost to life: a man who'd gone to sea and would never return, a vanished soul whose family would ever be waiting, hoping for him to come home. If she'd had any inkling of how to contact them, she would have made a point of finding them before she left the country, but that was something for another night, perhaps another lifetime.

The hours deepened and quiet settled. The pool emptied. The cabana closed and the lights turned off, and in the long darkness she was left alone, watching the boat, the pier, the surf. And when the tide had come in fully and began to ebb out, Munroe finally moved again.

According to the clock on her phone it was after three in the morning, that time when those who slept, slept deepest, and it was more easily possible for someone waiting on shore for her to return to have fallen asleep on watch. She removed her boots and socks, stuffed the socks inside her pockets, tied the laces of the boots together, slung them over a shoulder, and then, big cat on the prowl, left the safety of her shadow to slink from one hotel to the next between pauses and silences until she was far enough away from the pier that there was no way she could be seen from it, and there she slipped from hiding out onto the open beach and into the ocean.

The water was warm and the waves rolled gently up the sloping shore. With the cell phone gripped between her teeth and the boots draped around her neck, she waded out far enough that she could move among the currents without being seen from the seaboard and, using the cover of the water, reversed the half kilometer that she'd come.

As a precaution against the possibility that the trap that had not been sprung earlier might be laid for her here, she waited when she reached the pilings. Listened for any sign of life from within the boat and, hearing nothing, thumped the hull to see if noise might rouse the unexpected.

No response and so she thumped again, harder, louder, and then, as sure as she could be that she wouldn't be climbing to her death, swam aft and stretched for the ladder.

The metal groaned loud against metal. She climbed from the water and tipped over the side of the boat. Knelt and waited. Dumped the waterlogged boots onto the bench, and shielding the phone with her hand, guided its low light as a flashlight of sorts to check the fuel tank, which was half full, and the fuel lines, which were intact. The rifle was missing and she couldn't know if Sami had sold the gun or if whoever had killed him had taken it and left the rest of her supplies.

Munroe pushed the propeller into the water.

The engine's roar was a scream to the quiet, and if someone had been waiting for her, he was now fully aware that she had returned and was on the move.

LIGHTS BLINKED OUT over the water, and with them Munroe kept a steady distance from the shore; hugged the curves of the coast north toward Malindi in a patterned hum and rise and fall that once again drew long in the night, allowing the rage and violence that had followed in the wake of Sami's death to feast and fester and scheme into threads of possibility and action.

Taking the boat to Malindi would eat time. The faster plan would be to wait for dawn and find a quiet place not far up shore where she could scuttle the vessel—wouldn't be the first time she'd sunk thousands of dollars off an African coastline—but that would give Sami's killers nothing to play with. This way she would draw them away from Mombasa, provide an opportunity to mask the trail, and buy the opportunity to sort through options.

The same landmarks that Sami had pointed out those few days prior came into view shortly before dawn when the sky was purple and shifting through color and the small dots that were fishermen's skiffs or pirogues could be seen as blemishes on the water. Guided by the clues and working through trial and error, she eventually reached a small cove where the local fishermen congregated and the slow hustle of selling off the early-morning catch to households and restaurateurs had already begun.

The beach was spattered with small wooden boats dragged up and tied off, a miniature armada resting on the sand while the bigger vessels anchored in deeper water. The sun had already crested the horizon, and between the shouts and the cries of the merchants on shore, seabirds dove and squawked in a fight over fish offal.

Munroe neared the largest of the boats, a fiberglass V-hull nearly as long as hers with an improvised tarp under which five fishermen in cutoff pants, either bare-chested or wearing torn T-shirts, tended to nets and lounged in the developing shade. Munroe called out a hello in English and said, "I'm looking for the owner of your boat."

All of the men had already turned to watch her approach, but in response to her shout the youngest stood, and arms and torso ripped with definition, leaned against the side in her direction. "Why?" he said.

"I have a boat to sell."

He smiled and his head ticked toward her. "That one?"

Munroe returned the smile, sweeping her hand toward the bow. "How much do you want?"

"Are you the owner?"

"I'm the renter," he said. "But I want to buy my own."

His English was perfect, melodic and educated and proper with the British history that was part of the country's accent, an English more common in the big city, not the broken fragments of Sami's or the pidgin of the hotel staff, and she adjusted her own grammar accordingly. "Together with the engine and the fuel it's worth at least ten thousand U.S. dollars," she said. "I want five thousand."

He whistled. "I'll give you five hundred."

She laughed. "Let me talk to someone with money."

"Six hundred," he said.

Still smiling, she shook her head and said, "Do you carry a knife?"

He threw his arms wide. "I'm a fisherman! What a question."

"Sell it to me."

"How much will you pay?"

"How much is it worth?"

"Eight thousand shillings," he said.

"I'll give you four thousand."

"Deal," he said, and motioned her in closer, and when her boat had neared and she'd cut the engine, he used an improvised gaff with a cloth wrapped around the end to pull the boats together. His knife had a six-inch blade, clean and sharp, pointed and narrow and better suited for paring than hand-to-hand combat; was holstered in leather that had been resewn several times; and was worth far less than Munroe had agreed to, but it was a blade all the same, a weapon until she could return to collect those she'd left behind in Mombasa.

With the transaction complete, Munroe asked for the number of his boat's owner, and he fished around by his feet. Held up the stub of a blade-sharpened pencil. "You have paper?"

She pulled out her phone, punched through the controls to insert a new contact. "One better," she said.

He laughed again and recited a number and a name. Munroe entered the information. "A woman?" she said.

He motioned toward the other boats anchored just offshore. "She owns five of these."

"Is she difficult?"

"Of course," he said. "She does good business."

Munroe gave him a mock salute and he let loose the gaff, and when she no longer had an audience, the mask of her smile faded and the rage returned.

Another kilometer up the coast, where the shore was emptier, Munroe made the call. The woman was pure business and her questions were articulated with a solid knowledge of nautical terminology; she knew exactly what she wanted and what she could work with, and when Munroe had satisfied those concerns, the woman described the large concrete pier that Munroe could see from where she now floated and arranged to meet there in half an hour.

Lack of papers were going to be the biggest hurdle to the sale. Anyone who was anyone or who knew anyone could find a way to them, but even so, the buyer would play up the issue as a way to undercut the price. And that was okay. Munroe needed the cash, but selling the boat was more about misdirection and a way to keep the tracker on the move.

CHAPTER 15

In the wait for the buyer Munroe dialed Amber Marie; held through ten, fifteen, of the irritating pulse tones while the phone in Djibouti rang long and went unanswered. There was no voice mail or caller ID on the other end, no digital footprint to provide notice that she'd attempted contact, so Munroe let the ringing continue.

Long past the thirtieth tone Amber finally answered, breathing the energy of action, of having been awake for a while, from being on the move and throwing parts of a plan into motion.

"Have you found any updates?" Munroe asked.

"Yes," Amber said, and there was triumph in her answer. "As of late last night or early this morning, the *Favorita* anchored off the coast of Garacad."

The detail was so opposite of what Munroe had anticipated that she drew a sharp inhale and said, "Garacad? You're sure?"

"Yeah," Amber said, and a smile was conveyed so clearly through her voice that Munroe could see it spread across her face—as if after having been cut off from Leo completely, news of any kind, no matter how horrible, created the same sense of excitement as a promise that Leo was alive and coming home. Oblivious to the caution and reticence on Munroe's end, Amber rushed on.

"There's not a lot of detail just yet," she said. "The ship is anchored about two kilometers offshore—typical—crew still on board, about twenty pirates on as well. So far they're using skiffs to ferry supplies in and out."

In a bid to clarify what was surely a mistake, Munroe said, "Did the *Favorita* finally turn up on the AIS? Garacad is pretty far north of where the hijacking occurred. It could be a different vessel."

"Still nothing on the AIS, but the ship is definitely ours. Somalia Report broke the news. They had a couple of images and I compared them against everything we have. They're grainy, but it's the *Favorita*, no doubt about that."

What should have been progress created confusion instead.

Somalia Report was one of the leading sources of information within Somalia and, like Al-Jazeera was to al-Qaeda in the Middle East, an outlet as likely to be contacted by hijackers to report what they wanted disseminated as to report on them; a website that Munroe had repeatedly visited over the past few days and not one whose reporting she could dismiss lightly no matter how little it all made sense. She said, "How did they explain the weapons in the hold?"

"They didn't."

"Nothing at all?"

"Nope."

Munroe replayed the attack on the ship, challenged her own senses, her own experience, rewound and saw through less cynical and jaded eyes, but no matter how she cut it, those weapons in the hold and Leo's reaction to their discovery had been real.

"You're sure?"

"Yes, I'm sure," Amber said, and her tone had a bite.

Munroe didn't press. Amber had never wanted to believe Leo would involve himself in gunrunning, and still didn't want to believe it. She said, "What about ransom?"

"They want three million dollars for the release of ship and crew."

The payoff demand brought another wave of mental dissonance. This was normal and the normalcy was jarring and frustrating: The normalcy was wrong. If the ship had been taken as a way to get to the weapons, Mogadishu would have been a better bet for a port of call on its hijacked voyage—or any of the port cities controlled by the Islamic militancy, Al-Shabaab—or for that matter, anywhere along the coast where the hijackers could offload what they'd come for. If the *Favorita* had been targeted for the weapons, it wouldn't be in Garacad right now under the roving eye of Somalia Report correspondents while the hijackers demanded a payment of at least triple what the ship was worth.

"What about you?" Amber said. "Have you heard anything?"

Other than possibly salving her ego after Amber had written off her account of the hijacking, no good could come of telling her of Sami's murder or that Munroe had something the hijackers wanted. She said, "The people I'm talking to have better access than Somalia Report. It's just a matter of how long it will take to get them to tell me what they know."

"Well, we know where the ship is," Amber said, "and we know what the hijackers want. We can work with that."

"What's the status on the hostages?"

"They claim to have already killed two."

At least this was a detail that Munroe could correlate with her experience on the *Favorita*.

Somali piracy had long since moved away from the methods of the rogue fishermen turned criminals who rarely deliberately harmed or killed their hostages. In its current incarnation, piracy was calculated, ruthless business where hostages as pawns were routinely tortured and executed. But even so, the brutality, no matter how often threatened, was, barring an adrenaline- or drug-induced accident, typically saved until negotiations stalled and the pirates needed a way to amp up demands. Which meant the two dead had probably been killed during the firefight, and if that was the case, then they were part of Leo's team, not the ship's crew. But Munroe kept this to herself.

There were logical explanations for why the presence of the

weapons would have been kept quiet, but there were bigger details missing from the story. "What about armed guards," Munroe said. "Any mention of them having been on board? Because if these guys were the first to take an armed ship, they'd be all over that, gloating, maybe even exaggerating how big of an army they were up against. The news would be everywhere."

There was a long pause on the other end, and then with her speech slowed slightly, as if her thoughts had tripped over a crack in the sidewalk and this was the first Amber had seen of the incongruence, she said, "There wasn't any mention of our team, either."

Munroe tried to find a fit for this new piece of information and couldn't, and when she didn't speak, Amber, almost as if betraying a confidence and certainly betraying the reason she'd stayed on the phone this long, said, "Natan and I are preparing to drive down to see if we can possibly negotiate the team's release."

Munroe ran a palm over her face and then looked up toward the sky. "Do you have resources?"

"Not three million dollars."

"Do you even have a hundred thousand?"

Amber whispered, "No."

"How far do you think you'll get?"

"Through Somaliland at least, maybe to Bosaso."

"That's kind of out of your way."

"It's our best bet for finding someone willing to supply us with a military escort."

"You're going to need it."

"We could really use an interpreter," Amber said.

If she'd been asked even a day earlier, Munroe might have jumped at the opportunity for no other reason than the adrenaline charge and the linguistic and cultural challenges a drive through Somalia would provide. But Sami's death had changed her focus, had given her a private war to fight. Whoever had killed him was going to pay a price. She *would* find the murderer and she would take revenge. And although her goal and Amber's goal were intrinsically linked to the

Favorita, Amber's plan was nothing more than a way to be in motion, to provide the illusion of doing something, anything, under the guise of controlling a situation that was chaos.

"How long till you get your resources together?" Munroe said.

"A week, maybe. I'll pay for your flight if you come with us."

"That's kind of a hollow offer, don't you think? I was due a flight back anyway simply for boarding the *Favorita*."

"So in addition to the flight, what would you want?"

"I don't know," Munroe said. "Let me think about it."

"Does that mean you'll come?"

"Probably not."

"Okay, think about it."

"It's a huge risk for not much benefit," Munroe said. "Especially if you're planning to carry the cash down with you."

"We'll use *hawala*."

"Fine. So let's say you manage to get all the way to Garacad. And let's say that by some hypothetical miracle you manage to sweet-talk the local clan elders into getting you a sit-down with a negotiator or even the guy running the show. And let's say that miracle expands and you're actually able to negotiate a release. What happens when they start playing chicken and won't release the entire team—and you know they'll do that. What are you going to do then? Take Leo and leave the others?"

Amber didn't answer, so Munroe pressed on.

"Let's say you beat all the odds. You get down there, you negotiate, and you pay for the release of your entire team. What's your exit strategy? You, as the negotiator, are right there. You and the cash and the team have no backup anywhere else. The world's eyes aren't on you. There's no outside pressure to force them to deliver on their promise, nothing to guarantee that after you hand over the money you aren't all shot right then and there. Or on the way back out by another gang of thieves."

"What else is there to do?" Amber finally whispered. "There's no insurance contract. The *Favorita* is a couple of voyages shy of being broken for scrap, no one's going to try to ransom it, and you know as well as I do that nobody but the crew's families give a crap about them. I can't just sit around wishing and hoping that something will save him—that's its own kind of death."

And that was a point Munroe couldn't argue and wouldn't even if she could. Amber's plan was stupid, but at least it was a plan instead of waiting for magic to happen.

"You're willing to risk everything to save him?"

"Yes."

"Even death."

"Yes."

"Is he worth it?"

"That's a horrible question," Amber said.

"You should think about it."

"Just because you're pissed that he forced you to go with him?"

"Maybe I see a side of him that you can't. Maybe this is fate sparing you from something worse by him down the line."

"I'm finished talking about it," Amber said.

"All right then, you should try calling."

"What?"

"Go through Somalia Report for information," Munroe said. "Find out if the hijackers are even willing to deal with you before you make the trip. If they think you're bringing money, they might be able to guarantee your safety all the way down, and when you get there is when you tell them you're working with *hawala* instead. At least it gets you a safe one-way ride. You could also try forcing their hand and get them to bring the team inland. Get them to a larger city in exchange for the payment, then you'd have a better shot at making it out of there—even more so if you were able to secure a military escort in advance."

If it was possible to hear mental wheels spinning, then that was the sound of Amber's silence. "Talk to me before you go," Munroe said. "I have people asking questions and it will take me about that long to get some answers. At least this way if you decide to traipse off on your Hail Mary mission, you'll have better information on what you're up against. You have a pen and paper?"

"Yeah," Amber said. "Why?"

Munroe glanced toward the road that followed the coast. A blue Land Rover Discovery had parked at the base of the pier and a portly woman wearing a bright green-and-black-pattern muumuu stepped from the passenger side. The man who'd done the driving, who also appeared to play the role of bodyguard, stepped around beside her, and together they strolled down the pier.

"Here's a way to reach me," Munroe said. She recited her number for Amber, and then said, "I've gotta go. If you don't hear from me before you head out, call me."

CHAPTER 16

Munroe shut the phone and raised her hand in a wave for attention. The woman spotted her and swaggered slowly toward the nearest rail and, once within shouting distance, leaned out over the water and called, "This the boat for sale?"

"This is the one," Munroe yelled, and the woman pointed down the coast toward another boat headed their way. "My man is coming to check her."

This was the start of a negotiation as predictable as it would be tedious, part of the drawn-out haggling innate to a culture that placed little value on the concept of time; and in the wait, as the approaching boat grew larger and the sun rose higher and began to heat the air, the conversation with Amber, the proposal of driving from Djibouti to Garacad, tumbled around inside her head.

To most in the Western world, Somalia was a single lawless piece of dirt where the battle of Mogadishu and warlords and pirates and starving children all blended into one big impoverished blemish on the map. But geopolitically, Somalia wasn't one country, it was four or five.

For Amber and Natan, the problems would begin on the other side of Somaliland, the northwesternmost territory, which operated autonomously as an unrecognized nation with its own government, laws, and currency, and a serene prosperity far removed from tele-vised images of lawlessness; would begin after they'd crossed into the neutral zones that were neither Somaliland nor Puntland and then get worse when they crossed into Puntland itself, a territory that straddled the middle of Somalia and operated as an independent state without any formal declaration of separation.

Puntland was where most piracy originated. The elected government was weak and ineffectual, and Bosaso, a city of over half a million, was its capital. Beyond the big city, the land area was vast and mostly empty, and deep down in the remote and barren heart of the territory, along the eastern coast, was the town of Garacad—silent c—where the *Favorita* anchored.

Clan law kept a fragile order, but when assault rifles were more common than indoor toilets, when foreigners were viewed as a form of currency, two strangers without political connections and protection, who didn't speak the language or understand the culture, had a solid chance of ending up as hostages or dead, no matter what kind of military training Natan had.

The man with the boat arrived, cut his engine.

The bartering took more than an hour, and once the price was settled, the transaction stretched on for another hour while the driver-slash-bodyguard-now-accountant left to retrieve the money and finally returned with a fat envelope that the boatman ferried out. And when Munroe was satisfied, he returned her to shore.

Beneath the concrete pier, slightly shielded by the pilings, Munroe stashed and scattered half the money throughout her pockets. Then put on her socks, dry from the journey, and her still damp and water-damaged boots, and shoved the rest of the money down out of sight. She strode up the beach to the fronting streets, relatively quiet with the sleepy feel of a small coastal town.

THERE WERE FEW cars, and pedestrian traffic was light. Spread between palm trees and overgrown flower bushes were one- and two-story buildings with the flat rooftops, wide arches, and porticoes of the Mediterranean, painted in the bright colors of the tropics, as if the town couldn't quite make up its mind which continent it was built on.

A *tuk-tuk* pulled up and puttered alongside her as Munroe walked the dirt shoulder, the driver soliciting a ride at the equivalent of a dollar per trip. He drove her to the edge of the city's bus depot, a rut-gorged piece of dirt that clearly turned into a swath of muck and mud when it rained.

Buses in a range of sizes were parked in and around the depot, and crowds of people milled about them. A blue-and-yellow minibus readied for departure, its top overladen with bundles, the inside packed beyond capacity. Children with shallow buckets filled with packaged food atop their heads shouted up at those seated inside. Coins passed down from the windows and goods passed up until the engine revved and the bus began the slow crawl over deep ruts, out and onto the road, and Munroe crossed and stepped out of its way.

She wanted the first possible ride out of town, but based on the activity around her, the next bus to go would be a patchworked and beat-up monstrosity with its glass busted from a couple of windows and tires with little tread. If seats worn flat to the cushioning of wooden boards weren't enough of a deterrent to keep her from taking the ride, the idea of multiple breakdowns along the way was.

A tout told her of other buses that plied the route, fancier and labeled as luxury coaches, air-conditioned with toilets onboard, but they left from a different part of town, later in the day. Munroe opted for the middle ground: a minibus that appeared set to be second to leave. She figured it would be an hour, give or take, before it filled, so she paid for a seat and stayed out in the open air where she could watch the other buses in the off chance she'd chosen the wrong horse.

She dialed Peter Muthui at Kefesa, thanked him for his time, and canceled the meeting.

CHAPTER 17

The return to Mombasa was a four-hour stop-start that dragged on far longer than the distance and potholes indicated it should, a journey segmented by unofficial delays as the driver augmented his wages by picking up passengers from among those waving down buses and trucks from the side of the road and stopping again to let them off at unmarked junctions or tiny villages where wattle-and-daub homes stood behind vegetable stands, hanging bush meat, and handcrafted furniture.

Munroe dozed and woke with the rhythm and jolts, squished against the window frame, on a bench seat with one person too many, breathing in dusty diesel-filled air from the outside, which was better than the body and food odors from within. And when they neared Mombasa's North Shore, she studied the strip of hotels and restaurants, not expecting to find anything worth seeing but watching all the same, while the conversation with Amber and the questions of the morning played out again in an endless maddening loop.

There were priorities and there were *priorities*. Amber and Natan could drive down through Somalia in their pointless pursuit of Leo's freedom and Munroe wouldn't try to stop them, but if they were willing to throw away their lives, there were better ways to put them to use.

The bus pulled into Mombasa just after one, and Munroe stepped out into another dirt depot, into the searing afternoon sun and the hubbub of motion and smell and noise that accompanied loading and unloading.

She strode along the busy streets in the general direction of where she'd seen a cybercafé. Stepped into the cool air. She couldn't stay long, only a few rushed minutes to do the double-checking she'd had no time for in Malindi, to run queries and confirm what Amber Marie had told her. In the corroboration, lack of sleep scraped at nerves already frayed, limiting her ability to analyze. The AIS still couldn't locate the *Favorita*, there were no mentions of the weapons in the hold, and not even a hint that the ship had been taken in an armed conflict—nothing that would appear to indicate the attack had been anything other than a typical Somali hijacking.

Clarity turned into self-doubt, making it difficult to sort reason from fantasy, and impossible to think sharply enough to pull the threads together into any semblance of tapestry. She shut down the browser, and then in a hurry opened it up again to check her e-mail. There were several messages waiting, but the one that caught her eye was the one least expected, and having spotted it, she couldn't control the pounding inside her chest—and that made her angry. Mouse hovering over the icon for a moment, she clicked through.

The e-mail came without a subject or greeting or signature, but she knew the address, and more, she knew the words:

Samantha told me you contacted the office. You can't know how happy it made me to know you're still alive out there, wherever you are. Wish you would have given me a heads-up, I would have made sure to be near a phone so that she could patch you through. I've missed you, Michael. I still do. Home waits for you.

That one paragraph hurt more than a knife to the gut, and still she read the e-mail several times before logging off. It wasn't lost on her that Bradford had referred to Sam by her full name, but Munroe didn't reply. Couldn't. What was there to say? That she still loved him? That she was sorry and she was coming back? Why? So that she could hurt him and watch death swallow him the way it did everyone else she got close to?

MUNROE PAID FOR her usage and made her way to the Aga Khan Hospital to answer the question that had been crawling through her head ever since Sami's death. The conversation between the hijackers on the *Favorita* had told her that the captain's picture had been shown around, that he was important to them for something, and in the aftermath of Sami's murder, the same man whom she would just as easily have let die was now a prized asset.

Munroe walked through the hospital gates, past the foyer and reception, and up the stairs. Found the captain immobile and placid on his bed, as he'd been when she'd last left him.

She stepped inside and shut the door. Crossed to a straight-backed chair in the corner, carried it to the bedside, and sat there and studied the cypher, this mass of skin and bones for whom Sami had died. He was a man with a name and a ship and a history that cried out with secrets and lies; he had answers to the unknown, and whatever he knew, Munroe wanted.

She reached for his hand and touched cool, dry skin. Pinched his thumb for a reaction and got nothing. His chest rose and fell with methodical breathing, the body's autonomic nervous system continuing on while his mind lit up a vacancy sign. Munroe envied him the luxury of his bed, the quiet and solitude, the lack of pain and burden that unconsciousness must bring.

The minutes ticked on and in the silence his face became the object upon which she focused, wrestling with the facts as she knew them, turning them, twisting them, molding them into a plausible, hole-filled scenario that made the most sense. Occam's razor. The simplest explanation with the fewest moving pieces, and this man was at the center of it. She played the scenario against itself. Unfolded and rewrapped, but she didn't have enough to take what she knew and use those pieces to avenge Sami or save Victor.

Munroe stood and stared down at the captain. She had just two days before she was obligated to collect him and was tempted to take him with her now as a preemptive maneuver against those who would try to steal him from her, but until she'd established whether or not her own hotel and identity had been compromised, she had nowhere to put him, had no guarantee that in pulling him from this hiding place she wouldn't gift him directly to those who'd killed to find him, and she had no way to mind him and hunt at the same time.

Munroe dragged the chair back to its corner, left the room, and jogged back down the stairs. She would win, would figure this out, would find some sense of closure for herself, for Sami, and possibly for Amber. She wouldn't allow a nameless, faceless opponent to steal her catch—not after what he'd cost thus far, not until she figured out who he was and what he was worth and how well she could use him to barter for what she wanted.

Munroe stopped at reception on her way out and warned the hospital staff not to allow the captain any visitors, and when the response was casual indifference, as if they'd seen crazy people before and knew how to humor them, she described in graphic detail what potential disaster might follow if they didn't listen. Then, having done the best that she could to keep her loot safe for the next day or two, Munroe left the hospital for Nehru Road and the *hawaladar*.

CHAPTER 18

The same bodyguard stood in front of the wall when Munroe entered the alley, and this time she approached with the casual air of an old friend. Unhooked the knife case from her waistband and walked toward him with the heel extended. When she was within a couple of feet, he reached out and took it from her and tossed it on the ground behind him.

The man in the doorway watched with a barely concealed smile. Munroe nodded and gave him a half grin, and when she approached, he didn't hesitate as he had the first time, rather opened and motioned her forward into the hallway with its bare and solitary light-bulb.

Inside, the way to the *hawaladar* was blocked by the man on the stool, and instead of ushering her on toward the next door, he had her wait. Munroe slid down the wall to the floor beside him, and as the minutes wore on, the tin-topped and unventilated hall-way's air, stifling and thick, exacerbated the fatigue and lulled her slowly into slumber. A creak at the far end of the hall jerked her awake.

Ten seconds or ten minutes, Munroe didn't know. She pressed her palms to her eyes and pushed back the disorientation, stood to keep from succumbing again to the cotton stuffing inside her head. The door to the *hawaladar*'s office opened and a woman dressed fully in black, eyes the only visible part of her body, stepped out into the hall. Was halfway to the exit when the man on the stool nodded Munroe onward.

As she'd done the first time she entered the *hawaladar*'s office, Munroe took a chair from the side of the room and dragged it to the front of the desk. She sat and he said, "You don't look well."

"I haven't slept much in the past couple of days."

Tipped back in his chair, arms crossed, he studied her a moment and then reached for a ledger on a nearby shelf. Opened to the pocket into which he'd placed her thousand dollars and withdrew not half but all of the bills. Counted them out onto the desk like a banker exchanging currency and slid them toward her.

"Your money," he said.

She raised her eyebrows. "Somali financing paid for the hijacking?"

"You said you'd take the money and be on your way," he said.

She picked up the bills one by one, slowly, dramatically, to buy time, because no matter what his words said, there was something in his tone and in his body language that told her the conversation was far from over.

"It's hard to imagine you haven't heard anything."

"I learned enough to know that I don't want to keep asking questions."

She tapped the long edges of the bills on the desk to stack them and, avoiding eye contact, said, "Without specifics, tell me at least, was the hijacking financed by foreign investors?"

The *hawaladar* answered with a single nod that clarified what Munroe had suspected since the night of the firefight. She said, "And I suppose the financiers weren't your typical Yemeni or Kenyan venture capitalists."

"You would guess correctly," he said, and with this validation the puzzle pieces pulled more tightly together.

Munroe placed the bills neatly in front of him again and tapped them.

"I hired a boy," she said. "Took him on as an *askari* to watch my boat. I returned to the pier last night to find his throat slit. They left him out on the sand, dumped like garbage. Take the money, please," she said. "Tell me what you know."

"I don't know much."

"But you've heard the rumors and the gossip."

"Well, yes, there's plenty of that."

She nudged the bills closer to him.

"I don't need the money," he said.

"It's a matter of principle."

He nudged the bills back. "So is this. I'll tell you what I've heard. Not because of your *askari* and not for your money. I'll tell you because I don't like what I hear. Maybe you're in a position to do something with the information, maybe not, but either way I don't side with the pirates. They bring shame and a stain on my country and they are *haram*."

Haram. A repeat of his thoughts the first time: forbidden; against the tenets of Islam. "This hijacking is something else," he said. "Scapegoating, I think, and Somalis have had far too many years of that—as if the world thinks we're their latrine, that they can shit on us and walk away."

She sighed and said, "So if I've pieced this together properly, instead of dumping nuclear waste along your coast, or raiding your waters for fish, this time the foreign interests have used Somalis to hijack a ship carrying something they wanted, and now with their tracks covered, the foreigners who started the mess will simply disappear while the blame for the hijacking remains placed at the feet of piracy."

The *hawaladar*'s mouth opened a half inch. "If you knew this," he said, "why did you come to me under the pretense of needing information?"

"I only hypothesized," she said, and when he eyed her accusingly and suspicion cast a dark veil over his face, she added, "I was on the ship, I pay attention, and I've learned a lot from my own contacts within the past twenty-four hours."

"Then why are you here?" he said.

"Because I want to know who's behind the hijacking, and you're in a position to learn things that none of my contacts know."

"What would you do with this information if you had it?"

"Probably use it to find and kill a few people."

"Somalis?"

"I'm after the foreign investors. Maybe a few pirates depending on what happens with the crew aboard the ship. It's hard to say, but I'm world-weary enough to know that nothing is black and white."

"You're not CIA?"

"No."

"Armed forces of any kind?"

"No."

"Connected to any government?"

"No."

"Vigilante justice?"

"Something more like that."

He sighed and scratched the back of his neck. "Do you know what you're doing?"

"That kind of knowledge is relative."

"Now you're playing games," he said, and his expression hardened.

Munroe slipped slowly back from the desk, away from the bills, shrank as far into the chair as space would allow so that she would appear smaller and be less of a presence to interrupt his thought process.

"There are Somalis involved," he said. "Of course there are, nothing like this would be possible without local cooperation."

"That's not the same thing," she said, and when the resultant silence became uncomfortable, she refused to break it. Everything in his posture, in the guarded words he offered, and in what he left unspoken, said that he hated those who'd done this more than he distrusted her.

The seconds ticked on, and at last the *hawaladar* leaned forward. "There was the promise of a lot of money," he said. "The rumor comes to me thirdhand, possibly further removed than that, but I've heard it from two different people, so you can take what you want from it. I make no promises."

Munroe nodded and said, "Go on."

"Supposedly, about three or four weeks ago, the faction out of Eyl was approached by an intermediary offering investment for a hijacking." He paused, backtracking. "Do you know much about the state of piracy today?"

"Some," she said. "I'm not an expert. I know that every hijacking is financed, I understand the concept of shares."

"I assume you know that these days hijacking carries a greater risk than it used to? Many skiffs have been destroyed, a lot of supplies destroyed, investors are looking for more secure places to put their money."

"Yes," she said.

"There used to be a lot of money in these small towns, huge inflows of cash, and now they've dried up. It's addicting, you know? The money. It buys a lot of prostitutes and a lot of khat. So when an intermediary approaches with a proposal for an easy payday, people listen."

He paused and raised his eyebrows, and she said, "I'm still with you."

"The investors flew in, a group of four or five, and they outlined plans to take this ship. They knew the schedule and had a way to track the vessel exactly. Rather than capture the ship in the Gulf of Aden, where the military presence was strong, they would take it in international waters off the east Somali coastline, making the risk very small. The investors offered weapons and training, and when word began to spread that there was money coming into town on the promise of the capture of a valuable ship, others wanted in on the investing pool."

The *hawaladar* pushed back from his desk and stood. "Somali financing paid for the boats and supplies and fuel in exchange for equal shares of the ransom money. The foreigners provided the training and specialized equipment beyond what was already available." He began a slow pace. "Unfortunately, once the ship was taken, my countrymen realized, too late, that it wasn't worth what they'd been told. But the investors had already left town, they and their money disappeared. So it seems the foreigners got what they came for, but for the Somalis the only way to recoup the investment is through the ransom of an aging ship."

"So the talk of investment was just talk? Almost everything came out of Somali pockets?"

"It appears that way," he said.

Munroe blew out a low whistle. "So the pirates got screwed both ways."

"I won't say it doesn't serve them right."

"What were the foreigners after?"

The *hawaladar* shrugged. "I'm baffled," he said.

"Did they get it?"

"I don't know."

"But if the group was out of Eyl, what's the ship doing in Garacad?"

He shrugged again and put his palms up. "Who can say? Lack of fuel? A show of antipiracy by Farole's people to keep the money flowing from the West? I'm simply passing along what I heard."

"The shipowners won't pay out," Munroe said.

"How do you know this?" the *hawaladar* said, and, avoiding eye contact, as if he might give away some secret, he shut the ledger and replaced it on the shelf. In his attempt to shield his thoughts, he announced that there was something that drew him to this hijacking, something more than just an aversion to piracy or anger over his people having been scapegoated, and so Munroe pressed on, answering his question, guiding her words by his reaction to them.

"The ship doesn't carry K&R," she said, "and given the condition the ship is in, I expect it would be headed for scrap soon anyway. With the principals shielded through the charterer—they probably own it through bearer shares anyway—I can't see why they'd show up to claim it."

The *hawaladar* glanced at her again with that same sly, curious, concealed smile, as if his mind had already jumped topics and his calculations had run in an entirely different direction. "But the ship is seaworthy," he said.

"Yes, just old."

"That's an interesting thought," he said.

"Wouldn't be the first time an owner abandoned his crew with the ship."

"No, it wouldn't."

"Most of them are from the Philippines," she said. "A few Egyptians. Russian captain and Polish officers, I think, so there's not a lot of money to be had from the families. Maybe the Russian or Polish governments, though I doubt it."

He sat again, hands clasped together across his midsection, and he avoided eye contact by studying the midpoint of his desk.

She said, "Where did the investors come from?"

He nudged the dollars back in her direction and this time there was a sense of finality in his action. "That's really all I have," he said.

"Why tell me everything else and leave out the key detail?"

"I have children, and news travels both ways."

There was no answer to that, so she stood and left the money on the table. "Keep it for me," she said. "There are plans in motion and I might still need to make *hawala* after all."

"What kind of plans?" he said.

"Investor plans."

He half smiled and the smile widened into a grin that said he would welcome her back for another discussion at the least. She'd give him another day or so to mull over the situation, would press harder to pull from him this thing she sensed he wanted more than money, and exchange it for the pieces about the investors that he held back.

MUNROE RETURNED TO the streets and strode along what were now mostly empty sidewalks, judging shadows, and the people in them, and second-guessing her own analysis. Aside from what little rest she'd managed on the bus from Malindi, and the minutes she'd stolen in the *hawaladar*'s hallway, it had been thirty-six hours since sleep, and it was like having had one drink too many. The deprivation blunted her senses, slowed her reactions, took her to the edge of tipsy and slightly off control. She needed to stop, badly, but couldn't just yet.

At the *matatu* depot she found a van for Mombasa's North Shore, took the ride to within a half kilometer of the hotel, and asked the tout to let her out. Hanging from the open door, he banged coins on the rooftop, the signal to the driver to pull over, and Munroe squeezed past other riders into the night, where light bled from multiple restaurants and bars, where the smell of woodsmoke and music and laughter filled the air and almost as many tourists as locals walked in the dark along the roadway edge.

She walked along the paved turnoff that led to the hotel reception area and followed it past lampposts and manicured foliage toward the room she'd not visited since she'd first left for the city. Sleep beckoned with its siren song, but possessions were what called her back: pictures and passports and money and weapons that she'd left behind on the possibility she'd be searched going into the *hawaladar*'s office; items she didn't want to walk away from as long as she might still retrieve them.

She reached the small parking lot, still fifty meters beyond the lit reception area and the hotel wings that spread out on either side. Nothing in the air warned her in the way the gaps and silences had over Sami's death. Habit had kept her mindful when moving about Mombasa; she'd been careful to create no link between the hotel and the hospital and the *hawaladar*, but other than the nearly two kilometers of coast that separated the hotel from the pier, she'd done nothing to avoid connecting herself to the boat: If the violence that had killed Sami had traced her here, it would have come from that direction.

She opted for hiding in plain sight. Walked to the open reception area, past the front desk, where the staff was busy attending to an arriving family, beyond the handful of guests seated on the lobby furniture, their focus glued to wireless devices, and slipped through to the walkways on the other side, invisible in the normalcy. Once out of sight, she stepped off the path and into the treed and grassy area, slipped from shadow to shadow toward her room, and passed alongside her patio.

Found the glass door slightly ajar, the curtains askew, and far more brightness coming from inside than what the bathroom light could put out, which was all that she'd left on. Lack of movement and shape on the other side told her that whoever had been here had probably come and gone, but she was too tired to trust her own judgment and so left the place and slowly looped back to the front.

Even if every piece of the room had been torn apart, she needed to get inside to find out what had been left behind, but not now, not tonight; better to avoid the room until after she'd had a chance to sleep and pay her body the dues it demanded, and if indeed there was nothing left in the room for her to collect when she came for it later, she would report yet another stolen passport to yet another U.S. embassy and call on Miles Bradford to wire operating cash from her reserve fund.

Munroe returned to the lobby. It took three minutes at the front desk to instruct the hotel staff to ensure that no further housekeeping would be done on her room—long enough for anyone paying attention to confirm that she'd returned, yet the only way to prevent those with good intentions from disturbing the scene and stealing from her the only clues she had.

Conscious of every breeze, every whisper, Munroe left for the highway, for the *matatus* to the city where she could find another hotel and disappear for the night. Was halfway through the parking lot when the first warning crawled up her skin: notice that someone, somewhere, studied her intently. The sensation mixed together with smell and sound and heat and humidity to create the equatorial Africa of her adolescence: spiked a potent and powerful trigger. The past became the present, became the fight for survival that would once have sent her plunging into the dark to hide and hunt, to refuse to be the victim yet again. Munroe paused and drew in the night, breathed past the urges of years gone by, faced the darkness, and moved her fingers toward the knife sheathed on the makeshift belt.

CHAPTER 19

Munroe hunted for the source of the disquiet, scanned windows along the hotel wings, and found nothing to answer the rising warnings. On the road ahead she caught a shift in pattern beyond one of the perimeter lights, and when she turned to face the movement, two men emerged from the bushes and strode in her direction.

They were in their late teens, possibly early twenties, wore a mixture of tattered clothing that spoke more of life on the streets huffing glue than of the boys who sold overpriced curios to tourists on the beach. On another night she would have led them to the dirt track on the other side of the wall-like hedges, enticed them to follow her toward quiet and emptiness so she might at least take one of them alive and, assuming they were at all connected to the destruction of her room or Sami's murder, try to learn from him what she could. Being this tired, she'd only set herself up for a fight she couldn't win.

Shifting strategy and changing plans, Munroe retraced her way to the lobby. The men slowed when she retreated, hovered near the edge of the parking lot, far enough away from the front to avoid catching the attention of the *askaris*, but still close enough to say they weren't leaving. Munroe pointed them out to the watchmen on her way back inside.

Sitting out the night in the lobby or finding a place to hide on the hotel grounds was out of the question. The men in the lot hadn't targeted her by random coincidence any more than Sami had been killed by chance, and a few batons and nightsticks, possibly machetes, would hardly be a long-term deterrent to keep them away. She'd be no safer in the lobby than in her room, and staying until the evening deepened, when she was even further sleep-deprived, would only put her in a worse situation than she was in now.

She waited until the guards gave chase and the shouts had traveled far up toward the highway, then turned and passed back through the lobby to the beach side of the property. Leaving the path she'd just come from, she took long strides in the direction of the north edge, where she could find a way through the hedges and avoid whoever might be waiting down on the beach.

A shadow shift twitched in her peripheral vision.

Munroe increased her pace, and from the opposite direction a man stepped out several feet in front of her. He appeared slightly older than the two in the lot, but like theirs his clothing spoke of street life. He wore a raglike T-shirt and cloth tennis shoes, his toes protruding through holes, but new jeans and an expensive watch on each wrist, as if he carried his every possession on his body, no matter how mismatched, because it was the safest place to store things.

Munroe locked eye contact and attempted to walk around him.

He stepped fully in her way, and a whisper of movement brushed her from behind. She didn't turn, allowed hearing and instinct to see in a way that sight never could; knew the shadow she'd first picked out among the foliage had drawn closer and hemmed her in.

She unsheathed the knife, and the cold wash of the hunt bled up from the metal and into her hand, mixing violence and exhaustion into an aching thirst.

"Let me pass," she said, and the man who blocked her way took a step toward her.

He put off the odor of rotting garbage, of unwashed skin and unwashed clothes, and his eyes had the bloodshot glassy quality of one who'd fried whatever higher-thinking ability he'd once had through sniffing too much glue. She repeated the demand in Swahili and in response his fingers twitched and the curve of his mouth gave way the slightest bit.

"Where is the other *mzungu*?" he said. "The *mzee,* where is he?"

"I don't know," she said.

"You know. You were the one who took him."

"Yes, but he's gone now. You killed his *askari.* You scared him, so he left with the boat for Malindi."

Footsteps and rustling leaves, darting glances and a shift in posture, told her that others were moving in from the edges. The longer she stood here, the more advantage she gave away, so she took another step to the side, and the man in front matched her and blocked her way again.

"I want the *mzee,*" he said.

"You can have the old man if you go to Malindi."

"You take me to him."

"He left without me. I don't know where he is."

He continued to gape as if he didn't comprehend, as if she'd deviated from the script and he had no cue cards, no one to tell him how to interpret her words, which meant he was just a tool, not the leader of this little gang—not in any meaningful sense.

Glass shattered behind her and the pathway darkened, though light from other lampposts and from hotel windows kept the area from plunging into black. The knife, warm in her hand, begged to be used, and she held on, conflicted, wanting blood yet wanting even more to know whose bidding these men served and why they'd killed Sami to get to the captain.

In the near distance, laughter and conversation filtered back from the pool, and from farther beyond there was music, but no sign of the *askaris* or staff or tourists. She'd wandered too far toward the periphery to make a potential strategy out of waiting for an interruption from passersby. There was even less chance that if she called for help it would find her in time to do much—and the very thought of *that* offended her.

Another crunch of glass and another light out and the pathway fell into deeper darkness. She could sense the others encroaching now, circling from the shadows. Munroe breathed in the salt-tinged air and the darkness, and inside her chest the tempo quickened, a beat that answered the call of the blade and pleaded for release, for permission to be let loose. "Let me pass," she said. "I don't have the man you are looking for, and if we fight, you may kill me, but several of you will die first."

His shoulders shook with silent laughter, an answer that said he wasn't afraid of the knife, that he was equally armed and she was outnumbered, that what he did tonight would guarantee money to put him into another drug stupor, and that any thought beyond that became meaningless. Munroe turned from him. Wouldn't bother to counter what payment he'd been offered, because he'd demand the money immediately, and if she proffered it, he would attempt to take it from her and they'd begin again exactly where they were right now.

Others from the pack formed a loose circle. She counted five by their breathing, by their smell; assumed that there were still more to come; sidestepped through the closing gap and slipped from the pathway to the grass, to darkness, where instinct could rule where sight failed. Maneuvered from one tree to the next, darting through the dark as she once had through the jungle, while her pursuers tracked her, calling to each other like hounds after the fox.

They were fast and they were many, sprinting after her, dashes of shade and shadow winding along parallel and then in front, and by the time she'd reached the beach, they'd closed the circle again and she had counted eight.

Another man stepped front and center, different from the one who'd blocked her way on the path: shorter, better built, and his eyes were clearer, though not by much. In English he said, "Where is the old man?"

"I don't know," Munroe said.

"If you don't tell us, we will kill you."

She'd been dead many times already. There was nothing they could take that had not already been demanded, no pain that had not already been inflicted, no fear they might incite through intimidation. "You'll kill me anyway," she said, "and I can't tell you what I don't know."

"You have the boat, you have to know."

"Had," she said, measuring distance, judging threat, anticipating weapons. "I had the boat. I don't have it anymore."

Movement reached out from beyond her field of vision and she danced to the side with the speed that was her greatest weapon— dodged a hefty stick that swung and missed and circled back to strike again. There was no argument or rationale to be had, no option but to fight, to kill or be killed. The calm of the impending battle and expectancy burned through her veins.

"Where is the *mzee*?" the short one said again, and she didn't answer.

Like his predecessor, everything about him said that he, too, was just one of the crowd, not their leader, but even if he'd been the boss and could tell her what she wanted, trading from a place of weakness when she was in no position to protect her interests would only weaken her further. If she died tonight, the secret of the captain's location would die with her.

She was still too close to accidental witnesses, too close to the hotel that had her name, her passport information. If she survived the night, she'd be blamed and forced to flee before fighting the battle she truly wanted. Another of the pack stepped in, another stick, another dodge, another dance, and the lust for blood, euphoria in anticipation of the kill, rose higher, flooded her senses, took her to the point of no return.

She danced again, dodged again, ran farther down the beach into the dark space between hotels, where heightened instinct would work to her advantage. Couldn't outrun them forever.

Backed up against a retaining wall, she cut their advantage in half, and this time willed them closer. Searched for the leader, the one that she could take down first to cause the others to weaken, but there was nothing in their posture or formation to point to one who gave the orders. Another stick came at her in the dark and the pressure inside her chest tore free. History became the present, the nights of the past the now, and the first rush of the fight bled from her chest into her fingertips. She struck with the speed of survival, speed carved into her psyche one knife slice at a time, speed that had kept her alive, speed born from the refusal to quit or be conquered; she moved faster than the nearest man had time to react.

Knife plunged into trachea. Yelp choked into gurgle. Blood spread over her hands, warm and sticky, sending her soul into the ecstasy of a crack addict's high. A blow fell from the side and connected with her shoulder. Landed hard enough to drop her to one knee and she laughed with the pain.

They struck fast in the moonlight, blows crashing down, wildly crashing down. She spun and connected, dodged and slashed, and the pain built, intensifying with each blinding hit. She struck and dipped, lunged and parried, and the bludgeoning came again and again, unrelenting, maddening, blows to her chest, her back, her head, and finally brought her fully to her knees.

Sand to their eyes, she bought time and bought fighting space. Rose again and was struck down again, and knew then that the fight was unwinnable. She would die tonight. And still she fought. With each plunge and slice of the knife, regret welled up from a place deep and buried, rose from the secret place where thoughts that shouldn't be felt were locked away for safekeeping. Like Sami, there would be no way for those she loved to know; like Sami, she would be a man gone to sea and never returned while those who mattered ever waited for her to come home.

Sight failed and darkness descended and the knife in her hand, alive with its own passion, struck and struck again until consciousness faded and it was over.

CHAPTER 20

Suffocating. Drowning in sand. Drowning in blood.

Munroe struggled for air.

Couldn't find air. Move. Had to move. Turn from the blockage.

No arms. No legs. She fought for air. Found only sand. Only blood.

Suffocating.

Something seared into her side. Pushed. Rolled her over and her face was free and she found air.

Air.

She gasped. Sucked oxygen.

Pain reached into her chest and ripped out her organs.

A scream ricocheted through her body.

Hand to the knife. The knife.

There was no knife.

A shadow, a face, a body above her against the night.

She struggled for the knife, but there was no knife, and darkness washed over her and she was gone again.

WORDS. MAYBE WORDS. English words. Reaching to her, calling to her.

We are friend. We are friend. We are Sami friend.

Sifting. Rising. Falling. Hands reaching.

She fought to keep the hands away. Feeble attempts from arms no longer connected to her body.

She couldn't move.

The knife, where was the knife? Couldn't find her hands.

Try to crawl. Try to turn.

The night sky screamed again, rained acid tears, burned.

All of her burned.

We are friend. We help you.

HANDS ON HER hands. Vises on her wrists. Fingers prying against fingers and she knew then that they took from her the knife that she clung to yet couldn't feel or find. They pried fingers that she couldn't move, couldn't control, and gradually the weapon was no longer hers.

Somewhere out in the darkness she could taste and smell blood. Her blood. Their blood. Someone's blood.

She didn't know, didn't remember.

The hands lifted her and she screamed. Or perhaps the scream was only in her head, while pain racked her body beyond the point of bearable. She fought to see but the night swirled on in circles that made her stomach retch and perhaps she vomited, or perhaps it was the motion of the boat. Yes, a boat, a small boat that carried her away from the place of death—death that nobody had seen—or maybe it had been seen the way Sami's death had been seen.

The police would come. They would look for her.

Would they look for her?

AIR. MORE AIR. More pain. No sound. No sight. Movement. Hands grabbed hold and took her shoulders. The night sky screamed again; stars shed blood. Inside her head the chaos came, darkness and voices from the past, chanting, calling for action, propelling her toward bloodshed.

She reached for the knife again, but there was no knife.

There was no reaching.

Only in her head.

There was water. Water on her feet. Her fingers.

Hands, rough and gentle, transferred her from the boat, and the sting of salt water touched her and her feet trailed, splashing behind, and darkness descended and there was nothing.

MUNROE'S EYES OPENED to light streaming through vertical slats, woke to piercing pain inside her head, a pain that filled her so completely that she didn't know where the hurt began or ended, pain that pushed her toward the edge of insanity and said that someone had died in the act of inflicting it.

Waves of blackness rolled in and enveloped her with dizzy nausea.

In place of memory she had only fog, darkness, and pounding, so much pounding inside her head. Her eyes shut of their own accord and her hand fumbled for the side of the bed, to feel what she didn't have the energy to try to see. She touched dirt for the floor and on the dirt a pile of rags or material, and beside it the knife. Her fingers drew it closer and her fist wrapped around the handle. She pulled the blade toward her and rested it, clenched within her hand, upon her chest and fell back into the oblivion where pain only licked at the edges of awareness.

HER EYES OPENED again. The light was not as bright and her thoughts were a little clearer. That meant time had passed, and the urge to get up, to move, ordered out from inside her chest, but her muscles wouldn't respond. Her body shook and each breath brought the primeval urge to scream, screams that she held back while they rattled and ricocheted around her head. She had no recollection of how she'd come to be here, only the sensation of kindness, of favor, and that somehow she was safe.

Her head turned right, toward the slats again, and she squinted against the light, trying to focus, to find some solid image among the blur of shapes and shadows, until gradually the edges sharpened and it wasn't slats that the light streamed through but the spaces between the sticks that formed the outer walls of the room. Above her, thatch-worked fronds were the ceiling.

Her eyes rolled from ceiling to wall and back, and then shut. It took a moment to draw the connections, but they were there, threads of meaning, and then they tied together and she recognized in the walls and the ceiling the same wattle and daub of the houses and little villages that had fronted the Mombasa–Malindi road.

Her fingers felt for the mattress, old, thin, and lumpy, covered with a threadbare sheet and permeated with the smell of age and mildew, and she struggled to open her eyes again, to focus. Could see from the colors, knew from the scent, that the clothes she wore were not her own, understood that except for the knife, everything she'd had when she'd gone into the hotel, including the money in her boots, was missing.

She no longer had a way to pay for pain medication, and in the agony of that realization, despair and defeat crept toward the corners of her soul. Tears of desperation seeped out and she shoved them away; would have swiped an angry hand against her cheek if she could have found the strength to move it.

She would push through.

Despair was a mind killer.

Pain was temporary.

For two years she'd fought through the nights in the jungle, fought to kill before she was killed, fought the torment and the hope-lessness; she had become faster, keener, and she had won. The enemy today was not stronger or smarter than the ones she'd already destroyed. She would win again.

Talking seeped into her awareness and she turned her head. There was a half-wall and an empty space where a door would have been if this had been the type of house to have doors, and from the other side the low voices passed through. She listened; focused on the sound and drew into it until gradually she could separate syl-lables from white noise: Swahili spoken by two men in the room next door.

Eyes closed, Munroe worked her fingers, her toes, each movement made in screaming rebellion, but nothing was so broken she couldn't force it into submission.

Slid her legs over the mattress to the floor.

Managed to roll over and get to her knees before the darkness overtook her. She woke again with her face in the dirt.

She pulled back to her knees and, in a slow crawl, one painful limb movement at a time, got to the half-wall, and with the wall as support, pulled herself to her feet. Made it upright and into a stand before two shadows filled the doorway.

One caught her before she blacked out again. One of the beach boys that Sami had befriended, one who'd been there after the killing and who had fought in the circle of bystanders. "What you do? What you do?" he said. "You sleep. You no money, no go doctor. You rest. You drink. You eat. You sleep."

"I need to go to the hotel," she whispered. "Please help me?"

He and the other man tried to take her back to the bed. She fought them and then went dark again. Woke on the mattress with the two men standing over her.

She whispered her request again. Had to get to the hotel. Had to find out what was left behind when the room was ransacked. Was the only way to get to a weapon and cash—if anything had survived— the only way to get pain medication and medical care. She couldn't wait until new guests had taken over the room. Had to try the hotel first before she broke down and called Dallas to beg for help from the man she hadn't spoken to in nearly a year.

The energy between the men shifted. She understood pieces of their conversation: true concern for her condition. She would die trying to get back if they didn't help her, it would be better to take her.

In English the one she didn't recognize said, "Gabriel go get car. You wait. You sleep," and she let go again, and it was dark when she next opened her eyes.

SOUND IN THE front room drew her around again. A man and a woman were talking, and though it seemed as if she imagined it, a car's engine rattled somewhere outside. Sami's friend returned and she struggled off the bed. Hand to her elbow, he helped her up and her body screamed in protest and darkness returned and she passed out.

He must have caught her. She came to with her feet still on the ground and her back against his chest. Just to the car, she could hear the engine outside, she only had to get that far.

The other man opened the rear door. Sami's friend, Gabriel, supported her, walked her from the room to the outside. She bent to get into the backseat and a scream escaped her head, shattered the relative silence. She lay on the cushion with her face to the car roof, panting past the pain.

Gabriel shifted gears. The car moved. They were on the highway. She didn't give directions. Didn't know where she was. They knew where to take her. How they knew she wasn't sure exactly— from where they'd found her on the beach, or from Sami—the sense of it was out there somewhere in the fog, and with each lurch of the car with its worn shocks and struts as it dipped in and out of potholes, she screamed inside her head.

And then there was nothing.

Gabriel helped her from the car to the lobby, where she found her voice in a faint whisper, and he explained to the front desk what she could not. Munroe gave her name and room number, and with no strength to stand, collapsed again.

Gabriel propped her up. Was careful to use his chest to support her and didn't touch her with his hands, as if afraid to hurt her, afraid she would scream. She bit back the tumult and the shrieks; clung to him for balance.

The manager gave Gabriel a key.

The darkness descended and Munroe began to fall. Gabriel was there. And somehow she was in front of the room. He unlocked the door. The manager peered inside and confirmed what Munroe had described. The room was trashed, as she'd last seen through the curtains, the bed tossed and the lamp atop the dresser smashed. Damage that she shouldn't be held responsible for, but might.

Gabriel closed the door behind them and Munroe slid to the floor. Through half-shut eyelids, she took stock of the damage. Her backpack missing, everything gone.

She dragged herself to the foot of the bed and turned to Gabriel for help. "Please," she said, and tapped the frame. "Please lift the bed."

He knelt beside her, lifted the frame up high enough that she could run her fingers beneath the base of the bamboo bedposts. Felt the tug of plastic stuffed up inside the hollow footing, and with the plastic, relief. Her passport had been left undisturbed, as had the pictures in the ziplock, and with one bag secured she pulled herself to the opposite leg while the screams of agony chased each other in circles inside her chest. Or maybe out of her mouth.

She didn't know. Was delirious. Couldn't breathe.

She motioned to Gabriel again and he lifted again and Munroe tugged out the several thousand dollars she'd stashed. Gripped the money tight in one hand and pushed from the floor to her knees, and from her knees to her feet. Made the few steps to the bathroom and, hand to the wall for balance and support, fought the ever-present dizziness and the need to vomit.

Slid to the floor beside the toilet and, head tipped back against the wall, tapped the tank lid, and Gabriel lifted it off and his eyes grew wide when he peeked inside. The handgun and ammunition were still waterproofed in their bag. Munroe pushed to her knees to collect them, and woke with her face on the tiles and Gabriel beside her with a hotel washcloth in his hand and water from it dripping into her hair and down her face. Weapon retrieved, cash gripped tightly, she found Gabriel's face and whispered, "Thank you. I'm finished here. Please take me away."

Somewhere in between spells of darkness were flashes of clarity: They'd returned to the car, she'd been brought back to the place with the dirt floor and was on the mattress again. During one of the brief moments when she was fully cognizant, she tugged a fifty-dollar bill off the wad she'd shoved inside her pants and handed it to the woman of the house, who'd come to check on her. Asked for

Kapanol—morphine sulfate—she'd seen it on the shelf at the pharmacy in Lamu, and if it was available there, so far away from civilization, it would be easy to find here, even without a prescription. And ibuprofen. They called it Hedex here. She'd seen that, too.

"Everything is closed," the woman said. "When morning is come, we get."

CHAPTER 21

Munroe woke to a hand behind her head and plastic to her lips, and the instinct to strike died before she could give birth to it. She struggled to lift her hands and fought against motionless limbs. Understanding gradually replaced violence, and she grasped that in kindness someone meant to give her water.

Lips pressed together, she turned her head to refuse, and the plastic went away. Without knowing the source, it was too dangerous to drink. Fingers returned with a tablet and pressed it up against her mouth, and when Munroe struggled to keep free of this thing, a woman's voice said, "It is what you ask for, take it to help you pain."

Munroe winced and dry swallowed; strained to open her eyes. The face of the woman blurred into a halo of orange and purple, a cloth that wrapped her hair. Her eyes and the lines of concern etched across her forehead came into focus, and when Munroe's eyes opened fully and connected with hers, the woman nodded approval; she sat back on her heels, attentive nurse hovering over her patient, and beamed a smile.

She was possibly late twenties, skin soft and cared for, wore a knee-length skirt and button-down shirt, but was barefoot and held a dirty plastic cup. She put the cup to Munroe's face offering water again, and Munroe pressed fingertips to the cup and nudged it away, as gently as possible to avoid giving offense.

The woman stood and left and Munroe lifted a hand, studied her fingers, struggled to control joints and muscles, stretching one tight limb after another until she had some control over movement, and finally found a way to shift up onto an elbow. Her thoughts were a little clearer than the last time she'd been awake and the headache a little less nausea-inducing. How long had it been?

The woman returned with a sealed bottle of water, held it toward Munroe, another offer of a drink. Munroe reached for it, cried out from the stab that went through her, and the woman knelt and placed a hand behind her head again, helped her sit, and with water dribbling down her chin Munroe drank until the bottle was nearly empty and she could hold no more.

The woman smiled, satisfied, set the bottle beside the mattress, and sat back on her heels again. The house was quiet. Traffic sounds filtered in faintly from the outside. Lengthening shadows converged with light and streamed in through cracks in walls made from wood and woven switches.

"What time is it?" Munroe said.

"It is afternoon," the woman answered, as if that were all that mattered.

"What day?" Munroe whispered, and from the woman's response she pieced together the timing.

Frustrated and working against a body that hurt everywhere, Munroe attempted to sit. The seventy-two hours for retrieving the captain had expired and she needed to get back to the hospital before they turned him loose and she lost him forever—assuming he hadn't been hauled off and beaten to death at the same time that she'd been accosted.

"I need to go to the city," she said.

The woman placed the boxes with the Kapanol and Hedex tabs and the change in shillings beside the mattress. "How do you go?" she said. "You don't take *matatu*."

"I can pay for a taxi."

The woman shook her head. "You stay," she said, and only after Munroe settled back did she stand and leave the room.

Left with silence and muddy thoughts that filled in for memories, Munroe placed a hand on the rags by the side of the bed; slashed and shredded, they'd once been her clothes. She had no recollection of how they'd come to be that way, no grasp of what had happened to the gang who'd set upon her. From outside the house the woman's voice carried back with the tone of instruction, and when she returned she carried a steaming chipped ceramic bowl. She knelt and put the bowl in Munroe's hands and said, "You need eat."

The dish held broth with sparse chunks of vegetables floating about and some kind of meat or fat that Munroe didn't recognize, all of it boiled, cooked well enough to be safe. She blew and sipped steadily while the woman watched with approval, and when Munroe had finished nearly half, the woman, satisfied, left her.

Munroe angled her legs off the mattress and her feet to the dirt. For the first time she truly saw the clothes she wore, an embarrassing getup of ill-fitting pants and a button-down shirt, most probably spare pieces from the men who'd brought her to the house. Even being clean, they were dirty and stank with body odor from overuse, the by-product of poverty, which made the kindness in the gesture of having put them on her all the more eloquent. She searched the pockets for the money she'd collected from the hotel room, all of which seemed still to be with her—the result of being a guest of the household rather than an employer or neighbor of it. The gun and ammunition were still in plastic beside the bed next to the fisherman's knife.

Munroe made her way into the next room, a living area of sorts with mismatched furniture fitted so closely together there was barely room to stand. Every flat space was cluttered: a mixture of dishes, tattered books, a few towels and sheets, and a small TV with rabbit ears sandwiched between wooden cupboards with broken doors, as if all the family's worldly possessions were stored here.

The woman wasn't inside and so Munroe opened the front door, a solid piece of wood, overkill for what the rest of the place was built from, and stepped out into a wide yard, squinting against light that made her head hurt.

The house sat on a compound of sorts, the property hedged by lush greenery that opened onto what seemed to be the Mombasa–Malindi road. Chickens ran freely chasing bugs, and three goats were tethered to a stake off on the edge where the ground was still green and not barren and caked mud. There was another house to the right, with cinder-block walls and a tin roof—had to belong to someone better off than her host family. Smoke rose and twisted from a small lean-to built against the house, and because it had no door, Munroe could see the back of the woman as she squatted near an aluminum pot boiling over an earthen-pit fire.

The woman stood and turned, and noticing Munroe she smiled again. Put hands to hips and scoldingly said, "You go rest."

"I will soon," Munroe said, and perhaps because of the morphine, she smiled back. "What's your name?" she asked.

"Mary. And you name?"

"Michael."

"Michael a boy name," Mary said, waving a finger toward the overworn slacks as if contradicting her own statement. "You no boy."

"Not a boy," Munroe repeated. "But Michael is my name."

Eyes still hurting, Munroe squinted toward the sky and gauged maybe another hour of daylight. She needed to get to the captain and discover what had become of him. "I have to go to Mombasa," she said. "I have to get a friend from the hospital."

"You friend sick?"

"Hurt. Like me. But he can't stay at the hospital anymore. I need to bring him. I can pay you, like a hotel, if we can stay for a few days."

"How you go get him?"

"Help me with the car," she said. "I can pay."

The woman smiled again, a rich flash of bright white teeth. "Maybe," she said, and waved Munroe toward the house of wooden sticks. "You rest, I go ask."

———

THE SKY WAS fully dark, the inside of the house even more so, when Mary returned, her arrival announced by the *put-put* rumble of an old car with muffler issues, probably the same car that they'd used to take her to the hotel.

Munroe was in the doorway when the car shuddered to a stop and Mary stepped from the passenger side, laughing and joking with the driver. He was younger than she, taller, thin in the same way that most men in the area seemed to be. "This Gabriel, my brother," Mary said. "You know him. You remember?"

Munroe nodded.

"He take you Mombasa."

Munroe paused for a moment at the combination of names. Gabriel and Mary. Had the parents had any idea how strange those names played out when paired as brother and sister? The world tilted at an odd angle, and Munroe wrote off playing a biblical name game as the drugs talking. She shook hands with Gabriel, and whatever he said entered her head through a funny slow-motion haze that left her feeling far happier than the situation warranted. She limped back to the room to collect the money and weapon and drugs on the off chance she wouldn't return, left the few thousand shillings that had come as change for the prescription purchase; and with Mary already on the other side of the compound untethering the goats and talking to three of the children who'd returned home, Munroe eased into the passenger side of the car, and Gabriel shut her door.

The vehicle was a Toyota, spray-painted light blue, and twenty years old at the least, with bald tires, a missing window, and doors that had been dented and reshaped several times, one of them latched closed with wire. For a family at this end of the socioeconomic scale, the car was an incredible and costly luxury.

They crawled from the compound entrance to the highway, where buses, *matatus,* overladen trucks, and an array of cars from luxury vehicles to those decrepit like this one moved past, and Gabriel waited a long, long time for the road to clear. With emergency flashers going, he pulled out onto the highway. The vehicle gained speed slowly and only after he was up over thirty kilometers an hour did he turn off the flashers. The car never got much faster than that, but it was better than walking, and unlike many of the other cars on the so-called highway, the headlights worked, which limited the chance of hitting someone along the side of the road. Even if Munroe had had access to her own vehicle, she wouldn't have driven it. Not in the condition she was in, not driving on the left-hand side, everything opposite, and where in a road accident, no matter the circumstances or who was at fault, the white one was always to blame.

Gabriel glanced at Munroe several times along the way, and finally, when she in her chemical daze offered nothing to fill the silence, he said, "You very lucky."

She turned just enough to briefly catch his eye.

"I watch when they come," he said. Both of his hands gripped the steering wheel and he focused on the windshield and the taillights of the truck belching black smoke in front of them. "Six men. Seven men. Eight men. Three dead now. Three. Four."

Munroe tipped her head back against the cracked vinyl headrest. "I don't remember anything," she said.

Gabriel glanced at her again. "Nothing?"

"Nothing."

He sighed, and after a weighty pause the story unfolded in halting, measured, and broken English, and with his words flashes of memory returned, and then imagined memories rose to re-create what she could never have known unless he'd told her; that she'd fought for the kill, to die killing, unwilling to go to the grave in brutality or alone, that she'd fought until overpowered and bludgeoned, beaten unconscious and dragged toward the ocean to die.

"They want kill you," he said. "And then come light and shout from the houses, many *askari* from houses, maybe they hear and they come and the men, they scared. They run away." He paused. "You a very dangerous woman. I think you die," he said. "Me and Johnny get the boat. We are Sami friend, we think you die and we carry you to the boat, but you live and you scream in you sleep. Bring you to my sister house. You have very much pain, but we have no money for doctor. Sorry."

Munroe touched his shoulder, whispered, "Thank you for giving me help."

He smiled. "Very welcome," he said. "You think you be okay?"

"In a few days," she said. "Do you know the people who did this?"

He shook his head.

"Do you know who killed Sami?"

He shook his head again. "Maybe same people who try kill you."

"Do you know why?"

"I don't know," he said. "But very bad for business, very bad. Nobody come to beach, nobody buy when trouble come."

"You didn't see them do it?"

"I find Sami after."

"Thank you," she said again. Took fifty dollars from her pocket and offered it to him. He looked up, surprised.

"No," he said.

"For petrol," she said. "For the car."

He nodded and took the money.

CHAPTER 22

The hospital gates were closed when they arrived, and Gabriel honked the horn. An *askari* stepped from the pedestrian opening, scanned the car, acknowledged Munroe in the front seat, and opened to allow them entry. Gabriel waited in the car, and Munroe, grimy and hair still matted from the blood and the beating, eased out onto the pavement and walked barefoot through the front doors.

The receptionist did a double take and let out a small gasp.

"It's bad?" Munroe said, and the woman nodded.

She hadn't seen herself in a mirror. Could only imagine. "I'm here to collect John Doe," she said. "Dr. Patel wanted him released."

With her focus never leaving Munroe's face, the woman picked up a phone and punched a number for the doctor. It took him a few minutes to arrive, and he, too, stopped short when he saw her. She said, "I got mugged."

"I see," he said. "Are you here for yourself or for your friend?"

"I'm here to get him."

"Have you had any medical attention?"

She shook her head.

"Your friend is still resting," he said, and studied her face, his eyes tracking from her jawline to her hairline, as if he wasn't sure she was all there. "I want to look at you before I release him to you."

Munroe didn't argue; she followed him down the hall. The doctor opened a door, motioned her inward, and she inched up onto an exam table, went through his questions and prodding. He disinfected and stitched up the deepest of the lacerations that hugged the hairline at the back of her neck, and when he'd finished, he held up the needle and motioned to her body. "Do you have any others?"

"I think so," she said, and with effort inched out of the shirt. The doctor stared at her torso and it was difficult to tell if he was more shocked by the scars or the realization that she was a woman. "You get in a lot of fights?" he said.

She glanced down. "Those are old."

He didn't say anything, just numbed and disinfected the wound that ran from the side of her rib cage down toward her hip, a gouge considered superficial but which hurt like hell. He counted out the stitches as he tied each one off. Stopped when he reached thirty-three.

He wanted X-rays, and she went along with the request; fell asleep on the exam table while he checked the prognosis. Woke to the door opening. Fuzzy and without much concept of passing time, she smiled at the news, which was about as she expected: concussion, two fractured ribs, and a whole body's worth of bruising. "It could have been worse," he said. "Are you taking pain medication?"

Munroe nodded.

"I thought so," he said. "What are you on?"

"Kapanol and Hedex."

He shook his head in disapproval. "The anti-inflammatory is good; the morphine is a problem. Do you know what you're doing?"

She nodded, and he didn't say more. Between the scars and her odd request to sedate the captain—and now the fighting and self-medicating—he probably figured that whatever she was mixed up in was something he should stay far, far away from. He stretched a hand to help her sit.

"Take a deep breath," he said, and when she did, he wrapped tape around the upper portion of her torso and she winced. Even with the morphine, the pain was brutal. When he'd finished, he handed her the roll. "Keep it," he said. "You need to unwrap for a bit every day to make sure you're breathing deeply enough. The tape compresses the lungs, invites pneumonia."

"I've had broken ribs before," she said, and then she smiled, her way of apologizing for having bullied him into sedating the captain. "Thank you," she said.

He smiled back. Apology accepted.

"They're hairline fractures," he said. "Should be easy compared to the broken ribs. I'll write you a prescription for antibiotics." Motioned a finger toward her abdomen. "You don't want to take a chance with that." When she smiled again, he offered his arm as leverage so she could inch off the table. "Your friend is starting to come around," he said. "I think he'll make a full recovery."

Munroe nodded. That was good. As soon as the morphine was out of her system and she was back to being angry, she'd start asking the captain a lot of very pointed questions.

Munroe fell asleep in the lobby; woke when a nurse wheeled the captain in. He was back in his original clothes, which had, she was grateful, been laundered, and his facial hair had grown to the point that he had an aging, wild, crazy-man look to him. He sat slouched over, hands limp in his lap, and when the wheelchair turned to face her, his half-open eyes met hers and there was recognition on his face.

THEY TRAVELED OUT of Mombasa, routing around the city one wrong turn to the next while Munroe watched mirrors and traffic, until finally, convinced they'd not been followed, she asked Gabriel to take them home.

He didn't question when she'd made the requests for misdirection, and asked no questions now as he headed for the Nyali Bridge. Having witnessed Sami's death and then Munroe's beating, he knew as well as Munroe did the risk of bringing the captain home—and, of course, there was always Hollywood. Movies were the only examples that most in Africa would ever see of average daily American life, and this fit right in.

Gabriel pulled the car from the highway onto the dirt shoulder, slowed to turn into his family's compound, and Munroe asked him to switch off the engine and lights and wait awhile. Even medicated as she was, she could think clearly enough to see that there was little that the killers could have used to follow them to this hideaway: If they'd been able to trace her to the hospital and had found the captain, then they would simply have taken him, not laid a trap to find her—he was what they wanted, and as far as they knew, she was dead.

But being dependent on the kindness of others made the guilt burn inside. Her hosts were simple people who had done right by a stranger at their own inconvenience and expense with no expectation of anything in return, and all she could offer in exchange was the risk of bringing death and killing to their families.

Munroe checked the mirrors one last time and to Gabriel whispered, "We can go now."

He started the engine again but didn't turn on the lights; the car crept into the compound. Uncertainty tore at her. Painkillers made for poor choices, made for missing things that should be obvious. She watched the mirrors again, chasing phantoms. The car shuddered to a stop and Munroe waited in the passenger seat, eyes closed, head tipped back, while Gabriel went in search of his cousin. There was no sound or movement from the captain, and at some point she must have fallen asleep again, because she startled awake at the sound of laughter and conversation, and then Gabriel opened her door.

Johnny was with him, the other man who'd rescued her from the beach and gone with her to the hotel. He knelt to eye level. "Everything is good?" he said, and Munroe forced a weak smile for answer.

She watched and then followed inside the house as the cousins worked through the effort of hauling the captain's dead weight from car to mattress, and when he was situated, Munroe gave Gabriel another fifty dollars and asked him to find rope. This far into the evening she didn't expect he'd show up with anything new, so she wasn't disappointed when he returned an hour later with a twenty-foot segment that, from the smell and texture, had to have once been part of a longer line used to keep a boat moored to the shore.

Munroe knelt by the bed and grasped the captain's wrist, and his eyes snapped open. He had little strength to struggle as she wound between his hands a tight figure eight that he wouldn't easily slip free from, and his eyes shut and he said not a word as she tied the rope tail around her own waist and strung it through her belt buckle.

The doctor had said it would be another twenty-four hours before the sedatives fully wore off. He was loopy now, and disoriented, and although eventually he might try to get free, he wouldn't get far. Munroe eased down onto the bed. Swallowed another dosage of morphine, antibiotics, and another round of anti-inflammatories. With painkillers back in her system she lay on the mattress beside the captain, hand gripping the knife, trusting the instinct of the blade to keep her alive if for some reason he should touch her.

SHE WOKE TO a sun-shadowed room and to the captain's face less than a foot from hers, staring at her. Munroe's focus traveled from his eyes to the walls, and measuring the level of light penetrating in between the slats, she guessed at early afternoon. If only one night had passed, then she'd slept another fourteen hours give or take a few on either side.

With the captain still watching, Munroe struggled upright. Turned her back to him, took off the shirt, and unwound the tape from her chest. Breathed deeply and felt dizzy. Her focus turned toward the Kapanol beside the bed, tablets singing sweetly to her, calling out with more than one temptation, and with her focus resting on the box, she inched back into the shirt. It was a dangerous game, self-medicating for physical pain when numbing oblivion had once been her chosen method for muting the demons of the past.

Munroe nudged the pills away. Took a heavy dose of ibuprofen instead; she would last as long as she could without the morphine, measuring the minutes waiting for relief. She stood slowly, untied the rope from around her waist, and tied the tail off around a beam. Not perfect but enough that he wasn't going to get free in the next five minutes.

She collapsed back on the bed, screaming silently, breathing in shallow gulps to push past what the little effort had caused her, and when she could think again, Munroe hobbled for the opening.

There was no one in the next room, but on the cloth-covered table pushed up against and filling the back wall were a pitcher of water and a couple of chipped dishes with food: cooked dark and oily greens and a sticky white dough, both still warm. Over the dishes a swath of mosquito netting kept circling flies off the food, and on a scrap of notebook paper was a beautiful shaky scrawl that said *Please take.*

Munroe tore into the dough with her fingers; ripped off a bite-size piece and formed it into a ball, pressed her thumb into the center to form a spoon of sorts to scoop the greens; she tried not to shovel it into her mouth faster than she could chew. The texture and taste were a little different from what she'd grown up on in the houses of her playmates in Cameroon, but the concept was the same: thick starch and cheap vegetables; an acquired taste, a luxurious meal considering her last food had been the broth yesterday evening, and before that she had no idea.

Munroe stood over the table, swallowing until both dishes were empty, and although the food had most likely been intended for both her and the captain she ate it all without shame: The hungrier he was, the easier it would be to get him to talk, and regardless, he had an ample spare tire to burn for energy. He'd live.

Satiated, she stacked the dishes and re-covered them. Limped back to the room, and this time the captain was on his back, staring at the palm fronds above. She checked his neck for rope burns. She needed to get him water, needed to get herself water, but couldn't trust what Mary had left behind the way she could trust food that had been boiled to death.

Eventually the captain's eyes shifted from the ceiling to her face. "My name's Michael," she said, and his head turned in her direction. "I don't know if you remember. Your ship got hijacked."

His expression betrayed no understanding, no reaction, and he turned back to staring at the ceiling. She ignored him in kind and, with effort, lowered herself to the floor. Picked up the knife, the gun, and the drugs, carried them into the adjacent room to keep them out of the captain's hands, shoved the handgun into a crevice between cushion and armrest on the tattered floral sofa, and left the house for the late-afternoon sun.

The brightness brought the headache back full force and Munroe squinted against it. Three of the school-age children were in the yard area, and with them two others, little ones, half-naked and young enough that their potbellies still poked out. The eldest was a girl, one Munroe had seen with Mary the day before, about ten years old, perhaps eleven, and Munroe assumed she was Mary's daughter. The children stopped playing when Munroe opened the door, and then all of them, a group at the zoo flocking to the monkey area, came slowly in her direction and stood around in a half circle, staring.

To the oldest girl Munroe said, "You speak English?"

She smiled bashfully, looked away and then back again while her bare toes dug little holes in the ground.

Munroe held up a fifty-bob coin and every pair of eyes followed the money. Munroe palmed the coin and with a flourish and misdirection showed them her empty hand. Five sets of eyes grew wide, and wider still when she pulled the money from the oldest girl's ear, an old and boring trick but new here, and the children burst into squeals of surprise and laughter.

"Do you know where to buy water in bottles?" Munroe asked.

The girl nodded. Munroe handed her the money and then another two hundred shillings. "Bring me water," she said, "and I'll show you the trick again."

The children ran off in a chorus of excited chatter, and Munroe returned to the mattress; was on her back, eyes closed and ignoring the captain's unabashed glare, when the girl opened the front door and slipped inside.

Munroe picked up the box of Kapanol and struggled upright. The rest of the children huddled in the doorway, peering inside as if the house were strange and foreign and they expected their sister to be eaten by a monster. Munroe motioned for the water bottles, took them and the change from the girl, and set it all aside. Held up another coin and as she'd done earlier vanished the money and pulled it from the girl's ear.

The expressed delight was even louder the second go-around, and Munroe smiled, offered the coin to the girl, and when she reached for it, pressed the tiny fingers around the money. The children squealed again, crowded into each other to examine the shiny piece, and then the little herd ran off with their collective treasure.

Munroe shut the door against the light and drank half a bottle while searching through the broken cupboard for a clean glass. Found a chipped teacup and used its base to grind a morphine pill into powder, swept the powder into the cup and poured a few sips of water over the top and swirled it around: an amount of liquid small enough that the captain, thirsty as he must be, would drink it all regardless of the medication.

She took the water to the room, offered the captain the cup. He reached for it and drank unassisted. The drugs were a way of mitigating the risk of an escape until she could come up with something better. He handed back the cup and she filled it again and he drank that, too, and after several rounds back and forth, having met her obligations to keep him hydrated, she collapsed back into bed and into sleep while time marched on through the foggy haze.

CHAPTER 23

The direction of the shadows in the room said early morning, which meant Munroe would have slept fifteen hours or so. Another day of rest had done her mind good, though her body would take longer to heal.

Munroe inched upward. Balance was better, pain levels dropping if only slightly. She could sit without agony, and although her chest still hurt, the pain was mostly dull and only grew sharp if she moved the wrong way.

The captain, next to her, snored lightly and so Munroe rolled to the floor and pushed to her knees. First movement off the bed and his eyes snapped open. He still hadn't spoken since she'd collected him, but he woke when she woke, slept when she slept, and observed in a way that approximated the patience of one who had plenty of experience as a prisoner, or prisoner of war.

She took money from her pockets, stood and peered around the door frame where sound had reached out to her. In the crowded living room Mary tucked clothing onto a shelf. She turned when Munroe entered.

"How are you?" Mary said. "You sleep?"

Munroe nodded. "Thank you."

"You want eat?" she said.

Famished, Munroe shook her head no. She desperately needed

sustenance but didn't want to take any more from a family who gave so generously out of what little they had. "I have to go to the city," she said, "but I have a big problem. My friend will try to run away while I am gone." Munroe opened her fist and presented the five one-thousand-shilling notes she'd taken from her pockets, money that had seen more grime than the mattress on the dirt floor—a hundred dollars, give or take: a month's wages for a laborer.

"I need help to protect him," Munroe said. "It's very important that he stays in the bed and doesn't run away. If he leaves, the men who tried to kill me will find him, too, but he doesn't believe me. Please? Sit in the room with him until I return? A few hours, or maybe until dark."

As if under hypnosis Mary reached for the money and Munroe tightened her fist around it. "He may try to fight you," Munroe said. "I can give him medicine to make him sleep. Is there a pharmacy close?"

"Maybe one kilometer," Mary said.

Munroe asked for paper and Mary found a scrap and then a chewed-off broken pencil, and Munroe wrote down nearly identical instructions to what the doctor in Lamu had given her when buying supplies for the captain. She handed the slip to Mary, then offered more than enough money to cover the costs.

Munroe gave the captain water, then rested in the living room until Mary returned.

Seeing the syringe, the captain's eyes widened. He sat up and then, even against the bonds that kept him trussed and choked him when he moved, he tried to struggle to his feet.

Without the port Munroe would have to inject him directly, and if he struggled it would be an exhausting chore. "Don't fight me," she said. "It'll only be worse for you."

Then, lips twisted in a snarl as if he was pissed off that she'd forced him to speak, he uttered his first words since leaving the *Favorita*.

"What are you doing?" he said. His voice was hoarse and sticky from lack of use, his accent thicker than she remembered it having been.

"Sedating you," she said. "I have things to do and I don't want you going anywhere."

"Where would I go?"

"I'm sure you'll figure something out," she said, and tapped the air bubbles to the surface of the syringe. "Hold out your arm for me, will you?"

"I'm hungry," he said.

She nodded. "There's no food in the house. I promise that if you go to sleep I'll bring food back with me when I come."

His expression stayed hard, as if he pondered the options, as if there was no way in hell he'd trust her to inject him with anything, but the morphine in his most recent glass of water was in full effect, and although he pulled away when she took his wrist, he was weak from having gone so long without anything but the IV for food and he winded easily and gave up.

The pain of holding on, even with so little resistance, was excruciating, and Munroe pushed past it the same way she'd pushed past the pain those many nights in the jungle, just long enough to get her knee on top of his forearm and a fist on his shoulder so that she had him under control; enough to get the sedative into him, though his arm wouldn't be pretty tomorrow, and then she let go and collapsed onto the floor.

When she finally crawled to her feet, she took the tape and rebound her chest. Was tempted to beg Mary to find Gabriel so she might hire his car to get back into town, but she couldn't become dependent on him; the pain wasn't going away for a while, things were going to get a lot harder before they got better, and the only way was to push through. As long as she didn't use her left arm much, didn't breathe too deeply or turn too rapidly in any direction, the pain dissolved into a dull constant and became easier to ignore.

Munroe finished with the taping. Put the shirt back on and lay down to allow the exhaustion and breathlessness to subside. The captain's eyelids had already closed, his facial muscles had relaxed, and she envied his happy place; would gladly have traded places for the gift of drifting off into la-la-land. Instead she struggled to her feet.

Mary was on the sofa, an old torn paperback Bible in her lap. Munroe said, "You have a machete?"

"I have," Mary said.

"He's supposed to stay asleep, but if he wakes up, you might need it."

Mary stood. "I go get," she said, and Munroe patted the woman's shoulder, handed her the promised payment, and hoped she'd keep her word.

MUNROE WALKED A painful hobble out into the compound, found her stride, and continued to the road. Stood out in the heat under the shade of a mango tree and waved down several shared taxis before she found one with space.

The Safaricom store was her first destination, and like the receptionist who had gasped when Munroe had entered the hospital, so the proprietor grimaced when she opened his door. He was the same young Indian man who'd been there the first time, though she doubted he recognized her. She hadn't showered since before her beating and assumed that the smell was as repugnant as her looks. That she was barefoot and in other people's clothes didn't help.

Munroe went through the process of buying and setting up a new phone, and when she'd finished and had no more energy left to stand, she slid against the far wall to sit on the floor, and there in the shop with the manager eyeing her warily from behind the counter, she dialed Djibouti for Amber Marie.

She'd lost five days since the attack and braced for the possibility that Amber and Natan had already left for Somalia. But the phone rang just twice before Amber answered.

"Hey," Munroe said. "Did you call or leave a message?"

"Yeah, did you get it? We're leaving for Somalia in three days, we're set to go—will you come with us?"

"I can't," Munroe said, "but there's a complication—some stuff you need to think about before you head out."

If the warning and caution in her voice registered at all, Amber didn't react to them. "Okay, what?" she said.

"I need you to do something for me before I can tell you."

"Come on, Michael, I really don't have time for games."

"It's not a game, Amber. This is the difference between you getting out of Somalia alive and not, but I need to know you're going to take me seriously, that you won't blow me off, so I need you to read something for me."

"Fine. What am I looking for?"

"I'm going to give you a website," Munroe said. "You have a way to write it down?"

"Yeah, hang on a sec." Faintly in the background there was the shuffling and clacking of things being pushed around on a cluttered desk.

"Okay, go," Amber said, and Munroe spelled out the URL to a copy of a previous brag sheet, a list of prior jobs—the legal ones—a résumé of sorts, kept on hand for assignments where boardroom decision makers needed a fancy cover-your-ass dossier before signing a contract they'd already begged her to take. She hadn't had a reason to update the information in the past two years, but even the prior work history would be enough for Amber to see her as more than just a kid with a limited worldview.

"Got it," Amber said. "What is it?"

"Just check it out," Munroe said. "It's self-explanatory. Call me back after you've read it. And here, I have a new number." She recited the digits and Amber repeated them back, and Munroe hit the End button, drained of energy she didn't even know she didn't have.

The store was empty and the proprietor studied her with the same crazy-eyed look that everyone seemed to give her lately. She imagined she looked worse now than she had at the hospital, especially if the bruises had begun to mottle green. "I won't be here long," she said. "I got attacked and I'm hurting pretty bad. I just need to make a couple of phone calls and I'll go."

If the story made a difference, it didn't reflect on his face, but he said, "It's no problem. Stay if you need."

Munroe half-smiled in thanks, closed her eyes, and tipped her head back against the wall. The throbbing had started up again and she desperately craved the pain meds. Could push past it a little longer; would try to wait until she was back at the house before taking them. Must have dozed in the silence because she woke to the door opening, a customer entering, and a moment later the phone vibrated in her hand. Amber said, "I read the file, but I don't understand what it has to do with you or us."

"That file is me," Munroe said, and waited for the facts to settle, for Amber's mental dissonance to engage. "When I'm not off taking a vacation in some tiny-ass country like Djibouti, I'm setting up shop in developing countries and scoping out the political and socioeconomic climate for corporate investors."

Amber said, "What the hell does that even mean?"

Munroe sighed. "I'm a spy for hire, Amber. I travel to developing countries, dictatorships, banana republics. I analyze strategic threats to get a feel for what's going on on the ground—the stuff that news outlets don't report and governments try to cover up. Then I figure out who holds the true political clout, who to bribe and who to avoid, and if I'm paid well enough, I do the bribing and make sure my employer's name never sees print. It's dangerous. It's taxing. I've made enemies. You get the idea. And those are the jobs I've done on the record. The issue of the *Favorita* is right in the center of my work history Venn diagram, and there are few people in the world who can do what I do, so take me seriously when I tell you that driving down to Somalia is a bad, bad idea."

"Maybe it is, maybe it isn't," Amber said. "I don't know what kind of crap stunt you're trying to pull, Michael, but those documents belong to a woman and I don't have the time or patience to be on the blunt end of some kind of prank."

"Yes," Munroe said. "They do belong to a woman. Welcome to the truth."

"You're a woman?"

"Yes."

"You're a woman," Amber said, and this time her tone had the bite of temper rising, as if Munroe playing coy about her gender wasn't in a whole other universe than Leo's lying about the purpose of his armed transit contract, of bullying an unwilling participant onto the ship believing she might get killed, while at the same time cutting that unwilling participant out of the deal that Leo forced her into.

"I never told you I was a guy," Munroe said. "You all made the assumption and I never bothered to correct it, which has absolutely nothing to do with why we're talking right now. There'll be plenty of time to be pissed off later. Now that you know who I am and what I do, that I'm not some eighteen-year-old kid, will you listen to what I have to say and take it seriously?"

"I'm listening," Amber said, "but that drive down to Garacad is the only thing I have right now. If you're telling me not to go, if you're everything that those files say you are, then that means you have a reason, so yeah, I'll listen, but I want to know the reason, otherwise this is all just bullshit."

Amber's words choked off at the end, a tirade that might have kept on going if emotion hadn't intervened. Munroe felt beyond the anger, felt the unshed tears and knew the pain, the desperation of losing forever the one she loved; breathed it in as the fear of her own past losses. Separated by half a continent, Amber would risk everything to pursue what she loved most, while Munroe ran from the same, yet they were really not so different.

"My phone was stolen five days ago," Munroe said, "taken by a group of thugs acting on behalf of the people who hijacked the *Favorita*. They tried to kill me, and this is after they'd already killed a guy working for me. They're after something that they think I took from the ship, and if you left a message for me, then they know your intentions. They'll be waiting for you, and if they find you, I can pretty much guarantee that they're going to hold you hostage or kill you as leverage to get me to hand over what they want, but I can't do that."

"What is it they want?"

"Something they think I took from the ship."

"You already said that. What is it?"

"It's beside the point."

"Why can't you just give it to them?"

"Things aren't that simple."

"How could they not be that simple? You obviously have it. Just give them what they want and we get Leo back."

"No, you won't get Leo back. You'll get Leo killed. Leo is in Somalia. I'm in Kenya. The thing they think I have is in Kenya. Do you not see the issue?"

"Yeah," Amber said, and if Munroe heard properly, there were more tears somewhere in the background, part of the same up-down emotional roller coaster that Amber had been riding since she first got the news.

"Look," Munroe said, "I'm still working on finding out who they are and why they want it. If I can figure that out, then we'll have far more than just bargaining power—we'll have a way to play them and open up other possibilities to get the team off the *Favorita*."

"Why bother?" Amber said, accusatory and angry again. "You already have what you want. Why were you in Djibouti, Michael? Were we just a cover for one of your jobs? A convenient way to chase after this thing that both you and the hijackers targeted on the *Favorita*?"

"What? No!" Munroe said. "Are you insane? This is not a James Bond movie. How could I possibly know six months in advance that Leo would take this job? And if not for him threatening to fire me if I didn't go, I wouldn't even have been on the ship to begin with."

Amber blew out a long breath, was silent for a moment longer as if setting aside her sense of righteous betrayal to try to see the bigger picture. "How close did they get?" she said.

"To what?"

"To killing you."

"Pretty damn close," Munroe said, and left it at that. Recounting the details of the attack, relaying her current condition, would only lead to pity and sympathy and *that* was for the weak. "Whoever did this had the money and the smarts to use Somali pirates as a way to hijack the *Favorita*. They'll come after you in a heartbeat if they know who you are," Munroe said. "Watch your back."

"But we're not the ones who have what they want."

"It won't matter," she said. "They'll assume you'll know where it is."

"I can't just abandon Leo."

"I'm not asking you to, but what good will it do him if you go down to Somalia and get killed in the process? You ever think that maybe what he's holding on to right now is the idea that you're okay? That maybe fighting to get back to you is what's keeping him alive and motivated? If you're determined to kill yourself to go get him, then at least let me help you. I can figure stuff out and you have a better chance of staying alive."

"You'll do this to help Leo?"

"No," Munroe said, though her exact thought was something closer to *Fuck Leo.* "I would do it for you," she said, though that, too, wasn't the whole truth, and after a pregnant pause she said, "You told me you'd be willing to put everything on the line to help him, right?"

"Yes."

"What if that means going into debt?"

"Yes."

"No matter how much?"

"What are you getting at, Michael? I'm not going to put a price on his head. I'll do whatever it takes, but I don't like all the open-ended questions."

"There are other ways to get him out, but they're not going to be free. I just need a little time to plan and sort through how to do it."

"How much longer is a little time?"

"Three days," Munroe said, and with that commitment the impact of having to function with a body unable to keep up with her mind became the burden of a deadline she wasn't sure she'd be able to meet. "If I haven't called you by then, I'm either dead or useless," she said, "and then you'll have to figure it out on your own."

CHAPTER 24

Munroe left the Safaricom store to find clothes. Snickers followed in her wake, sidewalk merchants and street-store touts who noticed the bare feet and local attire, and she found them amusing; pickpockets were what concerned her. Every bit of money she had left was spread between her pockets, and here on these busy streets she was most at risk for having it taken from her.

She finally spotted a store, one street over, that sold imported clothes, and there found a pair of cargo pants that fit well enough and a couple of T-shirts that might, with minimal washing, last a couple of weeks. She changed into the new clothes before leaving, added a button-down for the layering, but without a shower the effect was something akin to dressing up a pig. Shoes and socks came next, and after that a pharmacy where she purchased soap and shampoo, antibiotic ointment, and another box of morphine. And when she'd acquired all that she could reasonably carry without straining, she found food, and then a taxi and asked the driver for a local hotel, a place that might possibly cater to the occasional backpacker but never the packaged tours.

The driver took her in the direction of the old city and turned off onto a dirt road just as pitted as the paved ones; pointed her toward a block-shaped four-story building with a hand-painted sign, bars on the windows, and wide deep green double doors. The lobby matched the outside, wasn't much more than a shoddily built desk and an empty space, cooler than the outside heat due to the thick walls, but still hot and humid. The clientele were those who'd be in from the smaller cities: merchants who'd come to buy supplies from items fresh off the boat or perhaps pull their own wares out of customs at the port. Cell phones were abundant and languages cluttered, and many of the guests loitered in the lobby or around the front and in the small restaurants next door. If there were women here, Munroe didn't see them.

Munroe paid for a room with its own shower. A boy in torn pants and slippers crafted from old rubber tires led her up a steep narrow stairwell to the third floor, an exhausting climb.

There were clean sheets on the bed, a fan, a little bit of space to walk from bed to bathroom, and a window that opened to the street below, where the noise of car horns and motorbikes lifted up with just enough breeze to keep the room from sauna-level heat. But the bathroom had a towel and running water and the water was hot, and this was why she'd come.

Munroe stood under the lackluster stream, hands to the wall, neck to the spray, allowing the heat to wash away the dirt and grime, and with the cleansing her body began to relax, and in the letting go came the memories and the emotion that she kept tamped down in favor of the rage and anger that pushed her toward survival. They bubbled up into pain worse than the fractures or the lacerations, and she didn't fight them, allowed the flow to take the history and the scars, the losses and the impossible choices, and wash them away, and when they were gone, Munroe shut off the valve and reached for the towel.

Above the small sink was a cracked and worn mirror, enough to examine the wounds that she'd not yet seen. Her face was mottled, but not the worst that she'd experienced—and probably looked better now that she was clean. The bruises on her shoulders and torso were extensive and deep, would be a long time in healing, and the laceration along her side would be another scar to add to the collection of slivers that crisscrossed her abdomen and back, mementos of the history that had taught her what it meant to fight for life.

She re-bound her chest with the same tape, dressed again, and lay back on the bed fending off the urge to sleep. The simple acts of making her way into town, getting the phone, shopping and showering, had depleted her energy, and the headache was back again. With the emotional clutter washed away and her thoughts running clearer, her mind circled around through the strategy at hand and then twisted dizzily along the scenarios and events that had brought her to this point, warped into a looping maze that had no beginning and no end.

She needed sleep.

Munroe took more ibuprofen and checked the time on her phone. Set the alarm. She could afford a few hours. The fan buzzed a hypnotic lure to the background of street noise against clean sheets and clean skin, and then one blink into the next the phone alarm pierced the melody and she lurched back into the rush of the world and the need for answers.

Feeling weak and hating the weakness Munroe took a taxi back up the highway. Exited several hundred meters before her destination and, on foot again, stopped to buy bananas and bread and bottled water from a small roadside stall, ate again as she walked.

Sunlight was fast fading when Munroe entered the compound, where she found Mary in the lean-to kitchen, squatting beside a charcoal fire and fussing over an aluminum pot. The woman glanced up when Munroe approached; smiled her trademark smile as if there was no reason to be concerned that she was here outside and not in the room with the captain where Munroe had paid her to be.

"He is sleeping," Mary said, and Munroe nodded and forced a half smile. Handed the woman a loaf of bread and the bag of Gabriel's borrowed clothes.

She expected to find the captain awake and working at his bonds, or missing entirely, but he was indeed as Mary had said, fully out and snoring in a way that only old men could.

Munroe set the remaining loaf and the bananas beside him and he didn't open his eyes. She dropped a couple of morphine tablets into a water bottle and put it beside the food. Didn't know if they'd dissolve but she didn't have the energy to crush them. Swallowing a half-dose of morphine, she drank heavily to rehydrate, eased down onto the mattress, and sank hard into sleep. Woke to sunlight, and to a shaking movement: to the captain upright and shoveling food into his mouth.

Only a small portion of the loaf remained, and none of the bananas. He'd probably be rewarded with vomiting considering he hadn't eaten solid food since she'd taken him off the ship. She lay watching until he registered her staring and turned to face her, eyes locked onto hers while he continued to feed bread into his mouth.

She stretched. Felt the aches a little less than yesterday and less still than the day before; rolled to the floor and to her knees, limped one room over, and confirmed that the house was empty. Opened the front door, peered out into the compound; and certain that they were as alone now as they could be, she pulled the handgun from the sofa cushion where she'd stashed it and carried the weapon back into the bedroom.

Standing in the doorway, she released the magazine, pushed it back into place. Pulled the slide, though her hand had barely enough grip to manage what should have been a straightforward maneuver. The captain stopped chewing and tracked her movements.

She walked to his side of the bed.

He put down the bread; swallowed his last bite.

She unhooked the rope that secured him to the wall and he blanched. "Where do we go?" he said.

"The latrine."

"You'll kill me there?"

"Only if you try to run," she said.

Although she'd never seen him do it, he'd been using the empty water bottle to relieve himself, and considering that until today he'd eaten nothing after their flight from the *Favorita*, the bottle had been enough, but wouldn't be for long; best to get him used to a new pattern.

Munroe nodded toward his makeshift urinal. "Might as well take that," she said. "Get rid of it while you have the chance."

The captain brushed crumbs off his chest and out of his beard. With hands still bound, he leaned over to pick up the bottle and twisted to get to his feet. His movement was agile for a man who'd been sedated and fed off an IV for a week, and Munroe took note of that; an assessment of what she'd be up against if he managed to run or take a swing. She motioned him toward the front door.

Rope in one hand, weapon in the other, she followed him out and took him around to the rear of the house, to the farthest edge of the property and another thatch-roofed wattle-and-daub structure. Its vertical sticks had been woven with horizontal ones and filled in with mud, and an open-hole doorway stood on the side that faced away from the houses and the kitchen. Inside was a dirt floor, a hole in the ground, the high-pitched whine of flies, and an unmistakable stench.

Munroe nodded the captain inward and let out enough slack so that she could keep hold of him without having to step in behind him. He sighed and walked to the middle. Even with his wrists secured he had the dexterity to dump the bottle and unzip his pants, and although it took him a while to get going, he did his thing and Munroe turned her shoulder to him, keeping an eye on him with her peripheral vision. When he'd finished, she nodded him to the nearby water bucket and scoop, where he washed his hands and then his face and neck, and she nudged him along and back into the house and to the bed, and when he was situated she said, "There are people looking for you."

He inched farther into the mattress and grunted.

"They killed a boy working for me and then nearly killed me to find you."

He lay back, put his bound hands behind his head, and studied the ceiling.

"They're not the only deaths over this, either."

She fastened the rope to the wall's supporting beam, keeping it taut enough that he didn't have much in the way of leverage to get off the bed, though if he got crazy he'd probably pull down the house.

"I kept you hidden and saved your life," she said.

The captain gave her nothing, not even eye contact.

"Your crew and the armed men you hired are still on the *Favorita*," she said, "under guard by pirates off the Somali coast—at least the ones that are still alive." She paused to allow for a response, didn't get one, and so stood over him so that he couldn't avoid eye contact without admitting weakness. "The vessel is pretty much worthless," she said. "The hijackers didn't go through all that effort to track and target the ship for the ship's sake. And it seems that for now nobody but you and your crew even know about your weapons cache down in the hold, so I can think of only one thing valuable enough to keep them hunting, and that's you."

He closed his eyes and rolled over, turning his back to her. She said, "When they didn't get you, they abandoned the ship to the pirates, which creates a problem for me because now the pirates are demanding three million dollars for the release of the crew."

More silence.

"I haven't got three million dollars to spare," she said, "but I do have the thing that started the hijacking in the first place, and that's something I can use to barter for the crew."

He rolled back over.

"I haven't decided what I'm going to do," she said. "I figure you don't want to go to Somalia to be traded off in exchange for the ship and the crew, so if you can think of anything that would work as an alternative, now would be a really good time to start talking."

"Where am I?" he said. "And who are you?"

"You're in Mombasa, but the real question is *Who* are *you*?"

He grunted again, rolled over again, and she let him be. There was no point in attempting to interrogate him while she was weak and more exhausted than he. She'd get her answers eventually; would crawl inside his head and figure him out, and she had tomorrow for that and the day after, but today she would leave him and pursue the last of the threads she'd left untouched in the city.

CHAPTER 25

Mary returned to the house late in the morning and Munroe greeted her with a smile and open friendliness. Accepted the offer of coffee and sat on the threadbare couch enduring the tedium of small talk until enough time had passed that she'd fulfilled social obligations and so offered another five thousand shillings if Mary would watch over the captain again.

She used the promise of real food and the last of the sedatives to put the captain under and stayed with him until his eyes closed. On the dirt floor, her back to the wall of sticks, she ordered and reordered pieces on a mental game board, fighting for checkmate against an invisible army and a king she couldn't see while on her side she had but three pawns: Amber; the captain; and the *hawaladar*, who, because of his connections and business, could just as easily be one of the financial backers in the *Favorita*'s hijacking or, for that matter, responsible for Sami's death.

Munroe left the compound for the highway, for another *matatu* into the city. This would be the last time. She'd already kept up patterns for longer than was prudent and every time she returned to her host family she increased the odds of bringing death with her. By tonight she'd have to have a better place to stash the captain.

Unwilling to squander what little strength she had, she stayed off her feet, took a taxi to the nearest Internet café, and there set out the chessboard again, pulling up satellite images of Mombasa. Hunted through the maps for Nehru Road and, finding her target, enlarged over Bishara Street, a smaller road to Nehru's west, gauging rooftops and building shapes, judging distance and pattern, searching out the closest match to what she'd come up against in the *hawaladar*'s alleyway.

She paid for printouts of the maps and, with the pages in hand, left for sidewalks teeming with the daily hustle; made another trip by taxi, this time to the mouth of Bishara Street, and from there followed the narrow road, crowded with smells and heat, squeezing between humanity: measuring, comparing, judging in person and in real time what she had scouted online until she located the match and stopped in front of a white four-story colonial building that angled off the road and stretched back far enough that it abutted against and possibly encroached on the buildings on Nehru Road.

Out of breath and hurting, Munroe found shade and a wall to lean against, dry swallowed another dosage of ibuprofen, and when she could finally push through once more she studied the printouts again, then folded a page and tucked it away. She was close. If this wasn't the building, one of the others nearby would be.

Munroe opened the door and stepped into a long and unlit hallway, where the smell of acrylic lingered, as if the place had recently been painted, masking the age and must that permeated every part of the building. Scuff marks and dirt streaks along the wall made a mockery of the effort at improvement, while high ceilings and transom screens kept the air flowing.

A baton-wielding *askari* was sitting on a folding chair just inside the door stood when she entered. He gave her a half glance and sat down again, asked no questions as she continued on, stopping in front of each door to take note of the businesses that lay beyond: details mounted on plaques to the side of, or painted onto, the doors, most of which were half wood, half translucent glass, like something out of an old detective film.

She found what she wanted at the second-to-last door—a solid door with import/export signage mounted to the wall on one side, and a law office plaque with several names in increasingly smaller print on the other. She took the *hawaladar*'s name off of both: Abdi Geedi Bahdoon.

Then opened the door and stepped inside.

The receptionist stood when she entered and as Munroe continued around her and peered down the hall, the woman stepped forward and then hesitated, as if unsure as to the most appropriate action. Half out from behind her desk and half in the hall, she said, "Can I help you?"

Munroe said, "I'm sorry, I seem to be lost."

"Who do you need?"

"Imperial Tea."

"One door to the right," the woman said.

With the mental map to the interior redrawn, Munroe left once more for the outside heat. She had to walk Bishara Street all the way back to its opening before she found another taxi, a slow effort that leeched off and stole energy she didn't have. The persistent weakness, like getting knocked out in a fight she'd never before lost, was bewildering and frustrating.

At Abdel Nasser Road she flagged down yet another ride for yet another visit to an Internet café and another round of searching. Never a substitute for feeling and touching and breathing, this was a shortcut: a point in the right direction, and in the shortcut she lost an hour to learning what little there was to learn about the man who'd provided her with information on the *Favorita*.

She had his name and from her interaction with him knew where he'd spent his school years, but names were different for Somalis than for people of many other cultures: no surnames of which to speak, rather first names from father and grandfather to act as middle and last names, and nicknames that at times took on a multigenerational legacy.

She found him through school records, followed those threads, adding to what she knew, and then having reached the point where the law of diminishing returns turned further queries into redundancies, she cleared the history and shut down the browser. Left for Nehru Road with enough knowledge to cold-read and bluff her way through to more.

The bodyguard straightened when she approached and she handed him the knife as she'd done a few days earlier; endured the same tedious procedure to get inside. There was no wait in the hall, and when she entered the *hawaladar*'s office, she closed his door with a shove of her foot, a little harder than necessary, and the slam reverberated loudly in the enclosed space.

She didn't drag the chair to the desk as she'd done the last two visits, rather strode to the desk and, refusing to react to the pain screaming in response to the unnatural movement, sat on it and leaned in toward him. He pushed back and away from her encroachment and his gaze assessed her, top to bottom.

"Someone sent a group of street boys to kill me," she said.

"It wasn't me."

"I didn't accuse you."

"All the same."

"Who did it?" she said.

"How should I know?"

"I'm not one for letting slights go," she said. "By my last reckoning, four of the men who came after me are dead. I intend to find the others. I want what you know about the foreign investors and if you refuse to give it, then I will treat you as if you're part of what happened. I won't kill you today, although I could. And not tomorrow, or even the next day, but there's nowhere you can hide that I can't find you and you have to ask yourself, is it really worth it?"

The *hawaladar* faced her, silent for a long while, and although nothing in his expression or in his body language betrayed fear, she could smell a hint of it on his skin and knew she'd made her point.

"I had nothing to do with any attack," he said, and she turned her back to him and stepped for a chair. Dragged it back, sat, and with her arms crossed stayed silent for a long moment to disguise the pain and exhaustion that stole the breath from her and made it impossible to speak without shaking. When she'd recovered enough to put forth an air of control, she said, "I'm listening."

He leaned forward, hands clasped atop the desk. "I extended you a hand of peace, I offered you the little information I did have and asked for nothing in return, and yet you repay me by coming here to threaten me under my own roof?" He stood, and palms to his desk he leaned toward her, lowered his voice, and said, "You've given me nothing but games and riddles and bullying—no reason to want to help you. Cameroonian you say, and yet you come in here so typically American, full of piss and vinegar and righteous fury ready to blow things up. If you think I had something to do with your attack, fine. Do what you plan to do. If you're here to kill me, then go ahead and try to kill me, otherwise you're wasting my time."

"You haven't hit your safety alarm yet," she said.

"You haven't tried to kill me yet."

"I don't want to kill you," she said. "I could do it, finish with it before you got to your alarm, but I think we'd both be happier if you stayed breathing."

"I don't know who did that to you," he said.

"Are you sure? Because rumor has it that *hawala* is a perfect vehicle for funding Islamist extremists and laundering pirate money. Seems like you'd be in a perfect position to know who did it."

He smiled wryly, sat down again, rocked the leather chair back toward the wall, and smoothed down his tie. "I've made my position clear and you either believe me or you don't."

"I'm not worth fucking with," she said.

"And neither am I."

She motioned to her face, her body, threw out another lure to see how he'd bite: "This is connected to the hijacking of that ship. There's something they want and they think I have it."

"Do you have it?"

"Seriously?"

He grinned, as if amused by his own joke. "It was worth a try," he said.

"But you have an idea then, Mr. Bahdoon, of what it is they want?"

His expression tightened in response to her use of his name. "You've been doing some reading," he said. "Was it a dossier from your CIA friends?"

"The name on the door of your office," she said. Stood and walked toward the rear of the room. Ran her fingers along the cinder block and dragged her hand in the direction of nearby shelving. "You'd never be stupid enough to conduct financial transactions in a place with only one in and out, and *hawala* is hardly enough of a business to keep a man like you completely busy. You should have a small army of accountants in here, but you don't. For whatever reason you do this yourself, so I figure the door is"—she paused, tapped the shelving unit—"right about here." She turned to face him. "It wasn't difficult to find you on the other side; you should be more careful."

His focus had tracked her as she walked, and he smiled now as she returned to her chair. "Why do you keep coming to me?" he said. "It should be obvious that I have no interest in getting tangled up in whatever it is you're after."

"But you are," she said. "You are very interested. More interested than any one man should be, and so far, you're the only one who hasn't tried to kill me."

"That you know of," he said.

She paused and returned his smile. "Your reaction to the off-putting American answered that for me," she said. "I keep coming back because you have what I want—I *know* you have what I want. *And* you're the only one who hasn't tried to kill me."

"You want to deal?" he said.

"I want to deal."

"And you have connections?"

"I told you, I'm not CIA."

He waved his hand as if bothering with denials was a waste of her time. "Can you get a job done?"

She nodded.

"What do you know of the law of salvage?" he said.

The question, a derailed train of thought, took her by surprise. "When divers go down to shipwrecks to find treasure," she said.

"Like that," he said. "Partially. Although that isn't always the case. You found my offices; therefore you know I have practiced law?"

She nodded.

"You know my specialty?"

"Admiralty solicitor," she said. "Maritime law."

"Very good," he said. "Your dossiers are accurate. Kenyan law is partially based on English common law. I don't practice here, but it helps in figuring out how to navigate the system. It's my office that you found, but I don't work there. I hire Kenyan lawyers, it's easier that way. As a Somali I'm not trusted here. Hated even."

She nodded out of politeness. Still didn't follow the train of logic.

"How much do you think the ship is worth as scrap?" he said.

"No idea."

"How many years do you think she still has in her?"

"It's not my area of expertise, but I could find out."

"You want to know why I am interested in her?"

Munroe smiled at the redundant question. "Would love to," she said.

"According to the internationally accepted law of salvage, if a ship is clearly in distress and she is saved—salvaged—the rescuers are entitled to twenty-five percent of the value of the ship for the risk and effort."

"The *Favorita* isn't worth the risk of getting killed for twenty-five percent."

"Ah yes, but if the owners do not pay, the ship can be put to auction," he said, and Munroe understood his intent. The chessboard inside her head shifted, and a new strategy arose. He offered to give her what she wanted, believing she'd go after the ship to save what he assumed were her people, provided she brought the ship to him in exchange.

"Does it always work that way?" she said.

"It's not guaranteed. Each country has its own laws, and a suit has to be brought against the ship. I'd have good odds under Kenyan law."

"So if the owners decide an aging freighter isn't worth coughing up the cash to redeem it, never show up, you'll take it all?"

"Yes, if the owners don't claim it."

"You might have trouble finding someone willing to go get it for you with that kind of lackluster guarantee."

"I might," he said, and he studied her knowingly.

"It's not just the twenty-five percent," he said. "If they choose to claim it, they'll also be dealing with the ship's crew, and families, possibly the governments of those families, local officials, inspections, and appraisals."

"And the corruption."

"It does come in handy at times."

"Don't you have connections in Somalia that would allow you to buy the ship off them?"

"Sadly, no. We are dealing with pirates after all. Not even the president himself could convince them to release the ship without ransom, and my connections don't go quite that high."

"Tell me about the financiers for the hijacking," she said. "If it works for me, then we can discuss the *Favorita*."

"There's a Russian delegation in town," he said. "Nothing unusual about that except that they flew in from Galkayo a little over a week ago. How does that work for your timing?"

She breathed down a sigh. Given the origination of the weapons in the hold, she'd suspected a Russian connection, had searched in that direction and turned up nothing, but if it had been Russian investment in the hijacking, then it was all the more relevant that she'd warned off Amber and Natan from traveling to Garacad, because Natan would have been dead as soon as he opened his mouth. "The timing works," she said. "I wish you would have told me this last time."

"I didn't know last time."

She didn't believe him but kept that to herself.

"Do you have names? Itinerary? Anything?"

"They're staying at the Royal Court Hotel," he said. "They are all men, and there are some people in and around Garacad who have nothing good to say about Russians right now." He shrugged, almost apologetically. "That's all I have."

"What were they after? Why go through all that trouble?"

He steepled his fingers and glanced over the top of them. "I think you're in a better position to answer that question than I am."

"I might be able to get you what you want," she said.

"When do you know?"

"Tomorrow. But it won't be free."

"Won't it?"

"There are some lines that won't be crossed, Mr. Bahdoon. I may be able to retrieve this ship for you, but outfitting a crew to do it is beyond my budgetary resources."

"And if you had the financing?"

"I could do it."

"Perhaps we have a common interest," he said. "We should talk."

Munroe said, "Maybe." Stood and took a step toward the door. "Is there a way we could meet away from this place? Somewhere we can speak privately?"

"We are in a space as private as you can hope to get."

"If I'm going to show you my cards, I want to do it in neutral territory where I'm not at a disadvantage, where I can get up and walk away without having to kill you to do it."

"I'm not sure I want to be anywhere alone with you."

"The mistrust runs both ways. Bring your bodyguards."

He smiled again and shook his head in a chiding fashion. "As you wish," he said. "Tomorrow afternoon?"

"The Royal Court Hotel?"

"You're mocking me."

"If I'm going to track down your Russian delegation, I can't waste my time gallivanting around town."

Truth, minus the added bonus that if they were seen by her prey, recognition would be easy to spot, both in the *hawaladar* and in anyone who might know him. He shrugged as if he didn't care one way or the other. "Royal Court Hotel," he said. "One o'clock."

Munroe made her way back to the heart of the city and, one floor up in a six-floor building, found a restaurant that promised Indian food and relative quiet, and put a large dent in the cash in her shoes. At a table near the rear, back to the wall where she could watch the door, she ordered food for two and during the wait dialed Amber Marie. Natan answered and said, "She's outside. I'll get her."

CHAPTER 26

When Amber finally picked up, Munroe said, "If you want to save Leo, don't drive down."

"This isn't news. I took you seriously the first time."

"But you're still planning to go."

"Unless you have a better idea."

"The people who hold the *Favorita* have been screwed over by a group of Russians. Natan goes down there, he's dead on arrival." Munroe paused, and when Amber didn't answer, she said, "What if I told you I had an idea that would not only get Leo but your entire team, the ship's crew, and possibly the ship, an idea that you and Natan need to be a part of in order to properly execute it—would you fly to Mombasa?"

"You're really who you say you are?" Amber said. "The person on that website with that résumé, you're the strategist who figured everything out, the one who made it in and out—that entire list of countries?"

"It's not up-to-date, not comprehensive, but everything there was me."

"You've done an extraction before?"

"Not like this one, but yes."

"And you'll stick with us till the end?"

"If I figure this out right, you won't need me to, but yes, I'll stick around."

"What do you want for it?" Amber said.

The question, switching tracks, took Munroe by surprise.

She'd had no interest in saving Leo for saving's sake; neither had she expected payment. Her continued involvement had turned messy, was a way to bring payback against those who'd sent the street thugs to kill her, a way to avenge a boy who didn't deserve to die, and possibly bring closure for Amber and so wash her conscience of the whole situation.

"We can discuss it later," Munroe said, "after you're here."

"I like to know what my debts and obligations will be before I sign."

"I haven't thought through to what I want or expect," Munroe said. "If you need me to figure that out first, we can waste a few days dickering over details that don't matter and lower the chances of Leo's survival."

"And if we come down, then what?"

"I have a list of equipment you'll need to buy and have shipped in."

"What are you planning, Michael?"

"To hijack the ship back."

Amber started laughing. Spontaneous laughter, as much from surprise as from the absurdity of the statement, and Munroe didn't blame her for that. There had, of course, been other pirate-held ships freed through land-supplied commando raids: scenarios that involved air support, and token local government support, and heavy artillery, and that still nearly ended in disaster. But this, slipping hundreds of miles up the Somali coastline, carrying with them everything they might need, going without backup and no inside intel, this was about as suicidal as driving down into Somalia to try to bribe Leo free. Except, in a country where nothing could be kept secret, if they played it right, they'd have the element of surprise and a way to get back out.

"Let me talk to Natan," Amber said. "I'll call you in an hour."

Munroe's food arrived and she ate until she couldn't anymore;

packed up what was left to eat later and continue the calorie and protein infusion that her body needed to repair the damage it had suffered. Amber called again before Munroe left the restaurant.

"We think you're insane," she said. "But if it's planned and supplied right it might actually work. You really believe this is the best shot we have?"

"Unless I turn up leverage from another direction, yes, this is the best we've got."

"Then we're coming down. What do we need?"

"You have a pen?"

"Yeah."

Munroe started down a mental inventory, items she wouldn't be able to easily acquire locally, if at all, and with each one Amber drew a subtle inhale that expressed what her words did not: The list wasn't short and the pieces weren't cheap; equipment costly enough to put her in the red for the next decade and create a hell of an issue when it came to prying them out of the hands of Kenyan customs agents—an issue Munroe would figure out when the time came. There was always a way and the right pocketbook to line.

Amber said, "Is that everything?"

"I'll try to keep it that way."

"What about weapons and ammunition?"

"I have a local source. It's not worth you guys getting arrested coming into the country."

"I need about a week," Amber said. "And I'm not sure about shipping time lags. I'll expedite what I can."

"It works," Munroe said. "I'll e-mail you a name and an address for the invoices and waybills. You'll fly directly into Mombasa?"

"Possibly Nairobi."

"Find a way to get here without hopscotching, it'll save a lot of headache."

"I'll see what I can do."

"Update me by e-mail," Munroe said; spelled out the e-mail address: "Michael@race-or-die.com. I'll arrange to pick you up. If you have to call at some point and I don't answer, please don't leave a message."

Amber was silent another minute, scribbling. She said, "Michael, you'd better be legit. If this is some throwaway plan you're setting up, using my love for Leo as a way to accomplish one of your assignments, I swear to God I will hunt you down and kill you."

Munroe smiled; tried not to let the smile escape into her voice. "I wouldn't blame you," she said, and then ended the call. Amber did well to be suspicious, but she and Natan would get what they wanted in the bargain.

Munroe sat staring at the phone for a long while. She could have purchased the items up front, handled the air freight herself; and considering the sum of money she had sitting useless, accruing interest in accounts on three continents, it wouldn't have cost her nearly what it cost Amber. But she couldn't do it. Wouldn't. She had no reservations about putting her life at risk but drew the line at paying to rescue the asshole who'd tried to get her killed.

Taking back the *Favorita* wasn't impossible, it just had the potential for a one hundred percent fatality rate. The regret that had filled her during the fight on the beach swept in again—a reminder of the things she'd left unsaid, the unfairness to those left behind if she never came back: those left to wonder and wait and who would eventually try to find a way to stop caring because the unknown was most painful of all. She'd accepted death more often than she cared to count, but things were different this time. There were conversations she'd put off for far too long.

Feet on autopilot, Munroe found her way to the Internet café.

The letters to family and surrogate family came easy: e-mails touched with humor that said nothing about what had recently happened or where she'd been; heartfelt love that hinted at where she was and, if they could read between the lines, the possibility that she might not return, ever.

But she couldn't do that to Bradford. Fingers resting on the keyboard, she puzzled over words that wouldn't come until the physical pain reached the point of being unbearable. She'd lived a life on the edge, without regret, with every choice, every decision no matter how awful, made in full acknowledgment of the responsibility she bore, and with fear fully conquered. Remorse, foreign and unfamiliar, now eroded her soul. She couldn't push him away, didn't want to, really; she just didn't want to feel, didn't want to care. What was the point of caring only to watch those who mattered die? Again. And again.

In reply she bled her heart, vulnerable and naked, onto the screen.

I've been running, Miles. From myself. From the world. But no matter how far I go or where I hide, I am still with me. I'm working again—back in Africa, though on the east coast this time. It's been good for me, but not without consequences. If I get through this job, I am ready to return, but I am afraid. Of myself. Of happiness. I know you understand. You're the only one who ever truly did.

Munroe hit Send without rereading; didn't want the opportunity to change her mind. Cleared the cache and her history and made a lackluster attempt at covering her tracks. She hurt too badly to think clearly anymore, and the desire for medication consumed her. Another minute. She could last another minute. And then maybe another minute after that. Just long enough to get back to the little house and make sure the captain was still there.

THE ROYAL COURT Hotel was a seven-story building that filled the corner of a block not far off Moi Avenue, a hotel that catered more to business guests than tourists, the hotel where, according to the *hawaladar*, the Russian delegation out of Somalia now stayed.

Munroe strolled past the building twice: first to scope out its location relative to the buildings around it, second to get a feel for security, which aside from the standard baton-carrying *askaris* was pretty much nonexistent. On both sides of the building, traffic kept the roads busy, and across the street from the main door, men hung out idly under the eaves that fronted a store with empty windows and a security grille pulled tight and padlocked. With cardboard for chairs, two of them squatted on either side of a *mancala* game, while others sat on concrete steps, smoking, staring at nothing, waiting for work if it should happen to arrive in any form.

Munroe entered the air-conditioned lobby, where white paint reflected the light that reached in from outside and the walls were filled with bright art deco, and the furniture attempted something modern. A handful of guests milled about, all of them foreigners. Munroe strode past the reception desk and wound her way inward as if she knew where she was going.

The architecture was colonial Africa, and no amount of renovation would mask the unmistakable fragrance of age, of a hundred years of humidity and seasonal rains and the resultant mildew that even air-conditioning couldn't prevent. She met hallways and a wide spiral staircase that circled up from the ground floor to the rooftop. Took the stairs one floor up, passed a small restaurant, and found the elevator, and there, accommodating the exhaustion that still plagued her, broke from her preference for traveling on foot and took the lift to the rooftop.

The restaurant up top was closed, so she continued through to the terrace and pool area and found a seat at the bar cabana. Ordered a bottle of water and watched a couple of travelers frolicking in the pool. The building was large enough, had enough rooms, that a simple inquiry at the front desk wasn't going to get her what she wanted, but being able to confine her search to just one building— assuming the *hawaladar*'s information was accurate and that he told the truth—made the hunt doable.

Munroe returned to the lobby, checked in, and wandered the halls again, upstairs, downstairs, kitchen and staff rooms, until the map of the layout had been branded into memory. She left the building through the staff side door, followed the alley, putrid and full of garbage and human waste, scouted the nearby streets, then returned and started over until slipping in and out of the hotel unseen from the front or by the hotel staff was a fluid process.

Finished for the day, she left the hotel and caught something familiar in one of the men playing *mancala* across the street; nearly stepped in front of an overladen bicycle as she strained to look.

He wore a new peach-colored button-down shirt but the same ratty shoes, squatting in front of the game, half turned away. The stockiness of his torso and the odd mixture of his clothes brought on a flood of memory. The bicyclist yelled at her and the *mancala* player glanced in her direction; didn't see or didn't recognize her and returned to the game.

Whether or not the Russian delegation had anything to do with the *Favorita*, one of the men whose hands were dirty with Sami's blood was outside their hotel. Rage and pain rushed through her senses and Munroe tamped down the driving urges that screamed for revenge and retribution. She turned in the opposite direction. This was a fight she couldn't win. Not now. Not in this condition. There were other ways to even the battlefield.

MARY WAS IN the room when Munroe returned, leaned up against the inside wall, arms wrapped around her knees, watching the sleeping man. She smiled when Munroe entered, and Munroe put a finger to her lips, a signal not to wake him. She peeled several bills off a small wad inside her pocket and paid the remainder of what she'd promised, and then beckoned Mary outside.

"I will leave tonight," she said. "Can you find Gabriel and ask him to come with the car?"

"I send for him," Mary said.

"Can you come with me? I can pay you. Five thousand shillings per day—" Munroe stopped and her voice caught. She'd offered Mary—had been paying her—the same money that Sami had asked for when she'd first hired him on.

"For how many day?" Mary said.

"I don't know."

The woman gazed out toward the house as if calculating numbers, trying to find a way, and she said, "Maybe Gabriel can do," and Munroe nodded.

Gabriel would have been the better choice regardless.

Mary called over her oldest daughter, and with discussion and instructions running in the background, Munroe returned to the captain and set about with the supplies she'd picked up at a pharmacy before returning. The captain jerked awake when she took his arm, jerked away farther when he saw the needle.

"What are you doing?" he said.

"Putting you to sleep."

"Is it forever this time?"

"Don't be stupid. I still need you in case I don't find another way to ransom the ship and the crew."

"Why?"

"Why what?"

"Why are you putting me to sleep this time?"

"So I can move you."

"To where?"

"You demand a lot of answers for a man in your predicament."

"Cooperation is better when I know what goes on."

Munroe snorted. Nothing he'd done so far had been cooperation—surveillance and intel gathering and waiting for a chance to slip away were more like it. "There are some Russians in town who want to have a look at you," she said.

The captain's eyes widened, his body stiffened, and his mouth moved as if he had words to say but no voice to say them with: the first genuine reaction he'd shown yet to anything she'd said. Munroe reached for his arm again to administer the sedatives and he jerked away from her, scooted as far away as the rope would allow.

The comment had been a throwaway, an opportunity to test the validity of the *hawaladar's* information against what the captain knew, to discover any obvious link between the Russian delegation and the *Favorita,* and his reaction answered far more eloquently than words.

Munroe let him flail. "This is what I get for answering your questions?" she said.

"Do not take me to them," he said.

"They just want to look."

"No, is not true."

She paused. A fake hesitation, as if the connection had suddenly dawned on her. "Are they the same ones who tried to kill me, you think?"

He studied her, weighing one evil against another. "What do I get in exchange?" he said.

She reached for his wrist again and he pulled away.

"You get a change in plans," she said. "And if you tell me why they want you, I promise not to give you directly to them."

"You give me indirectly?"

"I might still trade you for the *Favorita*."

"But not today?"

"You still have plenty of time to plot your escape," she said, and he glared and shoved his arm in her direction.

CHAPTER 27

There was a form of poetic retribution in hiding the captain in the same hotel where his hunters stayed: chicken in the foxes' den, the least likely place they'd look for him; and even if the killers had managed to get a scan of her passport from the front desk at her hotel on the North Shore, it was unlikely they'd recognize her even if they sat across from her at the dinner table.

Munroe and Gabriel entered the hotel from the alleyway entrance, navigated the captain through storage and staff areas to the hallways, and then to the elevator and up to the fifth floor. Far enough up that the captain would be a fool to try to go out the window—though she didn't put it past him.

The room, clean and efficient, held two double beds, a small desk, and a tiny TV, and was attached to a serviceable bathroom. Like most hotels in the West, and unlike most on the continent, the keys were magnetic cards, which would make coming and going a whole lot less of a headache. She motioned the captain onto the bed farthest from the door and gave the other to Gabriel. Munroe used the foot of Gabriel's bed to fasten the tail of the captain's rope, made sure his bonds were still secure, and left them with Gabriel cradling a hefty stick and a round of instructions given as much for the captain's benefit as for Gabriel's.

She took a detoured loop through the hotel's public space, scoping out the clientele to see if she might bump into anyone who resembled a Russian delegate, and, turning up empty, returned to the rooftop restaurant. She bought drinks she didn't want and a meal she didn't have time to eat, an excuse to mingle with the staff and tip heavily and listen to whispers and conversation that might give her what she needed.

The evening dragged on without profit, so she eventually returned to the room, gave the mostly uneaten meal to Gabriel, and left for the North Shore, for the hotel that had once been home, where the guests were tourists and dressed like it, where she knew the lay of the place and how to get inside rooms that weren't hers.

It took thirty minutes and slipping into four rooms, rifling through clothes and makeup, shoes and hair products, to commandeer the items she wanted: pieces that she would have bought locally if she'd had the time and if she could have found them. With her loot thrown into a bag also taken from one of the rooms, she strolled back through the lobby, took a taxi for the return into the city, walked the last distance to the hotel, and called it the end of an overworked day.

She slipped out of her shoes and lay beside the captain in the same clothes she'd been wearing for days. Dumped a heavy dosage of ibuprofen into her system, but no more morphine. She was done with the painkillers. Not because she didn't hurt, but because she couldn't afford the risk of taking them anymore.

MORNING CAME EARLY and Munroe woke with the sun. She handed Gabriel two books that she'd taken from one of the hotel rooms, something to keep his mind occupied while she was gone. She showered and used the stolen makeup to cover the remaining signs of damage on her face and neck. Changed into clothes that fit her well enough and hung the rest of the items in the closet. To Gabriel she said, "I need everything here. Please don't take anything. Not one thing."

"I don't touch," he said, but she wasn't sure she believed him. It was one thing for her items to remain unmolested while she was a guest in his house and under his sister's roof, another thing now that he was in her place and she was paying him. Left to his own devices and given enough time, he'd likely pilfer everything she had. This was the way of the continent, something to prepare for and deal with without judgment; it just was, like malaria and bad roads and lack of sanitation.

Munroe walked another loop through the restaurants and bar and rooftop and public areas. Tipped well again, and this time asked questions of the staff that eventually netted her eyes to watch and ears to hear; and then, since afternoon had not yet come, she made two separate trips out the front door, head down, glances darting for a look across the street, hoping to find the thug again, the one who'd nearly killed her, another waste of time and another empty quest.

If the delegation was still in the hotel, if they still had work to be done, the thugs would be around. She wanted them dead, but even more she wanted the handler, the local who passed messages one to the next, because surely the foreigners weren't dealing with them directly.

She reached early afternoon with no forward progress, returned to the room. Found Gabriel sleeping and the captain with his feet untied and working on his wrists. He froze when she opened the door and she shook her head and strode to Gabriel's bed and reached for the stick. He woke when she touched it, and seeing what the captain had gotten to while he'd been asleep, jumped to his feet and raised his stick in a threatening manner.

"Hit him," Munroe said.

Gabriel looked askance at her.

"Right there," she said, and pointed to the captain's shin.

The captain jerked his legs back, so Munroe pointed to his upper arm.

Gabriel swung hard—though not as hard as Munroe would have had she had the strength and mobility. The captain gritted his teeth and refused to cry out, though the blow had to have hurt.

"Next time it won't be a stick," she said, and the captain's face remained hard, defiant. "Next time I'll make sure he breaks something."

Gabriel stood with the stick raised in further threat, and Munroe resecured the captain, then tied the tail of the rope around Gabriel's waist so there'd be no getting away without an alerting tug. She rummaged through her things for the last box of morphine tabs. Crushed a dosage and scooped it into a nearly empty water bottle, handed it to the captain. "You drink it or I'm sedating you completely," she said.

He took the water and swallowed it down, continued with silence and closed his eyes. Munroe turned to Gabriel and said, "I'm grateful for everything you and your family have done for me, but this can't happen again. The men who are looking for him are the ones who killed Sami—this keeps him safe, it keeps me safe, and it keeps your family safe. You understand?"

Gabriel nodded and glanced away, an apology she didn't want, a humiliation he didn't deserve. This had been her fault for staying away so long. She'd make an effort to return more frequently, but at the moment she had to leave again for a lunch meeting she couldn't miss.

MUNROE FOUND THE *hawaladar* in the rooftop restaurant, seated at a four-person table in a corner with his back to the window, separated from two of his bodyguards by an empty table: far enough away that they were within reach but not quite within earshot.

She scanned the room before approaching: a restaurant half-full with the lunch crowd. From the cacophony of languages and the visual palette of skin tones, the diners were a mixture of visitors from outside the city and abroad with locals scattered in between. No Russians insofar as she could tell.

The *hawaladar* caught her eye; stood when she approached and greeted her with a handshake far warmer than she'd expected: different environment, different man.

She took the seat next to him instead of the one opposite and kept her own back to a wall. He'd already ordered a salad and half eaten it, and when the waiter approached she ordered the same and allowed the *hawaladar* to lead the conversation, which didn't turn to business until they'd finished the meal and were on the first cup of coffee.

"You've had a chance to discuss my proposal?" he said.

She nodded. "I can do it," she said. "I can arrange for some supplies, but you'll need to commit more than information."

"If I get you what you need, in exchange you bring me the ship?"

"Yes."

"Do you have an idea of what it would take?"

She pulled a piece of paper from her pocket and slid it across the table. He picked it up. Scanned it. "What are the odds you'll be successful?" he said.

"With the element of surprise we have a good chance. Without that, there's no point."

He folded the paper and slipped it into his chest pocket. "I risk losing my entire investment if it goes wrong," he said.

"I risk losing my life."

His lips turned up only slightly. "Just like piracy," he said. "The irony is hard to miss."

"Does that mean we have a deal?"

He handed her a business card. "It's my private line. We can haggle the finer details later," he said. "I have a meeting to get to."

She stayed seated and watched him go. Finished her coffee in silence. There'd been nothing beneath his words or hidden in his body language to point to lies or betrayal, but her trust in him ran only as deep as his own motivation, and when money was the driving force, loyalty was easily purchased by a higher bidder.

MUNROE LEFT THE hotel from the side entrance and cut through alleys until she reached dirt streets and wandered them, asking directions, being pointed along, and finally stopped in front of a construction site. Shielding her eyes, she scanned up the couple of floors to where workers toiled, some barefoot but with hard hats, none harnessed, pushing wheelbarrows filled with cement along wooden planks from one area to the next.

She found a boy at the edge of a pile of quarried stones. He was maybe twelve or thirteen, hustling for odd jobs that might pay him a few bob now and again. Munroe pointed out a line of rebar. "I want this," she said, "two pieces," and she showed him with her hands, measuring out more or less the length of her thigh. "Can you get it?"

"Three hundred bob," he replied, and she nodded.

He ran off and she waited in the shade where she could sit without risking a stray piece of scaffolding or unsecured stone falling on her. Twenty minutes passed and at last the boy returned with the rebar and she exchanged the pieces for money.

She'd been carrying the knife, having hidden the gun beneath the mattress while Gabriel was in the bathroom and the captain was asleep, but the knife was an obvious weapon; she needed something common, and these two pieces would suffice. She asked the boy directions and a few streets over she found a local market of sorts, an alley where artisans, barbers and welders, basket weavers and tailors, had set up makeshift shops and businesses. *Jua kali,* they called it, "hot sun," for those who toiled at their trade out in the open, wherever customers could be had, finding a way to repair or build or do without any formal licensing or education. She located a tailor, his threads and cloth strips set out on a cardboard table and in front of him a pedal-powered sewing machine that he worked with sandal-clad feet.

She showed him the rebar and described what she wanted, and while she sat behind him with a piece of cloth wrapped around her waist and a growing crowd of gawkers in front of him, he sewed thin pockets along the seams of her pant legs, then handed them back to her.

She checked the workmanship, searched for broken threads, and, satisfied, slipped back into the pants, and then, de facto entertainment over, the crowd slowly dispersing, she slid the rebar into the pockets, and paid the man. She had her weapons. This time she was ready.

HER TARGET IN the peach-colored shirt was in front of the hotel playing *mancala* when she returned, and on seeing him again, the rush filled her head, filled her lungs, sent her striding, long steps in his direction, fingers reaching for the pockets along her thighs. In terms of Amber, in terms of Leo, the driving impulse might wreck the entire mission. She didn't care.

Munroe pulled a stick of rebar from its sleeve and approached from behind, slowly enough to avoid drawing attention, fast enough that she had speed and momentum behind her: one chance to get it right, to strike fast and move out of the way and limit the attention from passersby, to avoid starting a riot and getting beaten to death in mob justice.

The man in the peach shirt, still squatting in front of the game, leaned forward on his toes to make a move, and in that moment she swung hard: a left-handed strike to limit the most severe movements to her undamaged side. She connected with every bit of strength she could find, struck his rib cage, felt the crack as it hit, and nearly screamed with the pain that charged through her when it did. He cried out and doubled over, and when the face of the other player rose to hers, she recognized him, too: the man who'd first stopped her on the path, the one who supposedly didn't speak English.

"Remember me?" she said, and through the breath-crushing agony pounding through her chest and arm, she smiled.

He stood, paused a comical half second as if torn between the idea of bolting or challenging her. She said, "Without your friends you're not so tough—just a little boy," and that seemed to fortify him enough to take a step in her direction. He paused again, glanced down at Peach Shirt, who'd since rolled into a ball on the piece of cardboard, then took another step in her direction.

She backed away. Not enough to lose him or allow him to think he'd won or made a point, just enough to keep a safe distance. And when he slowed in hesitation, she taunted him again. "You need eight friends to help you fight?"

The man in peach pulled himself to his feet, listing to the side she'd hit, arm wrapped protectively around his chest. She took another step in retreat, and they both picked up machetes and followed.

She slipped through a break in traffic and taunted them again from across the street, luring them toward the hotel, to the block where she knew every alley, every turn: houses with their doorways and the streets with their sewage, and places where she had walls and ditches for leverage.

They followed more cautiously than she'd expected, as if leery of a trick or a trap, and only after they were behind the hotel, in an area rank, fetid, and strewn with garbage, did they increase speed, and with more confidence closed the distance. She didn't have the strength and physical dexterity to fight them off, but she had the knife and she had the rebar, and all she needed was one really good swing.

CHAPTER 28

Munroe limped on. Turned a quick corner and scurried up on top of a welded cage that held equipment of some sort. Pulled the second piece of rebar from its sleeve and held both together. Waited for the men to come around the building, directly into her path, and with the force of her entire weight brought the metal down onto the head of the second *mancala* player.

He crumpled. Silent. Maybe dead.

The man in peach turned first to his friend, then looked up at her and took a cautious step backward.

She dropped off the cage and shifted the bars, one to each hand.

They were even now: damage for damage and one on one.

Except he held the machete and she had two sticks of metal.

He raised his weapon, took a step forward in challenge; she side-stepped, focused on his breathing, his eyes, the minute expressions of his body that would warn her and give her microseconds of lead time.

She jabbed him with the end of the rebar.

He swung the machete. She spun and slammed the bar down on his forearm hard enough that the reverberation stung her hand, and when he screamed, she did, too. He kept hold of the weapon and struck out wildly, madly, and with each attempt, she hit back.

Pain was out there, somewhere on the edge of awareness, shouting for attention, drowned and muted in adrenaline and the hunt as she struck again, and then again. Even in her weakness she was faster than her opponent.

She took him down in a battering, blow by painful blow, in the way the fists and sticks had nearly taken her life down on the beach, struck until he dropped to his knees and covered his head and pleaded for her to stop—as if he would have stopped had she begged that night when they'd come for her.

Out of breath, lungs stabbing glass shards, body seared with branding irons, she picked up the machete and tossed it into a gutter.

"Who do you work for?" she said, and in Swahili he whimpered, "I don't know."

She kicked him, and he screamed, "I don't know!"

"If you don't know, then you are worthless," she said, and she kicked again, his stomach, his groin.

Hands wrapped protectively around his head, he yelled, "Ibrahiin, Ibrahiin," and Munroe paused.

It was an Arabic name. "A Kenyan?" she said. "Somali?"

"Mix," he said.

She drew back her foot to kick again and he said, "I heard Anton. I heard Anton. I heard Sergey."

"Who are they?"

He was sobbing now. "I don't know."

"Why are you here at this hotel?"

"Waiting for more work," he whimpered. "Waiting for money. Maybe today. Maybe tomorrow."

"Who pays you?"

"Ibrahiin."

"What do you do next?"

"I don't know," he said, and he tipped his face up toward hers. Blood bubbles blew from his nose and he grimaced through a mouth without teeth. "Please let me live," he pleaded.

She loomed over this man who'd tried to kill her, who'd been part of what had killed Sami, who would be dead through glue and the streets soon enough, though only after more crime, more misery. By taking his life she'd be doing the world a favor, might save another in the process. One blow to the head would put an end to him, but she couldn't do it. Not like this. Not in cold blood with him mewling for his life.

She wished him up, wished him to try to kill her again, to fight for his life, to make a lunge at her and so allow instinct to overwhelm reason so she could finish him. But he didn't move. Not even a twitch. She turned away and he gave no evil last hurrah, didn't rise up and come after her in a final attempt at triumph. He stayed on the ground sniveling, defeated.

She lowered the rebar and felt then the first wave of crushing agony that had been but on the periphery in the adrenaline rush of the attack. The alley tilted at odd angles and her head went light. She had to either kill him now, or leave before weakness became her own undoing.

"If I let you live," she said, "then go away. If you return to Ibrahiin, if I see you again, if you talk about what happened here today, I will find you and I will kill you."

She didn't have the resources or the time to track him down, but he didn't know that. He nodded and blubbered and dripped more blood into the mud-slush of the alley. "I promise," he said.

Munroe turned from him, walked away, and the last she saw, he was crawling and pulling himself in the opposite direction, hopefully to die from the injuries she'd already inflicted.

She found a doorstep and collapsed onto it, fought hard to keep her eyes open in the wake of the adrenaline dump, trembled from the hurt as pain levels amped higher and took her back to those first days after the beating.

She needed to get to the hotel. Needed to get morphine back into her system. Stood with effort and limped down the street, one foot in front of the other, until eventually the service entrance was before her though she had no recollection of how she'd gotten to it, or how long it had taken; one foot in front of the other and then she was in the elevator, and then in front of her room and opening the door.

Stumbling, blinded by pain, she somehow found the box of Kapanol and swallowed down a dosage, and somehow Gabriel was beside her, and with the same intuitiveness that had brought him to her on the beach and that had helped her get into her hotel room to collect her things, he helped again now. Walked her to the bed and from the fog said, "Everything is good. You sleep," and she shut her eyes and descended into the dark.

THE RHYTHM OF a flutter pulled her steadily upward and Munroe opened her eyes to a room filled with the low light of the late-afternoon sun, and a book not far from her face, in the captain's lap, and the captain with his back to the wall, turning pages at regular intervals. He glanced down when she opened her eyes and exhaled as if disappointed to find her alive.

Munroe rolled onto her back, stretched through the stiffness, struggled upright, and shifted her feet to the floor. Gabriel, on the other bed, jumped toward her and offered her a hand. "You need help?" he said.

"I'm okay," she whispered, used his arm for leverage, and stood. Shuffled to the closet for an armful of stolen items and carried them to the bathroom. This pain would pass far more quickly than it had in those first few days after the beating, when every small movement was its own living hell and staying still made it that much worse; this was just a small step backward after so many forward, and bearable.

The heat of the water took the remnants of the opiate fog, took most of the stiffness, and when she'd lasted under the pounding stream as long as she could, she stepped from the shower and swallowed a double dose of ibuprofen to pick up where the morphine had left off. Changed into the first of the outfits she'd stolen from the hotel rooms: a loose blouse that allowed her to hide her bandages and a tight knee-length skirt that covered the largest of the bruises on her thighs and accented long legs where the damage had been minor.

Dressed, she stared at the moisturizers, hair product, and makeup she'd collected. Swiped a towel over the steam on the mirror and scrutinized the reflection. It had been a long time since she'd had any need for beauty products, and it felt awkward to apply them to a face she rarely saw anymore.

With fingers no longer as practiced as they had once been, she changed her hair back into something feminine; painted her face into what most people reacted to as beautiful. The transformation was striking—it always was—though for practical purposes the beauty that the stranger in the mirror reflected back was nothing more than a tool through which she could funnel reactions: a way to lower entry barriers because people were inevitably superficial and reacted differently to poison when it was aesthetically pleasing.

Munroe put down the brush, closed her eyes, and, against the exhaustion and low dull pain, drew in the role, the smiles and flirtatiousness, the poise and posture, the charm and seduction that had once been among her quiver of weapons used to beguile secrets out of statesmen.

It had been a long time; maybe too long.

The captain's head ticked up when she stepped out of the bathroom, and he studied her as she walked back to the closet to replace the stolen products. She returned to the foot of his bed and staring down said, "I'm just as capable of killing you while dressed as a woman as I was when I wore pants."

"Are you a woman?" he said.

"Shouldn't matter one way or the other," she said, and with Gabriel sitting watch, she left for the rooftop restaurant, for food and for the hunt, because as long as the Russians were still checked in— and according to the clues dropped to her by the staff she'd been tipping along the way, she believed that they were—as long as she continued to haunt the restaurants at mealtimes, inevitably her prey would have to show, and it was only a matter of time and probability before she ended up in the same place as they.

Munroe stood in the restaurant entrance and scanned the room.

Waited for a hostess, and once seated took her time ordering, and when the food arrived took longer still to eat: a way to drag out the evening and increase her odds that she'd be in the right place at the right time. She was halfway through the entrée when the first words, foreign and familiar, announced the arrival of her targets, and she toyed with her food while, without lifting her head, her eyes scouted for the voices that called her out to play.

The words came from a group of four men, two of whom she placed at early to mid-twenties, a third who was possibly late thirties or early forties, and the last in his fifties at the least, though possibly older. Clothing and hair and the four-day scruff on the younger two said civilians, but their posture and mannerisms and interaction said they were, or had all once been, military of some sort.

Munroe took smaller bites and, over a water-filled wineglass, studied them, five tables down with a couple from Uganda in between—enough distance that the only way to hear the conversation would be to strain: body language that would betray her before she was ready.

Munroe signaled the waiter, spoke to him in Swahili when he arrived. Glanced at the table where her targets ordered drinks and slid a five-hundred-shilling note onto the table. "I want to know what rooms they stay in," she said. "If you can get me that, then this is for you."

"How soon do you need this?" he said.

"Before my meal is finished."

"I will see," he said, and wandered off, and after another few moments of work he exchanged conversation with another staff member, and from there he moved out of sight. She took bites even smaller still and spaced further apart between longer sips of water while the body language of her target table continued to tell her a story, one in which the leader separated from the followers and said that the man in his late thirties was the boss.

When at last, even after the delay, she'd finished her meal and the waiter had still not returned, she ordered dessert and then after that coffee, prolonging the legitimacy of her stay, listening as she could to what few words of Russian wafted in her direction from men who seemed in no hurry to go anywhere, and who ordered drink after drink and slowly became louder.

The conversation was lighthearted: not a celebration but the relaxedness she would otherwise have ascribed to people on business that had been completed. If they were concerned about finding the captain, they certainly didn't show it.

She was on her second cup of coffee, losing patience and ready to move again, when her waiter returned. With the bill for the meal he included a slip of paper with four consecutive room numbers and beside each number a last name.

Munroe slipped payment for the meal onto the small dish on the table and a five-hundred-shilling tip on top of that, and with the waiter beaming a smile, she left the restaurant. She had time. Not a lot. Maybe enough to get through one room before the meal upstairs ended.

She took the elevator to the lobby. There were a handful of guests scattered among the seats and passing through, but none at the front desk. Munroe continued toward the staff, who, caught up in conversation, paid no attention to those who came and went.

Dressed as she was, she marked the male as her target and hands on the counter waited for his attention. When at last he stood and faced her, she smiled, a long, friendly smile, and said, "You're unlucky to have the night shift."

He smiled back.

"What time do you finally get to leave?" she said.

"At five."

"And then a two-hour walk home?"

"You know how it is?"

She nodded. "I've spent a lot of time here—have many friends who do the same. I lost my room key," she said.

He smiled again and asked for her name and room number and she quoted from the paper the waiter had given her.

"Do you have your passport?"

"It's in my room," she whispered.

He grimaced and hesitated, and she slid a twenty-dollar bill over the side of the counter and dropped it toward him. "You can take the bus for a few days," she said. "I don't want to make complications over a key—it's not a big thing."

He gave a nervous peek over his shoulder, confirmed that his deskmate had not seen the exchange, and then went through the process of magnetizing a keycard and handed it over with another smile, thanking the Russian upstairs by name.

She left for the next floor up, for the room she'd chosen at random off the list of four, and paused in the hall listening for voices, for the boisterousness that inevitably followed one too many drinks after a good meal.

In the ensuing hush she used the keycard to slip inside.

The room was smaller than hers: one bed instead of two, and it had been slept on or used as a bench since the maid had last put it back together. She perused the bedroom and bathroom, scanned through the many toiletries and trinkets left out on countertops instead of packed away in the suitcase that lay open on the floor, as if this person had gotten comfortable spreading out, the lived-in way of someone who didn't expect to have to leave on short notice.

She nudged among the items in the open suitcase and then flipped through the clothes hanging in the small closet. Stopped at the sight of the banana clip on the shelf, the AK-47 magazine that had been inside her backpack; picked it up and found familiar markings, and she knew. She'd found her target.

CHAPTER 29

Munroe searched through the rest of the room for more, but there was nothing else that belonged to her. Ear to the door, she listened for movement in the hallway and, in response to the silence, opened it a sliver and then slipped out for round two. Called Amber along the way.

"Things are set on this end," Munroe said. "Are you ready to move?"

"Made the last purchase yesterday and got the tickets. E-mailed you the flight information and a few other details. You didn't get it?"

"I haven't had a chance to check."

"We'll be there in three days. Have you made any progress? Do you know anything more about Leo?"

"I've learned a few things," Munroe said. "I'll update you when you get here. I've got it under control."

"Just tell me now."

"There's nothing about Leo, Amber, nothing that will help you sleep. It's just strategy and tactics and it can wait."

"Okay." Amber sighed and then ended the call.

Munroe took the stairs back up to her own room, a temporary detour from the evening's plans in order to inject another round of disequilibrium into the captain. Gabriel had his back to the wall and the stick in his lap when she entered.

By appearances the captain was asleep, though it could have been a ruse. Leaning over him, Munroe smacked his face.

He lurched and tried to take a swing. "*Dobroe utro,*" she said.

He twisted away from her, confused, glanced toward the window, where the sky was still dark. "Why?" he said.

"Your Russian friends want to see you." She tugged on his elbow as if to hustle him from bed, the movement made to keep him off balance while she calculated his response and fear levels.

He jerked away. "What do they want?"

"I have no idea, though I'm sure you do."

She reached for him again, and he scooted farther away. She motioned him up and he stared at her unblinking.

"Please don't push me to violence," she said. "One way or the other you're leaving this room, and I'd like to deliver you in one piece."

He still didn't move, so she straightened and sighed. "I'm tired of putting up with your escape attempts. It's better for everyone this way."

"Not better for me."

"You shouldn't have been such a pain in the ass—maybe a little more forthcoming when I asked you for help in solving this the easy way."

"They kill me," he said.

She motioned him up again. "They didn't go through the trouble of hijacking the *Favorita* just to kill you. If all they wanted was you dead, they would have blown the ship up."

He responded with silence and an empty expression that said he disagreed but wasn't willing to offer an explanation.

"Come on," she said. Measured his lack of response against how far she'd have to push before he called her bluff or caved and finally started talking. When, after a moment of waiting, he still refused to move, Munroe turned to Gabriel, who'd sat observing from one bed over and said, "I'll need your help. We're going to get him to the elevator and down two floors." She produced the keycard given to her at the front desk, room number scrawled across the sleeve; held it so the captain couldn't help but see it. "They gave me the key to where we're supposed to deliver him."

The captain flinched again, and when Gabriel stood to help get him off the bed, he took a swing with bound wrists and clenched fists. Gabriel dodged back.

"You won't take me," the captain said.

"We will," Munroe said, and she reached for him again, and when he lunged and tried to hit her, she struck back, elbow into the side of his head, base of her palm up under his jaw. He was knocked back against the wall with enough force that he stopped struggling and lay still, blinking up at her.

She swore in a low growl, turned her back to him, and stalked to the bathroom, where she could breathe through the hurt that the force and movement had brought on. Hands to the sink, head tipped toward it, she panted and hoped to hell that she hadn't just put the captain back into whatever head trauma he'd so recently come out of. Minutes ticked on and the hurt subsided, and when at last she returned to the room, the captain was spitting blood and Gabriel was on the second bed again, staring at the ceiling with a smirk that said he'd taken matters into his own hands.

"Aleksey Petrov," the captain said. "Alexander. Alexander Petrov." And Munroe said, "Excuse me?"

"Is information for you," he said and, hands raised to his mouth, swiped blood off with his wrist. "Maybe you take some time to find it, maybe postpone a little this meeting with new friends."

She glanced at Gabriel. "Keep watch on him," she said, and left the room.

So he'd given her a name—not one on the waiter's list—toyed with her just enough to send her hunting, to buy what he thought was time. The stress in his voice, his anxiety, told her that whatever this name meant, it wasn't a red herring.

It was too late in the day to return to an Internet café, and she wouldn't risk using the hotel's business center. She'd start chasing shadows in the morning.

The upstairs restaurant was empty and Munroe passed through to the pool and cabana bar, where music filled the rooftop and guests stood laughing and drinking in small clusters. She spotted one of the Russians among them, bought a drink, a prop to play with through the night, and wound her way to the edge of where he stood, avoiding eye contact and moving in from the side so that she never faced him directly and never encroached on his personal space.

He was one of the younger two, chatting in broken English with a German woman who seemed to be twice his age and whose English wasn't a whole lot better. Ham-handed come-ons and crude flirtatiousness passed between them in botched attempts at communication, and when the Russian, frustrated with the inability to communicate, said a word in his native tongue, Munroe took the opening. Face still turned toward the pool, she spoke loudly enough that they would hear; interpreted for him, Russian to German.

Both of them turned, annoyed. She smiled. Raised a hand and said, "Sorry." And so it went as their conversation continued, another word interpreted here, another there, until gradually the ice thawed and she became part of the conversation, and eventually the sieve through which the conversation strained, and at last the focus of the conversation so that by the time the evening had ended the other woman had wandered off, and the Russian had turned his aggressive hitting toward Munroe. She dodged the coarseness with a smile and an apology for an early morning at work and the promise of another evening. He grabbed a napkin and wrote his name and phone number, handed it to her with a verbal invitation to a party the following night, which she accepted.

She left him standing alone and glanced back once to wink, and walked away smiling. She'd found the Sergey over whom the man in the alley had sputtered blood bubbles; had already been in his room, could get back in if she wanted, now with or without the key.

ALONE IN THE quiet of her bathroom, Munroe stripped out of the trappings of femininity, let the hot water run long, and washed away the remnants from her hair and off her face, processing the conversation of the evening and the encounter with her first target until the pieces had been properly categorized. Dressed in the clothes she'd previously worn. Needed to find a way to get them clean, though at the moment smelling good was the least of her worries, and in this environment she blended in with every stink around her. She swallowed another dose of ibuprofen to soften the edges and lay beside the captain, counting on his movement to keep her from falling into deep sleep, yet exhaustion overtook her and when she woke the sun was high in the sky.

Even with the windows closed and the air conditioner running, the city noise from the streets reached up from below, life in full swing, gone on without her. Disoriented and sleep drunk, her body's protests louder than when she'd first lain down, she groaned and dropped her legs over the bed, rolled to get to her feet. In the bathroom she ran cold water over her head and, when finally fully awake, examined her bruises and tugged gently on the stitches that ran down her side to encourage them in their falling out and ease the itching. Then, already late for a day in which she had no time to spare, she paid Gabriel for yesterday's work and left the hotel for the hot and muggy morning, the belching dust and traffic, for Internet access a few blocks over and the name that the captain had used to pay for another night of captivity.

It took digging to uncover the trail. The name was common enough that it turned up more hits than she had time to sort through, but she stayed with news coverage, preferring the botched autotranslated versions to the tedium of trying to translate Russian Cyrillic into something her faulty wiring could interpret into sound. Within the mixed phraseology were scant details that led to clues—although clues to what, exactly, was difficult to say: Alexander Petrov, if she'd found the *right* Petrov, was a recently appointed first deputy minister with the Russian Ministry of Defense: the first connection she'd come across that even remotely tied the weapons in the *Favorita*'s hold to any other part of the hijacking or killings: Russian made, Russian sourced, the munitions that Leo had likely given his life for were the one puzzle piece all the players in this madness continued to ignore.

Munroe left the Internet café and on the way back to the hotel bought boiled eggs and fried plantains from a street vendor. Carried the greasy food wrapped in newspaper up to the room and gave it to Gabriel. He ate and Munroe sat on the bed staring at the captain. No words, and although at first he matched her stare, his eye contact became less consistent as the food portions dwindled until there were only a few bites of plantain and one egg left and his focus turned completely to Gabriel's breakfast and he said, "I too have hunger."

Munroe held out a hand toward Gabriel, motioning for what was left, and he brought it to her. "I'll be leaving again soon," she said. "If you want to shower, now is a good time."

He left them for the bathroom and Munroe set the food in front of her. To the captain she said, "First we talk, and if we have a good talk, then you can eat."

He turned from her toward the window. Looked out at nothing and said, "Am not so hungry to sell my soul for food."

"I think your soul's already been bought and sold a few times." She leaned forward and whispered, "Look, my only interest in keeping you is to find a way to get the crew off the ship and to track down the person who did this. You help me get what I need and we can forget the Russians—I'll let you go—you can walk away and continue on as you've been."

He shrugged, face turned up toward the ceiling and then back toward the food, and Munroe rolled the egg in her hands, peeled the shell in a slow succession of movements, then handed it to him. When he reached for it, she pulled her phone from her pocket and snapped a picture.

"Why do you do that?" he said.

"Proof that you're alive."

His cheeks flushed: anger or shame, she couldn't tell. Probably a mixture of both; she'd taken him by surprise, and the last thing someone in his position would want was a photograph floating loose.

"Who are they?" Munroe said. "These men who want you."

Mouth full of egg, the captain said, "I told you this already."

"You gave me a name," she said. "That doesn't get me very far, so it doesn't help you much if you want to avoid being turned over to them. I need more than that. Who are they? Why do they want you?"

In answer he sighed down words he wouldn't speak, never took his eyes off the soggy newspaper. She handed it to him. He shoveled the few bites into his mouth and the grease from the plantains dripped down into his beard. He rubbed the smear off with his sleeve and wadded the paper, clenched it in his hands, and said, "You let me go, not let me go, is the same. I never go back to the way before. Maybe I run and hide, but no more ships. You make that problem fix, then I can tell you everything."

She got off the bed. Took the newspaper from him and tossed it into the garbage. If she fixed anything she'd do it for herself, not to save his ass, and the clumsy attempt to manipulate her into cleaning up his mess would have been amusing if keeping him alive hadn't already left a trail of bodies. "You want me to fix it," she said, "tell me who you are and what they want with you."

He glanced up, as if trying to determine if she was actually capable of solving his problems, and in his hesitation was the sliver of an inroad she'd been waiting for. She turned her back to him. Strode to the bathroom; knocked on the door.

Gabriel opened, towel wrapped around his waist.

"You ready?" Munroe said.

"Very nearly."

Munroe closed the door and didn't so much as acknowledge the captain. He'd ceased to exist. As soon as Gabriel stepped back into the room, Munroe left for the hall. The abrupt end, walking away before the captain had a chance to articulate his lies and schemes, would give him time to stew without ever knowing how far he could push or if she even cared enough to negotiate at all.

CHAPTER 30

Munroe left the hotel by way of the staff entrance and stepped out to the front long enough to determine that the thugs hadn't returned. At the *matatu* depot she found an empty share taxi and haggled over a day rate with the driver. They drove north, another trip over the Nyali Bridge with the hot breeze and dust blowing through the broken windows; through traffic that slowed around car-size potholes, a fit of stops and starts until they were fully away from the city, up the Mombasa–Malindi road, past the hotels and resorts, up to where the stretches between buildings grew emptier and to where, although expatriates were likely, tourists were a rarity. She had no set destination in mind, only an idea of what she needed and the memory of what she'd seen from the boat on that first arrival in Mombasa.

A small cluster of makeshift structures dotted the highway edges up ahead, more stick than stall, and for these roadside sellers Munroe had the driver stop. They were markers pointing to the proximity of villages and population clusters.

In the slow banter of bargaining, Munroe inquired about empty houses, about owners looking to rent; a line of seeking that netted her questions and references to cousins or uncles or friends, but nothing solid, so she returned to the car with her items and they continued on again and then stopped again, vendor to vendor, while bush meat and dried fish and more fruit made its way into the car.

The tedium drew long into the afternoon, and the evening invitation that would bring her closer to the men responsible for Sami's murder and her own beating called Munroe back to the city. Without finding what she was after, she'd be forced to repeat this trip tomorrow, which was a problem insofar as Amber and Natan's arrival was concerned.

Munroe spotted another rack of drying meat ahead and asked the driver to pull over yet again. The vendor was a gray-haired man with leathery skin, knobby knees, and a red-and-orange cloth wrapped around his waist. With him was a young boy, perhaps nine or ten years old.

The alcohol on the old man's breath was strong and his eyes were cloudy, but in response to her question about houses, he stood and leaned against a rough-hewn walking stick, its top-knob polished by what had to be several decades of use.

In beautifully articulated English he said, "My son has a house to let."

She doubted that he'd accurately pegged the definition of "has," but as he offered to show the way, she offered the front seat of the car, and they left the boy behind with the rack of bush meat.

The driver followed the old man's hand signals down a dirt road that cut through thick foliage toward the coast, a kilometer at least before they diverted to a smaller turnoff, and came at last to a stone wall with an open metal gate and stopped in front of a single-story house.

Munroe stepped from the car and breathed in the air; knew the ocean was close from the smell. A barefoot young man in cutoff pants and a ripped T-shirt came from the house. Seeing the old man, he smiled, and the two conversed in slow sentences that Munroe didn't understand, and then the young man turned to her and introduced himself as James.

If he was the old man's son, then the old man had been busy late in life—the boy couldn't have been but seventeen or eighteen. When Munroe let go of his hand, she said, "Your father says you have a house available."

"I can give you keys," he said. "For how long do you need it?"

"Three weeks."

"I can give you for two."

If he was willing to hand over the keys, she was willing to talk money—she shouldn't need the property longer than a week, week and a half tops. "I'd like to look inside," she said, and he opened the door and invited her in.

The house had two bedrooms, one bathroom, and a windowless maid's room the size of a walk-in closet, semifurnished, with a generator and a functional kitchen and running water fed from a cistern on the roof. She walked from the living area through a back door that opened twenty feet shy of the sand, which sloped long down to the shore. There were no piers to tie off to, but they could make do without them. She negotiated the rate low enough that only someone without a vested interest in the property would have taken it, an informal arrangement made solely on a handshake. "I'll pay you by the day," she said. "You give me the keys now, I pay for today. I'll return tomorrow with the next payment."

James handed her a key and with it she locked and unlocked the front door to confirm it was the correct one. She left her many food purchases in the kitchen. Had a fifty-fifty chance they'd still be there when she returned, but she wasn't about to take them back to the hotel. Walked around the house and worked the lock on the rear door, then handed James twenty dollars' worth of shillings with the promise that she'd be back by tomorrow's nightfall.

Evening had fallen by the time the driver returned her to the hotel, and when she stepped inside the room, the captain turned toward her, face swollen, blood clotted near his forehead where he'd apparently taken a blow. Gabriel sat across from him, the stick in his lap, and Munroe said, "He tried to escape again?"

"Yes, and he try fight me."

Munroe stepped around to the captain. He winced and pulled away when she tried to examine a wound that was minor, if a bleeder. "Very nice," she said. "You keep getting knocked in the head and eventually you're going to go out again—that'll make my life easier but probably won't help you much." She straightened and turned toward Gabriel. "You did good," she said. "Thank you." Pulled out five hundred shillings and handed it to him. "I'll pay you for the work when you get back. Go celebrate a job well done, get something to eat."

He nodded and stood, took the money, and when he'd gone, Munroe sat on his bed and sighed. Pulled off her shoes, picked up the stick, and, resting her hand on it, lay back on the bed. Felt the captain's gaze boring into her. Eyes closed and face toward the ceiling she said, "I offered you a shot at freedom. Just take it. It'll be easier than getting beat up every day."

He was silent a long while and then said, "I agree to help you and you untie me, let me go?"

"We save the crew on the *Favorita* and *then* I let you go."

"Is still a death sentence."

"Maybe," she said, then opened her eyes and turned to look at him. "But it's still a better option than your Russian friends."

The tendrils of exhaustion wound up from the bed, pulling her downward. She closed her eyes again. "Why do they want you so badly?" she whispered.

The captain harrumphed and shifted, perhaps turned his back. She could feel that he'd stopped watching her, so she ignored him and allowed herself the luxury of falling in and out of uneasy sleep until Gabriel returned.

He sat on the captain's bed and she handed the stick off to him. Left for the shower and cold water to bring her fully awake, then changed into the next set of stolen clothes, and as she'd done the evening before, transformed her hair and face and drew in the mental shift, the character transformation, a change she could feel inside her chest, inside her head, as she pulled in each long breath.

Every run for information, whether the target was male or female, was seduction in the highest form: The conquest happened first inside the mind. Tonight should have been an afterthought, the type of routine work that in years gone by she would have done on the fly, invigorated by the challenge of triumph. Instead, the fatigue of indifference and the words from the book came back again: *What did it profit to gain the world and lose your soul?*

What would she give in exchange?

SERGEY WAS ALREADY in the lobby when she arrived, and although he'd told her that they would be partying with a group, they left the hotel alone. Traveling by private car outside the city, they took the Likoni ferry south to the party playground of tourists, to a beach-side restaurant tucked in among villas and stately homes that lined the shore. It was a place without a name, a place one had to know to find, which indicated either that the Russian delegation had been in Mombasa longer than the *hawaladar* had let on or that they had local connections who were familiar with the area.

The driver parked and opened the rear door.

Hand on arm, Munroe followed her date into the restaurant, where, even though it was still early by holiday standards, the party had clearly been going on for some time. The main room was one large circle, an oversize Tahitian-style hut with a ceiling at least thirty feet high and sides open to the night, screened in against insects, and lit by colorful lights.

Munroe nursed a drink through the first hour while those around her drowned in liquor and music and dance. Sergey became more inebriated, his coarse flirting with other women less veiled, and so she left him and wandered among the guests, listening to threads of conversation that had no common language or common tone and more often than not resorted back to English and banality and made a mockery of the time she'd wasted coming here.

Two hours in, the three other men from the Russian delegation arrived with an entourage of local women. Munroe watched her date, and when he left off his desperate vying for a brunette's attention to join his group, she exited her own conversation, timing her approach so that she arrived at the same time he did. Made it through another round of introductions, another round of drinks, placed faces to the names on her list; absorbed group dynamics and the women that had come along, and eventually singled out Alice, the youngest, who belonged to Anton, the boss of the group, and sidled up to her in a form of camaraderie.

From Alice, Munroe learned the patterns of the delegation, of the haunts that they visited and the money that they spent, learned what they ate and drank and how they occupied their time, what made them laugh, but most important, whom they wined and dined. And in Alice's recognition of people in the room Munroe began to assemble a map of threads and connections. This was consuming work that pulled her back to that different life and different time, a world of secrets and adrenaline and high-stakes information, and only when her date encouraged her toward the exit did she realize that six hours had passed. His interruption forced her up for air, and in breaking from the focus of the assignment, she felt her own fatigue.

Munroe followed him without protest; his car was the fastest and safest way to return to the city. In the backseat he pawed at her with drunken advances and in response she laughed and pushed him back, ran the fine line between encouragement and offense, seduction and aggression, an invitation to another night and the urge to slit his throat.

GABRIEL WAS AWAKE when Munroe returned to the room, holding vigil by the desk with the small lamp on and one of the books she'd stolen between his hands. He looked up when the door opened, and seeing her, he smiled and said, "You had good night?"

"Yes," she said, and glanced toward his bed, empty and inviting.

"You go sleep," he said, and so she stripped out of the blouse and replaced it with the T-shirt and lay on the empty bed. Eyes closed, she listened to the tempo of the captain's breathing, a slow and steady rhythm not nearly as slow or steady as it should have been, which told her he'd woken when she came in and preferred that she not know it.

She managed a few hours of rest before sunrise came, and then with a pillow over her head managed a few more after that until the effort became pointless and she rose and showered and reverted back to her old clothes. She ordered room service for Gabriel and herself, ate what she wanted and gave the captain what was left over, and with her obligations satisfied, left the hotel once more for the *matatu* depot.

It took fifteen minutes of asking around, of leads and phone calls and dead ends, to find a reliable van to rent for the day, and when she'd finally negotiated the rate and secured the driver, she had him take her to the Mombasa airport, where, among the many other parked vehicles, they waited.

The flight was scheduled to arrive at midmorning, and close to noon Munroe spotted them, Amber first, followed by Natan pushing a luggage cart piled high with suitcases and duffel bags. Amber squinted right, then left, shielding her eyes against the bright light of the outdoors, searching through the milling crowds, while touts and taxi drivers and money changers vied for her business and attention and Natan forcefully pushed them back to make space for the cart: all part of the maddening rush of arrival.

CHAPTER 31

Munroe left the van and maneuvered around bodies to move in Amber's direction, and when Amber glanced up again and made eye contact, her expression twisted between a smile and tears and she pushed toward Munroe and threw her arms around her neck in a hug that she never would have attempted in Djibouti.

Munroe's body revolted and the pain in her chest burned hot. She drew down a breath and patted Amber's back with as much warmth as she could muster and then when the hug became claustrophobic and suffocating, she gently pushed Amber away. Natan was beside them now, with the cart, and Munroe shook his hand. He gripped her hand far harder than was necessary, held on longer than was expected, as if making a point, and Munroe didn't need the act of dominance to feel the animosity.

She nodded at his ankle and he said, "It's good now."

Amber took Munroe's hand again and Munroe fought the urge to shrug her off, managed a good three meters before her fingers began to sweat and the claustrophobia kicked in again, and with the anxiety mounting, she had to let go. Munroe put her hand on Amber's back, guided her toward the van, while Natan followed.

The driver loaded their stuff and Munroe slid the side door open.

Amber stepped in and slipped onto the back bench. "How long do we have the van?" she said.

"Just today," Munroe said, and Natan lifted a duffel, knocked into Munroe as he put it on the floor by Amber's feet, and then climbed into the van and in the process brushed hard against her without even a pretense of apology.

She didn't have the physical strength to take him down and make a point, so she slid the door shut and let him have his passive-aggressive fit. Waited until the last of the bags were loaded in the back and climbed into the passenger seat. Using Swahili so that Natan wouldn't understand, a way to needle him by shutting him out, she told the driver to take them to the Royal Court Hotel.

They were five minutes down the road before Amber spoke. "Was that Somali?" she said.

"Swahili."

"You speak that, too?"

"Working on it," Munroe said, and the driver, checking Amber in his rearview, said, "He speaks very well."

The rest of the ride into the city was a mixture of silence and stories: Amber grilling for what little information Munroe had, and Natan sitting with arms crossed, staring out the window through sunglasses. At the hotel Munroe guided the driver around the block and down the street onto which the staff door led and, stepping from the van, said, "It's going to be twenty minutes at least before I get back down, so sit tight, okay?"

"Where are you going?" Amber said, and Munroe shut the door without answering. Headed inside and up to the room, where Gabriel, on the floor beside the desk, back to the wall and knees bent, struggled to stay awake. The look on the captain's face said that he'd been biding his time, just waiting for another opportunity to get loose, and that she'd inadvertently thwarted his plan.

Gabriel picked up the stick and got to his feet.

"Any escape attempts?" Munroe said.

Gabriel shook his head. "He has been good."

Munroe cleared out the closet and dumped her few belongings into a plastic bag and in Swahili that had gotten clearer as the days had progressed said, "I'm moving the *mzee* today. I think it's better that you don't stay with us. The people who killed Sami will be looking for us, and Mary needs you."

Gabriel was thoughtful for a moment, and she knew he was weighing risk against reward. In the end he didn't offer to continue working, so she closed out the matter. "Come with us until we have the *mzee* in his new home, and then I will take you home and pay you everything that I owe you."

"We go now?" he said.

She nodded. "Now."

Gabriel held on to the stick and picked up her bags and motioned the captain up. "Where are we going?" the captain said.

"On a little trip," she said.

A glimpse of panic crossed his face. "I will give you more information," he said. "Another name."

She took his elbow and nudged him upward. He resisted at first, but Gabriel stood beside the bed and held the stick high in the threat of another hit, so the older man grudgingly got to his feet and as Munroe prodded him toward Gabriel, he said, "Nikola Goran."

She nodded. Wasn't in the mood for playing guess who. Knelt beside the bed and loosened the sheets, and then slowly, to avoid straining, pulled them off, and repeated the procedure with the second bed. Wadded the bedding into tight balls and handed them to Gabriel. He opened his mouth in protest and she said, "They'll blame me, not you. They'll put the expense on my bill."

He took them, and fingers to the captain's back, Munroe prodded him toward the door. To Gabriel she said, "Check the hall. Tell me when it's empty."

"Nikola Goran," the captain said again. "It's my name."

Gabriel said, "It's empty," and Munroe pushed the captain onward again.

"Nikola Goran, Nikola Goran," he said again, and she said, "I heard you the first time," and that was when the first yelp came out of him, a scream for help, and Munroe slugged him in the kidney and regretted it for the pain she caused herself.

The captain sagged slightly and nearly tripped over his own feet.

"You can shut up now," she hissed, "or I'll cut off your ears and then take you directly to the people who want you."

"You don't take me there now?"

"No," she said, and shoved him into the hall.

A door opened behind them and Munroe turned for a quick look. Noted another guest and pushed the captain on faster and this time his pace picked up willingly. The Russians might spot her bringing him down, but they'd been up late, and from the conversation the evening before she knew they had no plans for anything until tonight; they, too, were in a holding pattern, waiting for something.

They made it to the staff exit, observed by both employees and guests, but without confrontation, and continued out into the alley to the waiting van. Munroe guided the captain into the far rear seat and had Gabriel sit with him as guard, then slammed the door and took the front passenger seat and in Swahili instructed the driver to take the bridge north.

They were on their way and pushing out of the city when Natan said, "Who are the guys in the back?"

"The reason the *Favorita* was hijacked," Munroe said, and if either Natan or Amber saw past the facial hair and recognized the captain from when they'd dropped the crew off at the port, they didn't mention it. "They both speak English," Munroe said, and for Natan's benefit added, "and the old guy speaks Russian." She smiled and turned her back to him and they rode in silence until they neared the turnoff for the property, and Munroe guided the driver toward the coast.

James stepped from inside the house when they arrived, notice that he had a second key, and Munroe left the van and paid him for it, and asked him to come see her again tomorrow evening; watched as he walked off with a lazy languid stride, and when he'd gotten far toward the beach, she opened the front door.

Amber and Natan followed her in while Gabriel waited with the captain.

"You guys can take the two bedrooms," Munroe said. "I'll room with Nikola," which was about the same as offering to share space in a dark closet, though she didn't plan to spend much time there. "I have a few sheets, but they'll need to be washed."

"We have sleeping bags," Amber said.

Natan dropped his duffel on the threshold of one of the rooms and walked the inside of the house, checking the windows and doors, and then without a word left for the outside, presumably to scout the security of the perimeter. When they were alone, Amber said, "I still don't understand why the old man is with us."

"He's the captain of the *Favorita*," Munroe said. "He's also what the hijackers are after and the best bartering chip we have for getting out if we run into trouble."

"Does he know this?"

"He has an idea."

"Which explains the guy guarding him."

"Yeah. I saved the captain's life, Gabriel saved my life," Munroe said, and she turned back to glance through the open front door to the van, where the driver stood leaning against the hood, smoking, and Gabriel and the captain were still sitting in the sweltering backseat. "What goes around comes around," she said. "I figure that between us we can keep the captain contained, so I'm sending Gabriel home today—I'd rather another bystander not end up dead from this thing."

"How many are dead already?"

"Not counting whatever mess is left on the *Favorita*, there's been one here in Mombasa that I know of—there could be others."

"And almost you," Amber said, though her voice inflected up, as if it were more question than statement.

"It's a long story," Munroe said. "I'll tell you all about it when you're settled."

Amber nodded, shrugged out of the straps of the backpack she'd carried in, and let it drop to the floor. Natan walked alongside one of the windows and continued on beyond the house toward the ocean, and in the uncomfortable silence both of them turned to watch him.

Munroe said, "You and I both know that as much as you care about the rest of the guys being held on the *Favorita,* you're doing this for Leo. What's Natan's reason?"

"For all of them, I think," Amber said.

"Loyalty?"

"Probably guilt or shame. He should have been there."

"We don't know if any of them are alive. We don't know if Leo is alive."

"Yeah," Amber said, and she sighed, and then, as if finding a way to change the subject, said, "What's your reason?"

"For you, maybe for the ship's crew."

"Not because it's the right thing to do?"

"The right thing to do would be to let Leo find his own salvation."

Amber crossed her arms and raised her eyebrows.

"He brought this on himself," Munroe said. "And everyone with him knew what they were getting into. They put their lives at risk willingly, unlike the ship's crew, who had nothing to do with it."

Amber stared. Munroe shrugged and looked out toward the van, where in the backseat the captain appeared to be getting testy. She turned and met Amber's gaze. "Let's say I was doing it for Leo," she said. "Is he worth it?"

"What do you mean?"

"You're about to risk everything for this man, Amber. From my perspective he's a douchebag of the highest order. You'll be in debt for the next, what? Ten years? Fifteen? And hopefully not dead in a week—all for standing by him. Does he deserve your loyalty?"

"You're an asshole, Michael."

"Agreed. But that doesn't answer my question."

"How do you measure what someone deserves?"

"Only you can."

"Yeah, well then, yes," Amber said, and her chin tipped up. "He deserves my loyalty."

"He'd do the same for you?"

"In a heartbeat."

"You're sure about that?"

"Enough to put my life on it, which I am."

"That's all fine and good," Munroe said. "But we go through all this, and I find out that a year later he's cheating on you, or beating on you, or that you guys are separated because of dumb married shit, I'll be pissed off enough to come hunt him down and finish off what we should never have started today."

Amber crossed her arms, defensive, defiant. "You'll never know him the way I know him."

"God, I hope not," Munroe said. "And I hope to hell he's worth it."

"I can only go forward," Amber said. "I refuse to live a life of loss and never knowing, always wondering if things would have been different if I'd fought harder. If Leo's dead, I'll come to terms with that—" Her voice caught. "Eventually. I'll come to terms with it knowing that I did everything I could, that I didn't roll over and play dead. Like you said, only I can decide if he's worth it."

"And?"

"I'm proving it with my life."

"And with mine."

"That's your choice. You seem to have your reasons. You're certainly not going for Leo."

"No," Munroe said, "I'm not," and she turned and strode through the front door toward the van, motioning Gabriel out. Pointed a finger at the captain and said, "Get out, walk to the house, don't try my patience, or I'll break your fucking leg."

CHAPTER 32

Munroe situated the captain in the windowless maid's room. Made sure he had water and had used the toilet before locking him inside and securing the door from the outside with a chair beneath the handle.

Amber watched from down the hall but said nothing.

"I've got to get back into town," Munroe said. "Need to get Gabriel home and run a few errands. If I manage to get back tonight, it'll probably be late—don't let Natan kill me coming in."

Amber shook her head and gave a half smile.

"I'm not kidding," Munroe said. "Do you have copies of the air waybills for any of the shipments?"

"Yeah," Amber said, and from her backpack she pulled out a small file folder and thumbed through a few pages, handed four of them to Munroe.

Munroe scanned the details and tucked the pages into a pocket.

"If you take your eye off the captain for even ten minutes," she said, "I guarantee he's going to try to run. Might be a good idea for one of you to sleep in the doorway."

"I'll take responsibility for him."

Munroe nodded. Fished the knife out of her plastic bag of belongings; debated taking the handgun, but it just wasn't worth the risk of getting caught with it, and she was never as comfortable with a gun as with a knife anyway. She hooked the knife sheath onto her makeshift belt, left the house, and climbed back into the van.

They stopped just north of Gabriel's family's compound and Munroe stepped out with him while the driver waited in the vehicle; they walked until they were out of sight and she paid Gabriel the last of what she owed him. Between the days that both he and Mary had helped her, she'd dropped at least a half year's wages in their hands, a windfall that would likely disappear into drink and gambling as quickly as it had come. She shook Gabriel's hand and then put an arm around his shoulders and said, "Be smart and stay safe, okay?"

"You do also," he said, and she nodded, turned, and left him there.

Perhaps in his intuition, in his daily experience of hustling those tourists brave enough to walk the beach, he'd developed the smarts and determination to defy the odds, would invest the money, use it to better their lives. Mary would have been the wiser choice for that, the women always were, but she hadn't been the one to do most of the work.

Munroe had the van drop her off at the mouth of Bishara Street. It was late enough in the afternoon that she expected the *hawala-dar* to have already left his alley office for his professional one, and although she could have called to find out, she wanted the surprise of showing up face-to-face as a way to gauge through his expression and body language what she still didn't trust from his words.

He offered a hand when she entered, and when she reached to shake it, he said, "No threats for me today?"

She grinned. "I have the base for loading supplies," she said. "You have the dhow?"

"I promised."

She handed him a slip of paper on which she'd written, turn by turn and landmark, directions to the house on the far North Shore, studied his reaction when he browsed the details, saw no hint of treachery in his expression.

Gifting him directions to where she slept, to where her catch was housed, was the same as handing him a knife and offering him an opportunity to stick it in her back. As vulnerable as this made her, hers was a preemptive strike against betrayal. If he would turn on her, better that he did it now than wait until she'd traveled several hundred miles up the coast and had no other way out.

"You still have a phone?" he said.

She nodded.

"I can give my men your number?"

"Yes, but if I don't pick up, they shouldn't leave a message."

"I will have them there tomorrow morning. Call me if there are issues."

"I'll need you to clear some supplies out of customs for me."

"When do they arrive?"

"Day after tomorrow."

"Do you have papers?"

"If you have a photocopy machine."

The *hawaladar* called for his receptionist, and Munroe handed him Amber's paperwork, documents that listed the *hawaladar* as the consignee and his company as the receiver. He shook his head in disapproval and she read the resignation on his face. "You've taken liberties," he said.

"Only small ones."

He turned one of the pages toward her and tapped the date. "Before we agreed to this venture jointly," he said.

"True."

He raised his eyebrows as if waiting for an explanation.

"I'll get the items myself if I have to," she said. "Same as I would have if you hadn't signed on for this. It's not too late to change your mind."

As with the directions to the property that she'd just given, if he was going to screw her over, this was cheaper than dying.

"Is there anything illegal mixed in with these items?"

"Not that I know of."

"It'll be easier that way," he said. He raised an eyebrow. "What are you getting out of this?"

"I get the crew back."

The *hawaladar*'s lips twisted in a slow rejection of the idea and he shook his head as if deep in thought. "I stand to make at least twenty-five percent of the ship's value," he said, "one hundred percent if the owners fail to claim it and pay me. But even knowing this you've never asked me for a cut, only information and the supplies you'd need to capture the ship." He paused and she stayed quiet. "I feel I am missing something," he said.

She smiled. "Would you like to cut me in?"

He smiled back and shook his head.

"Don't worry about me," she said. "If all goes according to plan, you'll get your ship and I'll get everything I need."

He continued to glance over the bills of lading and then grunted approval. "You've done this before," he said, and since it wasn't a question, Munroe didn't bother correcting him. His continuing to ascribe her actions to covert U.S. government involvement meant the less chance of him turning on her.

MUNROE LEFT THE *hawaladar*'s office, original waybills tucked into a pocket, and made her way to one of the Internet cafés she'd used a few days prior. Reached it minutes before closing time, offered the proprietor double the price if he'd let her stay an extra half hour, and when he agreed, she took a terminal and searched for the second name the captain had given her: Nikola Goran.

This was an easier trail to follow than that of the deputy minister. As with the first search, she found her answer in news coverage, war coverage: Bosnia during the height of Yugoslavia's coming undone in the early nineties, brutal coverage that associated the name Nikola Goran with genocide and mass graves, the name of a man who'd disappeared after the war and was still wanted for crimes against humanity.

There were pictures of Nikola as a younger man, most of them grainy, but the similarity was close enough that if Munroe took away the ocean-weathered skin and the facial hair and the paunch of age, this Serbian colonel resembled the Russian master of the *Favorita*. Which made absolutely no sense. Oh sure, that the men might be one and the same, yes. But that someone within Russia would have used pirates to act as cover to capture an alleged war criminal a quarter century after the war—no connection, not even an abstract one. It wasn't as though the guys in town were modern-day Simon Wiesenthals tracking down evil to bring it to justice. These guys were their own kind of criminal. And the only commonality that tied them together was the weapons in the hold, and that only by implication.

She printed enough to keep track of what she'd learned and then tried e-mail again, and this time a response from Bradford waited for her:

> *Home is where you are and what you make of it. It's a terrifying thing to taste happiness—to WANT—when the threat of losing what you want is always right around the corner. Trust me, I know. There's no shame in that fear, Michael. You once said that you're already dead and that every day is a debt waiting to be claimed. Maybe now it's time to burn the chit, maybe now it's time to choose to be happy, maybe now it's finally time to live.*

His few words said what no one else would ever understand, and she read the paragraph again, and then a third time, and although tempted to print it and take it with her, she wouldn't risk exposing the connection to him—not to the people who'd tried to kill her, not to Amber or Natan.

She had no words for what she barely understood, would write again when her thoughts weren't hijacked by emotion, but left him a reply.

> *I'm heading to Somalia in a few days. If I make it back, I will find you. As you say, maybe now it's time to live. If I don't turn up again in the next three or four weeks, then it's time to open my will. Please tell Logan I love him and that I'm sorry. PS: I haven't forgotten. I may have disappeared for a while, but always means always.*

Munroe paid the bill, nearly the last of her shillings, which meant she'd need to stop at a forex to change more dollars soon, and they'd be closed by now. And she was down to her last two thousand dollars. If she had any hope of getting out of the country on her own dime when this was finished, then only half of the dollars were available for expenses, which was about the same thing as being broke. She could access accounts from Europe, but none of the banks she used had branches in Kenya, which meant that from here on out money was going to be a problem, and she no longer had the luxury of hiring private cars and taxis.

Munroe found a grocery store still open, bought several boxes of packaged food and bottled water and, hiring help from a porter on the street, carried the boxes to the bus station. Counting out what shillings she had left, she negotiated the fare for a one-way ride.

IT WAS DARK when Munroe stepped off the bus. Still not healed enough to lift and carry the boxes, she left them on the dirt shoulder; waited until the bus had continued out of sight. Then, once certain she was alone, she shoved them by foot into nearby bushes and walked the rest of the way to the house.

Unlocked the front door and opened it to a gun in her face.

Remained motionless until Natan had lowered the weapon. "Killing me would be a bad idea," she said. When he'd tucked the weapon away, she said, "There's food for us out by the highway, but I'm not able to carry it." He hesitated a moment, as if he couldn't understand the why behind her statement, so she added, "I need your help."

Natan called out to Amber to let her know he was leaving the house, followed Munroe out because that was the only appropriate response she'd left him, and they walked in silence along the rutted track, between trees and foliage that grew thick along the sides, the crunch of dirt beneath their shoes loud against the buzzing mosquitoes and insects and the subtle sounds of coastal night.

They'd gone three hundred meters at least before Natan spoke.

"Amber has told me what she knows of the hijacking," he said. "She's also told me what she knows of you. It's not a lot."

The neutrality of his words was underlined and punctuated by the same simmering accusations that had accented his actions throughout the day; a tacit indictment that, spoken to someone else, might have invited defensiveness and far too much talking. Instead, their footsteps crunched in the silence.

They reached the boxes and she pointed them out.

"They're small," Natan said.

"Yes."

"You can't carry them?"

"No," she said.

He turned from the boxes to face her directly, took a step into her personal space, and her hand reached for the knife on her belt.

"Every day you climbed to the rooftop next door," he said, "and here you can't even carry these?" He leaned down, lifted the first of the two boxes, which probably didn't weigh but ten or fifteen pounds. "Turning into a girl did this to you?"

"No," she said. "Two fractured ribs did this to me."

He grunted. Stacked the second box on top of the first, picked them both up, and heaved them onto a shoulder, and they began the return trip to the house.

After several minutes Natan said, "You got the fractures during the hijacking?"

"After the hijacking."

"I don't understand how you got off the ship," he said: another subtle jab and not-so-subtle accusation.

"I went over the side and took one of the attack boats."

"Very convenient for you that it was there waiting."

"It was also very convenient that I speak Somali."

"You could have fought with them. You and your supposed skill. You could have made a difference."

"Yeah," she said. "Would have too, if Leo had agreed to cut me in, paid me what he was paying everyone else, you included."

"You abandoned your team," Natan said, and he spat the words with far more venom than the point required. "The plan to hijack the ship back, what is this? Atonement? Apology?"

Munroe paused, breathed past the rising anger. His rush to condemn wasn't bait meant to taunt or prod her into revealing information; his was a genuine smug self-righteousness, and it provoked the same rage as Leo's arrogant dismissal when she'd found the weapons and he'd denied her what was fair.

"They weren't my team," she said. "Yours, but not mine, and if you want to point fingers, point one at yourself. You colluded with Leo to put what you thought was an ignorant eighteen-year-old kid on the ship when you, just like Leo, knew the risks. You should have been there and you know it. Don't project your guilt onto me."

He turned and with his free hand jabbed a finger toward her chest. Instinct overrode caution and the threat of pain. She batted his hand away and moved into his personal space before she'd taken a breath, and it was clear that the response, which he should have anticipated based on what he now knew, took him by surprise.

He stood awkwardly, with one hand balancing the boxes on his shoulder, while they remained chest to chest and she read the calculation in his eyes. She stayed in his space, breathing his air, until at last he laughed as if she were a joke, exhaled, and took a half step back. "You are using Amber and me for something," he said.

"I'm going after the ship," she said, "for Amber, maybe Victor, for the ship's crew, who didn't have a choice in any of this."

"No," Natan said. "That would be altruistic. There is no such thing, not even for Mother Teresa." He jabbed his finger at her again, careful to keep it from touching her. "A feeling of goodness, scoring bonus with God, whatever the reason, even the saintly get something for the sacrifice, and you are no saint. You are not doing this out of goodness. You have a motive and it's not noble."

"You don't believe in altruism?" she said.

"No."

"Good. Neither do I, so we both agree that since Leo refused to pay me for my work, I was under no obligation to save his ass."

Natan's mouth opened, then shut, then opened again, and he said, "But you pretend to save it now."

"Confusing, isn't it?" she said, and she smiled a fake smile. "Like I told you, I'm going after the ship."

CHAPTER 33

They reached the front door and Munroe opened it. Amber stood in the hallway with a rifle raised toward the door, same as Natan had when she'd first returned, as if the two of them expected an assault on the house at any time—wariness that would certainly come in handy if the Russians did get wind of the hideaway. "I told you guys not to bring weapons," Munroe said.

Amber lowered the gun. "It was our call. Our necks if we got caught."

"There's food in the boxes," Munroe said. "Is the captain still here?"

"He's in the room."

"When did you last check?"

"When Natan left with you. He's sleeping."

"Supposedly. He say anything while I've been gone?"

"He's asked a few times who you are, but nothing more than that."

"Didn't ask about you and Natan?"

"Nope, just you," Amber said. "I gave him the same story you told us when you came looking for work." Then she paused. The absurdity settled in, and she snickered, and then the snicker turned into a snort, and then into laughter, and her laughter was infectious and Munroe laughed too.

Natan huffed and brushed past with a box under each arm and carried the supplies into the kitchen. Let them down with a thud loud enough that it filtered back into the foyer. When the laughter subsided, Amber said, "You look pretty rough. When's the last time you ate?"

When was it? Dinner yesterday? Munroe shook her head.

"Slept?"

"Off and on."

"I know there's a lot of tension right now," Amber said, and nodded toward the kitchen, where sounds of containers being dumped against the tiled counter reached out. "He's being a drama queen. Just let it go. And no matter what his problem is, I trust you—I appreciate what you've done so far, appreciate your sticking with us. After what Leo did to you, this really isn't your fight."

"Thank you," Munroe said, and left it at that. Amber's was an empathetic gesture, especially considering she wasn't even aware of the full extent of Leo's betrayal. Amber said, "If you want to sleep, I can watch your prisoner."

"I got it," Munroe said, and she moved for the kitchen.

Amber hovered and when Munroe glanced back, Amber said, "It's good working with you again, Michael. Wish the circumstances could be different, but I've missed you."

Munroe stood a moment facing her, then offered a small smile and continued on. Pain levels that had risen tremendously over the past hours had amped higher in her smack-back against Natan, and now that he was out of sight the full impact wound through her limbs and left her shaking. She needed rest. Needed food even more.

When she walked into the kitchen, Natan turned and left. Munroe ignored him. Running this rescue would be a whole lot easier if it didn't involve dealing with a grown man with the emotional development of a thirteen-year-old. She picked out a couple of eggs and a packet of *maandazi*, deep-fried dough pieces, the Kenyan version of doughnuts, which would have enough carbs and calories to bolster her energy levels. Opened a bottle of water, drank half of it down, and wiped her mouth on her sleeve, while in the living area Natan conferred with Amber in hushed clipped conversation, his hands chopping the air with angry punctuation.

AT THE WATERLINE the waves rolled in, low and slow in their long approach to the beach, and Munroe sat just beyond the water's reach and drew in the ocean air and the last of the calm of solitude. From behind, beyond the house, came an approaching rumble that broke the morning stillness. The heat hadn't started yet, but it would come soon. Another sunrise, another day alive, another debt waiting to be claimed.

She'd woken before the sun, and much as she had on the rooftop in Djibouti, she'd come to the water's edge waiting for the light to rise. She'd roused the captain when she'd gotten up, allowed him to bathe and to use the threadbare sheet from the bed as a sarong of sorts so that he could wash out the clothes he'd lived in for the past several days, and then returned him to his room and left him there, the door barricaded again by the chair.

The truck had already shut off by the time she reached the front of the house. The taste of burned diesel still hung in the air, and the three men who'd been in the snub-nosed cab had climbed out and now stood by the open doors in a silent standoff, their attention turned toward the front of the house, where Natan and Amber casually filled the front door's threshold.

There were no weapons visible, but they were surely at hand, both with the mercenaries and within easy reach of the visitors, somewhere inside the truck cab. Munroe called out a hello in Somali and all five turned to face her, an instant break in the tension. The man on the passenger side of the truck lifted aviator sunglasses and walked in her direction. Like his two compatriots, he was dressed casually, collared short-sleeved pullover shirt, baggy jeans that had seen extended wear, and imported sports shoes. No jewelry or watch, but there was an outline of a cell phone in his pocket, and he carried himself confidently enough that it seemed he was used to giving orders.

Munroe extended a hand, and when he reached her, he took it and said, "Are you Michael?"

She nodded. "Khalid?"

"Yes," he said, and his English was crisp and articulate with a tinge of British, like the *hawaladar*'s. Cousin, the *hawaladar* had said, although in this part of the world *cousin* could mean any member of the extended family no matter how far removed. Munroe glanced toward the back of the truck, dented and rusted, an uncovered shell with rails too high for her to view the contents from the ground. "May I?" she said, and Khalid took a step back as if to give her space.

She used the rear tire as a boost, a wheel lashed to the axle with a cut of two-by-four and rope instead of lug nuts, pulled herself up with her right hand so as not to put another round of strain on the weakened ribs, but getting up was still its own form of torture. She scanned the contents of the truck bed, then dropped off and dusted her hands on her pants.

The *hawaladar* had held true to his word: fuel, generator, air compressor, drinking water, food, and shade. Weapons would come later. She said, "Do you want to unload here or bring the truck around to the shore?"

"Let me see the spot first," Khalid said.

Munroe turned toward Amber and Natan, both still glaring and silent. The men showing up on the property wasn't a surprise; she'd briefed them on the truck's pending arrival, so it shouldn't have been an issue. Munroe waved and said, "I've got it. Relax."

Natan turned on his heels and stomped inside, and it was easy to imagine that he'd found someplace that he could use to keep an eye on the newcomers through a scope.

Munroe shook hands with the other two Somali men and they introduced themselves as Omar and Ali. Like Khalid's, their English was clean and articulate, though without the undertones of having been educated abroad. Amber left her perch by the door, approached the truck, and stood by Munroe, and when Munroe introduced her to Khalid, Amber held out a hand, and in an awkward shuffling he didn't accept, and neither did Omar or Ali.

"It's a cultural thing," Munroe said. One example out of thousands as to why she dressed and carried herself as a boy so much of the time. "Not personal."

Amber's brow furrowed, but she was smart enough not to say anything. The men might, in their own time, discover Munroe's gender, but by then the cultural and religious boundaries would already have been crossed so often that for the sake of the job they would continue as though nothing had changed. Munroe led Khalid down to the beach, and Amber followed a few feet behind.

THE DHOW ARRIVED in the late afternoon, a forty-foot wooden vessel with a high bow, twin engines, and a rattan roof on posts that provided shade for the back half. Calls and shouts that came from the outside pulled Munroe out of a hazy heat-induced sleep, and she rose from the rough-hewn bench that passed for a sofa. Locked the front door from the inside and then left the house through the rear. Stood on the small porch watching the arrival, shading her eyes from the afternoon sun, while the boat slowed and dropped anchor a few hundred meters offshore, just beyond the break.

The truck, which had been backed down to the edge of the sand since morning, had drawn the attention of nearby villagers. The number of onlookers had ebbed and flowed throughout the day and at the moment eight men and boys were seated under the shade of a mango tree at the edge of the property, staring at the parked vehicle and the lazy lack of movement as if the circus had come to town.

Amber left the house and stood beside Munroe, and then together they strode down to the sand and sat on the beach to watch while the two men on the boat lowered a pirogue over the side and one paddled in to shore.

"Where's Natan?" Munroe said.

"Up in a tree somewhere, maybe."

"He doesn't trust them?"

"Natan doesn't trust anybody."

"What about you?"

"You know what you're doing," Amber said. "That's all I need. Natan knows it too, he just doesn't like it."

The pirogue neared the waterline and the three men from the truck went into the water to push it up along the sand. They handled the little craft deftly, and Munroe studied their movements, gauged their ability to work together. They weren't strangers to the ocean, and that would be a plus; she waited until the men were back up on the shore and then stood and shook the sand off her pants. They knew what needed to get done and she'd only be in the way and cause animosity if she started handing out orders. She returned to the house, to the kitchen, and collected food and water for the captain.

She left the door open while he ate so that air could circulate and lessen the smell of sweat and body odor. He would have heard the commotion throughout the morning, and an information void was its own form of questioning. She allowed him time and silence and he made it halfway through his meager meal before he said, "Who makes all the noise outside?"

"We're preparing for the next phase of the project," she said.

"You are going to Somalia?"

"We. We are going to Somalia, unless you'd rather go to the Russians."

"There are no good choices," he said, and he continued to eat, so she let him be. After another few minutes he said, "You find the name I give you?"

"Both names," she said. "You've managed to stay hidden for a long time."

He nodded as if to affirm the obvious and said, "You believe everything you read?"

She'd proven printed facts wrong so often that she rarely believed *anything* she read, and that the people who wanted him had hijacked his ship some twenty years after he'd gone on the run only strengthened her lack of belief. "I'd be interested in hearing your version of events," she said.

He set the last of the food aside and drank down half a liter of water. "Nothing good will come from telling," he said, and wiped his mouth, lay back, and closed his eyes. "Maybe you figure it out by yourself. Then you know."

"Perhaps," she said, and stood and stepped into the hall.

Found Natan waiting there, weapon slung over his shoulder, leaned back, one leg kicked up against the opposite wall. It was as if he'd been listening to the conversation while waiting for her, suspicion and mistrust worn like a shirt, as if from his point of view every move she made was a potential betrayal, as if she'd just come from conspiring with the captain and the Somalis on the property were planning to kidnap them all and deliver them to pirates once they were under way.

Munroe shut the door and sent the captain back into darkness, resecured the handle with the chair, and when she'd finished, Natan straightened and took a step forward and in doing so blocked her path. She made to inch beyond him and he stepped directly in front of her.

Without the energy or desire to try to out-alpha him, she sighed and said, "If you have something to say, say it. Otherwise, get out of my way."

He glowered for several long seconds before stepping aside in a movement that wasn't deference but rather magnanimous wish granting.

Amber had moved to the porch, so Munroe sat next to her and, like the crowd of onlookers under the mango tree, lazed in the shade swatting away flies, watching as two of the Somali men paddled the pirogue out to the dhow, placed a fuel barrel within straps to be raised onto the vessel, and then paddled back for another turn loading: one slow trip at a time; the way of a continent where time and manual labor were the cheapest commodities of all.

CHAPTER 34

The truck rolled off the property before dawn, a belching, creaking, crawling lurch up the gutted track between trees and overgrown vegetation, and Munroe braced her feet against the peeling vinyl of the dash to keep from getting tossed about. They'd left Khalid and one of the men from the dhow behind. Omar, as driver and presumably the one in charge, had invited Munroe to take the passenger seat, relegating Ali and the second boatman to the truck bed.

Munroe called the *hawaladar* along the way, confirmed their progress, and updated him with details that Khalid would already have told him, and they rode the long journey into the city for the airport, an inconvenient trip that detoured them back onto the island, and then off again, west as if they were to make the slog to Nairobi, then south again toward the airport and the complex of stone and concrete walls and metal roofs that warehoused airfreight through the customs-clearing process.

Munroe stepped from the truck to an area dry and dusty, where even the aggressive grass and foliage couldn't compete with the trampling of far too many footsteps. Omar pointed out the *hawaladar*'s Land Rover, and Munroe walked in its direction while the men from the truck clambered out, found shade near the front tires, and sat there, content to wait.

The rear door of the Land Rover opened before she reached it, and the *hawaladar* invited her into the air-conditioning. She said, "I didn't expect to see you here."

"We're in a hurry and there will be a lot of hands to fill," he said.

"I figured you'd have one of your people handle that."

"It will be faster if I do," he said, and she knew what he meant.

The clearing process was a madness of pushing paper: multiple queues that amounted to mobs fighting for space in first-come first-serve lines that were never lines; seemingly endless rounds of paperwork transferred from authorized stamp to authorized stamp; money changing hands to keep files from becoming permanently stuck at the bottom of piles; money changing hands to revalue items and minimize duty paid; and eventually somewhere in the bowels of the process, money changing hands for access to those with the power to put an end to the ordeal, cutting days into hours by decreasing the number of additional desks the paperwork had to traverse.

It was never the knowledge of how it was done that shortened time and cost, it was always where the connections tied, and this was what had made Munroe valuable in Djibouti, though Leo and Amber could never appreciate how valuable.

"How long do you think it will be?" she said.

"If the right people are in their office today, maybe late afternoon."

She opened the door. "Have Omar give me a call before they head back. I need the ride."

"You won't stay?"

"There's no reason," she said. Stepped back out into the muggy humidity. "Soon as anyone sees a white face, the price will go up."

"I'll let you know," he said, and she shut the door.

Munroe found Omar on the ground in the shade of the truck, a mat rolled out beneath him, while Ali and the man from the boat whom the others called Yusuf were seated on a mat one over, pulling khat leaves from a plastic bag, cans of 7UP beside them: the first khat use she'd seen in the *hawaladar*'s men, and although irritating, it was better to be aware now before her life was in their hands.

She sat beside Omar and said, "No khat for you?"

He shook his head and she read disgust in his face and knew that she'd found an ally. "What about Khalid?"

"No," he said.

She nodded toward Ali and Yusuf. "There won't be khat when we travel," she said. "Will it be a problem?"

"I think no," he said. Shrugged. "Maybe."

She stood. A handful of khat addicts beginning withdrawals when clarity was most crucial would definitely be a problem.

"Let me see your phone," she said, and Omar handed it to her. She punched in her number and handed it back. "Call me before you go back. I'll be in the city. I need to return with you." She smiled. "Don't leave me here."

"I'll call," he said, though she had her doubts.

She left him for the guard shack that was the freight depot exit, continued past other parked trucks and men lounging in the shade the way the *hawaladar*'s men did now, continued beyond the exit, walked to the nearest junction, and under the shade of a palm cluster waited for vehicles to pass, utilizing the dichotomy of the continent and the privilege of white skin to hitch a ride with a car heading back to the city.

Her host was a portly man in shirt and tie, with sweat stains bleeding out where the air conditioner had left off. Confirming that he was headed in the same direction as she, he invited her into the passenger seat and filled the drive with friendly questions that she satisfied with generic answers twisted back into questions about his work and life so that she kept him talking. He wandered on about the Kenyan Wildlife Service, and her mind traveled elsewhere, filling in the blanks of conversation with just enough to give the impression of being present until they reached Mombasa.

He left her in the middle of Moi Avenue and she waited at the curb until traffic had swallowed him, then walked to the nearest tower and found a bistro on the ground floor; stayed long enough to eat and catch her breath. She called the Royal Court Hotel and asked for Sergey, was redirected to his room, and with the confirmation that the delegation was still at the hotel, she hung up before the line connected.

Munroe found a forex to change a few hundred dollars and then another Internet café. There, she sent the picture of the captain on her phone to her e-mail and from her e-mail printed it out; scanned through e-mail subjects before closing, caught another from Bradford.

Don't know if you will get this—just want you to know I'm thinking of you. Be safe. Stay alive. Assignment is ending here and I just got a call from a friend for a baby-sitting gig. I think I'll take it—I need a break as much as you do. Consider coming with me? Escape the world for a little bit?

She wanted what he offered, the idea of riding off into the proverbial sunset; a want that had haunted her over the years and that she'd fought against, always choosing the hard way because pain was comfortable and familiar, and in emptiness there was never a risk of loss because she had nothing to lose.

Munroe paused, fingers over the keyboard, and with an inhale and a sigh, typed the words that even now violated instinct and self-preservation.

Tell me where and when and if I get through this, I'll run away with you.

She hovered the mouse over the Send icon longer than necessary, closed her eyes, and clicked. Then shut down her session and cleared the history, paid for the page she'd printed, and made her way back, one busy street corner to the next, and returned to the hotel.

The street thugs weren't out by the abandoned storefront when she arrived, so she entered through the main doors and passed through the lobby, noting guests and staff, and took the stairs up a floor to the room for which she still had the key. Swiped the card to test the lock, and although she didn't expect the magnetic strip to still be active, the door clicked open.

She waited in the hall for a reaction—voices, movement,

something—but there was nothing, so she stepped inside and shut the door. The bed was unmade, belongings left carelessly about, tempting theft, nothing giving the appearance that the occupant would be moving anytime soon. She perused the items in the closet, the suitcase, took time to look under the mattress and in places she would have thought to hide anything worth hiding. Found Sergey's passport taped to the bottom of a drawer; thumbed through it. His was a Russian diplomatic booklet, with only a single page filled with stamps.

She slipped it into a pocket.

It might take him a few days to discover it missing, and without travel documents, he'd be stuck here for as long as it took to have it replaced. Nearest embassy was in Nairobi, so it could be a few days; it would buy her time. Given how much he drank, he could only blame himself for losing it.

She found five hundred dollars stuffed in a crack behind the air-conditioning unit and took that, too. Tracked back over the room to be sure she'd left it as she'd found it, then returned to the hall and then to the lobby.

Different staff members meant a different tack for obtaining a new key, so she strode to the desk and slapped the keycard down hard.

Both women's heads jerked up and in her direction.

"You gave me the key to the wrong room," she said. "Four rooms and you'd think you could get them right."

"I'm sorry?" the nearest woman said.

Munroe studied her chest long enough to be obvious about read-ing the name tag, then held eye contact and silence far into the terri-tory of uncomfortable, and when the woman glanced away and then back again, Munroe said, "This key doesn't open my room, Betsy. It opens the room next door to mine."

Betsy looked down at the card and at Munroe's fingers, which remained resting on top of it. "I apologize," she said. "We will correct that."

Munroe said, "Good." Slid the card in Betsy's direction and, tapping her fingers against the counter in a show of impatience, recited the name-and-room-number combination off her list. This time, Anton, the thirtysomething-year-old boss.

Perhaps rattled by the accusation or the display of impatience, Betsy didn't ask for identification, so Munroe didn't intensify the act or resort to another round of bribery. Instead, the desk clerk offered three minutes of blaring uncomfortable silence while Munroe huffed in obvious annoyance and Betsy fumbled and punched buttons and at last swiped the new card and with another apology handed it across the counter.

New key in hand, Munroe took the stairs again and let herself into the boss man's room. Anton, unlike the slob next door, had left his bed partially made and kept his belongings neat, not to the point of OCD, but close. She found her backpack in the closet together with the rest of her belongings, minus the magazine from the AK-47.

As she'd done in the first room, she scoured the hiding places, searching for another passport, documents, anything that might provide insight into who had instigated the hijacking, what they wanted with the captain, or how long they'd stay. In an unlocked attaché case she found personal papers and photographs and she pulled out the pictures and studied them, looking past the smiles and the faces for the secrets they held—these were the loved ones he cherished and they told a story about the man, though not anything that would draw the noose tight or speed revenge to a close. She replaced the pages and left the printed photograph of the captain on the counter.

Using a pen from the attaché case, she wrote across the bottom: *He is still here. Do you want him? Let us make a trade.* And with her purpose for this visit accomplished, she returned to the closet and took a change of clothes from her backpack. Stripped out of what she was wearing and swapped old clothes for new. Rolled the castoffs into a bundle, then fished out her knives and took those, too, and with more time flown than she'd planned, left for the hall and the staff exit.

A bundle would draw attention, so in an extravagant waste she dumped the dirty clothes just outside the exit and went back to the hotel front for one last confirmation that the street thugs had still not returned.

There were other men playing *mancala,* and not far beyond them others still who sat idle, staring into nothing, either drunk or high, but none of whom she recognized. Though it was possible that the fight in the alley had left the last of the street gang skittish enough to abandon future job offers, the more likely scenario was that the two she'd led into the trap had been in no condition to pass along the message, and if the others weren't at the front waiting, they were instead out doing dirty work.

Munroe left the hotel for Bishara Street and Nehru Road, for the *hawaladar*'s offices and the opportunity to feel what went on in his absence, and like the night that Sami had died, warning that something was wrong reached her before she arrived. The notice came through silences, through hiccups and broken patterns, in the way that those idling near the building watched the entrance, and the way that the building swallowed the sound and chaos of the street so that the melee of life continued everywhere but there.

Instinct tuning for threat, searching for the warning that someone had come looking for her and feeling nothing, she pushed open the door. The *askari* lay unconscious on the floor. Munroe released the knives and, scanning the hall and the doors, knelt, felt for a pulse. Feeling life, she continued on, a blade in each fist.

The hammer of typewriter keys clacked out from beyond the nearest office door, but beyond that, the building was quiet. The several doors along the hall were closed, unmolested, but for the *hawaladar*'s office, which lay gaping open, the door listing off one of its hinges as if it had been kicked in. Splinters of the shattered door frame littered the hall, and Munroe approached from the side, tipped her head in to get a look, and then followed into the reception area, where the one piece of art had been torn from the wall and the sofa shredded. The receptionist lay on the floor, blood seeping from a wound on her head, curled in a ball as if trying to protect herself from a bludgeoning.

As she'd done at the front, Munroe paused to feel for life, and sensing shallow breathing, she continued past for the first office, where file cabinets had been overturned and papers scattered, as if the hunters had been looking for documents, not people. She moved on, room to room, found more of the same mess but no more bodies, and finally reached the office that she assumed connected this building to the *hawaladar*'s place off the alley on Nehru Road.

It, too, was trashed, but not more than the other rooms. If the intruders had been looking for a way to the other side, they'd missed it completely, and unless this was a random act of violence, which didn't seem likely, there were few culprits at whom to point fingers.

Munroe crossed into the next room, also tossed and shredded, also without any additional victims, which was odd. She would have expected more people at work at this time of day. She stood, staring at the wall, processing the mess she'd wandered into, trying to place it within the larger puzzle, when a sniffle and the slightest shuffle of footsteps whispered in from far down the hall, perhaps outside the office itself.

The only way out was through the front, so Munroe backed into the wall beside the door frame. The footsteps neared, the sporadic sniffle grew louder, and she separated the sound into two people, at least. A whisper followed and, with it, furtive movement that confirmed that whoever had walked through the door had not come as a friend.

CHAPTER 35

Instinctively and without thought Munroe balanced her knives while, eyes closed, her ears drew in careless footfalls on the other side of the wall and measured movement by their progress.

Whispered Swahili carried to her, saying, "How many came in?"

"Only one."

Then a third voice answered, "Are you sure? Maybe he left already."

Poised for a strike, the knives grew warm in her hands, extensions of her body, comforting, soothing in the lullaby of death. In the anticipation of the coming attack, calm descended and the world grew silent and slow. A heartbeat carried out long. Clarity drowned in time while the broken stop-start squeak of rubber against the tiles announced a clumsy tiptoe forward and men near enough that she marked them by their breathing and the intermittent sniffle.

She smelled him first, other senses drawing in what sight denied her, felt him approach before the machete and hand appeared outside the door, and then ripped and torn pants. The shadow of his body filled the doorway. Heartbeat pounding with recognition, she waited for him to step fully into the room, working against rage, running the odds of taking at least one man alive to try to learn from him what she'd been unable to get from the thug in the alley.

He turned and saw her. Made eye contact, hesitated only a second, and swung the machete. Instinct overwhelmed reason. She stepped aside. With his own momentum, she pulled him fully into the room and in that same movement struck in self-preservation, plunged knife to throat and cut off his air, his scream: a fight over before he was aware of its having started; a fight already won a decade ago when speed and silence had kept her alive.

Adrenaline amping higher, she waited for the next to come, knew that he would because now his partner was missing. Felt the pain out there, somewhere, reminding her again that she was weak, and the urge for blood that blocked out the weakness heightened her senses, flooded her reflexes.

Another shadow, another body through the door, and she fixated on the movement, waited as he called out carelessly to his now-dead companion and so announced his presence, his distance, and when he stepped through, she took him down before he had a chance to raise the machete.

He dropped, one body on top of the other in an unnatural embrace, and she stepped over them and into the hall, where the footsteps of the last man called to her. He was in the reception area hovering over the woman on the floor, and he turned before Munroe reached him. With his head behind the desk, she couldn't see his face, but he saw the knives. The blood.

With papers in his hands, he turned and fled.

Munroe knelt beside the woman again, checked for a pulse again, and this time there was nothing. Heart still pounding, she strode into the hall, caught the slam of the door to the street, and ran to the exit, yanked it open. Scanned the road in both directions, strained to see the break in the pattern, finally spotted him heading toward the narrow end of the road, and ran after him.

He stepped into a car.

She moved off the sidewalk and into the street, where she could get after him faster. Shimmied between vehicles that blocked her way, and by the time she got clear, the car ahead was gone.

A horn blared. Munroe swerved and, seeing without seeing, stared through the windshield of the truck that had nearly hit her.

A man leaned out a window and cursed at her, and she stepped out of the road, breath laboring, pain laddering higher, and glanced again toward the invisible contrail left by the killer with his papers. The roads ahead would be crowded, the car couldn't have gotten far, but the ability to overtake him on foot belonged to the Munroe before the beating, would belong to her again one day, but now this was a time in which strength and endurance had been replaced with feeble limbs and a struggle for air.

She doubled over and knelt beside the road. Sheathed the knives without a chance to wash off the blood, and when she had the strength to pull herself up, could breathe without shards of glass shredding her insides, she stood and turned and hobbled in the opposite direction, replaying the scene in the office, attempting to brand to memory the finer details that would fade in the wake of the adrenaline dump.

She moved slowly up Bishara Street, waved down a taxi, sank into a worn and lumpy backseat. The trail of bodies was going to be a problem. Sooner or later even the most inept police department would have to start asking questions.

The taxi returned her to Moi Avenue, to the large, clean, and modern Diamond Trust Arcade, to the ground floor, where a slice of corporate America, grafted to the root stock of East Africa, greeted her in the form of the purple-and-orange FedEx logo and an air-conditioned shipping office designed to mimic what she would have found in the United States.

There was no one in line before her, and with a passport for identification she collected the three boxes Amber had shipped, already opened by customs inspectors: smaller than the crates that would be coming through the airfreight depot, larger and heavier than what she was capable of carrying; then she collected her own, a package she'd ordered during one of her Internet forays.

Munroe paid the import duty based not on the declared value

but on what the customs officers had claimed the items were worth, and went through the boxes, item by item according to the manifest, to ensure that nothing had been stolen. Then, having confirmed the contents, she begged tape from the counter clerk, resealed Amber's boxes well enough that someone would have to cut them open to get at the contents, and nudged the boxes out the door and into the atrium, where she dialed the *hawaladar.*

"Are you still at the airport?" she said.

"In a meeting. What do you want?"

"Do you have a guy working for you named Ibrahiin?"

"Not that I know of," he said.

"What about someone capable of passing as either Kenyan or Somalian? A dual national, maybe?"

"Several. What are you getting at?"

"Have you been to your office recently?" she said.

"Not since morning," and then again, "What are you getting at?"

"You have dead people in your office."

"What is that supposed to mean?"

"It means you have dead people in your office."

He was silent for a moment and finally said, "Which office?"

"The law office. I didn't check the other. I'll tell you more in person. I need you to pick me up."

"Who is dead?" he said.

"Your receptionist and a couple of other guys who were in there trashing your place. I'm at the Diamond Trust building. I'll tell you everything when you come get me," and without waiting for a response she ended the call.

In the thirty-minute wait, Munroe unboxed her package, a satellite phone and a multiplug. Ran through the instructions and set it charging until the *hawaladar* announced his presence by phone call and, at her request for help in carrying boxes, sent his driver to find her. The man made the first two trips out alone, and she followed him with the third. Found the Land Rover double-parked and blocking traffic, and when the driver shoved the last box into the rear, Munroe climbed in next to the *hawaladar.*

He ended a call abruptly and turned to face her, and though his expression was full of questions he didn't say anything, as if inviting her to speak, to tell him what she knew.

"You first," she said.

"It's as you described."

"Do you know who they were or what they wanted?"

"Dare I ask what you were doing there?"

"Covering my ass."

"Spying on me?"

"Yes," she said, because it's what he expected to hear and by giving him what he wanted she could redirect his attention. "The men who tore up your place were looking for something. Another got away. He carried off documents. I'd like to think you've got your nose deep in other crap and that this doesn't involve me or the *Favorita*, but experience tells me that would only be wishful thinking."

He turned from her as if uninterested in conversation and picked up the phone again. Even without seeing the screen she could tell that he clicked through links randomly, without paying attention, nervous energy needing an outlet.

"Who knows we're coming?" she said.

"No one knows."

She shifted in the seat so that she faced him directly, leaned in toward him so that he couldn't avoid her. "If you're wrong, if you're lying, your entire investment goes down," she said. "We only have one advantage, Abdi, and that's the element of surprise. Without that, if someone expects us, then your cousins, your men, all of us—we're already dead."

"I told you," he said, his voice rising a notch, and she scrutinized his every flinch, every twitch, searching for the lies and the uncertainties. "Nobody knows. Not even Khalid, Omar, the men I sent to you. They might assume, but even then, they can't be sure."

If he spoke an untruth, his body didn't betray him. "Your office wasn't trashed as a result of nobody knowing," she said. "They weren't searching through documents as a result of nobody knowing."

He didn't answer, so she shifted to face forward again.

"You're sure there's no Ibrahiin among your employees?"

"Where did the name come from?"

"A dead guy."

"I see," he said.

His phone rang, and the *hawaladar* listened, then rattled off a one-sided conversation in Somali and tossed the phone aside. "The crates have cleared," he said, and then to his driver, "We go back to the freight depot."

Munroe said, "Watch your back. Same people who killed my friend and tried to kill me will start coming for you."

"I can take care of my own," he said, and his focus turned back to his phone while his body language continued a story of agitation and stress.

Munroe tipped her head against the window. There was no way that attack had come from someone following her movements about town, could only have come by word out of Somalia, which meant that for all the talk of Russians having screwed over the pirates, the delegation—or someone with similar motives—was still connected to *someone* up north feeding information in this direction. Nothing in Somalia was ever a secret, and this had come because the *hawaladar* had been asking questions.

"How many people did you leave working in your office today?" she said.

"Only Aasiya," he said.

"Your receptionist?"

He nodded. "My niece."

"I'm sorry," she said.

He turned back toward the window and she said, "The guy who ran off with the documents didn't behave like a stranger, and he was dressed better than the others. You might want to look closely at the people working for you—by now it's well known that you were asking about the ship, and you're not the only one with connections that run both ways."

"I'll take care of it," he said, and his tone implied that he was finished with the conversation, so they made the return to the freight depot in silence. When they approached the truck there were crates on the ground behind it: Amber's crates—money spent that she didn't have, to save a man who might already be dead.

The driver pulled to a stop beside the truck, and the *hawaladar* stepped from the air-conditioning, as did Munroe, who first went to the rear and with the help of the driver transferred the FedEx boxes to the bed of the truck, then came to the crates on the opposite side of the *hawaladar.*

There were two wooden boxes five feet cubed, stuffed with packaging material, and like the FedEx boxes they'd been opened and torn through multiple times, courtesy of the men in the customs building. Omar lifted the lid off the nearest crate and, heads tipped together, they peered inside.

There was no obvious damage, though until they had a chance to unload and inspect they would be unable to know if every piece had survived the journey—or, rather, survived the customs-clearing process. With luck, they now had inflatable tactical boats, engines, mounts, and the tools to put them all together.

The *hawaladar* signaled for Omar to reseal the crates, and he was in the process of hammering the second lid down when a Toyota pickup arrived and pulled in beside the Land Rover.

Two of the bodyguards from the *hawaladar*'s alley stepped out, and the *hawaladar* left the crates to confer with them. When the conversation was over, he got into the backseat of the Land Rover with one of his men, and the two vehicles drove off in convoy.

Omar came and stood beside Munroe, followed her gaze to the dust kicked up by the tires, and when the vehicles were out of sight, he said, "We are ready."

The sun was red on the western horizon by the time they passed the guard shack on their way out of the freight depot, the sky completely dark when they reached the city, and the return trip up the coast was made longer because the men hadn't eaten all day and needed food.

Omar pulled off the road at a wayside restaurant just beyond Mtwapa.

The building was but a room, a patchwork of tin siding and a thatched roof where kerosene lamps blinked out from screened windows. Yusuf stayed with the truck while Munroe followed Omar and Ali into a cramped and crowded space, and amid the laughter and drunken conversation they found an empty table, a shaky wooden contraption covered with plastic and marked with cigarette burns. Smoke from a charcoal fire kept the mosquitoes at bay, and Lingala blared out from blown speakers in a radio roped to the rafters.

The rhythm of the room, which had hiccuped when Munroe walked in, picked up again when she nodded and took a seat, and the conversations loud and boisterous swirled with speculation about the lone white person, no thought given to the possibility that she might understand what was being said.

The food, when it arrived, was pilau, a rice pilaf, served without meat—the *hawaladar*'s men unwilling to eat what was not halal—and hot enough that pathogens should have been killed, though Munroe couldn't vouch for the silverware or cooking utensils or the water they'd been washed in. Although Kenyan beer flowed freely around the room, the *hawaladar*'s men also abstained from alcohol; in an odd contradiction, by religion they eschewed anything fermented yet accepted khat addiction as a normal part of the culture: both were mood- and behavior-altering substances, yet to them two distinct and separate issues, one forbidden, one not.

Food was sent out to Yusuf, the meal progressed, and so did the conversation as Omar and Ali began to relax, and although Munroe occasionally interjected a few sentences as a way to answer questions or elicit laughter and build camaraderie, her focus stayed on her new phone, and on the bleached-out colored plastic plate as she toyed with her food, interested not in the meal but in the interaction that went on across the table: the stories, the jokes, giving her the opportunity to unobtrusively learn and read these men in preparation for what was yet to come.

CHAPTER 36

Natan, flooded by the truck's lights, stood in front of the house, rifle gripped in his hand. Omar slowed to a stop and Munroe slid from the cab and walked ahead as a way to mitigate accidents from trigger-happy fingers, and then with Natan by her side, she guided the truck down toward the beach until the brakes squealed, the engine shuddered off.

Ali and Yusuf climbed off the truck bed, and watching them, Natan said, "Everything arrived?"

"Seems like," she said. "Smaller boxes need to go in the house—the crates can stay outside," and when he paused and stared at her, she motioned to her ribs and said, "Girl."

Natan smiled: the first crack in the ice. He unsnapped a flashlight from his belt, used a tire to boost himself up, and ran the beam over the crates. She left him there and wandered toward the small fire on the beach, where Khalid and the other man from the dhow had made dinner, and where the three from the truck had already joined them. Best as she could tell, the audience under the mango tree had gone home for the night.

Khalid stood when she approached, invited her toward the fire. Risking that he'd take offense, she declined on account of work that she still needed to do. "Have you heard from Abdi?" she said.

"This morning, yes. Before the truck returned to Mombasa."

"Good," she said. "We had a successful day," and left it at that. She'd expected that the *hawaladar* would at least have warned his lieutenant about the attack on the office, but there was no indication that he had.

She walked toward the house, and Natan, who'd hovered just beyond the light, joined her in silent company up to the grass and then headed to the truck for the boxes. Not far from the back door were thatched mats and blankets that Munroe assumed Khalid had laid out. She glanced at the clouded sky and anticipated rain at some point in the night, figured the men would move beneath the truck if it happened.

Amber met her on the porch, asked the same question Natan had.

"It's all in the truck," Munroe said. "Natan is getting the boxes."

"So, tomorrow?"

"Test run with the boats, a last run for supplies, make sure we have what we need. Then wait for the weapons and ammunition."

"And then," Amber said, and her voice trailed off, and Munroe followed her line of sight toward the ocean, where the dhow's single light lifted and lowered with the rhythm of the water.

"The captain tried to escape today," Amber said. "Rushed the door when I opened it to feed him. Knocked me over and ran for the front."

"He pretends to sleep a lot, but he pays close attention to sound and routine."

"Natan hit him pretty hard."

"Good."

"How bad do we need him?"

"Depends on the condition of the crew and the ship. If we don't run into too many walls, and the first mate is still alive, then he's only valuable as a personal trophy for me."

"And if we do hit walls?"

"We can trade him for freedom," she said.

Munroe slept on the living room couch where the air was fresher, woke before the sun, and left for the outside, for the water and the sand and the quiet of her own private cathedral until light in its many hues filled the horizon and noise from behind told her that the others had begun to stir.

THE LAND ROVER and the Toyota arrived in midafternoon carrying the *hawaladar,* his driver, and two of his bodyguards. They'd used shipping boxes as the disguise for the armaments, and the bodyguards transferred them from the rear of the Land Rover to the pirogue.

Munroe stayed on the porch and allowed the men their space, and when the *hawaladar* came to join her, she stood and shook his hand and, nodding toward the beach, said, "How many people know about the contents of those boxes?"

"You. Me. Khalid," he said, and he turned toward the largest of his bodyguards, the one who'd always faced her when she entered the alley. "And Joe."

She paused in response to the name. Raised an eyebrow.

The *hawaladar* smiled, almost bashfully. "Too many American movies," he said.

"So only us four?"

"Yes."

"If you're moving weapons, someone's going to piece it together. We lose the element of surprise, we've already lost the ship."

"Nobody knows," he said.

She offered him tea, which he accepted, a gesture made in conciliation, and toward trust and cultural bonding in a scenario where no one truly trusted anyone. He endured her clumsiness, which came from working with the house's broken pots and mismatched utensils, and they sat in the shade and talked of unimportant things for a time, until gradually she turned the conversation back to the office on Bishara Street and said, "Have you learned who came for your office, what they were after?"

"I'm still working on it," he said, "but I've told my people in Somalia that I no longer have any interest in the ship."

"Will they believe it?"

"I told them about Aasiya," he said. "They believe."

"Khalid doesn't know."

"It's better that way," he said. "You'll have less trouble keeping your army intact if they don't suspect anything other than victory. I have also withheld mention of your destination or why you go. When you are ready, tell Khalid. He'll inform the others."

"What about the papers? What went missing?"

"We've only put one room back together." He took another sip of tea. "We will figure it out."

"Makes the most sense they'd be looking for something related to the freighter. Did you file documents to seize the ship?"

"I've drawn them up," he said. "I haven't filed them. I won't file them until you're back in Kenyan territory—to be safe—in case someone *is* looking."

She smiled, acknowledgment of his perception, and he took the cue and stood. Extended a hand and when she shook it he said, "I expect to see you again," and in his statement was both threat and Godspeed.

"It's in my best interest if you do," she said, and when she released him, he placed his other hand on top of hers and said, "Travel safe."

Munroe walked with him to the front of the house, waited as he and his men got back into the vehicles, the truck included, and she stood in the middle of the track staring after them until all three sets of taillights had disappeared into the foliage. Then, mind switching gears to the work at hand, she turned to Joe, whom the *hawaladar* had left behind.

He'd yet to utter a word in any encounter she'd had with him.

"You have what you need?" she said.

He nodded, and walked from her to the beach and the rest of the men, bringing their hunting party to nine plus a prisoner.

In the house Munroe checked on the captain. She allowed him out of the room to shower and wash his clothes, and when she'd fed and watered him and returned him to his cell of a room, she dumped her few belongings out of the plastic bag and carried the bag down to the beach.

The inflatable boats were on the sand, and Natan and Amber were beside them, tools in hand, assembling parts from the crate while the generator ran loud and Khalid used the air compressor to fill the second craft. The rest of the men crowded around to observe. Munroe joined the circle, noted the progress, and then, bag held toward Khalid, said, "I need all the cell phones."

He glanced up, squinting against the sun.

"You can have them back when we return," she said. "If you have a problem with it, call Abdi and ask him. He'll tell you the same thing."

He stood and fished his phone from his pocket, dropped it into the bag, and she said, "It'll be easier if you get them from the others too," and so he took the bag and against groans of protest and brief arguments, collected phones from each of the rest of the crew. Joe was last, and with a smirk, eyes never leaving Munroe's, he too dumped his phone in the bag.

Khalid brought the bag to her, and while they watched, she pulled the phones out and one by one removed the batteries. "It's for your own safety," she said, though the bigger truth was that it was for her safety and the safety of the mission. From here on out, unless one of them had smuggled in a communications device, only she would have access to the outside world, and that would limit the risk of betraying their movement and position to the *hawaladar* or to Ibrahiin—whoever he was—and by proxy to the Russians or the pirates.

The work on the inflatables had stopped completely—even Natan and Amber had turned to watch her—so Munroe left them. Carried the phones inside the house, put them in a cupboard in the kitchen, and then continued on, out the front with her own phone, far enough away so that the captain wouldn't be able to overhear conversation.

She dialed Sergey and he answered with the tentative inflection of someone who didn't recognize a number, though that changed as

soon as she infused honey into her hello, and a reminder of the unfinished promises left behind in the backseat of the car.

"I'm in Kampala," she said. "Sadly. Stuck here thanks to idiot bureaucrats. I can't return to Mombasa for another week. Will you still
be there when I return?"

"A week?" he said. "Yes, I should still be here."

"Do I find you at the same hotel?"

"Sentrim Castle," he said. "Do you know it?"

"I can look for it."

"Call me when you get back," he said.

"Of course," she said, voice lilting and inviting. "We can finish
where we left off."

"I look forward to that," he said, and the hair rose on the back of
her neck, the telltale signal that she was being watched. Breathless
and full of sugar, she added, "I'll make sure that you do," and ended
the call, and without turning said, "What do you want, Natan?"

"You were speaking Russian," he said. Surprise underlined his
accusation.

"Yes."

"The people behind the hijacking of the *Favorita* are Russian."

"Yes," she said.

"*S kem eto ty govorila?*"

She turned to face him. "I'm taking care of business."

He walked toward her. Stopped just outside her personal space,
as if trying to read her or find some answer to an unasked question
while mistrust oozed from his expression and his posture. "What is
it you are after?" he said.

"Same as you."

"Not the same."

She shrugged, glanced beyond him toward the house. Wouldn't
play his game or get baited into a pissing match. "Either you trust
that I'm after the ship just as you are," she said, "or you don't trust,
and if you don't trust, there isn't a thing I can do to make you, so I'm
not about to try." She nodded toward the ocean. "When we get on
that dhow tomorrow, my life is at risk just as much as yours, as Am-

ber's. Stepping on my toes every leg of the journey isn't going to get you what you want, and it certainly won't get us safely back."

"Who are you?" he said.

"You know who I am."

"No. I know who those documents say you are. I know who you said you were when you first arrived in Djibouti. One was a lie, it could all be lies. Who are you?"

"I'm the person standing in front of you."

He clenched his jaw and his breathing shortened.

"You're playing word games with me," he said. "Why are you here?" He swept his hand toward the house, the beach. "Doing this?"

"We've already had that conversation."

"It's an unfinished conversation. There are too many holes and inconsistencies. Now you say that you haven't spent the last five years in Djibouti, that you aren't the child of English-teacher parents."

"Correct."

"But you speak Somali."

"Yes. And Afar."

"Did you study these languages? For your assignments? Your missions?"

Munroe sighed. Knew where this conversation was headed. "I learned them locally," she said.

"That works for your old story, not your new one."

Out of the corner of her eye, she caught the twitch of his fingers toward the gun holstered at his side. He said, "In the new version you were only there a month or so before you came to work for Leo."

"That's correct."

"You contradict yourself in lies." He smiled a triumphant smile as if waving the proof of her duplicity in her face. "You don't become fluent in a language in so short a time."

"I do," she said.

"Okay, supergirl, if that's what you say." His expression hardened and his lips drew taut. "One lie upon the next," he said, "and now you are keeping something from us. I don't trust you."

"Of course you don't," she said. "You and Leo lied to Amber, lied to me. After all of your own lies it must be difficult to believe someone else might be telling the truth. You screwed me over. You should be careful when this is finished."

"When this is finished?" he said.

"It only benefits me to hunt you down and kill you after the mission is complete."

Natan's eyes widened, as if in the many avenues she might be dangerous, that was one he hadn't considered.

She smiled. "I'm fucking with you," she said. "Don't be a self-righteous asshole, Natan. If anyone here doesn't deserve trust—doesn't deserve it from Amber or from me—it's you."

His shoulders lowered and his hands relaxed, and he looked toward the trees and shook his head. "That still doesn't answer the questions," he said. "You have other motives and you are keeping secrets." But resignation filled his voice, almost as if he said it to clear the air and get it out of his system.

"Supposing that's true, then that only makes us even," she said. "You're not the good guy in this scenario either." And with the heart of the conversation over, she walked toward the beach. Natan kept pace beside her, and they made it about twenty feet before he broke the silence.

"About the languages," he said. "Where did you learn Somali?"

"In Djibouti."

"And Swahili?"

"Here."

"Why do you keep telling stories?" he said. "In this it can't hurt to tell the truth."

"It is the truth."

"But it's not possible."

"What? To learn so quickly, to speak so many? Why not?"

"Nobody can," he said, and his response irritated her. Not the disbelief, which was fairly standard, but the small-mindedness from which it was born.

"The world is gifted with mathematical wunderkinds and musical geniuses," she said. "They're rare, but they exist. They are everyday people with neurological connections wired differently than yours. Just because you've never met someone who can do long math in their head faster than on a calculator doesn't mean it can't be done."

"I speak five languages," he said, and took on the tone of conversing with a toddler who needed slower talking and smaller words. "Every one of them took years to learn. You're not a cartoon, Michael, so stop with the pretend play, yes?"

She stopped walking and turned toward him. "You have your share of flaws, Natan, but until now I never mistook you for one of those fools who use their own inability and limited experience to measure what others can or can't do."

He stared back.

"You ever heard of Daniel Tammet?"

"No."

"He's a savant," she said. "Asperger's. High-functioning autism. He learned to speak Icelandic in a week—most difficult language in the world—did it for national TV to prove it could be done."

"You're not autistic."

She started walking again and Natan kept by her side.

"Heard of Timothy Doner? He's a teenager in New York who's taught himself over twenty languages, learned some in as little as a week. He's not autistic. What about Emil Krebs, heard of him?"

"No."

"Diplomat. He mastered sixty-eight languages and could translate from up to a hundred and twenty. What about John Bowring?"

"No."

"A hundred languages."

"You've made your point."

"Uku Masing."

"Just stop."

"Sixty-five languages."

"Mario Pei."

"I get it," he said, and so she stopped with the list, and because they'd reached the edge of the sand, she also stopped walking.

"It's a defect in human nature," she said, and turned to him again.

"Weak people do it, you know? Turn personal opinion into a fact worth fighting for. That's what differentiates me from you, makes me a better strategist. Don't underestimate your opponent by gifting him with your own weaknesses, Natan."

"Then you agree: You are an opponent."

"Either way your suspicion makes me one."

"My suspicion is well justified. You can say differently, but your motives are not as simple as you claim."

"Does it matter? We're here, going after the ship, going after your team. You could never have done this without me. I pulled this thing together out of thin air on short notice in a country where none of us have connections and your trust or nontrust made absolutely no difference. What's still at stake is the outcome—if you want to fuck *that* up, then keep riding my tail, otherwise just leave me alone and let me do my job." Munroe closed in on his personal space and said, "I don't need a baby-sitter."

"You've hijacked a ship before?"

She smiled wryly. "No."

He snorted. "Been on a hijacked ship?"

"The *Favorita.*"

"Besides that."

"Yes, actually."

He raised his eyebrows and then laughed, as if she'd offered him another of her *stories,* and she let him have that. He'd believe what he wanted to believe.

"I'll let you work," he said, "though you are just as guilty of using your own limitation to view the world. Not once have you asked me of my own history or experience with hijackings—you don't know what I know."

The underhanded conciliation was probably the best she'd get from him, so she met him halfway: sat and patted the sand beside her. "Come, sit," she said. "Tell me what you know."

CHAPTER 37

They left with the tide, an embarkation that had taken close to an hour to get under way in the early-morning dark, and Munroe stood at the gunwale looking out over the house, unlit and abandoned, the base of operations that had served its purpose and upon which she'd left the last twenty-dollar payment and the keys hammered to the front door.

The dhow picked up speed and with the increase in forward momentum came the rhythm, the pounding rise and fall, and the house became nothing but a blend of all the other darknesses along the shore. This boat was home now, and with them was everything they needed to make the twelve-hundred-mile round-trip. If they'd miscalculated on fuel or food or water, there were no fallbacks, no one to call in an emergency or for rescue.

Natan sat fore, face to the wind, and Amber beside him, an outline under the moonlit sky, head tipping up and down in conversation that Munroe couldn't hear. For the moment, Yusuf had the wheel, and the others had staked out territory in the open among the fuel drums and supplies where they could stretch out and sleep. She turned from them toward the canopy, where she'd stashed the captain, boxed in among the smaller supplies.

She'd delayed bringing him from the house until after most of the men had boarded, and she'd stood with him on the sand while the pirogue returned, using Joe with his imposing size to keep him from making one last mad dash to freedom. The captain's arrival on the dhow was the first that the Somalis had seen of him, and she listened for the nuance in their muttered surprise, searching for a giveaway that might point to a traitor in their midst so as to cut him loose before the journey began, but she found no tells.

Munroe shifted boxes to create space and lay beside the captain, close enough that she'd feel it if he got up to rummage. He turned his back to her and she closed her eyes. For the first time since leaving the *Favorita,* she had no reason to stay awake, nowhere to go and nothing to do, so she allowed heat and time and the rise and fall to lull her down into nothingness.

She woke and slept and woke again, knew time passing by the bodies that came in for water or to utilize the bucket surrounded by cloth as a makeshift head. The heat intensified and then waned again, and when dusk came once more, she rose, gave the captain water, and left for the bow.

They were far within Somali territory now, as much at risk from pirates as the *Favorita* had ever been, their position measured and guided by a pair of GPS units with batteries recharged by the sun. The relaxed atmosphere that had filled the boat at the outset had since been replaced by a subtle low-level tension, and the weapons, stashed and hidden while in Kenyan waters, had appeared in the form of Kalashnikov rifles and ammunition bands worn by each of the Somalis. Natan, not one to be outdone, had taken the display a step further, wearing two sidearms and combat knives sheathed and holstered around his pant legs.

Under other circumstances Munroe would have rolled her eyes, but here his peacocking couldn't hurt. The *hawaladar*'s men outnumbered hers two to one and she wasn't certain their instructions were the same as what she'd been led to believe. Trust in the *hawaladar* had come from necessity—perhaps desperation—certainly not out of confidence in his self-interest or loathing of pirates, no matter how much he professed this to be true.

Munroe wound her way to the bow and stood watching the distance and endless water, thoughts churning with the waves, until Khalid approached, stopped beside her, and offered a bowl of rice cooked in soupy broth. The food was cold, the last of the dinner from the night before, and she sat with him atop a fuel drum, scooping from bowl to mouth with her fingers as he did. His posture and the occasional catch in his breath indicated he'd made the gesture as a way to converse, but instead his face stayed lifted toward land, eyes tracking the scattered crags and rocky outcroppings in the distance, arrows pointing their way toward Garacad.

"You miss your home," she said, and he glanced toward her just long enough to nod before staring out toward land again.

"You're from the Mogadishu area?"

"Galkayo," he said. "It's not so long since I was there."

The rush of wind filled in for a reply.

"I didn't want to leave," he said. "I had work with the Puntland Maritime Police Force." He looked at her again and, as if he wasn't sure she understood the implication, added, "Fighting against pirates."

She nodded.

"When it ended, I tried other things, but there are few jobs and little money. Abdi has provided a better opportunity for me. I work for him and I send the money home."

"Your wife is in Puntland?"

He nodded again, continuing to gaze into the distance, as if the closer they got to his homeland, the more the air itself breathed a familiar song imbuing him with a sense of belonging. She envied him that, a place to which he was always connected, a land that was part of him, something she'd never had, never would have: *home.*

"Ali is going to be a problem," she said. "Yusuf also. Without khat."

Khalid leaned back and squinted in their direction.

The two men sat, backs to the gunwale—squished as they all

were among the supplies that filled the dhow—but even lazing in the shade playing a game that Munroe didn't recognize, they showed signs of agitation. The longer they got into the voyage, the more their tempers would wind up, and with weapons so easily to hand it would be a miracle if they made it to Garacad without a death along the way.

"I'll do what I can," he said.

With their meager meal finished and only silence to fill the space between the engine and the ocean wind, she stood and refilled her bowl. On her way back to the captain, she paused over Ali and Yusuf, and they blinked up with bloodshot eyes. She nodded and carried on.

When she reached the captain, he was nestled between boxes and the rear bench, on his back, watching Joe at the wheel. Kneeling beside him, Munroe took the knife from her belt and cut the bonds at his wrists and legs. He cocked his head and studied her, rubbed his thumbs over the bands where the rope had worn his skin raw, and then, as if he doubted his good fortune, he said, "Why? What do you want?"

"Nothing," she said, and handed him the bowl of rice. He hesitated a moment, then accepted it and scooped greedy bites with his fingers, slurping, chewing with his mouth open and dropping grains of yellow into his beard. Munroe turned from him slightly, disgusted.

"We're in Somali waters now," she said, "about three miles offshore. You can go overboard if you like. It's a long swim but doable, although I can't promise what waits for you if you manage to make it. You could also stay on the boat and try to fight for control, but there are nine of us and one of you, and no hostages here for you to take. Or you can eat your dinner and enjoy the ride and come with us when we attempt to take back your ship. We'll reach the *Favorita* in probably two or three days."

Wiping his fingers on his shirt, he set the empty bowl aside and said, "Will you succeed?"

"You're a soldier," she said. "You've commanded your own men. You've seen what we've done—the planning, the supplies—and you know what we're up against. Decide for yourself."

He harrumphed, as had been his way, but this time, instead of closing his eyes and lying back to ignore her, he ran fingers and thumb along his beard, combed out the food particles, and said, "Maybe for you there is a chance."

"Us."

He nodded, his focus out somewhere beyond Joe. "Yes," he said. "Maybe for us there is a chance, and when we come back to Mombasa, everything is good for you, but for my problem, she still exist."

"I'm working on that," she said, and his face jerked back to hers as if that was the last thing he'd expected.

"Is a possibility?"

"Could be," she said. "I haven't decided. The problem is this story has no good guys. Not you. Not me. Not any of the people on this boat, not the armed guards left behind on the *Favorita*. Not the pirates, and certainly not the Russians who want you. Maybe your crew," she said. "They didn't deserve this. But the rest of us, we're all scum of one sort or another. It's only a matter of degree of scum. You want your problem fixed, but maybe the Russians have a good reason for wanting you. Maybe by giving you to them I do the world a favor, I don't know. And until you talk, I have no way to know."

"What is scum?" he said.

"*Svoloch.*"

"Ah." He studied the open air again. "Swim," he said. "Swim or try to fight you, or take back my ship." He was thoughtful for another moment. "The ship, she is the one easier to come home alive."

"I would think so. How difficult will it be to get her moving if half your crew is dead?"

"Depend on which half. If both engineer are dead maybe I can get oil up, but then it must be someone else to run the bridge."

Munroe nodded. Paced through the scenarios. It didn't seem possible that the entire crew had been killed—not based on the news that had come across the wires.

He said, "I help you, we bring her to Mombasa, and yes, you let me go?"

"It's what I promised."

"And my problem?"

"I don't know," she said. "If I can solve it, I will. Not for you—I have my own reasons—but I still need to know why they want you."

He sighed, shifted, and fully stretched out, and with his hands now free, laced his fingers atop his belly and closed his eyes. Annoyed, she turned to leave. From behind, his voice said, "You know who is Aleksey Petrov?"

She swiveled back. Sat again. "First deputy minister with the Russian Ministry of Defense," she said.

"Yes, is who he is now. You know who he is before?"

"He had a military career, then went into the telecom business, and then the ministry."

The captain opened his eyes. "Is all good on paper," he said. "And Nikola Goran, you know who he is?"

"I know who they say you are," she said. "Serbian colonel wanted for war crimes, ethnic cleansing against Bosnian Muslims."

"Is not so good on paper," he said, and chuckled. His laugh caught in his throat and he hacked a cough. "I did many things during the war," he said, and elbowed back up into a half-sitting position. "Many things for which I have pride, and many things for which there is shame. But I did not make the mass graves and the killing and the genocide for what they say of me."

Munroe nudged space free against the nearest box, close enough that she could see the lines on his face, could read his expressions and body language, but not so close that she crowded him. He stopped talking when she shifted nearer, so she closed her eyes and tipped her head back against the boxes, waited for him to begin again, knew he would—everything she'd said and done to him over the past weeks had been to soften him for this moment.

"Do you know of Bijeljina?" he said.

She shrugged. Opened her eyes a sliver.

"And of the foreigners who came to fight in the war?"

She nodded. This she knew from the time she'd spent in that part of the world: the three basic divisions that had fought in the divided Yugoslavia, and the foreign support that came to them along the same ethnic and religious lines. Muslims had rallied to the aid of Bosnia and Herzegovina, Catholics to the Croats, Orthodox to the Serbs: long-standing ties and alliances that ran so far into history they'd been the start of World War I. The alliances hadn't changed much since and so beckoned foreigners into a war in which over two hundred thousand Muslim civilians were murdered and two million more were made refugees—volunteer armies and mercenaries fighting along historical fault lines.

Outside governments disavowed and distanced themselves from official involvement, but it was no secret that weapons and advice funneled in from abroad: Russian and Greek to the Serbs, Western European and U.S. to the Croats, and Muslim to the Bosnians.

"I was in Bijeljina during the killing," he said. "Is worse in life than what you read in reports. Serbians have close connection with Russia, you know this, yes? Aleksey Petrov, he is in Bijeljina also."

He paused, as if waiting for her to prod him for more or to ask for clarification, but she didn't. "Aleksey came as consultant," he said. "Soldier consultant. Unofficial, of course. No uniforms, no official documents, but he fight with us like soldier, same as us, courtesy of Mother Russia." The captain tapped a forefinger to his temple. "Aleksey is not so right in the head, I think. He likes the killing too much. Is sport for him, not war. Was not only Aleksey who did killing in Bijeljina, but he did much, and he gave orders and when at first soldiers don't listen, he make the first kill and then make many more." He paused again and when he still received no response from her, said, "Do you see?"

"I really don't," she said. "It's an interesting tale, but it doesn't answer the question of why your ship was hijacked. That war is twenty years old and last I checked, you, not Aleksey Petrov, are the wanted war criminal."

"There are pictures," he said.

"You have pictures of Aleksey in Bijeljina?"

"I know they exist. Before the war end, I go back and I find them. Was not so very easy, you think."

Munroe stayed quiet for a moment, processing, filling in the blanks of what he hadn't said, and in a roundabout way the attack on the *Favorita* began to make sense. "Nearly two decades," she said. "Why now?"

"You know," he said.

"Pretend I don't."

He sighed and closed his eyes, and annoyed at his sudden return to acting coy, she kicked his foot. He opened his eyes again and grinned, as if to say he knew he'd gotten under her skin, and as much as she played like she didn't care, he wasn't an idiot.

She said, "A man like Aleksey Petrov wouldn't care about being blackmailed—it's not like he *earned* that position or got voted into it. No one cares about anything he's done in the past—especially not something that happened in Bosnia when Russia sided with the Serbs in the first place. No one is going to fire or arrest him."

"Maybe arrest," the captain said. "If I take pictures to tribunal, maybe there is some problems for him. There are many pictures. Very bad pictures. Small problems for here, but in Russia small problem with right people is still a big problem for wrong people."

"The weapons in the hold came from him?"

"A way to make retirement," he said. "Sell to South Sudan, push through Somalia, and then I find an island and I am finished."

"Mombasa is an island," she said. "You got close."

He choked on a half laugh and waved at her. "You try to make funny."

"Sometimes it works," she said. Then, after a pause, "So Aleksey wants you dead."

"Maybe alive and dead at same time. As I say, killing for him is sport."

"You knew that before you tried to blackmail him."

"Yes," he said, and sighed. "I send him e-mail of few pictures. I don't know what will come of it, but he is in a good position to get me what I want, is an opportunity, I give a try. I use fake name and fake e-mail and fake phone. I work with people to make buffer so he can't find me."

Munroe understood then the purpose of the arms in the hold; the Trojan horse that led one piece of scum to another, and the reason no mention of the weapons had been made was because no one who knew about them even cared.

"Well, you got what you wanted," she said.

"Much more."

"How did they find you?"

He shrugged and his eyes cast downward, and for the first time in the conversation she picked up the shame of failure. In a double act of indignity, he'd been outsmarted by a man responsible for his own twenty-year run, and every day in her captivity had been a reminder of that failure.

She offered him an out. "Perhaps they used the AIS," she said. "Once the weapons were on their way to you, they would eventually have figured out that you captained the *Favorita,* and it wouldn't be too difficult to track you through the ship."

"I make the AIS disabled after we come around the Horn," he said. "That is the easy way to track, and is never good to make easy, so I disconnect it."

And that explained why the ship never turned up in any searches.

"Did you check the weapons, the crates, the pallets, for GPS tracking?"

"Certainly I check," he said, and huffed as if offended by the implication that he'd been a fool to make such a simple oversight. "In any case, the hold, she provide too much cover to transmittal. She is a dark zone with no signal."

"Then maybe one of your officers."

His expression tightened as if he hurt. "I know these men couple years," he said. "We work together on team, on same ship for two years. They know what we do, they help plan, they get paid good. But maybe, I don't know."

Munroe closed her eyes and rested her head against the boxes again. He had a good narrative, a good act. The plausibility filled in a lot of holes, but this was still just a story, one for which she might never know the actual truth—and she didn't really care. Whatever he'd left out—rivalry, hatred, a catalytic event that drove a decades-long thirst for retribution—someone had sent a delegation of Russian military men after the captain, had used Somali financing and Somali pirates to cover their tracks, had used Kenyans to intimidate and kill people they thought were hiding him. These were facts she knew to be true. Her interest in the finer points was to understand the strength of her enemy.

She said, "When we go after the ship, the tracker, wherever it is or whoever has it, is still there, and once we start moving, the people who did this are going to be watching for it, they'll be waiting."

"Is a problem," he said. "Is your problem."

It *was* her problem, but it was going to become his problem too if they got hijacked again.

CHAPTER 38

Raised voices broke the conversation, and Munroe leaned around the boxes, caught sight of Khalid and Natan facing off, hands gesticulating, each arguing in his own language while the other men crowded in from their places on the dhow, ants moving toward the ant mound, lines drawn and sides taken. Amber, ignored by the others because she was a woman, stood outside the circle. Braced against the bulwark for recoil, her rifle inching higher.

Munroe flipped to her side and scrambled over the supplies that blocked her way, caught her breath and choked through the wave of darkness that washed in with the pain: a stabbing reminder that she'd not yet healed. Slid a knife from its hidden sheath and, knowing she wouldn't reach the antagonists before someone did something stupid, yelled at them.

Her voice was weak beneath the drone of the engine, carried away by the hiss of the wind, but strong enough that the Somali men on the edge of the circle heard her and glanced in her direction. She continued forward, slowed by the boat's movement, yelled again, and finally Khalid and Natan both turned.

"Are you insane?!" she screamed. Waved a hand toward Khalid. "Get back," she said, and the same toward Natan in English, "Back!"

Neither man moved but she had their attention, and those who'd crowded around parted enough to allow her through. She got between Khalid and Natan, and in Somali, loud enough that all of the *hawaladar*'s men would hear, said, "Save the anger. You'll need it to survive when we get to the end of our journey."

Khalid didn't answer, nor did he concede territory, but his grip on the rifle relaxed slightly and his jaw unclenched. Munroe resheathed the blade burning hot against her skin; breathed past rage at the alpha chest-thumping that wouldn't permit either man to stand down—one-upmanship that could so easily become the death of them all. She turned to Natan and, as a way to allow him to step aside without surrendering, said, "We need to talk," then nudged him, using her body to crowd him away from the circle so that he was forced to move.

Out of earshot of the others, voice lowered and tone as neutral as anger would allow, she said, "Dick measuring is going to get you killed. Not me. You. And probably Amber, too. Tell me there's a good reason for whatever the hell that just was."

He shook his head. "Stupidity," he said.

"Did it start with Khalid?"

"With that one," he said, and nodded toward Ali.

She cut a glance over and watched the dispersing circle. "Khat withdrawal," she said. "It's going to get worse, okay? Working with it won't make you less of a man."

"Fucking barbarians," he said, and Munroe had no response that wouldn't reignite the tinder she'd just put out, so she turned her back and climbed in the direction she'd come. She squeezed by Amber, caught her eye, and in the steel of Amber's expression knew that there'd been no bluff in her actions: she would have put a bullet in every one of those men, perhaps even Natan, if a fight had threatened to derail the mission and get between her and Leo.

Munroe sat outside the canopy where she could observe the length of the boat and ensure that the squabble didn't pick back up again, played the knife against her fingers, stayed through the lengthening shadows, running scenarios, measuring threats, until the sun began to set, its light replaced by orange pinpricks and cigarette smoke. She scooted beneath the canopy. Joe nodded an acknowledgment and, although he'd certainly seen the ruckus, said nothing, asked nothing. Munroe sat beside the captain and closed her eyes. She'd wait until the evening deepened, would apologize to Khalid on Natan's behalf and do the same for Natan in the morning, damage control by reinventing the conversation—the benefit of being the only one able to speak everyone else's language.

THE DHOW NEARED Garacad late in the morning. Yusuf cut the engine and they drifted far enough out that despite the easy way sound carried over the water, the growls of the generator and air compressor wouldn't invite other players to the private party. Floating, rising and falling with the swells, tempers and the irritation of the past days transformed into impatient tension until the inflatables were filled and readied, weapons checked, ammunition prepared, and attack plan coordinated; then there was nothing more to do but wait.

The dhow grew quiet, and under the canopy and other improvised shade, they ate and napped through the high afternoon heat, waiting for the dark to come. When the first of the cooling arrived and the men began to stir again, Munroe ducked behind the curtain of the makeshift head and there wrapped her torso, loop after loop of medical tape, uncomfortable and constricting, forming it into a cast of sorts. She'd avoided ibuprofen for the duration of the trip, a way to ensure the meds were completely out of her system and reduce the chance of overdosing, but even with the maximum amount she could safely take tonight, she'd still run a fine line between agony and immobility until the adrenaline kicked in and drowned out her body's limitations.

Torso set, Munroe left the head for the nearest drinking water. Funneled it from the container into an empty bottle and brought the bottle to Amber, who was resting under the shade of a towel stretched between fuel barrels. Munroe offered the water and when Amber took it, Munroe sat wordlessly beside her. Amber unscrewed the cap, drew a long swallow, and, recapping it, tipped her head onto

298 / Taylor Stevens

Munroe's shoulder. After several long minutes Amber said, "The anticipation is the worst, you know? Misery in the waiting."

Munroe patted Amber's thigh and drew in her quiet sigh; she wouldn't offer words of comfort or reassurance though it would cost nothing to speak such small lies in a life of lies; Amber deserved better than that. "It'll be better when we get moving again," Amber said. "Once the fighting finally starts."

"I need to ask you a favor," Munroe said.

Head still tipped to Munroe's shoulder, Amber said, "I'm not staying behind with the dhow no matter how nice you ask or how much you beg."

Munroe smiled and leaned her cheek against Amber's hair. "Not as bad as that. I just need you to stay on the water until we secure the deck."

"Why?"

"I need someone to keep control over the captain."

"I thought he was part of this now."

"Supposedly," Munroe said. "But even if we take the freighter, his problems are only just beginning, and he knows it. Given access to one of the inflatables, he's more likely to use the distraction to run, to commandeer the dhow, make a return to Kenya on his own and try to disappear. It's what I would do if I were in his shoes. I can't risk leaving him alone, but I can't bring him onto the ship until we have a secure zone."

"One of the men can handle him."

"You're the only one I trust to do it right."

"My priority is getting on that ship, Michael."

"I know it is," Munroe whispered.

"Yeah," Amber said, and they were silent for several more minutes until she spoke again. "We don't need him," Amber said. "One of the ship's officers could pilot, could get the freighter out."

"If they're alive, then yes, but it's more than that. I need him."

"As a trophy?"

"As a trump card."

Amber was quiet again, her breathing slow and deep, and with each inhale her torso expanded to touch Munroe's skin, a connection that warmed and withdrew several times until at last Amber said, "If there's no other way."

"Would have asked anyone else if it didn't matter as much."

Amber nodded, lifted her head off Munroe's shoulder. "I'll wait ten, fifteen minutes. After that, I'm coming up. I'll send him ahead."

Munroe patted Amber's thigh again: camaraderie, the only person she trusted in this whole damn mess. Then she stood and left for the captain, the pawn upon which the game still turned.

THE INFLATABLES SLIPPED away from the dhow under the cover of late night, four people to a boat, moving slowly over the water to keep the sound of approach as low as possible and retain the element of surprise, assuming they'd ever actually had it. Munroe sat in the middle of her craft, opposite the captain, while Khalid guided the tiller and Amber, face blackened with camouflage paint, faced the wind. Lights from the shore winked like stars in the far distance blending sky and sea, and somewhere far ahead, still out of sight, the *Favorita* anchored as a ghostly fortress on the water: a vessel of death no matter what happened tonight.

Munroe clenched her fists against the invisible bloodstains and turned again toward the distance, drew in the impending fight while the voices from the past rose in a low whisper and her lips moved with the chant of violence: *I whet my glittering sword. My hand takes hold on judgment. I will render vengeance to my enemies and will reward them that hate me.*

A prickle of warning traced up the back of her neck and Munroe turned to find the captain studying her, and she shut him out. The invitation from Miles Bradford beckoned, countered the violence, wrapped tendrils of want throughout her chest, and she hated that it did. The path to survival, to fight without fear or hesitation, was to hunger for nothing, to enter battle already dead. To have a reason to live only welcomed the hand of fate to make a mockery of desire.

She shoved Bradford away. Breathed out the last of him and drew the empty night in to take his place. Tonight she would free her conscience so that she could pursue Sami's killers and then leave Africa forever.

The bulk of the dhow faded and then blended completely into the water. Ahead in the second inflatable, Natan was at the tiller, with three of the Somali men, their bodies hugging the gunwales to avoid casting human-shaped shadows. Natan's inflatable veered off—no point making a single target out of both boats—and eventually it, too, vanished into the night.

Joe and his one boatman had been left behind as the *hawaladar*'s guarantee that he'd get his investment back—and a fallback of sorts should tonight go horribly awry—though Joe and the dhow were a difficult safety net to trust. The man had kept to himself for the entire voyage, his body language fluctuating between guarded and friendly, making him hard to read, and Munroe had yet to hear him speak.

She ran her fingers over the satellite phone and confirmed it was secure, then checked the two-way radio; made sure neither could be knocked off her belt through sudden movements. The two-way was the emergency backup for communication between the boats, the tether that would keep them connected within a thirty-mile range if the world went to shit. In place of accurate intel they had history, news reports, and combined experience, and through this they anticipated a contingent of at least twenty pirates, probably more, possibly an interruption by a supply skiff from shore, and hopefully khat, ample supplies of khat.

The advantage would go to the men on the high ground: better armed, protected by the bulk of the ship, with hostages to use as human shields, and backup from the shoreline to flank and attack the invaders from the rear. Without the gift of a stationary vessel even an attempt to take back the ship tonight would have been unthinkable. Stealth and surprise were their friends, but beyond those, the entire crapshoot would depend on tenacity and the favor of the gods.

Ahead lights on the floating fortress winked a welcome, the ship not lit fully, but enough to provide a beacon and guide Munroe's inflatable in for approach. Khalid cut their speed again and they crawled forward with a nearly inaudible whine. Munroe used a spotting scope to scan the bridge wings for shadows against the light and found nothing. The bridge itself was dark, as were all of the windows in the tower, and with the darkness came doubt: Everything the *hawaladar* had said, everything the news sources had delivered, indicated the hostages were being held onboard, but the only sign of life came from the splotches of shadow and movement on the deck that pointed to a moving patrol.

They covered the distance, rising, falling, over four-foot swells, and, engine off, guiding the craft with oars, Khalid brought the inflatable amidships beneath a narrow fixed accommodation ladder that crawled halfway down the starboard side toward the waterline. Amber acted as point man, rifle to the bulwark some eighteen feet above, and Munroe, on her knees for balance, extended a telescoping ladder, rubber-coated grappling hook on the end.

The boat pitched, and straining against the sway of the tube, Munroe missed the first connection. Recent wounds screamed in protest, and she swore to the night. The swells pushed the little boat away from the ladder. Oars against the hull, Khalid braced the inflatable from heaving into the rusted metal. Amber, at the boat's bow, shoved the rifle down by her knees and worked with Khalid, guiding the inflatable back into position.

A man short because of the captain, they needed the extra body to provide suppressive fire should a patrol start shooting, needed the extra hands to get the ladder hooked—couldn't trust him with either. Forced to ignore him, forced to hand him a weakness with which he might lunge for a weapon, Munroe focused on balance, on the grappling hook. Losing strength, screaming silently through gritted teeth, she strained to control the shifting weight. The captain sat intentionally unhelpful as if he had hatched a greater plan or didn't care which way the war turned tonight. The inflatable slipped back into position.

CHAPTER 39

Holding nothing back for yet another try, Munroe pushed up off her knees. Shed the weight from her arms when the grappling hook connected with the ship's ladder. She half collapsed, dragging in air without the luxury of a chance to pause to catch her breath. Swung nylon line into a knot around the tube of the bottom rung, cleated the line through one side of the inflatable, flung the tail to the other side, and knotted it there again: a solid tether between boat and ship as long as the grappling hook held.

Blade between her teeth, hand over hand, Munroe slipped upward, racing the pain, fighting for balance on the twisting pole as if it were some impossible-to-win amusement-park game of skill. Found respite on the frame of the ship's ladder and, tears smarting, panted shallow breaths. Weight fully borne on the bottom rung, the ladder groaned, gave slightly; metal scraped against rust. Munroe paused, strained to see above; caught only the haze of light against sea spray. Continued up, working far faster than was prudent, not trusting the strength of the ladder, unwilling to risk a patrol coming to inspect the noise and shooting down at her. She flattened on the top landing, eyes at deck level, scanning for the patrol while the ladder groaned yet again and gave further with Khalid's added weight.

On the deck were four men, splotches against the lights, working a slow pattern in quadrants of sorts. There was none of the casual khat-buzzed indifference Munroe had hoped for, but neither was there a frantic alertness. If the patrol anticipated an attack, their stride and posture and the number of men on deck didn't speak to it, and this sliced a thick layer off her distrust of the *hawaladar*. In keeping his own men uninformed, he'd guaranteed that the whispers through the Somali gossip network wouldn't reach the ship before they did.

Munroe gauged the direction of each approach and found the gap in the timing between footfalls. Slipped over the rail, ran for the shadows of the nearest coaming, and there, hidden in the quiet space, she knelt, motionless, palms to the deck while subtle reverberations of the ship at anchor fed into her skin. Pain drowned out all else and she waited it out, counting down precious seconds, breathing through the same way she had on so many nights as a teenager when she'd proved to herself that she could, that she had what it took to survive.

Out in shadow beyond the bulwark, the dome of Khalid's head rose from the ladder framing eyes she couldn't see, waiting for an opportunity to feed from one slab of darkness to the next. Somewhere on the other side of the ship Natan and two of the *hawaladar*'s men would already have made the upward climb while they left the fourth behind to guard the inflatable. Their luxury of an extra man was one Munroe couldn't afford. If all went to hell and she had to return to her getaway boat, it would, in spite of the airtight chambers designed to keep it afloat, likely be worn raw and punctured from having been tossed against jagged paint and crusted hull, retrievable and repairable but not in time to save her sorry ass if she needed to escape this floating death trap.

The patrolman in the foremost starboard quadrant walked closer, grew clearer: black cargo pants, black T-shirt, ammunition band crisscrossed over his torso: half commando, half sea ruffian. She tracked him as he strode along the bulwark where Khalid lay, to where the boat, black against the water, floated beneath his feet. Palms to metal, Munroe rose, runner on the starting block, ready to bolt into him if needed, but he continued on, oblivious and blind, and then he turned again, and in that gap Khalid slipped over, rifle in hand, and ran, one shadow to the next, out of sight, somewhere closer to the hostages and the target.

Seconds ticked on, counting down to when Amber would abandon the water and send the captain up before her. Munroe continued through shadow to the coaming of the next hatch over: hunting ground familiar from warm nights spent exploring the ship. Glanced around the corner just long enough to get a bearing on the patrolman, checked aft for the other, and continued beside the long edge, following the patrolman far enough to duck around the fore side of the hatch.

The adrenaline uptick fed into her system, dulling the pain, clarifying thought, slowing time. She waited as he reached the end of his patrol and turned to walk aft again. Counted out steps in her head until he met her line of sight. Lunged from her place of hiding, dragged him back in with her, and slammed him into the edge of the coaming to stifle the yell still gurgling its way out of his throat. In the second of his hesitation when shock flooded his senses, before he'd fully rebounded from the metal into his face, she twisted his rifle from his hands and smashed the butt to the side of his head.

He dropped to his knees and she struck again and again, brutal in the attack until he was bloodied and unconscious, merciful because if she'd used the knife he would already be dead.

The air whispered behind her and Munroe spun, rifle stock to her shoulder, finger a hair away from the trigger.

Khalid froze. Hissed the signal not to shoot.

She lowered the rifle and turned back to the lifeless lump on the deck between the hatches.

"You kill him?" Khalid said.

"No," she said, knelt and felt through enemy pockets until she found a cell phone. Took it from him, opened the casing, and removed the battery. Tossed the pieces and reached for the knife that she'd dropped when she'd grabbed the rifle. If Khalid wanted the pirate slain, he'd have to do it himself. Her kills were primal, instinct that overrode logic and morality, blood and violence made flesh in the rage-induced defense of herself or another, a visceral reaction from the animal brain of the cut and bleeding girl she'd once been, the animal brain that took control and refused to die.

Munroe pulled the second knife and with blades in each fist snuck into Natan's territory, where both patrolmen still plodded in their respective courses. No sign of Natan. No sign of the *hawaladar*'s men. She'd taken the easier route onto the ship to accommodate healing ribs, had left Natan with the harder, longer climb and no ship ladder to cover half the distance, but without the handicap of the captain or a broken body, he and his men still should have made it to the deck first.

Munroe slipped along the port side between the number two and number one hatches, putting herself fully into Natan's territory, at risk of being mistaken for one of the pirates and killed by her own team should they happen upon her. Had to do it. The missing patrolman's absence would flash a silent warning to the others, and the boarding party held but a small window to take them down before they came looking or raised the alarm.

Munroe moved fore, tracking behind the nearest patrolman in an attempt to close the distance and take him by surprise. Not yet finished with the stretch of his patrol, he turned, as if he'd sensed or heard an anomaly and caution and curiosity drew him toward it.

She froze, relying on the shadows to keep her invisible.

The patrolman strode in her direction.

In close contact she was always faster than the hand that drew the gun, but there was too much distance, too much exposure, to fight a man with an automatic rifle. With each of his forward strides, she crept backward, inching for the corner, where she could move out of his line of sight and shield herself for an attack of her own.

He moved faster than she, closing the distance, and although his focus had not yet turned directly toward her, he raised the rifle in her general direction.

Too far from the corner to reach safety, she stopped completely, flattened into the coaming, adrenaline amping higher while she danced the tightrope stretched between surprise and discovery.

He drew nearer, and the sound of his footfalls amplified inside her head as she marked him, tracked him. Munroe shifted tension to her thighs, readied to toss a knife onto the deck as a distraction, to use sudden movement to throw off his aim, to buy enough time to charge into him before he fired.

A rush of whisper stopped her.

The disruption in pattern came as black against black moving behind him, and as if sensing this, the patrolman paused, began to turn, and in that pause two hands reached over his head and yanked a garrote tight into his throat.

The patrolman dropped the rifle, threw his hands to his neck, grasping, flailing, while his feet kicked. Then the struggle stopped.

Natan released his weapon, and the body, throat slashed, dropped to the deck. The kill had taken seconds, had been made with cold professionalism.

Munroe inched away. Natan had come for the fight, for the hostages, for absolution. The men who'd taken this ship were not her enemies the way they were his enemies; they simply stood in the way of what she wanted, and the less blood she shed in getting it, the better. This was Natan's war now.

He reached for the dropped rifle and glanced over his shoulder. The *hawaladar*'s men followed over the foremost bulwark like flecks of dust, barely perceptible against the limited light. Scaling the ship at the bow had given them better cover but a more complicated boarding, explaining the delay.

Munroe scooted backward another several inches and Natan caught her movement. Rolled the rifle in her direction.

She hissed at him, the same signal that Khalid had used with her.

He lowered the weapon and wordlessly turned from her, bled forward until he disappeared into shadows of his own.

Munroe shielded her eyes against the two lights off the bridge, tried to make out shapes and shadows. Had to assume there were watchmen farther up, but if there were, they were either asleep or distracted; otherwise, the alarm would already have been raised.

She crossed the ship again. Came to the body of the Somali she'd bludgeoned, now dead and naked. Khalid was missing. She followed aft in the direction he would have gone, to where the light was better and where the other patrolman, head twisting, body turning, had clearly picked up the absence of his compatriot. The patrolman shouted a name and his voice carried far in the relative silence, a cry picked up by his equal on the other side of the ship. Khalid, dressed in the dead man's clothes, stepped into the light.

The guard flashed a wave of acknowledgment.

Khalid continued, casual and confident, toward the patrolman and as he neared turned slightly, pointing fore, hiding his face and forcing the patrolman to come closer to hear the words, and then he struck, without warning, butt of the rifle up into the man's jaw, a knee to the groin, fist to his opponent's weapon: practiced moves, hand-to-hand combat skill courtesy of the foreign security company that had trained the Puntland antipiracy forces.

The patrolman's rifle went skittering. No rallying cry rose from the other side of the ship: Natan had made fast work of the last man on deck. Munroe paused to listen. Held back while the invading pack moved toward the tower's deck-level door, which was open, showing no sign of light or life from the inside, as if the patrol had been guarding a ghost of a vessel while the hostages had been spirited elsewhere.

CHAPTER 40

Munroe turned from the hunting pack and slid over the gunwale at the ladder. Amber was on her knees in the inflatable, stance wide for balance, her back to the tiller, rifle pointed at the captain, who, at the base of the tube ladder, had his face to his knees and his fingers laced behind his head.

Amber glanced up in response to the motion above her.

"Send him up," Munroe said, and Amber shifted. What words she spoke to the captain were carried away on the wind. He unwound from the protective ball and, with Amber's rifle tracking his movements, reached for a rung and made the swaying, shifting climb.

Munroe met him at the landing. "I told you not to fight or run," she said. The ladder groaned again, and Munroe sheathed a knife, took his elbow, and nudged him onto the deck, continued with him toward the tower.

Amber followed up and reached them with quick strides. "Have you seen Leo?" she said.

Munroe shook her head and nodded to where Natan and his men readied for the breach. Amber brushed past and Munroe caught her arm. "Send me Khalid," she said.

Rifle in hand, head down, Amber ran. Reached the men, and a

half minute later Khalid broke from the group, turned for Munroe, and met her eight meters out.

"We go up," she said. "Take the rear, guard the old man."

The captain's gaze followed Khalid's, tracking up to the perch where, less than four weeks prior, he'd been master of the ship. Hand to his back, Munroe pushed the captain forward, and then, as if broken from a reverie, he matched her stride, needed no encouragement to move up the ladder, and Khalid fell in behind them.

Munroe took the ascent at a steady clip, was winded by the time she reached the halfway point. Paused on the fourth landing. Waited. Listened.

No sign of shooters from above. No sign of anything.

She paused again on the bridge wing and put a hand toward the captain to keep him from following.

The bridge was dark, and from this height the few lit ship lights threw uneven shadows across the deck, casting the hatches in a cloak of splotchy black. Munroe moved deeper onto the darkened wing. The nests that Leo had used for protection had been dismantled, the contents strewn about, leaving shards of wood and a trail of sand. At some point someone had built a fire and scattered the remains of charcoal and bones on the wing deck.

One careful footfall in front of the other, Munroe circled the bridge and, finding the area deserted, returned to the bridge door. The handle gave easily and she slid the door open. A wave of humid rot washed over her, and even from the threshold she could see that the control room floor had been used as a campsite and one of the walls as a urinal. The glass of two windows was shattered and hung precariously in place. Munroe paused, confirmed the captain's and Khalid's locations, then continued in.

With the generator running to power the lights, the pilothouse should also have had power, yet it was unnaturally dark. She paused again; inched into the room and away from the glass to avoid making an easy target against the ambient light. Followed the wall. Heard the noise then, not so much a noise but a whisper ducking from one shadowed crevice to the next, of bare feet slipping along the floor, a brush of air moving fast and in her direction, and she dropped before the machete came crashing at where her head had once been.

She swiped her legs out. Connected with shins. Kicked balance out from under the attacker. He fell hard with a clatter, and she struggled against lack of mobility to get to her feet faster than he did. Wasn't fast enough. The machete swung wildly. Again. And again. She dodged. Crab-crawled backward. Instinct overrode thought, overrode reason, found opportunity, anticipated the strike, and she rolled.

He neared again, she lunged. Connected knife to skin, metal to bone, and with the taste of fear and the scent of blood, euphoria rushed through her veins, feeding the addiction into a peace so sweet that if he should rise from the dead and kill her now she would drift away happy: another death on her hands that she hadn't asked for, another ghost to haunt her sleep and stain her soul. She scanned the room for other attackers. Found his weapon on the floor in the far corner. Released the magazine and brought it out empty. Ran the bolt. Tossed the rifle aside. Like the man on the water who'd brought her to the fuel boat those several weeks ago, the watchman in the tower, away from the action, hadn't been armed the way the main contingent was armed.

Lack of funding? Lack of foresight?

With her feet she shoved his body into the corner streaked with urine. Then she stepped out and urged the captain and Khalid onto the bridge, into the critical time window before the alarm was raised, when they still had a chance to get off the ship. If they weren't going to be able to get the *Favorita* moving, they needed to get the crew off. Now.

The captain, reacting to the stench and the heat, paused at the threshold, and Khalid prodded him forward to the instrument panel, where he stood neither moving nor speaking, and Munroe's impatience bubbled up into words. "What kind of shape are we in?" she said, though she knew the answer to half the equation without a response.

"I need oil pressure," he said.

Even with the captain on the bridge, even with power to the ship, the engine couldn't run until the oil was up, and that would take twenty to thirty minutes beyond however long it took to get the oil pumps working—provided an engineer was even alive to make that happen.

"I'm going after Janek," she said. "Khalid stays with you to keep you from leaving the bridge. I just watched him kill two men, so don't be an idiot. Do what he wants and he won't shoot you in the legs."

The captain glared and she held eye contact. Then she turned to face Khalid and in Somali said, "Until we're under way, nobody comes through this door. If they insist, shoot them. Even if it's me."

Khalid gave her a mock salute. The captain moved forward and fiddled with a switch, and the panel came alive, casting a macabre glow over his face and much of the room. He nodded approvingly. Stretched for another switch but Munroe said, "Don't turn on the lights."

His hand stopped. "I'll get you your oil," she said. "Just get the ship to Mombasa and you can disappear."

MUNROE WAS ON the third switchback down when, from somewhere deep inside the tower, the first rifle reports rang out, thunderclaps suppressed by their containment: enough to know that the element of surprise had been lost. She raced down the last two levels, crept through the hatchway that Natan and his men had breached.

The interior of the ship was dark, and although the air was not as rank as the bridge's, it was stale and mixed with old smoke and body odor. She closed the hatch behind her and sealed it shut. Listened for sound, hoped for noise, some indication that the interior had been secured and the hostages rescued, but got only silence and darkness.

The *Favorita* had no true citadel, no safe room built to withstand explosives, to protect the crew with food and water and communications equipment as they holed up and hoped for rescue. That would have been expensive to build, cost prohibitive for this wreck of a ship. The so-called citadel for the *Favorita* was instead an oversize berth on the engineer's level, fine for the crew to put themselves out of harm's way while the armed guards fought it out with invading pirates, but once the ship was taken it would have turned into a prison of its own making and eventually a tomb.

If there were hostages in the safe room now, they would be dead.

Munroe paced in the opposite direction, down a long passageway, peering into spaces where anything not welded, riveted, or bolted down had been dismantled, presumably offloaded, meaning that hostages had probably never been kept here; was interrupted by another short burst of gunfire and then pounding against a bulkhead. She crept upward, found Ali on the crew's landing and Natan at the end of the passageway slamming the butt of his rifle into a door that wouldn't open. Instant assessment told her they'd taken the deck and whatever pirates had been here had locked themselves inside a berth. Amber and Omar were missing, so Munroe took another level up, the time crunch bearing down on her. The pirates locked in the berth would have phones, would have notified their commander on shore and called for rescue.

Thirty minutes to get oil up; less than that for boats on shore to launch and reach the ship. Had to find Janek.

Another burst of controlled rifle reports echoed in ricochet along the walls. Escalating fire was returned, not nearly as controlled. Munroe turned down another passageway, slid along the base of the wall in the direction of the staccato, adrenaline floating her into the precious calm and focus of battle, the ethereal peace she strove for and never found in her months of quiet running. Behind her the wall reverberated with pounding and carried muted cries for help.

She spotted Omar in a nook, hissed for his attention. Spoke with her hands; hoped to hell he didn't later mistake her for an enemy; then felt her way along the wall, fingers guiding her as the vibration intensified.

Omar crawled from his hiding place and Munroe lost sight of him. A muzzle flashed from outside a berth, a rapid waste of ammunition that made a joke out of the dead guy on the bridge with his empty rifle.

Munroe reached a door where the pounding was strongest. Groped for the lock, a hastily engineered contraption that kept the bolt from moving; hit the hilt of the knife against it until it gave way. Slid flat against the wall and reached out to the side to push the door open. Waited for movement from within the berth, for anything that would tell her she'd picked the wrong one. Another burst of gunfire broke from down the passageway, and Amber yelled for Omar.

Slowly the door swung inward. Near the floor, so close she could have touched it, a head poked out. The face of the cook squinted up. His eyes met hers, and he let out a yelp and darted back inside. She followed after him. Tried to make sense of the bodies inside the darker room. Couldn't count them, but from the air and the smell she knew that there were far too many for the space in which they'd been contained.

"Janek," she said. "Where's Janek?"

"Not here," a voice said, and she recognized it as Victor's.

Munroe knelt and crawled over bodies in his direction, close enough to see his face. Victor met her eyes and though his mouth opened, no words came out. His face was haggard, he'd lost considerable weight, and his thigh was wrapped with rotting cloth and crusted with dried blood.

Leo was on the floor, his neck in an improvised brace, stabilization that kept him immobile. Victor said, "He cannot move his legs."

"Where are the engineers?"

He shook his head. She stumbled over arms and legs to get out, fleeing the stench, but more, desperate to find the men who could keep this night from growing far worse than it already had.

CHAPTER 41

Two more doors, two more busted locks, two more timid entries and crawling between rifle bursts and screams, of not knowing who was still alive, of a single-minded focus pulling her through the tightly wound urban warfare that went on around her until Munroe found the door to the berth that housed the engineer.

She grabbed Janek, shook him. "We need oil pressure," she said. As if grasping the situation, understanding her intent if not the words, he stumbled over the others in the berth and crawled after her. Threw himself to the floor when the fighting got so close it was deafening. And on they went; a mile it seemed, and then they were free of the war and ran down the dimly lit passageway to the engine room.

Munroe shut the hatchway, sealing them into silence, and Janek, indifferent to her presence, turned on an emergency lamp and methodically surveyed the room, assessing, inventorying what hadn't been pilfered, muttering words that got louder and more vitriolic as time wore on.

She watched him, anxiety welling up and threatening to suffocate her. Down in the windowless room, shut off from the action, she was helpless, could only watch as he made increasingly frantic gestures. She wanted to run. Wanted air. Wanted to know the status of the fight, to see for herself as the enemy boats approached, to strategize the defense against the oncoming assault, but she had become Janek's personal bodyguard. Couldn't risk leaving him yet because no matter what else, as long as she had the captain on the bridge and the engineer at the oil pumps, they could get the ship moving. Maybe.

Time clicked on, hours to the minute, a full day perhaps, while Janek swapped wrench for screwdriver, thumbed through empty supply drawers, cannibalized parts from smaller machines, then sighed and shoved. How long had they been down in real time? Ten minutes? Fifteen? The oil pumps rumbled to life and he smiled. Gave her a thumbs-up, and the weight of anxiety shed from her like unwanted skin.

"How long?" she said, and when he didn't answer, she tried Russian.

"Maybe we have enough pressure in twenty minutes," he said. "But it's no guarantee."

Her body remained still, her mind frantic. She couldn't stay here; had to stay here. Fought the urge to pace the room. A crackle from the two-way on her belt broke through the mania: Amber's voice and the all-clear, and Natan, a hurried exchange and then radio silence. They had the ship. She could leave Janek long enough to do what he did best. She would send Rodel to help, would get a bearing on what was coming at them next.

Munroe unlocked the hatchway, stepped over the threshold, and stopped at the ringing buzz of a busted speaker. Janek reached left, yanked a receiver off the wall. She stayed to catch a whiff of the conversation, something about bunkers, the tons of fuel the ship still carried, heard enough to confirm that the captain was still on the bridge, doing his job, and when the conversation turned back to the urgency of oil pressure, she left.

The deck was windblown and quiet, and in the lapping silence of wind and waves, Munroe scanned the shoreline with the spotting scope. Lights blinked in and out, clustered and patterned in a way that denoted heavy activity. She didn't find boats on the water but wouldn't rule out the possibility that they'd already launched, were on their way, but in the vastness and the crests and swells of the water she'd not seen them. She strode back inside to where the passageways were still dim and, without the rush and panic of trying to find Janek, had the presence of mind to realize that most of the bulbs had been stolen.

She passed Natan in the hall. "Where's Amber?" she said.

"Up," he said, and brushed past.

"They're coming," she said, and Natan paused, turned back.

"The munitions are in the number one hold," she said. "Dead center, about three bags down. How many men are aloft?"

"Two of mine, some crew."

"Get the hatches open. I'll send them to you."

"What about the engine?"

"Twenty minutes to find out if everything runs," she said. "Maybe longer."

His lips drew taut and he stalked toward the deck.

Munroe returned to the berth where Victor had been. Found the room empty but for Leo and Amber, who was on the floor with one of Leo's hands in hers. His other hand was on her face, thumb wiping away tears while Amber laughed, and they whispered in a conversation Munroe couldn't hear, didn't need to hear to feel, and for that small moment she didn't despise him. She paused in the entry. Leo met her gaze and then turned away. Amber looked up.

"We need all fighting hands," Munroe said. "Boats are coming from shore."

Amber leaned over, kissed Leo's forehead, and without a word stood and left him. Outside the berth Munroe said, "Natan's already working to get the hatches open. Where are Omar and Ali?"

"Interrogating the pirates, collecting weapons and phones."

"And the others?"

"Emmanuel is dead. David is missing—we don't know."

"Victor? Marcus?"

"Somewhere," Amber said. "I lost track after we secured the ship."

"We're going to have to arm the crew," Munroe said. "They can fight or die. There won't be second chances."

Amber said, "I'll take the upper decks," and with rifle in hand she headed for the ladder at a run. Munroe started down, strode berth to berth, opening hatchways, seeking out the crew, who had already scattered throughout the ship, and with the urgency of another fight bearing down on them sent them to the deck, where Natan was at work.

Victor, weapon in hand, found her in the helmsman's quarters, and although his eyes expressed delight at seeing her, gratitude that she'd come for them, they had no time for sentiment. Through him, Munroe learned the damage: The first mate was dead; the second mate had been tortured for information on where the captain was hiding. Rodel, the second engineer, and one of the crew were also dead, and of Leo's original team, only Marcus had made it through unwounded.

Several of the cell phones that Omar had left piled up in the passageway rang and vibrated, their screens lit up like flashlight beams in the dim corridor, omens warning of what was to come from the shoreline. Uncertain of the alliances among the *hawaladar*'s men, unwilling to allow the opportunity for one of them to let loose the pirates they'd just captured, Munroe sent Omar to the deck and left Victor in his place, guarding the berth where they were now stashed.

ON THE DECK outside, splotches of shadow milled around the number one hatch, and from the tower, the last of the crewmen well enough to walk spilled out the hatchway, unwillingly mustered into service by Amber's rifle.

Natan had already brought up Yusuf from his inflatable, and together with Marcus, they'd utilized the deck crane to improvise a davit to haul all three hundred pounds of wet rubber and engine onto the ship. If Munroe could have spared the manpower, she would have sent Yusuf and Ali to retrieve the other craft, but in the moment, collecting the boat wasn't worth the risk.

On the two-way radio she attempted to raise Joe on the dhow. Reached his boatman. "The counterattack is on the way," she said.

The reply came delayed, the message having been passed one man to the next.

"We confirm to follow the plan," the boatman said.

The dhow would move in closer, prepare to rescue whoever managed to escape the ship if jumping overboard was what it came to.

From the dark, in the direction of the shoreline, the first muzzle flashes sparked against the black, light followed by the distant clap of gunfire that carried easily over the water.

Another five minutes and the boats would be within lethal distance.

The crew, spurred into action by the noise, worked to raise the anchor, scrambled down into the hold, where, under Natan's direction and aiding the deck crane, which couldn't do the job fast enough or with enough precision, they created a chain to remove the bags of rice and uncover the munitions.

Munroe stood still for a moment, watching, processing, strategizing, and in that moment of quietness, pain that had dulled in the adrenaline of the fight returned, ramping higher, and then higher still, leaving her hands shaking. She turned from the action and slipped toward the stern, into shadow. She had put the captain in position. Gotten Janek to where he needed to be, and the oil pumps now built pressure somewhere beneath her feet.

The staccato on the ocean was closer now. Three minutes, maybe.

She drew a long inhale to settle the trembling. She was empty, fading; stumbled for the ladder to take her down to the engine room for one last strategy reassessment.

Janek's face jerked up when she opened the hatchway. His face and arms were covered in grease, and parts surrounded him on the floor.

"What?" she said.

"The engine," he said. "Repairs." The stress in his voice told her what she needed. Munroe closed her eyes and slid down the wall and into the calm of finality. Not defeat, not surrender, simply the acknowledgment that for now, her job was finished. In the state she was in, she'd be useless up on deck—a casualty waiting to happen—and no matter how hard the men above her fought, if Janek couldn't get the pieces reassembled and the engine operational, all was for naught anyway.

The broken speaker buzzed again. Janek reached for the phone. Grunted monosyllabic answers and then in response to what could only have been the captain's alert that the attack was closing in said, "I'm moving as fast as I can. I will have her for you by the time the oil is ready."

Munroe drew slow breaths, focused on her extremities, on the rumble of the oil pumps, on the sound of Janek's methodical assembly; and in the minutes that ticked out long the pain dulled to a constant throb and the shaking subsided and she opened her eyes. Half the parts on the floor were gone, and Janek, focused on the task at hand, remained oblivious when she stood and left him for the war above her head.

On the deck the floodlights were off and under the clouded sky the musical score of combat came in fitful bursts, weapon reports that lit the night in all directions, an orchestration that kept the attack boats from drawing too close, kept them circling like sharks waiting for weakness while the music rose higher, faster, and in crescendo came the whoosh expulsion of a rocket-propelled grenade, and then another, and Munroe smiled and slid down the wall and closed her eyes while the symphony played on.

The first two grenades missed their targets, but the explosion of the third lit up the night with timpani and crashing cymbals, and a frantic answer rose from afar. Another roar from the percussion section, another flash of light, visible even with her eyes closed. As long as the attackers didn't have a way to get close to the ship, as long as the RPGs and ammunition supplies held out, as long as none of the attack boats managed to sneak men on board, as long as Janek could get the engine running, they would make it out.

The booming of the symphony rose higher as the minutes extended far beyond the twenty that Janek had promised, and in the music of war Munroe found the patterns. Too much focus in some directions, not enough in others. She stood. Braced for pain and ran the deck to the number three hold. Followed the shelter of the coaming until she reached the first shooters and, through hand signals, was pointed toward the rifles and ammunition they'd unburied. Found a weapon. Loaded a magazine, seated it, charged the rifle, and returned to the shadows, watching and waiting for the inevitable.

CHAPTER 42

Munroe scanned the length of the ship, waited three minutes, four, before the first head peered up from the ladder: starboard, facing away from shore, away from where Natan and Marcus worked target practice with the grenade launchers—a replay of the maneuver from the first night of attack, when the men had come silently while distraction lit up the night on the opposite side of the ship.

Munroe slid through the shadows, crept closer for accuracy, pain intensity returning with each foot gained. She pulled the two-way off her belt, risked detection, gave notice of the impending boarding. Amber responded from the bow; was farther from the targets than Munroe. No response from Natan.

The first man slipped onto the deck, silhouette of a rifle in hand. Two heads rose behind him. Pushing forward against shortened breaths, Munroe crab-walked nearer; knelt for stability and, hands shaking with a trembling she couldn't control, depressed the trigger. In response to the fusillade, the first man retreated back over the gunwale. Munroe crawled forward again. Gave up another five rounds. Didn't make a hit, but the suppressive fire drove all three men farther down the ladder.

And then the shudder.

Noise. Movement. The ship groaning as the propeller kicked on. Munroe called for Natan again.

No response.

Emboldened by the minimal defense, spurred on by the ship's movement, the men slipped back up and rushed the deck. Munroe didn't have the accuracy to take them down one hit at a time, sniper-style, had no strength to track after them, hunting through shadows to kill before they killed. Rifle stock to her shoulder, eye lined up to the sight, Munroe gave up another three rounds and scored a torso hit on one of the targets. He jerked, twisted, fell. The others scattered toward the holds, and she lost them in the dark, where they would be confused for her own men, set free to sneak among and kill the unsuspecting.

Without options, with no response from Natan, Munroe stood to follow after them. A rip of gunfire answered her movement: bullets tracing the night, aimed not at her but in the direction the attackers had fled. From the shadows an outline of arms and legs flailed into a heap and the second figure bolted from its hiding place. The gunfire continued. The runner yelled, twisted a near full circle, and stumbled; crawled forward, rifle swinging from one point to the next spraying ammunition, trying to find his enemy, until his gun went silent and Amber stepped from the shadows and stalked forward, firing one deliberate round after the next until she reached him. Stood over him. Plugged a last bullet into his head; moved to the next man and did the same. Stood over the dead for a half moment and then, face turned up into the dark in Munroe's general direction, tipped fingers to her forehead, turned, and strode back toward her position on the bow.

THE SHIP TOOK up speed slowly and the attack boats gave chase, a mile or two or three, kept at a distance by the RPGs until, after what felt like a century, the muzzle flashes stopped, the rocket fire ceased, the air fell silent, and the water went dark with the symphony's end.

Munroe stood on deck breathing in the night, the collective sigh on the ship, and the dawning realization that, though there could yet be new attacks as word of the *Favorita*'s recapture spread, they truly had a chance of making it to a port of safety. She turned toward the bridge and, with legs and hands still shaking, started up.

The captain nodded when she entered.

"What's the situation with the fuel?" she said.

"We travel slow, we make to Mombasa."

"How slow is slow?"

"Six, seven knots," he said, and she groaned. At that speed, they'd be targets for the entire length of the journey.

"Khalid will stay with you," she said. "As soon as we figure out what supplies are left, I'll have food sent up, but you can't leave the bridge."

He looked at her fully then, wore an expression that wasn't quite pain or concern but came close, and offered silent questions in place of words.

"They're dead," she said.

"Both of them?"

The second mate had been blinded in the torture. She simply nodded.

"They weren't the only ones," she said, and turned from him. Paused at the door but had nothing with which to articulate the spite stuck inside her throat. He'd taunted fate by using blackmail to get the weapons, taunted fate again by attempting to deliver them to a buyer off the Somali coast. Men without options had died for his failed conceit.

Hands resting on the control panel, face to the broken window so that he avoided eye contact, the captain said, "You keep your promise?"

"Yes," she said, and left him. Returned to the deck, where the crew, released from duty by Natan, trudged back toward the tower, two of them dragging a bag of rice, perhaps the only food left on the ship. By the railing, Amber shoved the bodies of the men she'd killed and with her feet pushed them one by one beneath the bottom rail and dumped them overboard. Munroe came to stand beside her, and together they stared down at the water, where in place of the ladder and inflatable there was only blackness and a river of red ink on Amber's balance sheet, everything likely torn loose when the ship began to move and the damaged boat became a trawl.

"Do we have the fuel to get us all the way?" Amber said.

"Supposedly."

"Leo is paralyzed," she said. "No feeling from the waist down. He needs medical care."

"Will you get help in Mombasa?"

"I don't know," Amber said, and then leaving the conversation unfinished, turned for the tower. Munroe followed, slower, craving rest and a way to allow the pain to subside. Instead, she pulled the satellite phone and powered it on. Caught a signal. Waited until she was certain she wouldn't be overheard and dialed the Sentrim Castle, the hotel Sergey and the Russian delegation had moved to after she'd dropped off the first picture of the captain.

At her request, the front desk connected her to the room of Anton, the boss man, and, voice groggy and angry, he answered after several long rings.

"Hello," she said. Used English because it would give him the fewest clues to her identity. "Did you enjoy my gift, the photo of the friend you have been so desperate to find?"

"Who is this?" he said, his words thick with sleep.

"Nikola Goran," she said, mimicking his accent.

"You are not."

"I do have him," she said. "If you still want him."

"Yes," he said, and the sleep was gone, his tone alert and wary.

"We should make a trade."

"What do you want?"

"Five hundred thousand in U.S. dollars by wire transfer. Half now, half upon delivery."

"Is not possible," he said, but his voice betrayed a measure of doubt, which she had expected. In the grand scheme of things she'd not asked for a lot, and their calculations would be based on the up-front money—they'd never plan to pay the rest.

"You should speak with your boss about it," she said. "If he says no, then your friend will be given a passport and put on the next flight out of Nairobi. You will never find him again."

A pause and the heavy breathing of thought. "I need time," he said.

"I'll give you an hour."

"If I can make an arrangement, then I must have proof that you do have this man."

"Not a problem," she said, and ended the call.

She waited out the hour in the coaming shadows of the number three hold, back to the deck, face to the stars, occasionally catching sight of Natan and Marcus, Omar and Ali, all four of whom patrolled on high alert for the first sign of another attack, though if it came, like the ones before, they'd probably not know it until too late.

The gentle rocking of the ship pulled her in and out of sleep, and when the hour had passed, she stood and walked toward the bulwark, where, without the clutter of the deck crane, the signal was better.

Anton picked up the phone on the first ring. "We will trade you money for Nikola," he said.

"You'll have your proof in the morning," she said. "Check with the front desk for a fax. After that you have twelve hours to wire the money. If it's not there, Nikola is gone. Do you have a pen?"

"Yes," he said.

She recited routing details from memory, swift codes and account numbers, said, "No payment, no prize." Then the hair on the back of her neck rose, the animal instinct of being watched. The boss man grunted, acceptance and confirmation, and Munroe pressed End.

The air shifted behind her.

She said, "What now?" but spun before the words were fully out of her mouth. Blocked Natan's blow with her forearm and felt the impact down into her chest.

"Traitor," he hissed. "Selling us out."

"No," she said, and shifted, danced to slip from another blow, and then another as he struck again and again. Battle-hardened and a brutal fighter, he drove her back against the bulwark and, without the strength to do more than hurt herself if she tried to strike back without a weapon, she struggled to dodge, to block the beating, and still he pressed on.

"Stop," she said. "There's no point to this."

He struck, she swerved; his follow-through connected with her cheekbone.

Munroe's head rang, and she shook it off.

"Tonight I finish the misery I should have the first time," he said, and in the menace beneath his words she understood that with the ship secure, he didn't need her anymore, had every intention of succeeding where Leo had failed.

She reached for the knife without thinking, and in the heat of the moment, her hand on the blade, the jungle rose in the darkness and took her back to where weakness had made her strong. Warmth crept up her arms and the bloodlust rose, the desperate need to finish the fight, to strike before struck, to draw blood before her own was shed.

Natan kept at her, blow by blow, pain rising higher in the background of her consciousness as she dodged and blocked and sliced a blade into his arm trailing a gash that made him jerk back and pause.

Dizzying euphoria rose in answer to the connection and the war drum pounded harder, louder, drowning her senses, drowning out reason, filling her with Pavlovian need.

"I don't want to kill you," she panted. "If you keep at me, I won't be able to help myself. Please stop."

He hesitated just out of reach. Looked at his arm and the blood that flowed freely; shock, perhaps, that she'd managed to connect a blow, or shock that she'd actually cut him. She took the knife to her own shirt and sliced a ribbon off it. Grabbed his hand and wrapped the fabric tightly to stanch the flow, and there, while her hands were busy tending to his wound, he struck again.

The blow hit her chest, a punishing pain that rivaled the worst of the beating on the night she'd almost died; it dropped her to her knees. The world tilted at odd angles, the color of her vision shifted to gray. Unable to stand, she watched his feet as they approached, senses measuring time by each heartbeat, lengthening and distorting her vision, blood in her ears rushing out all else but the thirst for retaliation. Another second, another step, and he would be close enough.

He neared, and in response the blade came alive.

From behind came footsteps, and a clink of metal on metal, and Victor's voice saying, "No warnings, Natan. Stop or I finish this."

"Rescue with one hand," Natan said, "stab in the back with the other." He pivoted slightly, his face turned toward Victor. "There is more to this than you see, Victor. You should never meddle in things you don't understand."

When Victor didn't answer, didn't move, Natan flung an accusatory finger toward Munroe. "A traitor," he said. "Using us, using Amber, to take the ship. Using us to get to something else."

Munroe closed her eyes, drew in a long breath, and held it until her lungs burned with want of air.

"Step away," Victor said, and his voice was closer now and Munroe could see his feet. She exhaled and pushed away the need, the fire, the death. Drew in another long breath and let the poison seep out with her exhale.

Victor stepped around Natan in Munroe's direction. "Even if it's true," he said, "we would be rotting in wait with no rescue." He knelt. Offered Munroe an arm and helped her stand.

Upright, she turned to Natan.

"He takes the wise in their own craftiness," she said, "and the counsel of the cunning is carried headlong."

"What is this?" Natan said.

"I told you to let me work. You in all your smartness will get us killed."

"You are lying."

"Think what you want," she said, and with her arm on Victor's, turned her back to him, fighting the pain that wouldn't simmer.

In the passageway outside the Somalis' berth, where two of the ship's crew waited as guards in Victor's place, she reached for one of the cell phones piled up outside the door. Had to kneel to collect it and, with Victor helping her, made it upright again; allowed him to lead her to an empty berth and settled on the bed, adrenaline dumping, body burning.

He lingered in the doorway as if unsure if it was safe to leave her. "You be all right?" he said.

"Yes," she whispered, and when he'd shut the door, Munroe powered on the Somali phone and, hands shaking, dialed the *hawaladar*.

CHAPTER 43

The trajectories of the dhow and the *Favorita* converged, vessels traveling in convoy, a slow chug several miles off the Somali coastline, lights off, ship dark to avoid attracting attention, still very much within the high-risk area. Head on the pillow, Munroe closed her eyes listening to the background chatter of the two-way, following the progress until she drifted into sleep.

At some point Victor returned, and as Mary had done not so long ago, he pressed a tablet to Munroe's lips and followed the pill with water. The opioid wrapped her in warmth and she drifted into oblivion where time ceased to exist. Then woke with a start, blinking against natural light, disoriented and gasping for air, urged to rush onward because no matter what the hour, the daylight told her she was already late in delivering her proof to the Russians.

Munroe pushed up, rolled her legs off the bed, and, wincing against the stiffness and pain, unbound the tape that braced her chest. Used her T-shirt to dry her skin, which was mottled with sweat and itching with heat rash, and pulled the shirt back on. Pushed both phones into her pockets and, still woozy, opened the door to the passageway.

Victor was on the floor several meters down, rifle across his lap, keeping guard outside the berth that housed the Somali prisoners.

He tipped his head back when she stepped out, bushy beard and wild hair turning his smile into something ghoulish. "You sleep good?" he said.

Munroe forced a half smile, the best she had to offer, and at the sound of his voice a rumble picked up from behind him: banging and shouting, muted by the door and wall. Victor slammed the butt of his rifle into the door and swore in Spanish.

"How many are in there?" Munroe said.

"Eight."

"Have they had water?"

Victor shook his head. "There is no unity in the decision of what to do with them, so I wait."

"Just make the decision yourself."

He shrugged. The banging continued. Victor sighed. Stood. Opened the door and the tumult picked up volume. He motioned Munroe to have a look and she peered into the filthy room where once the crew had been kept captive and now what pirates still lived held bound hands out in the universal sign of prayer, pleading for water and for mercy.

"Amber is with Leo," Victor said. "She is not concerned with them. Marcus and Natan call for executions."

"And you?"

"They showed no pity to us."

"Would you dump them overboard?"

"I would," he said.

"That would make you the same as them."

"I have no problem with that."

Munroe shut the door and Victor continued to stare after it.

"It should be the captain's decision," she said, "as the master of the ship."

Victor snorted.

"At least give them water," she said.

Victor's beard twitched again, and without a word he handed her the rifle. She stood watch until he returned with a sloshing bucket and a single plastic cup; stayed with him until he transferred the water into the room and secured the door again; and then she left for the bridge.

The captain was in a chair, dozing, and Khalid nodded a greeting when she entered, then returned his focus to the ocean ahead, as if the two men had been playing tag team in this way during the long last hours while the ship's autopilot handled the navigation. Bowls of rice littered the desk space—someone else having made good on the promise Munroe had failed to deliver.

Munroe knelt in front of the captain and snapped a picture with the satellite phone. He startled awake at the resultant beep, expression blank for a second as if dusting away mental cobwebs, and then said, "Why?" Same question he'd asked when she'd taken the picture in the hotel room.

"Making good on my promise," she said, and now that he was awake and subtlety was no longer an option, she opened drawers and dug through them, found a permanent marker, and said, "Give me your arm."

"Why?" he said again.

"Just do it," she said, and although he eyed her suspiciously, he offered his wrist. She scribbled the day's date on his forearm, said, "Hold it by your face," and when he did, she took another picture.

"What's it for?" he said.

"Your freedom."

He continued to study her, his face creased with exhaustion and disbelief, and rightfully so, and to break the silence and make her exit, Munroe said, "What's our position? How many hours to arrival?"

The captain stood and walked toward the panel. Scanned the instruments and then squinted toward the ceiling as if running calculations in his head. "Ninety, more or less," he said.

"Fuel?"

"At this rate, yes, we will make."

"And you?" she said. "Are there any crew members capable of standing watch so you can get some proper sleep?"

He hesitated a moment before answering, as if waiting for a trick or a trap, and when none came, he nodded toward Khalid. "We do okay," he said.

Munroe repeated the question in Somali for Khalid, whose attention was still entirely on the swath of ocean ahead. He turned only long enough to confirm agreement, so she left them for the bridge wing and a better signal.

The dhow traveled some seventy meters off port, and Joe stood shirtless under the sun by the fuel drums, siphoning fuel into a container. Munroe watched him from the rail, waiting for the satellite and phone to sync, and eventually Joe looked up, saw her, and acknowledged her with a wave, and she waved back. Marcus and Yusuf patrolled the deck below, and although Munroe couldn't see him, she supposed that Natan, even if he slept, wasn't far away.

The phone vibrated in her hand.

She sent the captain's photo to the hotel's e-mail, impatient through the slow connection, and eventually, when the transmittal was complete, she called the hotel to confirm its receipt and sweet-talked the reservationist into printing the image and having the page delivered to the Russian boss man's room. The delay would have set him on edge and worked to her advantage.

Munroe waited another twenty minutes, then called the hotel again and asked to be transferred directly.

Anton picked up on the first ring.

"You've received your proof," she said. "You have twelve hours to wire the first half of the payment. No money, no prize."

"I understand how it works," he said, and she hung up, cutting him off before he'd finished.

TWELVE HOURS FROM the phone call brought Munroe to four in the morning Somali time; at five hours behind Singapore, it didn't leave much of a wait for her bank to open. At the start of business hours she made the call to verify that the transfer had arrived into her account, and then, with the knowledge that payment had been received, another piece on the chessboard moved into place and she returned to the berth to sleep until the alarm on the phone pulled her awake again at seven and she called the *hawaladar*.

She'd not spoken to him since they'd taken the ship, and that conversation had lasted only long enough for her to confirm that they'd secured the *Favorita* and ensure that he received the news directly from her because she suspected that Joe, as the *hawaladar's* insurance toward getting his investment back, had his own way of communicating the details.

The *hawaladar* answered as if she was now long overdue. Munroe gave him their estimated time of arrival as per the captain's calculations, and he countered with news of the Russian delegation.

"I've had men watching them," he said. "They're working with the port authorities and I fear they're expecting the freighter. This might make it difficult to seize the ship."

An undercurrent of accusation ran through his words, and with the accusation an unwitting confirmation that whatever had allowed the attackers to track the ship from the beginning was with the *Favorita* even still.

"Define difficult," she said.

"This would depend on what they want and why they are interested," he said, and paused. Finger-pointing permeated his silence, and when she didn't rise to defend herself, he said, "To the Kenyans, I am Somali. It doesn't matter that I'm a British citizen, I remain the enemy. My contacts only go so deep and they are fickle. Depending on how well these Russians are connected, or who in the government they involve, this could end badly. Personally I stand to lose an investment, but you risk losing more."

His toying annoyed her. She said, "In what way?"

"Rumor has it that the crew and captain will be arrested as soon as they arrive. You are crew, are you not?"

"If the Russians are expecting the ship, it's not from me," she said. "Have you already filed?"

"I continue to wait."

"Thank you for the warning," she said. "I'll make contingencies."

"And you will bring me my vessel?"

"I gave you my word."

The *hawaladar* ended the call, and Munroe closed her eyes, let the wind and the salt air fill her thoughts, then turned from the bridge wing and headed down. She dialed again for Anton.

"The money has arrived," she said. "You fulfilled your end, so I fulfill mine. The *Favorita* will arrive in Mombasa port within the next seventy-two hours. Nikola is the captain. If you intend to collect your prize, you'll need your men. All of them."

"Nikola is with the ship?" he said, and his voice betrayed anger and disbelief, as if he'd been played the fool. "I cannot believe this."

"You want your man and I want the rest of my money," she said. "I'll notify you when the ship is close. Be prepared to deliver the remainder before boarding."

THEY WERE IN Kenyan waters, five miles off the coast, when the vessels cut power and under Natan's guidance the *Favorita*'s crew reopened the hatches and all able hands offloaded the munitions. The inflatable became the raft to transfer to the dhow what few pieces were worth keeping and the rest they dumped overboard, ridding themselves of the certainty they'd go from prisoners of Somali pirates to prisoners of the Kenyan legal system. What the Russian delegation might plan was a different issue that Munroe kept to herself.

When the transfer was finished, Munroe sent Yusuf and Ali back to the dhow, where there was no opportunity for them to interfere with the pirates, who, because of indecision, were still on board the *Favorita* and at this juncture more likely to be handed over to the authorities when they reached Mombasa than to be dumped overboard. And with the inflatable pulled back onto the freighter and the ship under way once more, Munroe went in search of Amber.

The door to Leo's room was closed and Munroe knocked, opened it without waiting for an answer. The berth was still rank with the stench of unwashed bodies, but not nearly as bad as it had been when she'd first stumbled into it.

Ignoring Leo, Munroe knelt beside Amber.

"You still have a two-way," she said.

Amber nodded, and Munroe handed her the satellite phone. "Hold on to this," she said, "and always keep your radio with you."

Amber's expression clouded with questions.

"Just trust me," Munroe said.

Amber reached for the phone and Munroe held on to it for emphasis, their fingers touching, connected by the chunk of metal and plastic, and when Amber nodded, Munroe let go and left the berth for the bridge, where she could time the increments of their journey as they headed toward Mombasa.

CHAPTER 44

North of Malindi, in the predawn mist, while the captain looked on from the bridge and the crew slept, Munroe and Victor secured Natan's inflatable to the deck crane and took the boat over the side. Munroe rode the chain down to the water, then used the oars to keep the inflatable from washing into the ship while Marcus rappelled down the side to join her, and then, turning the nose of the inflatable toward shore, they continued wordlessly in the direction of the lights until they crossed the break and Marcus worked them forward with the oars.

When the bottom of the boat scraped sand, Munroe slipped over the fore gunwale and waded the rest of the way up, and by the time she glanced back, the boat and the man in it had already blended into the dark, leaving the fading hum of the engine as the only evidence they'd been there at all.

At the grass line Munroe sat; stared out toward where the *Favorita* drifted, invisible in the night. She'd handed the issue of the Somali captives over to Amber Marie to free Victor of the burden, then tasked him with backing up Khalid in guarding the captain. Shoes back on, she trudged inland, met a dirt road, and followed the edge south until the sun was fully over the eastern treetops, and at last a car passed and she flagged the driver. He slowed and she negotiated a ride to Malindi. Once in the city, in a near repeat of what she'd done just weeks prior, Munroe secured a ride to Mombasa and returned to the hotel where, in the aftermath of her brush with death those many nights ago, she'd found a temporary haven to shower and sleep.

She'd carried with her the Kenyan satellite phone, a two-way radio, and the bag of clothes and items that she'd bought and stolen along the way, shuffled from hotel to beach house to dhow and finally retrieved during the ferrying of light arms off the *Favorita*. The hot water washed away the dirt and stink of more than a week without bathing, and she scrubbed at the death in Garacad, a stain that wouldn't wash away, until the soap was gone and her skin was raw, then she left the shower and dialed Sergey.

When he answered, she oozed sugar into her voice. "I'm back in town but only for a night," she said. "My boss is calling me home and I fly to Nairobi tomorrow."

"Then we must party," he said, though from the lilt in his tone, the party had started some time ago.

"Sentrim Castle," she said.

"I'll be in the lobby at eight," he said, and with a hint of playfulness added, "No, perhaps not. You will have to find me."

"The hunt is on," she said, and ended the call. Images of Sami, dead on the beach, bubbled back to the surface and the anger she'd set aside to utilize her pawns in a long-term strategy to checkmate became the driving force once more.

Munroe dressed again. She'd ditched the handgun—she was safer that way—strapped the knives to her thighs under the knee-length skirt, applied moisturizer and makeup over her sunburned skin. Studied the transformation in the mirror, staring into gray eyes from which the spark had long ago died, and turned away from this thing she had become.

She arrived at the hotel ahead of schedule and wound her way among large potted plants and the mostly foreign hotel guests, found Sergey and the older delegate on a patio together with a blonde, each man with two empty glasses on the table and a third in hand, Sergey flirting shamelessly with the woman while she sipped something orange.

Munroe continued on, returned to the front desk long enough to charm the number of the boss man's room from the staff, and then resumed the hunt, approaching Sergey's table, flashing a radiant smile, and inviting herself into the open chair.

Sergey mirrored her smile. "You found me," he said, and drained his drink and knocked his glass hard onto the table.

Munroe crossed her legs in a long, languid movement, draped an arm over the back of her chair, made her fingers into the shape of a gun, winked, and pulled the imaginary trigger. "Bang."

Sergey smiled again, charming and nauseating, and pushed back from the table. "Now that you are here," he said, and stood as if they were all meant to leave. By way of a passing wave he introduced the blonde. "She is Olivie," he said. "She only speaks French."

As if somehow that was supposed to mean something.

They left as a group for a waiting car, only the four of them, and in response to this Munroe, playful and wide-eyed, squeezed Sergey's biceps and said, "Where are your other friends?"

He reached to open the car door. "They come later," he said, and ushered her into the backseat with Olivie. The driver took them to an open-air club on Nyali beach and Sergey spent the length of the trip running his fingers along the outside of Munroe's thigh and up her rib cage, unwanted and uninvited physical contact. She batted him away in ersatz playfulness, surrogate for the urge to slit his throat.

The car stopped, and free of him and away from his touch, Munroe made for the bar under the pretext of needing a drink, would have downed a couple in quick succession had she not needed to think clearly. Instead, she drank water until the tactile overload subsided and the pounding in her chest had been pushed down into a tiny knot; she returned to Sergey's side, drink in hand, tuning the strings of her behavior, vibrating between coy and flirt until the arrival of the rest of the delegation broke the rhythm and the alcohol flowed heavier and the night drew longer.

She'd come for conversation, for snippets and clues and nuance in the unspoken. The *Favorita* was tracked; she'd told them that the captain was on board. These men knew the ship would soon arrive, and alcohol was a horrible gatekeeper to secrets no matter how well they were guarded. The evening continued with smiles and come-ons, indifference and distraction, Munroe shrouded in the role that Sergey expected until, at some point between drinks, Anton took a phone call and twenty minutes later another man joined the group, bringing with him a shock of recognition and providing Munroe answers to the question of Ibrahiin.

Anton moved away from the group to a table off to the side while the *hawaladar*'s bodyguard, the one who'd sat inside the doorway and who'd come with the *hawaladar* to the freight depot, walked with him.

Laughter and conversation continued on around while silence filled Munroe's ears and a rush of images shifted perspective and the chessboard inside her head rotated and the pieces moved into check. She avoided eye contact with the bodyguard, feigned exhaustion and the need to sit in order to move closer to the satchel that had transferred from his hand into Anton's, and because Sergey went with her, Munroe closed her eyes to block him out, to block out all but the whispers of conversation that reached out from behind her back.

In the satchel were the *hawaladar*'s papers, copies of the legal filings to make the claim against the freighter for salvage. She'd expected betrayal to come from somewhere, hadn't anticipated its coming so late. Her thumb caressed the strap beneath her skirt, and realizing what she'd done, Munroe pressed her palm flat on her thigh.

Money changed hands and then beside her Sergey's body language shifted and for the first time in the evening he ignored the women. Focus entirely on the newcomer, he left Munroe and walked toward his boss. He stood behind Ibrahiin, and with the implied threat of Sergey's presence, the boss man's conversation darkened into demands for information about the captain.

Munroe turned slightly to observe the interaction. If the bodyguard was cowed, he didn't show it. He flashed a smile and to Anton, the only one of the delegation who spoke fluent English, said, "It takes more time, but I will get you what you want."

Munroe turned away, toward the water and the small breaking waves far out in the distance. The bodyguard was a good liar, he told the white men what they wanted to hear, but they'd never see him again; this was truth betrayed in subtle tics that went unnoticed by those blind to such things.

The bodyguard said good night and stood, and Sergey didn't stop him. A half beat of silence and the conversation started up again. They spoke of finishing the job tomorrow, of Anton's boss wanting to see for himself, and as easily as flicking ash off the tip of a smoldering cigarette, they reverted to the inanity of moments before and laughter followed and Sergey returned to Munroe, ran his fingers along her hairline and nuzzled at her neckline, shutting down the calculations running through her head.

Overpowering desire urged her to strike him. "I'm going to use the restroom," she said, and scooted away, knowing he would follow.

She entered the ladies' room and he came in after her. Ordered the other women out, and when they were alone, Munroe leaned back into the wall and smiled. Had he been less drunk, he might have seen the welcome for what it was.

He tipped in to kiss her and she drove her forehead into his face. Knee into his groin.

Mouth gaping, he slid down the wall, and by the time she stepped over him the knife was already in her hand.

Gasping for air, he reached behind his back for the weapon holstered in his waistband. She stabbed his shoulder. Plunged the knife through. His right hand twitched and flailed and he clawed with his left. She yanked the knife up. Through cartilage. Hit bone. Stomped his groin with her foot. Took a knee up under his jaw and slammed his head back into the wall. Beyond the bathroom door, the thump of the music and the deep bass notes played on.

His eyes glassed over, alcohol mixed with trauma, and she fisted his hair. Ran the blade from ear to ear, deep enough to satiate the lust for blood and yet still let him live. Held the blade to his face so he could see the crimson that stained it, then wiped the knife across his shirt. Straightened, then stepped over him and walked out of the club and into the night.

CHAPTER 45

Munroe strode along the roadway edge, followed dirt inland toward the highway that would lead back to Mombasa and kept to the shadows on the chance that one of the other men would be foolish enough to come after her. Another kilometer down the road, she flagged a car. Offered to pay for the ride but the three inside wouldn't hear of it. They took her to the Sentrim Castle, and after she assured them that she was fine, they left her there.

Munroe accessed e-mail from the business center, lingered only long enough to reprint the original photo of the captain. Scrawled a note on the bottom: *He is coming to you, as promised, will arrive with the* Favorita *in the morning. If you intend to claim him, wire the remaining payment before boarding.* Slipped the page under the door of Anton's room and left the hotel for her own.

She set the alarm on her phone, fell asleep in her clothes, and woke before the sun, before the alarm. She made the call to the *hawaladar.*

"Have you heard from Khalid or Joe?" she said.

"The ship should arrive in a few hours," he said. "Where are you?"

"Mombasa."

"Why are you here already?"

"I'm hunting for Ibrahiin," she said.

"Have you found him?"

"Perhaps. Did you file the papers for claiming the ship?"

"Yesterday."

"The Russian delegation got copies last night."

"Excuse me?" he said.

In slow and measured tones Munroe walked him through what she'd seen, and when he'd heard the details, he argued back, insisting she was mistaken. She sighed and closed her eyes, tipped back onto the bed, head on the pillow, and searched his words and tone for clarity. As a man who'd sent his underling to double-cross, to collect his own payment for her catch while also intending to collect on the ship, he was either a fantastic psychological player or he'd been betrayed as thoroughly as she had.

"Why now?" he said. "Why like this? They could have had the ship when it was in Somalia."

"They're not interested in the ship."

"They ransacked my office," he said, tone rising, exasperation in every word. "They've killed my niece, they've stolen the loyalty of my cousin, obtained copies of multiple documents relating to this venture. What are they after if not the ship?"

Munroe sat, swung her legs over the bed, planted her feet on the floor, and stood in the middle of the last act, the outcome toward which every moment, every turn over these last weeks, had pushed her. "I promised you the *Favorita*," she said. "I *will* fulfill my end of the bargain, and Abdi, I need the dhow."

"Now?"

"Tonight."

"If you guarantee me the freighter, eliminate our current hassle, you can have the dhow."

"Then be at the port to seize your ship."

"What of the Russians and their plans?"

"You're in a better position to answer that than I am," she said. "Which agency officials have they been courting?"

"Foreign Affairs and Ports Authorities."

"And what does that tell you?"

"They plan to hijack the *Favorita,* this time legally."

"They don't want the ship," she said. "They want to board it."

"Only a fool would put so much effort into something so easily obtained."

"They want to board before the ship is cleared, before the port authorities inspect, to get on and off without anyone looking at what they bring on or take off."

"I see," he said, though his tone wavered with unasked questions.

"Be there," she said. "Bring an extra car and an extra driver—and whatever you decide to do with your cousin, this Ibrahiin, keep him far, far away from any information about today."

"He will be far," the *hawaladar* said, though darkness filled his voice and he might as well have said dead.

MUNROE LEFT THE room with the sun just over the horizon, took a taxi to the port, and walked from the drop-off point down to the wharf, where a wide expanse of bulk freight filled the concrete docks, separating two- and three-story buildings from the water. The morning heat had already settled, and in the distance, the day's labor long begun, stevedores loaded bales into waiting trucks.

She kept to the shade. Moved slowly in the way that everything moved slowly in the sweat-drenching humidity, familiarizing herself with the port facilities and government offices, and when she'd seen all she needed and, based on the *Favorita*'s size and cargo, surmised more or less in which segment of the port the freighter would berth, she purchased water and small snacks from a vendor and sat in the shade, napping, until a convoy of six cars and a bustle of movement roused her from the heat-induced coma.

Four men stepped from the two rear cars, three of them from the delegation, expressions gaunt and postures strained, a far cry from the comportment of the men she'd drunk and laughed with the night before. The weapons they carried were well concealed but obvious all the same, submachine guns and whatever smaller hardware they'd stashed on their persons.

Sergey was missing, leaving them one man short, and that brought her a hint of satisfaction, as did their body language, which spoke of deference and fear of the fourth man, her target, who was broad-shouldered and imposing, an older and better-kept version of the pictures she'd seen of Aleksey Petrov. He lifted an arm toward the ocean, giving orders she couldn't hear.

With the arrival of the delegation, a signal that the *Favorita* was near, Munroe raised Amber on the two-way and waited for the satellite phone to boot up.

Eight more men stepped from the lead cars to the pavement, most of them in suit and tie, and by their dress and mannerisms Munroe separated government officials from entourage and drivers, counted two men of any importance, and assumed one had come from each office the delegation had courted. The two groups mingled, handshakes and conversation were shared between the bosses, and then they walked in the direction of an empty berth. Beyond them, almost inconspicuous in contrast to the size of their crowd, the *hawaladar*'s vehicle drove toward the dock: vultures, all of them, circling the dying animal in an easily predicted dance of wants and ordered priorities.

A police van and two cars arrived, and armed more poorly than the delegation, ten uniformed men joined the greeting committee, adding weight to the *hawaladar*'s warning that the crew would be arrested when the ship arrived.

With all the players come to the game, the weapons numbered, the strategy set, Munroe dialed the satellite phone. "There's an entourage waiting to make arrests as soon as the ship docks," she said.

"Lovely," Amber said. "What'd we do this time?"

"I figure it's weapons smuggling."

"We're mostly clean, we can dump the rest."

In the distance the *Favorita*, piloted in, grew ever so slowly. Another half an hour, perhaps, before she was fully docked. No sign of the dhow, which was good, which meant Joe had at least followed the original instructions.

"They'll make the arrests anyway," Munroe said.

"What for? They won't find anything."

"Oh, they'll find something," Munroe said. "They need a reason to get you out of the way, and once the Kenyan government has you, they have you. Is proving your innocence worth the money and months of fighting to get free?"

Amber sighed. "You're the fixer, Michael. You've never brought me a problem without a way out, so I know you didn't call just to give me bad news."

"Let's just say we've run up against a wall," Munroe said, repeating a sliver of their conversation on the dhow. "Let's say now's the time to trade the captain for freedom."

"It'll work?"

"He's what they're after, but the guys coming for him are armed foreign military, and if they take him, there will be nothing standing between you and arrest. We can outmaneuver them, but only if you have the cooperation of everyone on board—you'll probably get it faster if you let them see the greeting committee for themselves."

"I'll take care of it," Amber said. "Just tell me what I need to know."

"All right then," Munroe said. "Get Victor, and get a pen and paper."

MUNROE KEPT TO her spot in the shade, waiting out the heat while the ship came fully into port, angling in for berthing, and those expectant on the wharf began to agitate in anticipation. Twice the *hawaladar* left his vehicle for the port authority office, and on each return he glanced in Munroe's direction and shied away just as quickly, as if having spotted and recognized her, he couldn't help himself.

Munroe dialed Anton's cell phone, a number she'd lifted off Sergey the night before. In the distance he fumbled through his pockets trying to get the call, squinted at the unknown number. Munroe said, "Nikola is here, as I promised."

"What do you want?" he said.

She ignored the bite of mockery. "I have brought you your prize," she said. "It's time to make payment."

He scanned the docks, right, left; turned and looked behind him. "I have no guarantee Nikola is on that ship," he said. "You'll get your money after we claim him."

"Our agreement was half up front, the rest before you board. Pay now if you intend to claim him."

"The agreement has changed," he said.

"That's a mistake."

Anton put his arms wide and turned in a circle, searching her out, inviting her to have at him, and, smiling, almost laughing, said, "You've been paid well enough. There's nothing more for you."

"If you don't pay, he won't be there for you to claim," she said, and hung up before he could reply. Tucked the phone away.

Anton glanced along the wharf again, then leaned in toward Petrov, passing on some message, and they both laughed and turned to face the *Favorita,* where the crew threw the mooring lines and the dockworkers secured them.

The gangway slid toward the dock, and when at last the metal connected with concrete, the delegation quickened forward and the crew above slipped away. The policemen spread out on the wharf along the length of the ship.

Munroe stood. Dusted off her pants and strolled toward the freighter.

By the time she reached the *Favorita,* all four of the delegation had gone up the gangway and were long since out of view. The officials and their entourage remained on the dock, an expensive barrier against lesser bureaucrats questioning the series of protocol and legal violations. Munroe continued toward the gangway, pace increasing as she neared. Two of the policemen blocked her rush forward and motioned her away from the ship. "I'm sorry I'm late," she said, harried and out of breath, and attempted to push past them.

One of the uniformed men put a hand to her shoulder and shoved her from the gangway. Munroe half tripped a step closer to the officials and turned to the suited men, twisting her expression into anguish and bewilderment. The arrangement guaranteeing Anton's men access to the ship, preventing anyone else from disembarking, also left a gray area. "Anton is waiting for me," she said. "He's already angry at my delay."

The collective response was uncertain hesitation, so Munroe shifted into deference and supplication, held her phone toward a short portly man, the one she'd marked as the most senior government official, and said, "Please, sir, call Anton if you must confirm. I am late and he is angry, please call him."

With his authority questioned before those surrounding him, the man lifted his hand in ego-salving and face-saving and flicked a two-fingered wave toward the policemen. They stepped aside and Munroe rushed a thank-you in sycophantic gratitude, and hurried up.

The deck was empty when she stepped aboard, a ghost ship without a crew. Anton and Petrov raced up the ladder for the bridge, two steps at a time, and had already reached the fourth level, while Sergey's counterpart, weapon drawn, stood guard at the base. The other was out of sight, had likely gone to where he could cover additional exits and ensure that no one slipped off the ship.

Munroe slid along the coaming for an access hatch into the number one hold, found it unsealed and blocked open as requested. Following the rungs down into the dark, nursing a body that stabbed her if she moved too fast or at the wrong angles, she clambered over rice bags, following the bulwark aft. Dug for the rifle and magazines she'd stashed before leaving the ship. Secured the spares tight into her waistband, slung the weapon over her shoulder, then headed back up. Using a leg of a deck crane as cover, she held back, counting the seconds for Anton to make his next move.

CHAPTER 46

Munroe waited less than a minute before Anton and Petrov hurried out on the bridge, running down the ladder, stopping at each landing long enough to try to force the hatchways open and then, unable to gain entry, rushing onward, yelling to the man below, voices carrying far along the ship. They needed to get inside. The captain had been warned, there were lines leading from the ship, he had another way off.

They reached the main deck, forced through the shoddily constructed jamb on the only door that would open, believing without hesitation what they'd been told on the bridge, because Munroe, in the demand for payment, had primed Anton to accept it. Weapons ready, they cleared the breach military style. Passed through to the interior.

Munroe rose from her hiding place and, wary of the missing man, moved from coaming to coaming, then ran the final stretch to the tower. Reached the entry without spotting the stray shooter and followed through, into the stomach of the ghost ship. Slid along the walls tracking the same route the delegation would have taken, down to the second deck, detouring along a different passageway and continuing beyond them, intending to loop back and approach from their rear.

Victor followed her. She knew him by the familiar pattern the wounded thigh created in his footsteps, by his breathing, his smell. Paused for him. Motioned topside. One was still out there. He nodded, fingers filling in for words: Marcus and Khalid were on the hunt. He handed her the 9 mm she'd left behind and she traded him for the rifle and spare magazines, then with him at her back moved forward more quickly, down another ladder, another passageway, toward the engine room.

Stopped when she reached a blind turn.

Voices echoed out and with them the subtle clink of hands shifting against weapons, the sound of nervousness and uncertainty, and slurs and mutters that spoke of a standoff between far too many people for the enclosed space. Natan's voice was clearer than the others, meaning his face was toward her, and the delegation, if properly distracted, if properly outnumbered, would have their backs to the opening.

Amber and one of the ship's crewmen slid into place behind Victor. Together with Natan and his men, they outnumbered the Russians three to one. Munroe glanced back once and nodded. Moved through the door, smooth and silent. Put the muzzle of the handgun to Anton's head before he'd registered her presence.

Petrov stole a look in her direction, his expression blank, unreadable. "This one I don't need," Munroe said to him. "Will you sacrifice him while you decide what to do?"

In microsecond slivers, his every movement, every blink and breath, bled out as a story, advertising intent, and in the heartbeat that his finger twitched toward the trigger, Munroe shifted the gun from Anton's head to Petrov's arm and shot him.

The report echoed deafeningly in the enclosed space, and Munroe fired again, a round to Petrov's knee. Two bullets, less than two seconds, and he screamed and his legs buckled and he began to swing his weapon toward her. Munroe put the muzzle to his head. Her hearing blown from the discharges, she spoke loudly, formed the words clearly for his sake. "Chances are, I won't die before I pull the trigger again," she said. "It's certain that you will."

The room remained frozen in calculation, hesitation. Anton lowered his weapon; Sergey Two did the same. Victor pried the firepower from their hands. Petrov's gaze rose to meet hers, and in that pause Natan slammed the butt of his rifle at his hands, disarming him. "You were told to pay before boarding," she said. "You should have listened."

Muzzle of the gun back at Anton's head, Munroe nodded at Natan. "We have this," she said. "There is still another topside."

Natan backed away, his small contingent following, while Amber and Victor and the crewmen surrounded the delegation and Munroe pressed the muzzle to Petrov's thigh. "I need you alive," she said, "but I don't need you in one piece. I've got seven rounds left, so tell me, what's your arrangement for getting off the ship?"

He glared, shaking, and slid down the wall, and when her finger moved from trigger guard to trigger, Anton answered for him.

FIFTEEN MINUTES FROM the start of the incursion and, weapon to Anton's spine, Munroe walked him to the main deck, following slightly behind in an ostensible act of respect that allowed her to keep the weapon out of sight while she guided him down the gangway toward the waiting officials.

Munroe kept the pace calm, casual. Smirking, she leaned nearer his ear and whispered, "Relax," and when they reached the portly man, Anton stuck out a hand. He was far stiffer than what she wanted, but it was the best she'd get from him.

"You have our most sincere apologies," he said, tone overly formal. "Our intelligence is incorrect; this is not the ship we have been expecting."

The officials were quiet for a moment, disappointed perhaps that there'd be no show, no excitement, and no contraband to confiscate and later sell on the black market. The portly man said, "There are no weapons?"

"The weapons exist," Munroe said, and nudged Anton from behind.

"They do exist," he said, stilted and forced. "But this is not the ship. We are investigating the error and will seek an appointment with your office when we have gathered better facts."

"Our team will leave momentarily," Munroe said, jabbing Anton again.

"Yes," he said. "And we are grateful for your graciousness and assistance in this grave matter. There is no work for your policemen here today. Unfortunately."

The unspoken matter of payment hung thick in the air, and unwilling to risk Anton's working off script, Munroe said, "Regardless, we will contact your office to secure for you the remainder of our agreement."

Anton nodded, and although the portly man's expression showed doubt and his body language spoke of irritation, he shook Anton's hand again. Munroe stood together with Anton on the gangway, unwilling to let him move until the policemen had been called off and the entire assembly had started on their way to the vehicles. Only when they'd drifted far enough away did she march him back to a supply room where there were no portholes or hatches and where the reports of gunfire would be muted should she have to shoot someone again.

His companions had already been stripped down to their underwear, socks, and shoes, and Munroe had Anton do the same. Victor handed her the stack of passports he'd collected, and with the delegation bound and gagged, they left the room and sealed the door. Munroe rifled through their phones and wallets for a quick look, then set those pieces aside. They had but a small window to finish what they'd started. The rest could wait.

The crew, gathered in the passageway, observed silently as Munroe flipped through the passports, scanned the pictures, and, based on the facial features that were the closest match, handed out three sets of passports and clothing, and then tossed Sergey's passport to a fourth man. Disguises weren't necessary—they'd be leaving the country on their own documents. If any of the officials had chosen to remain behind, none were familiar enough with any member of the delegation to really know who was who—bribery at its finest—and this was a show, the men who'd boarded now leaving the freighter, a precaution to avoid scrutiny. She'd get the rest of the crew off the ship after dark.

Munroe walked Petrov's passport to the berth where the captain waited under guard. His face creased with surprise when she stepped in, and she handed him the booklet. "I've given you a head start, a way to disappear again," she said. "Do with it what you will."

The captain thumbed through the passport, stopped at the data page, and studied Aleksey Petrov's picture for a long while. A slow dark smile spread across his face, and within that unguarded flash of triumphant gloating, he gave up his inner sanctum.

Munroe turned from him, disgusted.

By fulfilling promises made to avenge a boy who hadn't deserved to die, in returning to Amber the man she loved, by washing her conscience of the tugs of obligation, she'd waded into a history between two men that ran deep, that coursed personal and ugly. For all she knew, by fulfilling her side of their agreed exchange, she would allow the devil to walk free.

"You have his passport," the captain said. "This means Aleksey has come to Kenya." He smiled again and his voice lilted with hope. "He is dead?"

Munroe didn't answer. Wouldn't gift him the knowledge of what had happened belowdecks or what would happen next. The captain had wanted Petrov out of the way so that he could continue his run for freedom. Well, fine, he could run, hide, and chase shadows until he figured events out on his own.

Munroe opened the door and paused at the threshold. Despicable as it was for a captain to abandon his ship and crew, his final act of perfidy would rid her of him. "You have ten minutes to be dressed and ready to leave," she said. "After that, I can't guarantee your safety."

MUNROE LEFT THE *Favorita* together with the new delegation, walked them to the waiting cars. With borrowed identification and hotel rooms, they had enough to make it through the night, could find a way to get to Nairobi and find their embassies.

She stared after diminishing taillights, and when at last they were fully on their way toward the city, Munroe dialed the *hawaladar* and returned with him to the office of the port officials, buying time and paying for temporary loyalty.

THE TEAM ON board waited until nightfall, and until money had changed hands, to get the rest of the crew off the ship, and then, with the help of an improvised stretcher, while Amber guided the blinded second mate by the arm, Khalid and Marcus carried Leo off to the *hawaladar*'s waiting vehicle. Munroe gave the driver directions to the Aga Khan Hospital, the start of the path to finding help for both men, if help could be had.

Amber slid into the front seat and Munroe, standing beside her, stretched out a hand. Amber stepped back out and wrapped her arms around Munroe's neck in a hug. Whispered, "Thank you, Michael," and, releasing her, clasped Munroe's hands in a good-bye that was, perhaps, not really a good-bye.

Munroe kissed her forehead and stepped aside for a look into the rear. Leo caught her eye and held contact for a moment, two, then tipped his fingers in a salute—probably the closest she'd ever get to receiving thanks.

She turned away and smiled. To Amber she said, "I need the inflatable. I'm willing to pay whatever you paid for it."

"You'd do that?"

"It's not a favor."

"Then it's yours."

"Check the business accounts in a day or two. I'll wire the money in."

"Thank you," Amber said, and Munroe waved her off. Walking for the gangway, Munroe said, "I told you, it's not a favor."

The favor would be the rest of the money that she sent along with the payment for the boat, courtesy of Anton and Aleksey Petrov, enough to cover medical expenses and the lost equipment and put Amber back into the black.

Off the Coast of Somalia, South of Garacad

Munroe leaned against the gunwale, observing as Marcus and Natan lowered the inflatable from the dhow into the water and, at gunpoint, nudged each of the Russian captives, still stripped down to underwear and socks, overboard into the smaller boat. Sergey with his lightly slit throat and destroyed shoulder was the lucky one. He'd never come to the port, had never been taken captive.

The wind picked up, leaving the swells choppy and violent, and Munroe glanced at the sky and the sun that had dipped beyond the midpoint, allowing them about four hours of daylight.

Petrov, hobbled by his injuries, was the last overboard, his descent more fall than climb, and when he had settled, Natan dropped a pair of oars to waiting hands. Munroe tossed down several water bottles, and then, against the captives' rising protests, Natan and Marcus shoved the inflatable away from the dhow.

There was enough gas in the engine for the boat to make the trip to shore, enough to get them a bit farther if they chose to go in the opposite direction. The oars would get them farther still, if dehydration, starvation, and exposure were the course they plotted.

Victor waited until the boat was several hundred meters off port and the dhow was back on its way to sea, then shot a flare into the sky. Somewhere on the coast, courtesy of the *hawaladar's* information network, an envoy waited. Men who had nothing good to say about Russians, who'd gladly take hostages of value in exchange for forgetting that an old and aging ship had been stolen from them. Unlike the crew of the *Favorita,* these captives would likely produce a ransom. Or perhaps not. Only time would tell. Either way, the fate of the delegation, and the success of the strategy birthed those many moves before—convincing Amber and Natan to come to Mombasa, trading the *hawaladar* the ship for his men, and negotiating the payment for the captain's delivery—all brought a sweeter satisfaction than exacting death in revenge for Sami's blood.

In the distance, the men in the inflatable fought over oars.

Munroe whispered, "Checkmate," and turned away.

They headed north, armed with the Russian weapons they'd transferred off the *Favorita* after crossing into Kenya, prepared to battle against another hijacking attempt should so small a vessel attract pirate attention: a return to Djibouti, where those who remained of Leo's team could sell off the vehicles and supplies, close down the operation, and follow their own way.

Munroe left Victor for the bow, for the wind and the salt air, and he trailed after her, stood beside her, traced her gaze out over the open water. He put his arm around her shoulders and she sighed, allowing the intimacy of contact that he would never have attempted before discovering she was a woman. "And you?" Victor said. "Where do you go?"

Munroe glanced toward the sun, pointed her finger high, and drew an arc toward the west. "I'm riding off," she said, "into the proverbial sunset."

If you're a new reader to this series, I'm so glad you discovered Vanessa Michael Munroe and were willing to take a chance on her most recent adventure. I truly hope you've enjoyed, and I would love to hear from you if you have. If you're a fan or a former reader back for another round, I can't tell you how happy I am to be able to share this world with you again. Thank you for keeping Munroe riding.

Now that this series has grown to five and a quarter books, I've begun to receive more frequent inquiries about the chronology, as well as questions asking if it's necessary to read the series in order.

The short answer is no. I do my best to keep each story self-contained, providing just enough backstory that it's possible to fall into any book in the series and pick up from there, but not so much as to annoy those who've started at the beginning and heard it all before. When it comes to plot, each book is a standalone and one could read a single volume, or all of them, in order or out of order, and each story will work well in isolation.

There is, however, an arc that flows from the beginning, where the characters—just like real people—are affected and changed by prior events. For readers who read primarily for plot and thrills, the chronology won't matter. For those who read as much for character as for plot, there will probably be a richer reading experience by including at least the first book, *The Informationist*, at some point.

In order, the books are:

The Informationist
The Innocent
The Doll
The Vessel (a novella that ties up loose ends from *The Doll* and leads into *The Catch*)
The Catch
The Mask

In addition to the Vanessa Michael Munroe stories, I also share extensively about the publishing industry, the mechanics of storytelling, behind-the-book research that has gone into each volume, and my path from growing up as uneducated child labor in the communes of the apocalyptic cult into which I was born to becoming a bestselling novelist.

If you'd like a more personal connection, or would like to go beyond the book, I welcome you to join me on this journey. You can find me at: www.taylorstevensbooks.com/connect.php, and I look forward to hearing from you.

ACKNOWLEDGMENTS

Writing is a solitary endeavor; getting a book published is anything but, and I've been blessed with a team that does an amazing job at making me look a whole lot smarter than I really am. To everyone at Crown Publishers—those in publicity, marketing, sales, foreign rights, production, audio, design, and more—all of you who put in so much effort on my behalf: thank you!

I'm especially grateful to Christine Kopprasch, my editor. Not only for wielding her fierce and fantastic powers of all-around awesomeness on my behalf, but because when travel and scheduling got in the way of deadlines, and I submitted this book only eighty percent written, she didn't even blink. We played tag-team while the clock ticked down, editing through the writing process—or, perhaps it was writing through the editing process. Together we got the job done *and* were able to get the manuscript into the production stream on time. Score one for team Christine!

Love and appreciation to my agent, Anne Hawkins—without her I would have no career, and possibly no sanity. Anne is the best thing that has happened to me in publishing; she has become my advocate, confidante, and friend, and every day I wake up grateful that she has my back.

I also want to say thank you to Captain Max Hardberger, the world's baddest badass, without whom we would have never had this story—or if we did, it would have been a very different story. He is one of the most fascinating people I have ever met, and I've been the honored recipient of Max's time, generosity, and friendship. Any details in this book that I got right concerning the ocean, ships, the maritime industry, maritime law, and even some of the parts that deal with Somalia, are because of him. Anything I got wrong is my own doing. If you're interested in hearing just a smattering of the stories this amazing man can tell, you can find them in *Seized: A Sea Captain's Adventures Battling Scoundrels and Pirates While Recovering Stolen Ships in the World's Most Troubled Waters.* It's a fantastic read. I highly recommend it.

Appreciation also to Abukar Abraham, linguist, educator, and certified Somali language tester and developer out of Atlanta, for double-checking the Somali in the text and tweaking it for accuracy and spelling (www.somalitranslator.com).

To my family and friends, thank you for putting up with my long silences, and for not taking it personally when I drop off the earth for months at a stretch or when I become flustered by the phrase "we should do coffee when you have time." Also, my children, for begrudgingly letting me do what I do; I promise that one day it'll all seem more impressive than it does right now. Hopefully you'll forget that I live in my pajamas.

And to my fans—and especially my "cool kids" who found me at www.taylorstevensbooks.com/connect.php—who bolster me daily with love, support, and encouragement, I thank you all.

You make what I do possible.

ABOUT THE AUTHOR

TAYLOR STEVENS is the award-winning *New York Times* bestselling author of *The Informationist*, *The Innocent*, *The Doll*, and *The Mask*. Featuring Vanessa Michael Munroe, the series has received critical acclaim and the books are published in twenty languages. *The Informationist* has been optioned for film by James Cameron's production company, Lightstorm Entertainment. Born in New York State into the Children of God, raised in communes across the globe, and denied an education beyond the sixth grade, Stevens was in her twenties when she broke free to follow hope and a vague idea of what possibilities lay beyond. She now lives in Texas and is at work on the next Munroe novel.

Read on for an excerpt from
New York Times bestselling author
Taylor Stevens's latest book, *The Mask*.

CROWN PUBLISHERS
NEW YORK

AVAILABLE WHEREVER BOOKS ARE SOLD

DAY 7

The attack, when it came, opened the floodgates of rage. Sound compressed. Time slowed to a water drip plonking into a puddle, echoing a musical note off concrete walls and floors; tires whooshing against the drizzle on the street outside as a car passed the parking garage exit; laughter pealing from the playground down the block. And footsteps, three sets of footsteps, moving in cautiously behind her back.

Vanessa Michael Munroe waited beside the motorcycle, one knee to the pavement, focused on the reflection in the bike's red fairing. Behind her head, shadows against the evening's light dropped hints of metal pipes protruding from raised hands, elongating and stretching as they drew nearer.

She counted heartbeats and felt the rhythm.

The muscles in her legs tensed and the chemical surge of adrenaline and anger loosed its addictive calm.

The metal bars came down hard into the empty space where she'd been a half heartbeat before: metal against concrete ringing loud in the enclosed space, symphonic in the thunder of war.

She came up swinging, helmet chin guard in hand, all her weight, her full momentum thrown into that backward strike. The man on the right ducked too slowly, moved too late.

The swing smashed helmet into head.

He stumbled. Munroe grabbed the pipe and tore it from his hand. She whipped up and downward, to the back of his knees. He hit the ground and became a barrier between her and the two other men. Boot to his shoulder, she shoved him prostrate and then boosted over him, swinging hard.

The attackers swung, too, and hit for hit she countered, connecting the pipe with their bodies in solid beats because speed was her ally and speed was her friend, in and out and around, until they separated, becoming not one target but two. They were cautious now, angry and, perhaps for the first time, fully aware of the strength of their enemy.

Movement from behind told her that the man on the concrete had pushed to his knees. Munroe rotated back, struck hard, and he collapsed.

She faced the other two again, predicting move against move, guarding the rate of her breathing, conserving strength for a battle that had only begun.

The men shifted, foot to foot, and tensed for the attack and parry. They gripped their weapons, fingers rising and falling along the pipes in slow motion like spiders' legs along the ground.

She waited for them to come at her again.

Instead, they exchanged glances: nervous with the uncertainty of foot soldiers marching to someone else's beat in an evening that had gone off script.

The pounding inside her chest groaned in understanding.

The drive for release, for pain, pushed her at them.

She pointed the metal bar at one, marking territory, intended pocket for the eight ball, then strode toward him in misdirection and distraction.

He took several steps in retreat.

A shadow moved in her peripheral vision: his partner flanking and closing in. Munroe pivoted, swung, and connected the metal bar to his shoulder: small pain, a half second of diversion. He retaliated and opened himself up like a fool. She dodged and dropped, then drove the metal bar across his shin: crippling pain, unbearable pain, she knew.

In the beat between his shock and agony, she wrenched the bar from his hand and with two pipes to his none struck his rib cage. He doubled over. She knocked him flat and rotated toward his companion, who, in those same seconds, had backed away another few steps.

She feinted toward him. His eyes darted from her to his partners, and then he turned and ran. The crippled one dragged himself backward, out of immediate reach. He put up a hand, shielding his face in a show of defeat, and Munroe stood in place, rocklike and solid, eyes tracking him, breathing past the urges that drove her to strike again, to move in for the kill and finish what he'd started.

He grimaced and struggled up. Never turning his back to her, arms wrapped protectively around his torso, he hobbled toward the garage opening and then, moving around the corner, he was gone.

The condensation dripped another *plonk* into the puddle, another musical note echoed along concrete walls; another set of tires whooshed against the pavement beyond the garage exit; laughter in the distance morphed into the squeals of multiple children; and, with long, slow breaths, the violence of the moment ebbed and faded.

Munroe hefted the pipes and checked her hands, and then her clothes and boots. No blood. That was progress. She walked toward the unconscious man and stood over him, then put a boot to his torso and shoved the body over so that his face turned upward.

He was in his very early twenties, maybe five foot seven, all bone and sinew and stylish hair. She stared out toward the daylight where the other two had gone. Boys like this, full of bravado and without a lot of skill, had no business coming after her. They were a piece of the puzzle that didn't fit. She couldn't guess who had sent them, and that raised questions she hadn't begun to ask. This wasn't the beginning.

Sometimes it was impossible to start at the beginning.

When the story was complicated and the origin far back in a seemingly mundane pattern of daily life, the only way to make sense of it was to go back to before the beginning, to before the first hint of trouble.

Munroe wiped down the pipes for prints.

In the echo of the garage, footsteps shuffled and clothing rustled: movements small and cautious.

Munroe knelt and placed the pipes beside the body and, without turning, said, "You can come out now."

The opaque doors of Kansai International's immigration hall opened to a wall of bodies and a polite crush of expectant faces: the international arrival's rite of passage. Munroe scanned the crowd and, dragging the small carry-on around the metal rails, continued into the thick of the waiting throng.

Airport lights in the night sky winked through large plate-glass windows, marking another city and another time zone—this one a long, long stretch from the puddle jumps she'd made out of Djibouti, on the horn of Africa where the mouth of the Red Sea kissed the Gulf of Aden, then through the Middle East and into Europe.

Frankfurt, Germany, to Osaka, Japan: sixteen hours in transit and now the traveling, the running, was finally over. Munroe shoved the backpack's slipping strap up her shoulder and turned a slow circle, searching, seeking.

For more than ten years, across untold airports and arrival destinations, strangers had peered beyond her with the same hopeful expressions, ever eager to spot a glimpse through closing doors of loved ones still on the other side. Across five continents she'd come and gone, ghostlike and invisible, while others welcomed family home, but this time—this time—a home waited to welcome her.

Not the country, or the city, or the land, or things built upon it, no. If there could ever be such a thing as *home* for a person like her, Miles Bradford was that home, and her gaze passed over the crowd again, seeking him out.

She spotted him finally: a splash of white skin and red-tinged blond hair leaning against a window, his face toward his phone, framed by parking lights and tower lights and shadows. She paused, drinking in memories that laughed and babbled like a brook over pebbles of pain, then maneuvered forward through legs and shoulders, suitcases and luggage carts, and the melee of joy that inevitably accompanied reunions.

She was halfway to him when he glanced up. His eyes connected with hers and the volume of the arrivals area shushed into white noise.

He stood motionless for a full second, two, three, phone paused in its descent to his pocket, grinning as if he'd just unwrapped a much-longed-for Christmas gift. She continued in his direction and he strode toward her, and when he reached her, he scooped her up, spun her in a circle, and drowned her smile with a kiss. She laughed as he set her down and didn't resist when he lifted the backpack off her shoulder and took the carry-on's handle.

"Good flight?" he said.

She nodded, unwilling to speak lest she break the spells of touch and feel and smell that whispered against her senses. She breathed him in to make a permanent memory and breathed out the dirt and grime and lies and death that had brought her to him.

Bradford dropped the bags and wrapped his arms around her again. He held her for a long, long while, just as he'd held her in Dallas the night she'd walked away, when he'd known she was leaving and had spared her the agony of saying good-bye. He kissed her again, hoisted the backpack, grabbed the carry-on, then took her hand and said, "Let's get out of here."

She followed him to the elevator, fingers interlinked with his, and he glanced at her once, twice, matching her grin each time he did. He hadn't changed much—a few gray hairs added to his temples, deeper wrinkles in the creases of his smile, and maybe more muscle mass beneath his shirt, though it was hard to tell. He looked good. Smelled good. And in a mockery of their eight-year age difference, she'd aged five years in their year apart—still bore the remnants of conflict that had prematurely ended a maritime security company at the hands of Somali pirates—hadn't yet fully healed from the assault in Mombasa that had nearly killed her.

A four-day layover in Frankfurt had allowed a respite of hotel luxury; given her time to scrub away the worst of the weather wear, the dust, and the salt-spray, and the effects of wide open spaces; and made it possible to trade sun-bleached clothes worn threadbare over the last year for new pieces, better suited to less demanding environments.

She'd come to Japan for him because he'd asked her to. Because she'd known happiness with him, and loved him, and running from that terror had only brought more pain and death instead of the nothingness she'd sought.

They left the terminal for warm air, thick with the promise of coming rain. Bradford rolled the suitcase between endless rows of cars and finally stopped behind an off-white Daihatsu Mira so small it could have fit in the bed of his truck back in Dallas.

Munroe looked at him and then the car.

"Don't laugh," he said. "This is the country of itty-bitty things."

She took a step back and, in an exaggerated motion, turned her head left and then right, where up and down the rows on either side were a vast number of vehicles much larger than the Mira.

Smiling, Bradford shook his head and opened the hatchback. He stuffed the bags into the tiny storage compartment and slammed the door to make sure it shut. "You think it's funny now," he said, "you'll be grateful later."

"It suits you," she said.

"Trust me, I asked for something bigger."

"No, really, it's very cute."

He nudged her left, toward the passenger side. He said, "Just keep on stroking that masculine ego."

Munroe sat and buckled, and when Bradford was behind the wheel with his seat pushed back as far as it would go, she stared at him.

"What?" he said.

"Cute," she said, and then she laughed.

He smiled, tucking a strand of hair behind her ear, kissed her lips, and then, palm cradling the back of her neck, rested his forehead against hers.

She breathed him in.

The parking garage, the bridge to the city, and the bright green neon on a giant Ferris wheel became a backdrop, and the last year a waning history, and it was as if no time apart had ever passed between them. This was contentment and peace. This was home.

That part never changed, in spite of everything else that would.